T0153144

No ONE But YOU

Catherine Maiorisi

BELLA BOOKS

2017

Copyright © 2017 by Catherine Maiorisi

Bella Books, Inc.
P.O. Box 10543
Tallahassee, FL 32302

All rights reserved. No part of this book may be reproduced or transmitted in any form or by any means, electronic or mechanical, including photocopying, without permission in writing from the publisher.

This is a work of fiction. Names, characters, businesses, places, events and incidents are either the products of the author's imagination or used in a fictitious manner. Any resemblance to actual persons, living or dead, or actual events is purely coincidental. The publisher does not have any control over and does not assume any responsibility for author or third-party websites or their content.

Printed in the United States of America on acid-free paper.

First Bella Books Edition 2017

Editor: Medora MacDougall
Cover Designer: Linda Callaghan

ISBN: 978-1-59493-548-0

PUBLISHER'S NOTE

The scanning, uploading, and distribution of this book via the Internet or via any other means without the permission of the publisher is illegal and punishable by law. Please purchase only authorized electronic editions, and do not participate in or encourage electronic piracy of copyrighted materials. Your support of the author's rights is appreciated.

Other Bella Books by Catherine Maiorisi

Matters of the Heart

Acknowledgments

Thanks to my wife Sherry for her ongoing support and encouragement. Her willingness to tolerate my spending so much time in my head with my characters is a gift.

And to friends Lee and Judy and sister-in-law Joan, thanks for cheering me on.

I'd also like to thank the hardworking board of the Golden Crown Literary Society for providing a community for authors and readers to meet and discuss books and writing. As one of its services GCLS provides a list of members willing to be beta readers and it was from that list that I found the beta readers for *No One But You*. Thank you Cindy, Betty and Ruth for your willingness to put your own work aside to read *No One But You*. Your thoughtful comments helped make this a better book.

Working with editors can be painful because often they highlight things the author would rather not deal with. But heartfelt thanks to Medora MacDougall for her gentle encouragement and for teaching me about deepening. Medora, you actually made the editing process for *No One But You* challenging and, gasp, interesting.

Kudos and virtual hugs of gratitude and appreciation to all the Bella Book Gals who work tirelessly behind the scenes to make this author's dreams a reality.

And, dear readers, I thank you from the bottom of my heart for taking this journey with me. My stories come from my heart and I hope they touch yours. Enjoy.

About the Author

Catherine Maiorisi lives in New York City and often writes under the watchful eye of Edgar Allan Poe, in Edgar's Café near the apartment she shares with Sherry her partner, now wife, of thirty-nine years.

In the seventies and eighties while working in corporate technology then running her own technology consulting company, Catherine moaned to her artistic friends that she was the only lesbian in New York City who wasn't creative, the only one without the imagination or the talent to write poetry or novels, play the guitar, act, or sing.

A number of years later, Catherine found her imagination and writing. Writing is like meditating for Catherine and it is what she most loves to do. But she also reads voraciously, loves to cook, especially Italian, and enjoys hanging out with her wife and friends.

When she wrote a short story to create the backstory for the love interest in her two unpublished NYPD Detective Chiara Corelli mysteries, Catherine had never read any romance and hadn't considered writing it. To her surprise, "The Sex Club" turned out to be a romance and was included in the *Best Lesbian Romance of 2014* edited by Radclyffe.

Another surprise was hearing the voices of two characters, Andrea and Darcy, chatting in her head every night, making it difficult to sleep. Reassured by her wife that she wasn't losing it, Catherine paid attention and those conversations led to her first romance novel, *Matters of the Heart.*

No One But You, Catherine's second romance grew from thoughts of a child on a beach into an exploration of what happens after the happily ever after.

Catherine has also published mystery and romance short stories. Go to www.catherinemaiorisi.com for a complete list and while you're there sign up for her mailing list.

An active member of Sisters in Crime and Mystery Writers of America, Catherine is also a member of Romance Writers of America and Rainbow Romance Writers.

To Sherry again. And always

CHAPTER ONE

December–Lily

Lily glanced at her phone. Still four o'clock. And she was still here in Micki's city, in Micki's church, waiting to become Micki's wife. But still no Micki.

Her nearest and dearest had gone silent an hour ago. Now they studiously avoided looking at her, even though the incessant tapping of her foot like a metronome marking the minutes was probably driving them crazy. The tension in the room was palpable.

A Christmas wedding. Micki's dream not hers. After two hours in the stifling room at the back of the church, her lovely white dress was stained with perspiration and dotted with black cinders from the crackling fire. Sickened by the smoke, the smell of pine, and escalating anxiety, her stomach gnawed at itself.

The muted rumble of the ninety-five guests who had been told two hours ago there would be a slight delay drifted in from the church along with Mendelssohn's "Wedding March." The organist played it over and over as if she didn't know any other music. Lily glanced at her phone again. She should have heard from Micki by now. Something was seriously wrong.

She jumped when the notes of the wedding march burst from the cell clutched in her hand. Micki's ring tone. All eyes swiveled to her. She stared at the phone, not sure whether she would be happier to hear Micki had been in an accident or had just forgotten the time. She turned away, seeking a little privacy. "Are you all right?" She spoke softly. She could hear breathing, but Micki didn't speak. "Micki?" There were voices in the background, but the only words she could make out were "Just do it." "Is this Micki?"

"Yes. I'm sorry, Lily. I, uh, I can't get married."

A chill inched up her spine and splinters of ice cooled her blood. "What? Why?"

Micki plunged ahead. "Everything of mine is out of the apartment, and I left a check for half of the expenses in the kitchen. I'm planning to take the honeymoon trip, so I'll pay for that. Please apologize for me, tell everyone I'm sorry."

Not dead. Not injured. Not late. Jilting her. "You're sorry? That's it?" The rage bubbled. "Apologize for y'all?" She tried not to yell. "Why the fuck don't y'all get y'all's cowardly ass down to *y'all's* church and apologize y'all's self?"

She heard Micki's sharp intake of breath. "Well, well, the Southern princess *can* get angry." Micki hung up.

Stunned, Lily held the phone to her ear as if Micki was still talking. Her already heated face burned with shame. She forced herself to breathe. She would not cry. She would act with dignity. Then she would find Micki and murder her.

After a few minutes of deep breaths, she said "goodbye." Lowering the phone, she swung around to face her mamas, her sister and brother, her two closest friends from Chicago, and her only New York friend, Annie, the girlfriend of Micki's best friend Tina. "Micki changed her mind. She doesn't want to get married." Ignoring the burst of questions, she handed her veil to her sister Bella, stood, then smoothed the silk of her gown. "I'll tell everyone."

Del pulled her into a hug. "Oh, baby, y'all don't need to face this right now. Let me or Cordy do it."

"Yes, I do, Mama." Lily pushed her shoulders back. "I need to face them now or I'll never be able to." She met the eyes of each person in the room. "But I intend to tell them and leave without answering any questions or hearing how sorry they are. So I would appreciate all y'all coming out there with me and staying to answer questions after I leave. Annie, I'd like your help getting a cab." Dry-eyed, she led the angry group into the church.

When she appeared in her flowing white wedding dress with her troop of supporters, the church went silent. "I know everyone has been worried about Micki. So have I. But she's fine. In fact, she just called to say she's in good health—"

Lily put her hand up and silenced the outburst of relieved chatter. "But she really called to say she doesn't want to get married. At least not to me."

The crowd gasped. A rush of whispers followed. Lily waited stoically for the room to quiet again. "I'm sorry we put all y'all to so much trouble, especially those who flew in from other cities. The reception is paid for, so please go to the restaurant and enjoy dinner and dancing on me and Micki." She started to leave, then stopped. "Oh, while we've been waiting for her, Micki cleared out our apartment. I don't know what she took, but I'll return any gifts she left behind. Thank you."

She gathered her train. Head high, she strode up the aisle to a stunned silence rather than the glorious exit march they'd selected. Annie followed her out and hailed a cab. "How shitty of Micki to do this to you. And where the hell's Tina been during all this, I'd like to know?" It was freezing, and since they'd expected to travel from place to place in a limousine neither had a coat. Annie wrapped her arms around Lily's waist, trying to warm them both. "I don't think you should be alone right now, so if my connection to Micki hasn't tarnished me, I'd like to come with you." A cab pulled up. Annie opened the door.

"You're still shining bright, Annie. But I need to be alone right now. Please tell my mamas and the rest of the wedding party to go to the reception in my place. And I want you all to come to my apartment for breakfast at ten tomorrow morning." She kissed Annie's cheek, then slid into the cab, gave the driver her address, and asked him to raise the heat.

Twenty minutes later she arrived at her apartment building. Lewis, the doorman, opened the door of her cab. He'd been smiling and teasing this afternoon when he helped her into the limousine to go to the church. And then he'd probably helped Micki move out. While she was sitting in the rear of the church still thinking she was getting married, he knew Micki was jilting her. Her faced flamed again. Not meeting her eyes, he helped her out of the taxi and walked her to the elevator. It wasn't until she stepped in that he whispered, "I'm so sorry, Ms. Alexander. What she did was wrong." With her back to him, she nodded, but she didn't turn until the doors had closed.

Lily wandered through the apartment. Except for the sound of the train of her wedding grown dragging behind and the heels of her white satin shoes echoing on the parquet floors, it was silent. It felt empty, hollow, like her. The office, her office, looked untouched, as did one of the extra bedrooms. Micki's queen-size bed, dresser, night tables and lamps were missing from the second extra bedroom. The third bedroom, where the wedding gifts had been stored, was mostly empty except for the suitcase Lily had packed for the honeymoon she wouldn't be taking. As she suspected, Micki had taken the wedding gifts sent by her friends and family. *Good.*

In the master bedroom, she touched the empty hangers in the closet as if needing confirmation that Micki's clothes were gone, then peered into the bathroom. Her cosmetics, her bath gel, shampoo, conditioner, moisturizer, and powder looked pathetic on the spacious shelves without Micki's many and various beauty products. *Dammit.* Micki didn't even leave her the toothpaste.

A wave of exhaustion hit her without warning. She sat on the bed and struggled to unzip the dress. Thankfully she didn't have a million tiny buttons to undo by herself. She kicked off her shoes, stood, and stepped out of the dress, then dragged her slips, pantyhose, and bra off. She started to hang the gown then noticed, the stained underarms, the black dots left by the cinders from that damned fireplace, and, ugh, it stank of her sweat, smoke, and pine. She let it fall to the floor. As far as she was concerned, it could go right in the garbage, but she was sure the mamas would want to give it to some needy bride. Feeling a sudden urge to get the stink of her non-wedding off her skin and out of her hair, she stepped into the shower. Under the streaming hot water, she scrubbed herself with her rosemary bath gel, massaged rosemary shampoo and conditioner into her hair, and let the tears come.

Done with washing and crying, she wrapped herself in one of the new large bath towels she'd bought and used a smaller towel to dry her hair. On her way to get something to put on, she pulled a drawer out of Micki's dresser. Empty. What had she expected? She moved to her dresser and grabbed a pair of warm socks, her most comfy sweatpants and sweatshirt and pulled them on. She ran a comb through her hair, then leaving her wedding stuff in a pile on the floor, she went out to get a drink.

She reached for the brandy, then remembered the Christmas gift she'd bought for Micki, Miss-Only-The-Best-For-Me. A glance at the Christmas tree, dark and sad in the corner by the window, confirmed that her presents for Micki were still piled on the left side, but the right side, where Micki's presents for her had been, was empty. She tore the wrapping paper off the bottle of Old Rip Van Winkle 'Pappy Van Winkle's Family Reserve' Kentucky Straight Bourbon Whiskey 15 years old but hesitated before opening it. Feeding into Micki's grandiose idea of her worth, she'd spent almost fifteen hundred dollars on this bottle. If she didn't open it, she could return it. But she'd already spent the money so why not use *the best* to drown her sorrows.

As she poured a hefty glass of bourbon, it occurred to her that Micki had moved a lot of furniture and other things in a few hours. Where had she taken it? Had she lied about giving up the lease on her apartment? Had she rented a new one? How long had she been planning this? It didn't seem like a spur of the moment thing. And who was going on the honeymoon with her? She didn't attempt to stop the tears or the sadness. *Oh, Micki, how could you?*

Alone in her new city, in her new apartment, on her new sofa facing the windows overlooking Central Park, Lily stared at the lights across the park on the East Side. Her wedding day. Micki was crazy for a Christmas wedding, so she'd sold her apartment in Chicago and at the beginning of December moved into this apartment on Central Park West. She'd loved the apartment the first time they'd seen it, but Micki had balked at buying, saying her money was tied up in the market, so she couldn't contribute. Was that a clue? Maybe she should have been paying closer attention to Micki. Instead, she'd insisted on using her savings combined with the appreciation on her Chicago apartment to make a hefty down payment. She'd bought it thinking it would be theirs together. Now she would forever associate Christmas and this beautiful apartment with the shame of public rejection.

She sipped her bourbon and thought about the relationship. The friend who introduced them had said Micki was a player who loved the chase. Lily had initially been cool to the idea of dating her, but Micki had been persistent and she was flattered. Once they were seeing each other, she'd suspected Micki was also seeing women in New York, but she never confronted her. She chose, instead, to believe Micki's professions of love and desire to commit for a lifetime. Her mamas' coolness toward Micki should have alerted her.

Micki's parting comment, about the Southern princess feeling anger, offended her. Of course she felt anger. She was angry at the church, wasn't she? She sipped. And she was always angry when Micki called her "tubby," then said she was only kidding. So what if she never expressed it? She hated the shouting and distorted faces and the threat of violence. Nothing wrong with keeping the peace. But her anger had passed. Now she felt sad and abandoned, but mostly she felt embarrassed. How could she ever leave the apartment? How could she ever face Lewis and the other doormen? It was probably a good thing that the only New Yorker in her life now was Annie. Annie wouldn't judge her.

She glanced around. Micki had not only removed all of her furniture, but also some of the new pieces they'd purchased together. Lucky for her, Micki had deferred to her taste in decorating the apartment, or she'd probably be sitting on the floor, surrounded by echoes.

She sniffed and dried her tears. In the short time she'd been here, she'd grown to love this apartment and this vibrant city. She could write anywhere, and there was nothing to draw her back to Chicago. So she'd stay as planned. Being in the same city as her agent and editors was a plus. Speaking of agents, she wondered what Irene had thought of today's fiasco. She giggled. Her agent believed pain and suffering was grist for the writing mill, so she was probably doing fist pumps right about now.

More to the point, what was *she* feeling? Was she in shock?

She dug deep, trying to get in touch with her feelings. Hurt. Sad. Teary. Sorry for herself. And mortified at having been so publicly rejected. But mostly she was upset that she'd ignored her doubts and hadn't trusted her feeling of unease about Micki. She would have to think about why she'd let that happen. But she didn't feel devastated about losing Micki. She felt…

She stared out the window puzzling over her feelings. Did she really feel relieved? She swirled the expensive bourbon in her glass. *Relieved. That's interesting.*

CHAPTER TWO

December–Robin

Robin stared at the high-powered businesswoman in her sophisticated suit weeping across the table from her and wondered how they'd come to this point. She knew she'd been clear up front. She always was, but somehow it often ended this way with accusations, tears and pain. The very things she dreaded.

"I'm sorry, Gina. I told you on our first date that I'm into having a good time, not commitment. And you said that's what you wanted as well." She handed her handkerchief to Gina and signaled the waiter for the check. This was too intense. It took all her resolve to stay and deal with the woman.

Gina dabbed at her eyes, obviously trying to salvage her eye makeup. "I didn't plan on falling in love." Gina blew her nose and glanced at the nearby tables. "This is embarrassing. I'm not usually the one groveling, but won't you give our relationship a chance?"

"I don't do relationships. I'm sorry." She hated this, hurting women, reducing them to begging. She hated feeling their pain. From now on, no more than three dates with anyone unless she sensed the woman was uninvolved. She gripped the table to keep from bolting, but she was desperate to get away. She pulled her phone out. "I'm texting Tanya to bring the car around. She'll take you home."

"What about the Christmas party?"

Robin signed the check. "I'm sorry, I'm not feeling very jolly at the moment." Her phone vibrated. "Tanya is out front. Let's go."

She retrieved their coats and helped Gina into hers. She dried Gina's tears, then handed her into the car. Her eyes met Tanya's in the rearview mirror. "Please see Ms. Gordon home, Tanya."

Gina grabbed her arm. "Aren't you coming?"

"I need to walk. And it's better if we don't see each other again, Gina. I'm really sorry that I hurt you." She pulled away and as she closed the door, Gina burst into tears again. Robin watched the car drive into traffic, then blew out her breath, tucked her hands in her coat pockets, and started walking.

Two hours later she found herself in front of Katie's brownstone in Greenwich Village. She wasn't surprised. Katie was her rock and she gravitated toward her whenever she felt needy. She rang the bell and smiled when Katie appeared looking like...oops, like she'd just had sex. "Sorry...am I interrupting anything?"

Katie yawned. "Just postcoital snuggling." She eyed Robin. "What's wrong?" She pulled her into the house. "Let me tell Michael you're here, then we can talk."

Robin could hear the murmur of voices from the bedroom as she paced in the living room. Not for the first time, she blessed Michael for understanding her relationship with Katie and accepting it. Most men would be jealous.

The television went on in the bedroom. Katie joined her, taking her hand and pulling her down on to the sofa. "Okay, spill. Why do you look like you just lost your last friend?"

Robin rubbed her hand over her face. "Sorry, I didn't mean to intrude."

Katie grabbed Robin's other hand and pulled her so they were facing each other. "C'mon, Robin, you know you're my priority."

"And Michael?"

"He knows the score. I told him up front and he's cool with it."

"So how come you told him the rules, and he understands and plays by them, yet when I tell women I'm not interested in a relationship, that I'm not into commitment, that I only want to have fun, they nod and smile, then ignore me?"

"Gina?"

"Yeah. We had a big scene at the restaurant tonight. God, Katie, I hate hurting people. I feel so bad." She swiped at the tears. "I don't know how I can be any clearer."

Katie pulled her into a hug. "The problem, Rob, is that besides being beautiful inside and out, you are intelligent and witty and playful. Oh, and rich. And though they don't know it, soon to be even richer. How can any woman resist falling for you?"

"You did."

"Well, other than the fact that I'm a paragon of strength, I'm also straight, and though I love you, our relationship is different. Maybe if I met you today in all your splendid glory, I would succumb. But I'm not the issue, am I?"

Robin kissed her cheek. "No. But you are the most important woman in my life, and I need you to help me figure out how to deal with this stuff."

"Do you ever think about settling down, Rob?"

"Occasionally. I sometimes fantasize about falling in love and having a relationship like you and Michael, but I haven't met anyone I want to be with forever."

"Maybe you're looking in the wrong places, dating women who live off their looks like models and starlets, and business executives like Gina who are attracted to your power and money. You need someone with more depth, someone who could match your intelligence and humor and playfulness, someone not interested in your financial statements."

"You're the only one I know who fits that description."

She patted Robin's cheek. "As unique and wonderful as I am, I'll bet there's at least one other out there. Let's keep our eyes open."

"I've decided I'm not going out with anyone more than three times unless I'm sure they're not interested in a relationship. What do you think?"

"It'll solve your immediate problem, but it makes me sad. You deserve so much more, Robin. Do you believe you deserve to love and be loved in a forever way?"

Robin stood and pulled Katie up into a hug. "Thanks. Now go back and snuggle. Give Michael a kiss for me." She hoped Katie didn't notice she hadn't answered the question.

Katie leaned back and glared at her. "Gee, and I thought I just asked whether you deserve a forever relationship?"

She should have known. Katie never missed a thing where she was concerned. She shrugged. "I'll think about it."

Katie squeezed her and kissed her temple. "You're sad. What can I do?"

"What you've always done, O Paragon. Let me cry on your shoulder, give me some loving, show me there's hope, and always be here for me." She turned to the door. "See you in the office tomorrow."

As she walked for another hour in the cold to reach her apartment in Battery Park City, Robin considered the question. Did she deserve to love and be loved forever? She wasn't sure. She wasn't even sure that was what she wanted. In fact, she spent a lot of time running from women who wanted that with her. Nearing her building, she was brought up short by a sudden realization that she was totally passive when it came to dating. She met the women she dated at various business or gay and lesbian events, and they sought her out. Never the other way around. She couldn't remember the last time she'd met someone who interested her enough to make her want to pursue her. Maybe in graduate school?

She leaned on the railing and stared out at the Hudson River. If she'd been as passive in her business life as she was in her love life, she'd probably be working as a typist someplace rather than running a multibillion-dollar business. Maybe Katie was wrong about her looking in the wrong places. Maybe the problem was she wasn't looking.

CHAPTER THREE

March–Lily

"I know it's been three months, Mama, but I'm really not in the mood to date." She listened. "Uh-huh. Yes, of course I have time to speak to Cordy." She held a finger up, letting Annie know she would be another minute. "Hey, Mama. You didn't call to gang up on me, did you?"

She rolled her eyes. "No, Mama. As I told Del, I'll know when I feel like dating." She listened again. "No, I'm not wasting time grieving for that fickle female fucker, and yes, I'm feeling better every day. In fact, Annie and I were just discussing going out for dinner and dancing later." She held the phone away from her ear, laughing. "Tell Del I got the message, no need to yell in the background. I promise I'll think about dating. Love and kisses to you both."

She smiled at Annie. "Sorry, Annie, they call me at least once a week and, as you heard, Del is pushing me to start dating. They send their regards."

"Your mamas are wonderful. And inspiring. I hope someday you and I will find relationships like theirs." Annie meant it, Lily knew. She'd told Lily that she hadn't liked Micki much but had tolerated her because she was the best friend of Tina, her girlfriend. Who became her ex-girlfriend after Tina had confessed she knew the night before the wedding that Micki wasn't going to show and had even helped her move out. Annie had broken up with her in disgust, not wanting to have anything to do with someone who could be so cruel and casual about hurting another human being. Lily was the kind of person she wanted in her life, she'd declared, and they'd become best friends.

"Don't we all." Lily ran her fingers through her hair. "They complement each other. Del is all emotion and fire while Cordy is analytic and cool except for her passions—mathematics, music and her family. They believe love and marriage are forever, even though they weren't legally married until last year." Her gaze went inward.

Annie frowned. "Why do you suddenly look so pensive? Did talking about your mamas upset you?"

Lily pulled at the lock of hair that she couldn't keep out of her eyes. "No. Yes, I guess. It just hit me. I never once thought Micki and I would have the kind of relationship they have. It's what I want for myself yet…I need to think about that. Sorry for disappearing."

"As long as you're not avoiding going out. Shazarak, the new place on Third and Eighty-ninth, combines fine dining in the front room with an active bar and a big dance floor in the back. They bring in a DJ at eleven. We could eat, then hang out and dance for a while." Annie held her eyes. "You do have to start to socialize sometime, Lily. If you're not comfortable, we can leave."

"Do you think Micki will be there?" She dreaded running into the woman who had publicly shamed her and had not made even a small gesture toward making amends. "It sounds like a perfect place for sexual conquest."

Annie ran her fingers through her newly cropped hair. "What the hell, better you hear it from me. Actually, she's spending a lot of time in Denver now. She just got engaged. Again."

Lily's face flamed. "She what? That bitch. I'll bet she was dating her while we were making wedding plans." She collapsed into a chair and bent over, her shoulders trembling. From under the cascade of her hair she saw the concern on Annie's face and realized Annie thought she was crying. She looked up, her face contorted with the laughter now bubbling out from deep inside her, loud and raunchy. Annie stared, confused, and then she convulsed too. Belly laughter can be contagious after all. It seemed like they would never stop, but finally, gasping for air, they smiled at each other. "Are you okay, Lily?"

"Actually, I am. It suddenly struck me funny that I'm so happy she jilted me. Otherwise I'd have wasted years dealing with her sleeping around. Thanks for telling me. You think I should try to warn the new woman?"

Annie shook her head. "If I know Micki, her version of the story makes her the victim. The best way to get revenge is to forget her, get on with your life."

"You are so right." She thought about the discussion with her mamas and her last phone call with her agent, Irene. Everyone was pushing her to date. Well, she didn't know about dating, but she was definitely in the mood for dancing and fun. She'd just be clear with anybody she met that she was looking for fun, not commitment. She no longer trusted herself to read the signals, her own or another woman's, and she doubted she'd ever be able to commit again. Lily stood. "Let's do it. But if you meet someone you want to hang out with, don't worry about me. Depending on how I'm feeling, I'll stay or come home."

* * *

Shazarak had delicious food and attentive service. Best of all was the short stroll to the active bar and great dance music. Lily moved with the beat as they made their way through the crowd of mostly women to the bar. She leaned over to speak into Annie's ear. "Do you want a sauvignon blanc? I'm buying the first round to reward you for bringing me to this wonderful place." Annie nodded.

When Lily turned back from the bar with Annie's white and her red, Annie was already dancing. A minute later, a short crew-cut butch wearing a black suit and a red and black plaid bow tie bowed and held her hand out. Lily put the two glasses of wine on the bar and allowed the woman to lead her onto the dance floor. Three dances later she excused herself and joined Annie at the bar. Miraculously their drinks were still there. As she sipped her cabernet, Lily eyed a shapely woman in a red dress, a good dancer who laughed a lot and danced every dance. Just what she was looking for tonight. *Here goes.* She downed her wine, put the empty glass on the bar, and went to claim her on the dance floor. The woman in red grinned, waved bye to her partner, and moved in concert with Lily. The next dance was a slow one, and they moved together. "Hi, I'm Lily. I hope I didn't interrupt anything."

"Toni. And, no, she's a friend. So what brings you here tonight?"

"Dinner and dancing. I'm looking to dance all night and go home alone."

Toni nodded. "Not looking to get laid?"

"No. So I'll understand if you want to move on."

"Is there any chance I could change your mind? I have some pretty good moves." She wriggled her rear and pulled Lily closer.

"That feels real nice, but I'm a recovering almost-bride. So I'm just looking to dance tonight."

"I appreciate the heads up. How about we dance until I spot somebody who looks more amenable to what I have planned for later."

Lily laughed. "Sounds good."

They moved really well together, and Lily was sorry when Toni danced her to the bar and kissed her cheek. "Thanks, Lily. Maybe another time."

She turned to order a drink and found herself face to face with a blond butch.

"Hey, lovely lady. Buy you a drink?"

"Sure. But, um, I'm just here to dance and have fun tonight. Nothing later."

"Thanks for telling me up front, easier on the ego later." The butch smiled. "Dancing and fun sounds good to me. I'm Frankie, by the way."

"Well, Frankie, I'd love a drink." As Frankie placed their order, Lily checked the dance floor. It looked like Annie had hooked up. She was going at it hot and heavy.

Lily and Frankie talked and flirted. It was her first experience with a fast-talking, sophisticated New York lesbian other than Micki, and she was pleased to find she was able to hold her own. They danced almost every dance, and it felt good to lose herself in the music. After a couple of hours, Annie left with the woman she'd met. Frankie claimed an early meeting and left soon after. Lily was not alone for long. An hour before closing, she leaned on the bar waiting for another glass of seltzer. She'd had two glasses of cabernet early in the evening, then switched. If she was sober when she got home in the wee hours, she could sleep late and still get in some work time, but if she got high, she'd be too fuzzy-minded tomorrow to write. She was thinking of leaving when a very warm body pressed her from behind and arms wrapped around her waist.

"I recognize that perfume. So, Ms. Red Dress, you couldn't score tonight?"

Toni spoke softly in her ear. "No one was as sexy as you, so I waited hoping you missed me enough to change your mind about—"

"I appreciate your persistence and your tempting body, but I'm still only offering dancing and fun." Lily turned so they were facing each other and gently pushed Toni so there was space between them. "Then I go home alone."

Toni grabbed Lily's seltzer, drank some and smiled up at her. "Will I least get a good-night kiss?"

"A friendly one."

"You drive a hard bargain. Let's dance." Toni led Lily onto the floor. They didn't sit out a single song. The last dance was another slow one. Toni pulled her close. "You sure?"

"Yes. And believe me, I'm doing you a favor because I'm such a mess."

Toni's hands moved over Lily's body, stirring feelings she thought were dead. "Just tonight. No strings."

The music ended and Lily stepped back. "Sorry, I don't do no-strings. But thank you, I had a great time. Maybe some other time." She kissed Toni lightly on the lips and pulled away fast before she could make it something more.

They retrieved their coats and put them on. "Can I give you a lift home?"

Lily put her hands on her hips and grinned. "So what don't you understand about 'alone'?"

Toni put her hands up and laughed. "Okay, okay. Got it. Thanks for a great time."

Toni waited with her until she got into a cab, then kissed her lightly. Lily waved as the taxi pulled away. What a great night. She'd danced almost every dance, been honest with everyone, and, not for lack of invitations, was leaving alone as planned. She could do this. Moving to the music had put her in touch with her body and made her feel sexy again. She'd reclaimed her ability to laugh and play. And any doubts about her attractiveness had been wiped away by the number of women who had come on to her tonight. As the taxi whisked her across Central Park, she vowed to get out more.

CHAPTER FOUR

March–Robin

Appalled at what she was hearing from two of her senior managers, Robin leaned on the podium in the small auditorium at DiLuca Cooper Technologies International.

"After all we're the decision-makers, they're just the workers. It's logical to limit the number of shares they receive." Simon scanned the conference room, expecting the other managers to jump on his bandwagon.

"Yes." Frannie chimed in. "I mean they're easily replaced, and if we give them too many shares, they'll probably leave anyway once they cash out." Frannie frowned and glanced over her shoulder, seeming uneasy with the continued silence.

Robin winced. How had she not noticed that they didn't really believe in the company's values? Happily, she, Katie, and Jan held all the stock in DCTI and would distribute stock options as they saw fit when their private company went public. "And how did you two get to be senior managers?"

Simon frowned. "We worked hard, and you thought we added value and could grow the business."

She took a second to make eye contact with each of the senior managers in the room. "Uh-huh, and we have grown it, and we've all been paid extremely well for our work, haven't we?"

There was a murmur of assent.

"We've earned it," Frannie said.

"Every single employee in this company has earned their salary by working hard and contributing to that growth. Those who didn't no longer work here. Our philosophy of sharing profits, fostering a team environment, and growing our people has resulted in the highest productivity and the lowest turnover rate in the industry. Right?"

Another murmur of assent. Frannie and Simon looked down.

"If we do what you two are proposing, the IPO will make us," she waved an arm around the room, "the senior managers, multimillionaires, but the employees will hardly benefit. How fair is that? And what impact will it have on the corporate culture that's made us so profitable?"

She moved to stand in front of them. "We're still working out the details with our IPO advisors, but we intend to allocate a substantial number of shares to everyone, not just senior managers." She looked around the room. "Thanks, everyone, have a good weekend."

She lowered her voice so only Fran and Simon could hear. "I'm disgusted by your greed."

"But—"

"We'll talk about this privately next week." She left them open-mouthed and walked back to her office. Jan, her assistant, friend and minor partner, handed her a stack of message slips. "Katie's meeting ran over, but she confirmed for dinner tonight at your place. Want me to order something sent up?"

Robin nodded. "Italian, please. Don't forget to have one of your slavies pull all the employee records and the financials I requested."

"Already in your briefcase, lovey. I confirmed Wanda for the LGBTQ Charity Ball tomorrow night. She expects you to pick her up at seven thirty. So is she a lesbian?"

"Interested?"

"Nope. Tall, gorgeous models don't do it for me. Why do I always have to remind you, men or women, I go for grunge and tats and muscle?"

"Really?" Robin raised her eyebrows. "Remind me again how you got through Human Resources? I distinctly remember telling them to hire lesbians, gays and straights, no bisexuals."

"Yeah, yeah. Maybe because you never hired me, I just moved in with you and Katie and neither of you asked. This is your fifth date with Wanda. Do I hear wedding bells?"

"If you do, you need an ear doctor." Robin laughed. "Happily, Wanda doesn't do commitment."

"Oh, that actress you met at the opening of her show last week called. Do you want me to set something up?"

"Lorna? Yes, dinner and dancing. There's a new lesbian restaurant I hear is very good, and they have dancing later in the evening. Shazarak, I think it's called."

"I'll find it. What about that other actress, Donna? Is she still on the roster for events or has she hit the three-date wall?"

"She's reached her expiration date, and we've parted ways." She grinned. "So if you're thinking of switching teams, she's available. You have her number?"

"Hahaha. I appreciate your interest in my love life, boss, but don't you have work to do on this IPO?"

"I don't understand why it's all right for you to poke your nose into my love life, but I can't do the same."

Jan stuck her tongue out. "You need me to help you filter the hordes and keep the date tracking spreadsheet updated. But do you need me at this meeting tonight?"

"Yes. Your warped perspective is always helpful. Oh, oh." Robin noticed Simon and Fran moving down the hall in her direction. "Could you also pull the files of the senior managers in Fran and Simon's divisions? I'm going to work on the IPO now. Absolutely no interruptions, please."

Jan's eyes followed Robin's glance. "Go. I've got this."

CHAPTER FIVE

June–Lily

Enjoying the brief respite from her date, Lily took her time strolling from the ladies room to the table where she'd left her. A celebration of some sort near the bar caught her eye, and she stopped to watch the happy crowd dancing around someone in a tux. Lily's body moved of its own accord to the beat of the music, and she longed to be out there dancing with them instead of listening to boring Glory. When the fast song faded to a romantic ballad, she sighed and returned to her table. Her blind date, Gloria, "call me Glory," resumed her monologue even before she sat. Lily wondered whether Glory had been speaking to her empty chair while she was in the ladies room.

As Glory went on and on about herself in excruciating detail, Lily's eyes darted to the dance floor. Ah, the someone in a tuxedo was an exuberant butch surrounded by hugging and kissing women, several of them actresses Lily recognized, a number of obvious models, given their height, carriage and looks, and a sprinkling of sophisticated businesswomen wearing expensive suits or sleek come-hither dresses. The sexy-as-hell butch was at the center of whatever it was they were celebrating. And unlike Lily, the butch and everyone with her seemed to be having fun.

Her eyes flicked to her date, still droning on. "I've taken my writing to a new level and this book is much better than anything out there. It will definitely go to the top of the bestseller list if Irene would just get off her ass and find an editor to buy it."

Damn Irene. Whatever had made their mutual agent think this egotistical idiot would be a good match for her? A cheer drew Lily's eyes back to the butch, now prancing one table away from them with her arms in the air like a winning boxer. The butch grinned as their eyes met. Lily couldn't help but grin back.

She'd make a dynamite hero for one of her romances. What was it that made her so damn attractive? Her height? She must be almost six feet. Her carriage? So debonair in the tuxedo and white silk scarf. The short black hair swept back from her face like that of a gothic hero, the startling green eyes combined with the creamy olive skin and the sexy smile—they were a good part of it, of course. Add in the high energy and the playfulness Lily could see and feel as she pranced mere feet away, and she was irresistible. At least to Lily, who felt drawn to her like steel chips to a magnet. And judging by the women vying for her attention, Lily wasn't the only one. Her hero had charisma.

Just then a slender, light-brown haired woman and a taller, heavier, dark-haired woman with tattooed biceps, a green streak in her hair, and, judging by the glint, a pierced eyebrow, separated her hero from the pack of fawning beauties and pulled her into a group hug. A cheer went up from their crowd, and the hero lifted their arms in the air for a second, leaned over to kiss each of them, then threw her arms over their shoulders. The tattooed woman shook her hips, grabbed another tattooed woman standing nearby, and boogied onto the dance floor. The handsome butch kissed the slender woman's forehead and turned her toward the bar where a man in a suit embraced her and offered his stool.

Her eyes fastened on the butch, Lily saw a flash of vulnerability, a moment of uncertainty and loneliness. Then a group of willowy beauties enveloped her, and the lost look disappeared so quickly from her hero's face that Lily almost thought she'd imagined it. But she knew what she'd seen and tucked it away to think about later. Right now she was enjoying watching her, enjoying the flush of pleasure each time their eyes connected, enjoying the fantasy of being swept off her feet.

A black-clad waitress stepped between Lily and the object of her study, interrupting her reverie. She placed a glass of champagne in front of her. Lily blinked. "I didn't order—"

"Compliments of Robin," she pointed, "the lady in the tux." She placed a glass in front of Glory as well. "She's celebrating tonight and she wants everyone to celebrate with her. She picked up your check as well."

Robin. The name fits. "What is she celebrating?" Lily was dying to know.

The waitress shrugged. "Some big business deal."

"Please tell her we appreciate her treating us and send our congratulations on her deal."

"How intrusive." Glory frowned. "Does she have to be so noisy about it? I can barely hear myself talk. It's annoying, isn't it, Lily?"

Lily picked up the champagne and turned toward Robin, surprised to find her staring. Their eyes locked and those emerald green orbs seemed to pierce Lily. Her heart did a somersault. Robin flashed that sexy smile and lifted her glass in a kind of salute. It took a few seconds for Lily's brain to connect with her hand, but she lifted her glass and silently toasted Robin.

Robin held Lily's eyes, mouthed "I love you," blew a kiss, and sipped her champagne. Lily grinned, then returned the kiss. Definitely the perfect romantic hero who could get the heroine to swoon. At least this heroine.

Glory stood. "Let's go."

Lily half-turned toward her. "What?"

"It's noisy. And it's getting too frenetic for me." She walked toward the exit.

Hoping for rescue, Lily whirled toward Robin. Apparently Robin had lost interest in her, had switched her attention to the high-spirited crowd of youngish casually dressed women and men surrounding her. With a sigh, Lily picked up her purse and reluctantly followed Glory out. In the cab, she berated herself for not having the balls to tell Glory to leave without her. Well, Irene be damned, she wouldn't spend a minute longer than necessary with this self-absorbed pain in the ass.

She leaned forward and spoke through the divider. "Two stops, please. First, Central Park West and Seventy-fifth." She turned to Glory. "Sorry, all that noise gave me a headache." She didn't say the noise was Glory's monologue. "I need an aspirin and some sleep." She didn't give a damn whether Glory believed her. At her stop, she handed Glory money for half the fare. "Nice to meet you," she tossed over her shoulder. Glory leaned forward and gave the driver her address. Thankfully, she didn't ask to see Lily again.

In the elevator on the way to her floor, Lily debated with herself about whether to go back to Shazarak, then decided she was making too much of what was probably a drunken gesture. She sighed. Maybe in another lifetime. It was fodder for the writing, but romantic things like that didn't happen in real life. At least not her life.

CHAPTER SIX

June–Robin

Surrounded by old and new friends and acquaintances, many of them the actresses and willowy models she liked to sport on her arm when she appeared at events for DCTI, Robin DiLuca was celebrating taking her company public. As of today, she and Katie were officially billionaires, but she was having a hard time wrapping her mind around the concept.

As she danced and played and whooped, she noticed a sultry blonde watching the dancers and moving her incredible body to the music. Although she was the hottest woman in the place, she seemed lonely, wistful. Robin watched her watching and saw her turn down the many women who approached her. Just as Robin decided to go claim her, she turned and walked to a table where a woman sat with her face buried in her cell phone.

Of course, she was with someone. Robin knew she shouldn't flirt with a woman who was taken, but she couldn't help herself. Whatever she was doing, whomever she was talking to, her eyes were drawn back to the seductive woman with the warm golden-brown eyes, who, despite her date, seemed to be equally fixated on her. She couldn't have been more different from the tall, thin, elegant fashion models or the beautiful actresses or the stylish cool business types who usually attracted Robin. Her beauty was natural, her breasts full, her body all curves and softness. She oozed sensuality. Robin felt a rush and a sudden longing to bury herself in that voluptuous body. She tried to keep herself from staring, but each time their eyes locked some empty space deep inside Robin filled with warmth. Weird. No doubt it was due to her heightened state tonight. Or maybe since she rarely drank alcohol, it was the half glass of champagne.

Katie and Jan had been dancing, but now stood one on each side of her, arms encircling her waist. "We've done it, Rob. Can you believe we're billionaires?" Katie kissed Robin's cheek.

Robin lifted their arms in a victory salute. Their friends cheered as she twirled the three of them around, then dropped an arm over each of them. "A billionaire. It's hard to take in."

"And you, little Miss Runaway Jan, are a multimillionaire." Katie leaned over and kissed Jan's check. Robin kissed both of them.

"Hey, just because I was a loser-teenage-vampire-wannabe-runaway from Ohio doesn't mean I didn't know how to pick the winning horses." Jan wiggled her hips and shimmied away with a woman who was standing nearby.

Katie followed Robin's eyes to the blonde. "Ooh, slow sizzle. Seductive. I might consider switching teams for someone that hot. Not your usual fare, that's for sure. Interested?"

"Very, but she's with someone."

"Actually, Michael and I have been watching her. She can't take her eyes off you, and her friend hasn't stopped talking. Go over and flash those gorgeous green orbs of yours, and she'll drop that woman like a three-week-old fish."

"It wouldn't be right, Katie."

"Okay, Ms. Prim and Proper. Send her a drink at least."

"Great idea. I'll send her a drink, then go over and introduce myself." Robin waved the waitress over and indicated the table. "Bring those two champagne. Tell them I'm celebrating and I'd like them to join me. And include them in the checks I'm picking up." She watched the waitress deliver the drinks and the message. The blonde picked up the champagne and turned toward her. Their eyes locked again. Robin fell into the golden pools and experienced a full-body flush that made her knees weak. She managed a smile, mouthed, "I love you," lifted her glass to acknowledge her, then blew a kiss. The blonde silently toasted her and returned the kiss. As the blonde half-turned to say something to the woman she was with, Robin used her phone to snap a picture. She was about to go introduce herself when a group of their newly wealthy non-management employees showed up to celebrate. Despite Simon and Fran's objections, every employee had received stock and benefited financially from the IPO. After greeting them, Robin turned to find the blonde, but she was gone. She made her way to the bar where Katie was sitting with Michael. "Did you see where she went?"

"Her girlfriend dragged her out. But she sure looked like she wanted to stay and play."

Robin scanned the room, not quite believing the woman would have left after they...They what? Had a fun moment? If that's all it was, why did she feel like a kid watching the ice cream truck drive away just as she arrived to buy her cone? She hoped her tacky behavior, flirting with another woman's date, hadn't triggered the blonde's abrupt departure.

"Too bad. She would be a nice change from your usual stick-thin models and self-involved actresses."

She brought her attention back to Katie. "How do you know *she's* not self-involved?"

"One, because she put up with that woman who was so self-involved she didn't even notice that her date only had eyes for you. And, two, she only had eyes for you, but she was polite to her self-involved date. Or something like that." She kissed Robin's forehead. "Sorry, hon, I know you've been looking for someone."

She fingered the phone in her pocket, grinned, then did a little soft-shoe, moved her hands in front of her and sang a made-up song. "How deep is the ocean? How high is the sky? So many women. Oh my, oh my."

Katie frowned. "Are you drunk, Robin?"

"High on life." She threw Katie a kiss as three women surrounded her and pulled her onto the dance floor. After all, she didn't even know that woman, so what was she upset about?

CHAPTER SEVEN

June–Lily and Robin

She'd been cavalier about the missed opportunity to meet the sexy blonde she'd flirted with, but those seductive eyes and that sensuous body had haunted her thoughts and her dreams since that Friday night a week ago. Unsettled by the unfamiliar feeling of aching for someone, she'd taken her entourage dancing at Shazarak every night, hoping sex with another woman would blot out Blondie, but no one tempted her. It wasn't until she was walking to her apartment after working late today that she'd admitted to herself that she'd been going to Shazarak looking for Blondie, not any other woman. And having admitted to herself her desire to find Blondie and take her to bed, she'd hailed a taxi on the chance that the woman only went out on Fridays and tonight might be her lucky night.

Now, leaning back on the bar, scanning the crowd in hopes of seeing the sexy blonde, Robin felt uneasy. Was she stalking the woman? Was this what obsession felt like? Should she leave and try to forget her?

* * *

Lily arrived at the bar hoping to see the beautiful green-eyed butch she'd interacted with the previous Friday. The more she thought about it, the more she regretted not dumping her blind date and finding a way to meet her. She hadn't been able to get her out of her mind. Had even dreamed about her.

She'd never done anything like this, but then again, she'd never felt such an intense attraction to anyone, an attraction based on thirty seconds of eye contact and a few flirtatious moves. She knew she sounded like the heroine in one of her romance novels, but she actually felt as if their souls had touched and they were destined to be together. What if she never found her again? What if she was already committed? Wait, hadn't she sworn off commitment herself? She decided it didn't matter. She could still have fun, still wanted to have fun, dance and sing and play, and Ms. Butch looked like she could be her good-time girl.

This was the third time she'd been back looking for her, for Robin. Did this constitute stalking? Maybe she should just go home. She hesitated. Maybe Robin only went to bars on Friday nights. A quick glance around, then she'd leave. She surveyed the tables and the dance floor, then turned her attention to the bar. Her breath caught at the sight of the slender figure towering over everyone, her black hair glistening in the soft light around the bar, her green eyes flashing as she laughed with someone standing next to her. No tuxedo tonight, just jeans and a pale green T-shirt that showed her nicely muscled arms and flat stomach. She looked even more delectable than Lily remembered. And she'd had a haircut, leaving her neck bare and vulnerable looking. Lily was mesmerized. She imagined kissing those lips, caressing that neck, running her hands over that body and—

Piggy, she chided herself. She'd never ogled another woman before. Should she go over to her? Was she with that woman? Screw it. She wasn't going to make the same mistake twice.

* * *

Robin joked with the woman next to her, who was waiting for her drink order. When the woman walked away, she turned to order another glass of seltzer, but a hand on her arm stopped her.

"Hey, Robin, I believe y'all were staring at me the other night. Have we met before?" The husky voice with traces of the South oozed through her body like warm chocolate. She shivered and looked down into the inviting gold-flecked brown eyes of the woman of her dreams. Her heart skipped a beat.

"No, we haven't, but let's remedy that. I'm Robin DiLuca. And you are?"

"Lily Alexander." She stuck out her hand.

Robin took the offered hand and, with her eyes locked onto Lily's, brought it to her lips.

Lily laughed, a joyous sound from deep within. "My, you're smooth."

Robin spoke into her ear. "My only smooth move of the night, I assure you. You addle my brain." And that was the truth. Up close like this she was sexier than Robin remembered. And the herbal scent of her shampoo mingling with the light fragrance of her perfume was truly heady.

Lily shivered. "Sweet talker too." She looked down at their clasped hands. "I'm feeling a little light-headed myself. Shall we get a table?"

Robin squeezed her hand. "See what I mean, forgetting my manners. Would you like a drink?"

"Cabernet sauvignon, please."

Drinks in hand, they found a table and stared at each other without speaking for a minute, then both spoke at the same time. "I'm glad I found—" They laughed.

Robin reached across the table and took both of Lily's hands. "Are you single?"

"Smooth *and* direct. Yes. And you? Was there someone special amongst all those gorgeous women hanging on you the other night?"

"Ah, so you *were* looking. No one special...until now."

"Romantic, too. So where do we go from here?"

Robin grinned and wiggled her eyebrows. "Your place or mine?"

"Whoa. Smooth *and* direct *and* romantic. *And* aggressive." Lily squeezed Robin's hands.

Robin flushed. "Sorry. It's just..." She looked down.

"Just what?" Lily ran her thumbs over Robin's hands.

Robin's heart raced. "You're so…I feel like a moth drawn to the light. I've wanted to take you to bed since I saw you."

Lily flushed. "I feel the same, darlin'." She brought Robin's hand to her lips. "But what will we tell our kids if we jump right into bed? We need to date, get to know each other before we make love."

Robin frowned. "So we're going to have kids?"

"I'd love to have your babies. Two would be perfect."

Robin's body flared. "That's the sexiest thing anybody has ever said to me." She pulled her chair so they were face to face. "But you're spooking me. I don't do…have never done…commitment well. In fact, I don't do commitment or relationships at all. I'm all about having fun."

Lily nodded slowly. "What are you afraid of?"

"Wow, no one ever asked. They usually just ignore me when I say that." She cleared her throat. "What if I'm not happy, what if I want to leave? I hate screaming, tearful, painful breakups. I hate causing pain."

Lily touched Robin's cheek. "Sweet Robin, know I would never cage you. Or anyone. And, truthfully, the last thing I'm interested in right now is commitment. Having fun sounds like…well, like fun. But who knows how I'll feel in a month. Do you have a pen and a sheet of paper?"

Robin extracted a pen and a small leather-bound notebook from the back pocket of her jeans, tore a page from the notebook, and handed it and the pen to Lily.

"A fountain pen? It's lovely."

"I collect them, you know the old ones. Most people don't notice how beautiful they are."

Lily raised her eyes to Robin's. She kissed the pen. "Lovely. Like you."

Robin shivered.

Lily uncapped the pen and began to write. When she was finished, she capped the pen and handed it and the paper to Robin.

I, Lily Boudreaux Carlyle Alexander, promise that should Robin DiLuca and I decide at any time for any reason to terminate our relationship whatever its nature and no matter how long we've been together, I will let her go without screaming, crying, accusations

*and hurtful language. I also promise that I will cherish whatever
time we have together, strive to make it fun, and mentally and
physically fulfilling, and that forever after I will remain her friend.*
     Lily

"For real?"
Lily smiled. "For real."
Robin folded the note and put it in her wallet, then put her arm
around Lily. "Let the dating begin." She breathed deeply, taking in
Lily's scent again.
"Wait." Lily put her hand up. "Since we're stating terms, I
have to say I find you incredibly attractive, attractive enough that
I came back here looking for you, but if all you're interested in is a
quick roll in the hay or casual sex, I'm not your gal. I've only slept
with a few women and that's after spending time together, getting
to know each other." She could barely breathe as she picked at a
thread on her jeans and avoided Robin's eyes.

Lily made her nervous. She said she was into fun, but it sounded
like she wanted commitment. Well, she enjoyed a challenge, and
Lily wouldn't be the first supposedly reluctant woman she'd
seduced. She put a finger under her chin and lifted her face. "I hear
you. Just dating. No sex." *For now. No sex for now.*
Lily's obvious relief and her sweet smile touched Robin. She
leaned over and kissed Lily lightly. "They're playing our song. Is it
okay to dance on a first date?"
Lily tilted her head, listening. "Our song?"
Robin pulled her out of her chair and whispered in her ear.
"Can't you hear? Bette Midler is singing "Be My Baby." She
moved them out onto the dance floor and sang along with Bette,
serenading Lily.
They danced nearly every dance, fast or slow didn't matter,
stopping only to drink something cold now and then. They laughed
and flirted and played.

CHAPTER EIGHT

Lily and Robin

After the DJ played the last song, a slow one, they sat close, holding hands, looking into each other's eyes, grinning.

"That was fun. I love to dance, but I never expected we'd have our own song on our first date. I'll bet you sing that song to all the women you seduce."

"Not true. When I seduce a woman we usually don't waste time dancing and singing, we get right to it. You're special, Lily." She lifted Lily's hand to her lips. "Believe it."

Lily studied her for a few seconds, wanting to believe but not quite trusting this gorgeous, slick New Yorker wasn't trying to get her into bed tonight. "We'll see."

"We will, but since this is our first date, we still have a lot of history to cover." Robin lifted Lily's hand to her cheek. "Be honest. And no googling. We tell each other what we want when we want. Agreed?"

"But if you're a serial killer, you have to say it up front. Agreed?" She squeezed Robin's hand.

"Damn. Okay, I am…not a serial killer. So, tell me. Where have you been hiding? I would have remembered if I'd seen you before." She kissed Lily's palm again.

Lily's body fluttered in response to Robin's warm breath on her palm. "Keep that up and I'll be just a gooey puddle at your feet." She shivered. "I just moved to New York City from Chicago in December and I haven't been out much."

"Is Chicago where you grew up?"

"I grew up in Alabama and California with two moms, a lesbian sister and a straight brother, twins. I graduated from the University of Chicago, then spent two years getting a masters of fine arts at the Iowa Writing Workshop before moving back to Chicago."

"Your moms are lesbians. Cool."

Lily laughed. "It was cool as I got older, but I got hassled a lot as a kid in Alabama. They're great parents, though, and it was worth it. What about you?"

Robin sucked in air. "Grew up in Florida. Mom, dad and two older brothers. I went to Harvard, then Stanford for a PhD."

"Ah, doctor, is it?"

"Want to play?" She wiggled her eyebrows again.

"Uh-uh, sweetie." Lily shook her head. "No playing doctor." She held Robin's eyes. "Yet."

"Hey, this is our first date. You can't call me sweetie."

"Of course, I can. Didn't we agree I'm going to have your babies?"

"It's just not done, calling somebody sweetie on the first date."

"Hmm, you may be right, sweetie. It's too soon to call you sweetie."

Lily followed Robin's lead and kissed the hand she was holding. "So what do you do when you're not seducing women in bars?"

Robin wiggled her eyebrows again. "Well, when I'm not seducing them, I'm usually home having sex with them, but I don't have high hopes for this evening."

Lily giggled. "Geez, Robin, I hope you don't think that wiggling-eyebrows thing is seductive. Anyway, I meant what work do you do?"

"Are you sure?" She wiggled her eyebrows again.

"Definitely. Work?"

"Ah, yes, the old work question. I guess you haven't seen my picture in the paper?"

Lily laughed. "Oh, are you famous?"

"I own a technology company. What about you?"

Ah, yes, the business deal. "I write."

"Hey, even a techie like me figured that out when you mentioned your MFA from Iowa. What do you write?" She put a hand up. "Wait, I know. You're a famous author of torrid romances, and you had to move to New York to get away from the hordes of fans hungry to ravage you."

"Wow. You got it on the first guess. Seriously, what do you like to do when you're not partying?"

"Other than partying and working, I read or workout or go to a movie with a friend."

"What do you read?"

"Some fiction and almost any non-fiction. What about you? What do you do when you're not seducing unsuspecting women in bars?"

"Actually, I'm really not into bars at all. I write, of course, and read lots of fiction, biographies, history, and some political stuff. I do yoga, I love dancing, and walking and hiking. I also volunteer at a soup kitchen and teach writing to underprivileged kids."

"Do you like swimming, the beach? Maybe we can—"

"Um, Robin, it looks like they're closing up here. Time to go."

She handed her phone to Lily. "Okay, Ms. Alexander, type in your telephone number and address so I can find you again. But give me your phone first." They typed the information and exchanged phones again.

Lily frowned at Robin's entry. "What does 'Robin, the Dad' mean?"

"Remember I said I'm not into commitment, that I just want to have fun? Well, that extends to our kids. Being responsible for bottles, changing diapers, walking the floor in the middle of the night, or any of those kinds of things, is not for me. I fit into more of the Dad model of parenting. Dads have less responsibility and are seldom around, so I'll focus on my work and occasionally do fun things with them."

"Is that how it worked in your family?"

Robin looked uncomfortable. "Mainly the seldom-around part."

"I see. My family worked differently." *And we're definitely going to have to work on your model of parenting when the time comes.* "So? Dad? Seriously?"

"Seriously. Now let me take you home as is proper on a first date. But first…" She waved the waitress over. "Check, MJ, and would you take a couple of pictures of us?"

She handed over her phone and pulled Lily close to her. "Smile."

"That's cute. Do you take pictures with all your girls on the first date?"

"Nope." She pocketed her phone, signed the credit card receipt and handed it to MJ. "Never done it before. Right, MJ?"

MJ glanced at the receipt and smiled. "Not on my watch. Good night, ladies."

Robin hailed a taxi outside the bar and gave the driver Lily's address. They stared into each other's eyes and held hands during the ride across the park. Outside her building, Lily turned to say good night.

"Wait, I'm coming up with you." Robin paid the driver and they got out.

Lily had expected Robin to drop her off. "You're not coming in, you know."

Not now, but soon. Robin steered her into the building. "Of course not. But proper first date behavior requires that I escort you to your apartment door."

As they had in the taxi, their hands and eyes kept them connected. The sexual tension that was a constant between them seemed to increase with each ding marking another floor. By the time they reached sixteen and walked to Lily's door, they were both flushed.

Robin put her hands on Lily's shoulders. "Do you kiss good night on the first date?"

Lily stepped closer. "That depends." She spoke softly and Robin tipped her head to hear.

"Depends on what?" She was breathless.

"On whether I want to or not."

"Cheeky little thing aren't—"

Lily's hand brushed Robin's neck and then pulled her head down to kiss her. It started as a sweet good-night kiss but quickly morphed into a passionate searching for each other. Robin pulled her close. Lily's arms circled Robin's waist and she leaned into her. When Robin gently pushed her against the door, Lily pulled away from the kiss. "I think," she panted, "we've reached the outer boundaries of first-date contact." She leaned her head against the door.

Robin held Lily close and covered her face with soft kisses. "We need to keep this dating thing moving. How about dinner tomorrow?"

"Dinner sounds wonderful, but we have to go out so we don't get into trouble."

Robin grinned. "I prefer to face trouble head-on, but if you insist I'll pick you up at seven fifteen for dinner. A fancy restaurant. Dress accordingly." She leaned down and brushed her lips over Lily's. "How will we know when we've dated enough?"

"I'll know." Lily leaned against her door, too weak to turn and open it, and watched Robin walk backward to the elevator and blow her a kiss as the doors slid closed.

CHAPTER NINE

River Café

At exactly seven fifteen Lily's doorbell rang. Her breath caught when she saw Robin's beautifully tailored black pantsuit and a silk shirt the exact green of her eyes. Robin's appreciative glance left no doubt that she approved Lily's choice, a clingy wrap-around of brown silk with golden highlights that displayed enough cleavage to keep Robin's eyes from straying in case any models were nearby at dinner.

Robin helped her into a waiting Lincoln Town Car, then instructed the driver. "The River Café, please, Tanya."

"Are you trying to dazzle me? An exclusive restaurant with terrific food, I've been told, and a chauffeured car." She inhaled the new leather smell. "At least it's not one of those ostentatious long limousines. A Lincoln Town Car seems more your style. Comfortable and classy."

"You think I'm classy?" Robin's thumb circled Lily's palm. "Don't forget the lovely view of lower Manhattan and the romantic atmosphere. I *am* trying to seduce you after all."

Lily caressed the buttery leather seat, then smiled at Robin. "I'm weakening."

When they arrived at the restaurant, a former barge moored under the Brooklyn Bridge in the East River, Robin leaped out of the car and dashed around to open Lily's door. She took Lily's hand and helped her out. Lily gaped at the flower-lined entry, the sparkling lights and the view of Manhattan just across the water. "It's spectacular. I can't thank you enough for bringing me here. I love it. I didn't expect it to actually be in the river."

Robin squeezed her hand, loving her out-there, enthusiastic appreciation, so unlike the blasé response of her usual self-consciously sophisticated dates. "We can walk in the garden later if you'd like."

The maitre d' greeted Robin by name and whisked them to a table next to the windows.

"Come here often?" Lily widened her eyes as she sat opposite Robin.

Robin blushed. "For business mostly. It's on the must-see list for a lot of our out-of-town clients."

"Uh-huh?" Lily's tone was teasing, and though she raised her eyebrows at the presumption of Robin's hand lying expectantly palm up on the table, she didn't hesitate to place her hand there. Thoroughly enchanted by Robin, she wasn't naïve enough to think she was the first woman Robin had set out to seduce. And she was charmed—the fragrant bouquets of flowers, the lighting, a pianist playing romantic ballads, the view of the Manhattan skyline, and Robin smiling across the table.

"Champagne, red wine, beer? What's your pleasure, Lily?"

"Whatever you're having."

"I'm having seltzer and lime. Here's the first secret I'm sharing tonight. I rarely drink. That first night was the exception because I was celebrating, and even then I only had half a glass of champagne. So?"

Lily studied Robin. "You don't mind if I have alcohol?"

Robin laughed. "Not at all."

"Then I'll have champagne because this is a celebration-worthy night."

Robin squeezed her hand. "I'm glad you think so." She waved the waiter over and ordered for them. "A glass of your best champagne and a seltzer with lime. We'll order dinner later."

"Okay, Lily, your turn to share a secret."

"A secret, huh?" She stared out the window. "I didn't come to New York to escape hordes of fans who want to ravage me. I moved here to get married, but she never showed for the ceremony and left me to explain it to our ninety-five guests, most of them her family and friends whom I'd never met."

"Whoa." Robin sat up straighter. "How'd you get involved with someone who obviously has her head screwed on backward?"

Lily shrugged. "Poor judgment combined with gullibility and neediness." She sat back, pulling her hand away from Robin. "She chased me so long and so hard I believed her when she said she was in love with me, and I convinced myself I was in love with her. She never bothered to explain, so I still don't understand what happened." She picked up her glass, gazed out the window, and downed half her champagne.

Robin gave her a minute, then took her hand again. "Is that why you're commitment shy?"

"You might say that." She offered a shaky smile as she turned back to Robin. "Sorry to be so dramatic. I guess I'm still raw." She straightened her silverware. "The good news is that after the shock of being humiliated in front of almost a hundred guests wore off, I realized I was relieved she hadn't gone through with it, that I had fooled myself into thinking I was in love with her. The bad news is I no longer trust my feelings. Or what others say they feel for me."

"With good reason. So why did you stay in New York?"

"I'd sold my townhouse in Chicago and used it as the down payment on the apartment we were going to live in and make mortgage payments on together, but really it was because I fell in love with New York."

Robin nodded "It's a great city. Do you think you'll ever trust again?"

She gazed into Robin's eyes for a long minute. "I hope to, some day."

Heat surged through Robin. She had never responded to anyone the way she did to Lily. She rubbed her thumb over Lily's hand, imagining slowly undressing her, caressing her everywhere with her fingers and her lips and her tongue.

"Where did you go, Robin?"

She looked up. "What? Oh, sorry, just," she flushed, "thinking." She met Lily's eyes. "About what I'd like to do to you."

"Oh." Lily waved her hand in front of her face as if she needed to cool down.

Their eyes held. "Sorry, I didn't mean to upset—"

"You didn't upset me. You do things to me without actually doing anything and make me feel things without touching me. I've never experienced that before." She took a deep breath. "Um, tell me about your family. Are you close?"

Robin smiled, but her eyes were sad. Recalling the moment in the bar that first night when Robin looked so vulnerable she regretted asking the question.

"Well, my mom died a long time ago, so it's just my dad and my two brothers and me. They live in Florida. I haven't seen any of them in years. What about your family?"

Lily wanted to know more. What had happened to her mom, and why wasn't she close to her dad and brothers, but clearly it was a sensitive topic so she dropped it. "My moms, Delphine Boudreaux and Cordelia Carlyle, met at the University of Alabama where Cordy, as she's called, was in her first year of teaching mathematics, and Del was a graduate student in journalism. They fell in love and settled nearby after Del graduated. I have a younger brother and sister, twins Bella and Ben. Del is our birth mother, and Cordy's twin brother Cornelius was the sperm donor, so all three of us also have the same dad. Cornelius is also gay. He lives and works in Hong Kong and we see him occasionally."

"Is Alexander a pseudonym? Or were you married?"

"Neither. When they started having children, they decided we all needed to have the same name so they changed their names to Alexander. We all have their previous last names as our middle names."

"Yesterday you said you were from Alabama and California, but now you just said Alabama."

"Right. When I was sixteen, Cordy was offered a position at Stanford and we moved to California."

Robin sat up straighter. "The brilliant Dr. Cordelia Alexander is your mom? I took as many classes as I could with her when I was a graduate student at Stanford. How's that for six degrees of separation?"

"Did you like her? Do you think she'd remember you?"

"Maybe. I was always bugging her with questions and theories and ideas, and she kindly and patiently responded. She's brilliant. So what does your other mom do?"

"Del was a journalist, but when we moved, she had to leave her job, so she started writing novels."

"Delphine Boudreaux is your mother?"

"One of them, yes. You've read her?"

"Yes. I love her books."

"You made the connection really quickly. Are you sure you didn't google me?"

"Absolutely. It's an unusual name and you mentioned it. Besides," she patted herself on the shoulder, "I have a rather high IQ and I'm quite good at solving puzzles."

"Well, la-di-da." Lily noticed the sky outside changing colors and realized Robin had timed their reservation so they could watch the sunset. "Wow, what a gorgeous sunset. You are quite a romantic, Robin DiLuca." Their eyes connected again, and she reached over and gently trailed a finger along Robin's jaw. Suddenly a light flashed and she and Robin both jerked back.

Robin jumped up. "What the?"

The photographer ran toward the door, but Tanya and another woman cut her off and escorted her out. The maître d' rushed over. "I'm so sorry, Ms. DiLuca, I don't know how she sneaked by us, but she's gone now."

"Someone on your staff must have tipped her off since only my chauffeur and my assistant know I'm here tonight."

"Please let me comp your dinners."

"Not necessary. Just leave us and make sure there's no one else lurking."

Tanya, the chauffeur, appeared at the table and held up a small square. "I got the memory card, boss, so don't worry, no picture."

"Thanks, Tanya. Where are you?"

Tanya pointed to a table further back.

Robin waved at someone sitting there. "Give Mel a kiss for me and enjoy your dinner."

"Will do." Tanya smiled at Lily. "Sorry for the interruption."

"Not your fault." Lily was puzzled by the incident and the fact that it didn't seem to be the first time. "Why are you being stalked by a photographer?" Then, seeing that Robin was rattled by the incident, she held her hands out. "Give me your hands and look me in the eye. Are you in trouble? Are you a married politician or public figure? Or married to a politician or public figure?"

Robin shook her head. "I'm not in trouble or married. It's nothing bad I assure you. I just wanted to know you a little better before we talk about it. At least Tanya saved us from having our picture in the gossip columns of the *News* and the *Post* tomorrow or, worse, plastered on the front page of some skuzzy supermarket magazine." Her shoulders drooped, and she turned to look out the window, clearly trying to figure out what to say.

Lily squeezed her hands to get her attention. "Let's enjoy our dinner. Tell me about it whenever you feel comfortable. I always enjoy a bit of mystery." She sipped her champagne. "I am curious, though. Your chauffeur is having dinner here with a date?"

"She's not my chauffeur. She's an entrepreneur. She owns the car and I hire her when I need to be driven. I feel bad asking her to sit in the car and wait when I eat, so she eats too. Sometimes, like tonight, Mel is available to join her."

"And you pay?"

"Of course."

"Wow. That's really nice of you. Technology pays well, does it?"

"Yeah, it does. Let's order. Is the tasting menu okay with you?"

"Sure."

Robin waved the waiter over. "We'd like the tasting menu." She looked at Lily. "More champagne or a glass of wine?"

"Red wine please, something full-bodied, bold and rich."

Robin raised her eyebrows. She conferred with the waiter and he departed. "I like bold and full-bodied," her eyes slipped down to Lily's cleavage, then back up, "too."

Lily's body flamed and she hoped her full-body blush wasn't visible in the dimly lit restaurant. She glared at Robin. "You may not know this, but bold can be offensive."

Robin had the good grace to look embarrassed. "Sorry, I'm not usually so gross, but when I'm near you all I can think about is sex."

Lily couldn't help smiling. She felt the same way. "Now tell me a secret, something no one knows about you."

Robin looked up and seemed to relax when she saw the smile. "Right, a secret." She looked out the window for a few seconds, then cleared her throat. "I was supposed to be named Rosaria Anna but somebody changed it to Robin Ann on my birth certificate.

I sent silent thanks out to the universe every day when I was a teenager. Except for my dad and brothers and my friend Katie, and now you, no one knows that."

"Rosaria, huh? Would you like me to whisper Rosaria in your ear when we get around to making love?"

"You're a tease, you know? I don't care what you whisper as long as we get around to making…having sex soon. Your turn to tell a secret."

It didn't escape Lily that Robin changed her "making love" to "having sex," but she filed it away for future examination. She tapped her fingers on the table, thinking. "I write romances as Lily Boudreaux, mysteries as Lily Carlyle and literary fiction as Lily Alexander."

"Wow. So how many books have you written?"

Lily laughed. "The more relevant question is how many have I published. Seven romances, three in a mystery series, and two literary novels."

"Don't you feel hemmed in by the rules of romance? You know, girl meets girl, girl loves girl, girl loses girl, then girl gets girl and they live happily ever after. Seems it would be boring to write."

"It doesn't bore me at all. There's lots of room for originality and creativity if you want to keep it fresh. Besides, I don't always stick to the rules. Sometimes I'm so into my characters that I want to know what happens after the happily ever after, so I interrupt it with a tragedy or a conflict that causes the relationship to fall apart." Lily sipped her wine. "Then I have to solve the problem and get them back together for the real happily ever after. It challenges me and, I hope, makes it interesting for the reader." She paused. "Mystery has rules too."

"Like?"

She ticked them off on her fingers. "The good guy or gal has to catch the killer. You have to play fair with the reader and give them the clues so they can solve the crime along with the detective. The killer has to be involved in the story and not be pulled out of the hat at the last minute. And all the loose ends need to be tied up by the final scene. Both romance and mystery are harder to write than they seem."

"What's your favorite?"

"I love them all, so I usually have a couple of books going at once. Which is why I instituted blackout days, like tomorrow. No phone, no Internet, no distractions of any kind. Just me and my computer in my apartment, writing all day. "

"But we need to have another date."

"The blackout ends at six p.m. so the evening—"

"Sold. I'll pick you up at seven p.m., informal attire. Now let's eat."

The waiter placed the first of their six courses on the table, and it looked and smelled delicious. They ate slowly, enjoying the food and each other. For dessert Robin surprised and delighted her with a chocolate version of the Brooklyn Bridge, which gave her an idea.

They walked out of the restaurant hand in hand.

Lily brought Robin's hand to her heart. "It's a beautiful night. Let's walk over the Brooklyn Bridge."

Robin looked down at the three-inch heels that brought Lily eye to eye with her. "You're going to walk in those shoes?"

Lily shrugged. "If they hurt, I'll go barefoot."

Tanya pulled the car up next to them.

"I don't know. Wait a second." Robin leaned into the car and said something. Tanya got out, dug around in the trunk and came up with three pairs of sneakers. Robin showed them to Lily. "We have Tanya's, Mel's and mine. What size are you?"

"Nine."

"Here, Mel's are nine and a half. I have some clean socks in my gym bag and you should be all right."

Lily leaned into the car. "You don't mind, Mel?"

"I'd be honored. And, believe me, you'll feel a lot better wearing them than going barefoot on the bridge."

Lily sat on a bench outside the restaurant and put on the socks and sneakers, then Robin helped her into the car. "Drop us at the entrance to the bridge. I'm not sure how long it will take us to walk across so we'll get a taxi home."

It was a beautiful night and they strolled arm in arm, stopping now and then to kiss. "This is lovely, Robin, thank you for indulging me. Have you walked it before?"

Robin smiled down at her. "I'm a bridge virgin just like you. And I should thank you. It is lovely. And romantic."

Lily's smile was mischievous. "Something new to add to your repertoire?"

"I don't think so. Most of my dates wouldn't be caught dead walking and definitely not someplace where there are no expensive stores." She leaned in for a kiss, then propelled them forward again. "Is there something you would love to do but haven't done yet?"

Lily hesitated for a second. "Travel. More than anything, I want to see the world, taste different food, meet different people, enjoy different cultures, and spend part of every year doing it."

Robin spun her around so they were facing each other. "I'd love to do that too. I've been so busy going to school, then working, that I've never taken time off to travel." She kissed Lily's palm. "I think we're destined for each other."

Lily caressed the back of Robin's neck. "Spend New Year's Eve with me in Paris?"

Robin took a step back. "It's July. We've just met. How can we commit to being together on New Year's Eve?"

The intensity of her attraction to Robin was making her loopy. Right now she wanted them to spend the rest of their lives together. But she could see she'd made Robin nervous. Well, she'd started it, might as well finish it. "Can you do a week? I'll make the reservations tomorrow."

Robin rocked heel to toe. "What if I can't or don't want to by then?"

"Hey, didn't I write you a get-out-of-jail contract? You can stop seeing me at any time. I'll take someone else." Where was this coming from? Neither of them was ready to commit, and yet she was pushing for a commitment for a date six months from now.

"Well, then, I would love to spend New Year's Eve with you in Paris. A week sounds lovely."

At the end of the evening, they were back in the hallway in front of Lily's door. Robin's kisses were gentle and passionate and erotic, and every nerve in Lily's body tingled and yearned for more. Robin's lips moved down her neck and slowly made their way to her cleavage while her hands slid down Lily's hips and cupped her butt. Lily felt faint. She slid her hands under Robin's jacket, enjoying the feel of the silk as her hands traced Robin's firm body, then aware of the sound of the elevator moving up, she pulled away, panting. "This is harder than I thought it would be."

Robin lifted her head, her eyes were hooded, her chest heaving. "We've dated long enough. I'm all for phase two right now."

"Not yet, but you need to go now or you'll need a mop to get me off the floor."

Robin grinned. "You have a real way with words. You must be a writer."

"Go." Lily pushed her toward the elevator. "It's an accurate description, though maybe not romantic enough to include in a book."

Robin leaned in for a quick kiss, then again walked backward to the elevator, her eyes on Lily. She backed in and blew a kiss as the doors closed.

CHAPTER TEN

Boat Ride

Lily looked down at her sundress, then back at Robin in her khaki shorts, green T-shirt and green sneakers. "Um, I didn't realize you meant that informal." She glanced back into her apartment. "Should I change?"

"You look fabulous just the way you are, but sneakers might be better and you might need a light sweater or a sweatshirt if it gets chilly."

"We're not going jogging, are we?"

Robin's green eyes twinkled. "No, my Southern belle, we are going out for the dinner I promised. So grab your things and let's get going."

She returned with a sweater and Mel's sneakers in a bag. "I don't wear sneakers with dresses. Will I be okay with sandals?"

Robin took her hand. "I guess I'll just have to hold onto you, then."

"Doesn't sound so bad."

Robin helped her into the car. Tanya drove downtown on the West Side Highway, then east to the South Street Sea Port, where she parked the car and the three of them walked out onto the pier.

"We're having dinner on a boat?" She'd read about these Hudson River boat rides where there was dinner and music and dancing, but she thought they left from somewhere on the West Side. And those boats were more like ferries with a couple of enclosed decks with tables and tablecloths. The few boats she could see looked like sailboats.

"I hope you don't get seasick."

A woman walked down the gangplank of a boat as they approached. "All set here."

It was Mel from last night at the restaurant. "Hi, Mel. Thank you for lending me your sneakers. They're in the car."

The four of them boarded. Robin escorted Lily to the rear of the boat, where a waitress stood with champagne for her and a tall glass of seltzer and lime for Robin.

Robin put an arm around her and pulled her close. "Smile for the camera."

"What?" She looked up.

The waitress pointed a small camera at them. "Say 'cheese.'"

Robin stared down into her eyes making it hard for her to breathe, but she managed a smile. She glanced at the front of the boat. Tanya and Mel, each holding a champagne flute, were at a table. *Nice work if you can get it.* Robin was a generous employer. The captain and the other crewmember were in the middle of the boat. She hoped they weren't drinking.

Robin lifted her glass. "Here's to a wonderful third date."

She touched her glass to Robin's then sipped the ice-cold champagne. She sneezed as the bubbles tickled her nose. The waitress placed a tray of hors d'oeuvres on the table.

They sat across from each other. She kicked off her sandals and put her feet in Robin's lap, then leaned back and closed her eyes, enjoying the briny smell of the East River and the breeze in her hair. Robin's gentle foot massage was a turn-on. "Ah, that feels wonderful, thank you." She opened her eyes. And was blinded by a flash. "Please, no more pictures tonight."

Robin put her hand out, and the waitress gave her the camera.

"So what's with the camera?"

Robin plucked an hors d'oeuvre from the tray on the table and attempted to feed it to her, but she pushed it away. "The camera?"

"Well, I, um, don't have any memories of my childhood, and I have no pictures of me or my family. When Katie, my..., one of my college roommates, heard that my freshman year, she decided I needed to build a history for myself going forward. We took lots of pictures in college and grad school but not so many since we started working. A month or so ago she brought it up again, but until I met you there was no one or nothing I wanted to include in my history."

Tears stung Lily's eyes. "I'm glad you want to make memories with me." She smiled. "Our children will need them."

"Of course they will." Robin brushed her arm across her eyes.

"Are you okay?"

"I'm fine." Robin hesitated. "I just remembered a nightmare I had after you said you wanted to have my babies the other night. It freaked me out because it was so violent." She looked away. "Because *I* was so violent."

Lily sat up. "Is the thought of children so horrible?"

Robin grinned. "Just my sadistic subconscious reacting to the shock of hearing you say it. Though I've never thought about having children, your wanting my babies is a turn-on."

They ate by the soft light of a lantern. The food was light and delicious and as they lingered over coffee and dessert, the waitress moved to the front of the boat, leaving them totally alone. "What a beautiful evening. Eating outside by lantern. Gliding on the river with the glow of the lights of Manhattan. The quiet. I love it. Thank you."

Robin moved her chair away from the table and then pulled Lily up and into her lap. They kissed long and deep, and the heat between them was so strong Lily wondered if they could feel it up front. Then she lost touch with everything but Robin, her mouth, her tongue, her hands. "No, no, Robin, not here. Please stop." Lily pulled away and stood.

Robin looked stunned. She rubbed her face and groaned. "Oh, God, Lily I'm so sorry. I feel like an out-of-control teenager."

"It's not just you, sweetie. I am so ready. Can we just hold hands for now, though?"

Robin nodded.

Lily sat on her lap again. Robin wrapped her arms around Lily and pulled her close, her warm breath on Lily's neck like a caress. Inflamed by the feel of Robin's strong body, the fragrance of her spicy cologne, and the passion of her kisses, Lily burned with desire. She'd never felt this turned on, this challenged intellectually or this joyful with Micki. What was she waiting for? She ran her fingers over Robin's arm. "I think we've dated enough. I know it's Sunday and you have to work tomorrow but would you stay over tonight?"

Robin's arms tightened. Her breathing quickened. "I'd love to, if you're sure."

"I'm sure. But, just so you know, I have plans to spend tomorrow through Friday with a really good friend from Chicago, Dawn, and she'll be staying with me. I'd cancel, but she came for the wedding and I didn't spend any time with her." She turned and kissed Robin. "But I'd like to take you on a date Saturday, if you're free?"

"No dating all week?"

"Not until Saturday. Are you free?"

"Yes, definitely. When and how should I dress?"

"Eat breakfast before you come, wear something you won't worry about getting dirty and meet me in my lobby at nine thirty. In the morning."

"What should I wear tonight?" Robin grinned.

Lily caressed her cheek. "Nothing, of course."

The four of them walked to the car and as they settled in, Lily's phone rang. She pulled it out to answer and saw four texts from Dawn; now she was calling. "Dawn, I was on a boat and just saw your texts. What's up?" She listened. "Um, just a minute." She put her hand over the speaker and spoke to Robin. "She was supposed to stay with her sister tonight, but there was a fire in the building and they can't get into the apartment. Her sister and her two roommates are going to stay with friends, and she's asking if she can stay with me tonight. I'm sorry."

Robin kissed her temple. "Saturday night then?"

Lily grinned. "You got it, sweetie." She took the phone off mute. "Sure. I should be home in about forty-five minutes, but if I'm not there when you arrive have a seat in the lobby."

CHAPTER ELEVEN

Soup Kitchen

Robin looked a little bleary-eyed when she arrived Saturday morning. *She must have been out late partying with one of her beautiful models.* Lily shook her head. They'd said no commitment and it was none of her business. Still she didn't want to date anyone else, and a part of her hoped Robin didn't either.

Robin interrupted her thoughts. "Where to?"

"Broadway and Ninety-third."

"Oh, I'll get a taxi." Robin stepped off the curb.

Lily pulled Robin back onto the sidewalk. "I'd like to walk, show you the neighborhood."

"But it's eighteen blocks." Robin sounded incredulous. "And what happens when we get there?"

"We're volunteering at a church that has a free soup kitchen on weekends and we're going to cook and serve lunch, then clean up. It's hard work, but you can leave at any time, including now."

Robin put her hands on Lily shoulders. "Hey, are you trying to get rid of me?"

"No, but I just realized that I should have given you a choice when I invited you. Maybe you don't want to volunteer." Lily started walking.

Robin followed. "Sorry, I don't mean to be a princess." She took Lily's hand. "I've never done it before, so I don't know how good I'll be at it, but I'm willing to give it a try. You can ask me to leave anytime if I screw things up."

They strolled along Central Park West, the park to their right, apartment buildings on the left. Lily stopped in front of the Museum of Natural History. "Have you even been here?"

Robin's eye's lit up. "No. I've read about it, but I've been so busy with work. I guess we can't go now?" She looked like a kid.

"No. But it's something to do another day." She started walking. "And that attached glass building is the Rose Center for Earth and Space. The planetarium is in there."

Robin couldn't take her eyes off the building and crashed into Lily when she tried to steer them left onto Eighty-first Street. "Oh, sorry. It's just…I read so many books about the museum and the animals and the planetarium and the stars when I was a kid that I can't believe I've been this close to it and never came here." She looked longingly at the park outside the Rose Center. "Where are you taking us now?"

"I thought we'd walk up Broadway." They walked across Eighty-first Street and made a right on Broadway. Lily pointed across the street. "Zabar's—good bagels, lox, cheeses, prepared food, and a great housewares department upstairs if that's what turns you on."

Robin pulled Lily close. "Let's be clear. *That* is not what turns me on."

Lily laughed and pulled away. "Come on, we don't want to be late." As they walked she pointed out the Children's Museum on Eighty-third Street and the French Roast, a restaurant open twenty-four hours seven days a week, and the stores. "We have Talbots and Chicos and Victoria's Secret, Brooks Brothers and Banana Republic and—"

"Okay, I get it. The Upper West Side has everything, even Starbucks. Oh, and lots of chain drug stores and banks. And look at Barzini's, the huge fruit and vegetable store across the street."

Lily punched her arm. "Don't make fun. Three more blocks."

Robin hesitated when they got to the entrance. "Before we go in, would it be all right with you if I get a picture or two of us while we're there?"

How strange. I think we're going to have to have a talk about why you don't have any pictures of you or your family. "You're really serious about this picture thing, aren't you?"

Robin flushed. "Yes."

Lily brushed a wayward lock of hair off her face. "I don't want to get in the way or make anyone uncomfortable, so let me check with Sonia, the woman who runs the kitchen."

Sonia gave them the go-ahead as long as they were sensitive to what was happening and didn't include any of their guests in the pictures. Lily introduced Robin to the rest of the staff and the other volunteers, then the chef assigned them tasks to prep the ingredients for the beef stew they were serving for lunch. While Lily cut beef into chunks, Robin chopped several heads of celery. Everyone chatted as they worked together, taking on various tasks such as chopping onions, potatoes or carrots.

At one point, Sonia popped over. Robin whispered to her and handed her camera over, then Sonia snapped a picture of the two of them hard at work at their separate tasks. Lily looked up and her eyes met Robin's. Sonia snapped another, handed the camera back and went to supervise the storing of items just delivered.

Lily watched Robin apply herself to the job at hand. She knew Robin would be a conscientious worker. Often she'd look up and find Robin staring at her, and their eyes would meet, sending a chill through her. Other times, Robin would be deep in conversation or joking with one or more of the other volunteers.

When the stew was bubbling, the salad prepped, the dessert baking and the coffee percolating, they moved to setting the tables and laying out dishes and serving implements. Just before noon, the volunteer servers arrived and after being introduced, one of them, Theresa, zeroed in on Robin. "You look really familiar, Robin. Have you volunteered here before?"

Robin looked uncomfortable. "No. I probably look like someone you know."

Theresa looked Robin up and down. "I doubt that. Don't worry. It'll come to me."

Lily thought Theresa was hitting on Robin, so she walked over and put an arm around Robin's waist. "How are you doing, sweetie?"

Robin kissed her temple. "Great."

Just then, Sonia opened the doors and the hungry diners filed in. And kept filing in all afternoon. Lily and Robin pitched in to serve, then clean tables as they turned over. Throughout the afternoon, Lily observed Robin conversing with the people who had come in for a free meal, calming an unruly man, laughing with a table of two men and two women and listening intently to people who probably hadn't had anyone pay much attention to them in years. And, unlike many of the other volunteers, Robin didn't avoid the homeless people, some of whom smelled so awful that it was hard to keep from gagging. Lily was impressed and proud of her. When everyone who showed up had been fed, the doors were locked, and they pitched in to clean up. It was five thirty when they walked out, blinking in the late afternoon sun and breathing deeply to take in fresh air.

Lily took Robin's hand. "Are you as hungry and tired as I am?"

"If you're starved and exhausted, the answer is yes."

"Okay, I'm buying you an early dinner as a reward for all your hard work."

"No, let me."

"No way. This is my date and I know just the place." She led Robin downtown on Amsterdam Avenue to Fred's, a basement restaurant with a few outdoor tables on Eighty-third Street. "Here we are."

Robin followed Lily down the few steps and past the busy bar into the cozy dining room. She looked around warily.

Lily could almost hear her thoughts. A basement, every inch of wall space filled with pictures of dogs in all shapes and sizes, how good could it be? Robin tried to look interested rather than put off by the décor, but Lily saw right through her.

"Don't be such a snob. It's a neighborhood place and, as you can see, they invite people to bring pictures of their dogs. The food is good and the prices reasonable. You're not one of those people who think it has to be expensive to be good, are you?"

"I'm open to trying it."

Lily poked her. "You damn well better be, because I'm not one of your high maintenance models who likes to see and be seen while nibbling on a lettuce leaf. I enjoy real food, all kinds." Her grin was mischievous. "Besides, I don't want our children to be snobs."

"Our lives are being controlled by these kids, and we haven't even had sex yet."

The people at the next table laughed and turned to look at them. Robin turned red. Lily laughed. "All in good time, sweetie." She patted Robin's hand. "Ready to order? I'm starving."

Robin took a bite of her burger and made an appreciative sound. Lily sipped her beer. "So, how was the day for you?"

"Good."

"Can you be a little more specific? And it's okay if you hated it."

Robin took another bite and chewed slowly, thinking. "I didn't hate it. It was a…profound experience. I rarely think about people who need to be taken care of and people like you who take time out of their lives to help them. I'd like to help. Maybe give some money."

"Sonia really struggles to get contributions to buy enough food. Sometimes they have to skip a day because they're short."

Lily took a bite of her burger. Once again, she noticed people staring at them, whispering. Was it the fact they were obviously lesbians or something else? They talked quietly while eating, then walked back to Lily's apartment, where they kissed passionately in the hall.

"Um, Lily, can I get a rain check on the sleepover? I'm exhausted, and I have to pick up a European client arriving at JFK six a.m. tomorrow morning and spend the day on sightseeing duty. I also have commitments Monday and Tuesday nights. I'm sorry."

"Between kissing you and being so tired, I'm about to fall flat on my face too. But I want to reward you for being such a good sport today. Will you join me at Shazarak for dinner and dancing Wednesday night?"

"You're getting mighty aggressive, madam, inviting me out again so soon. Not that I didn't enjoy myself today, but fun is always a good thing, so I accept as long as," she wiggled her eyebrows, "I can sleep over after."

"Really, Robin? Still wiggling those eyebrows? As long as you promise there will be no wiggling of eyebrows, the sleepover is on. Pajamas optional." Lily kissed her again. "My best friend Annie just got back from a two-month dig in China and I haven't seen her yet. Would you mind if I invite her to join us? For the first part of the evening, I mean, not the sleepover."

"I only have eyes for you but invite anyone you want and I promise to be civil." One more kiss and they parted.

* * *

As the taxi made its way downtown to Battery Park City, Robin wondered what it was that kept her coming back to Lily. Clearly, not just sex. This was their fourth date and the second time the sex got put off. Wednesday wasn't that far off. Normally, she would have dumped Lily by now. After all, if it's all about having fun, why delay the payoff? But Lily was different. Other than Katie and their four Harvard roommates, no one had ever invited her into their life, no one had ever insisted on taking her out, no one had ever wanted to do something for her. Usually, they wanted her to do something for them. She liked it. She paid the driver and turned toward her building. Sex wasn't the only way to have fun. She stopped walking. Did she just think that?

CHAPTER TWELVE

Shazarak

Lily's heart picked up its pace as Robin sauntered to the table, and while she was able to refrain from running to greet her, she couldn't repress the grin. She turned to Annie, but Annie was already watching Robin wend her way through the dining room. "That's her."

"Duh. I could feel your excitement the minute she came in. And I see why. Not only is she good looking, but she has a commanding presence. And I'm not the only one taking notice."

Lily looked again and Annie was right. Women were staring and whispering. Well, why not? She had when she saw her that first time. "Oh, she's so much more than a pretty face, Annie. You'll see."

Lily stood. They embraced and kissed lightly. "Robin, this is Annie."

"Glad to meet you because I'm anxious to hear all about your dig." Robin kissed Annie's cheek, then sat.

"Ah, Lily, you're right. She is a charmer."

Robin blushed.

Lily took Robin's hand and squeezed it. "Yes, she is."

"Okay, ladies. Remember I'm sitting right here. Have you ordered drinks?"

"We have. I ordered you a seltzer and lime."

They talked through dinner about Annie's work at a site in China where they turned up many mummies, clothing, jewelry and artifacts of daily life. It turned out that Robin was interested in archaeology, especially mummies, and had read voraciously on the subject, so she and Annie had a great time while Lily looked on. Every once in a while, Robin would check in with Lily to see if they were boring her, but she was fascinated watching Robin holding her own with Annie, a professor of archaeology at Columbia. It wasn't until they were drinking coffee and sharing a warm brownie with vanilla ice cream and a dab of whipped cream that the conversation turned to books and music and theater. Later, when the DJ began spinning in the bar area, Lily felt Annie's eyes on her, questioning. She assumed Annie was worried about having engaged Robin's attention for so long.

Annie stood. "Ladies room, anyone?"

Lily had given the waitress her credit card before Robin arrived to ensure she didn't try to pay the check, so she stood. "Me." She tilted her head at Robin. "You?"

"I didn't drink as much as you two. Hurry back, I'm looking forward to dancing with two lovely ladies on my arm."

In the ladies room, Annie hugged Lily. "I'm sorry I monopolized Robin, but it's rare I find someone interested in and so knowledgeable about what I do."

"Actually, I enjoyed watching her with you. Up to now, we've been alone and it's nice to see her in a different light. So what do you think?"

"She's wonderful. Intelligent, funny, articulate, gorgeous and... and tell me again why you're hesitating?"

"I'm not, but it seems the fates are keeping us apart. I haven't even told her mama Del is staying at the apartment tonight."

"Better not to spring it on her later. Tell her now. And don't keep her waiting too long, honey, she's obviously into you, but somebody will scoop her up soon. Go. I'll wait a few minutes before coming back."

Robin was practically dancing in place when she returned. "Thanks for dinner, Lily." She pulled her into a hug.

"Um, Robin, my, um, my mama Del arrived in town unexpectedly last night, and she's staying with me." She flushed. "I know we said we'd have a sleepover—"

"You could come to my place."

Lily paled. "I'd rather not get Del on my case. She can be a little intense. She'll want to meet you. And I don't think we're ready for that."

It was Robin's turn to pale. "No, we're not ready for that." She looked up and smiled. "Ready to dance, Annie?"

"I don't think you two need a chaperone, so I'll leave you to it."

"But we do need a chaperone to keep me from ravishing Lily on the dance floor. Stay. A beautiful redhead like you won't be alone long. Sit at the table for one dance and if you're still alone after that, the three of us will dance together." She lightly punched Annie's shoulder. "Come on, you need some fun after working in the desert for two months."

Annie shook her head. "You have the gift of blarney, Robin. Are you sure you're not Irish?" Annie looked at Lily for permission.

She smiled and nodded. "Stay."

Robin was right. Before the first dance was over, Annie had a partner and the few times she wasn't asked, Robin pulled her up to dance with them. Fast or slow, Lily and Robin danced. Lily enjoyed the fast numbers, but she loved the slow ones when Robin fit their bodies together and ignited her with gentle touches and soft kisses.

At the end of the evening, they dropped Annie off at her building and Robin escorted Lily up to her apartment. They made out in the hall for a while, then Robin pulled away. "Time to leave." Her voice was husky, her eyes dark. She cleared her throat. "Thanks for dinner and a really fun time tonight. My turn now. Dinner Saturday, dress up."

Lily nuzzled Robin's neck. "You know, this was easier when we were dating and sex wasn't allowed. Now it's damned frustrating. Mama is leaving Saturday afternoon. Neither snow nor sleet nor overnight guests will keep us from having that sleepover Saturday night."

As Lily got ready for bed, she wondered if she should have gone home with Robin. Her body was definitely in favor of the idea, but her mind and her heart knew mama Del would make life miserable until she met the woman she was sleeping with. And that would be disastrous for commitment-phobic Robin. Brushing her teeth, she admitted to herself that deep down she was also afraid if she slept with her Robin would walk away with her heart.

CHAPTER THIRTEEN

One by Land

One by Land, Two by Sea. Another expensive and romantic restaurant where the maître d' greeted Robin by name and immediately escorted them to a prime table. Heads turned and whispers swirled in the air behind them like leaves dropping from trees in the fall. Were people whispering Robin's name, or was she losing it? Robin seemed oblivious. As they sat, she asked the maître d' to bring them a seltzer and lime and a glass of the bold and rich red wine Lily loved.

Lily sipped the wine the waiter placed in front of her and glanced around. No. Judging by the surreptitious looks thrown their way, she wasn't losing it. Was Robin someone famous? Or infamous? When that photographer took the picture on their first date, Robin had promised to explain why, but somehow they'd never gotten around to having that discussion. And since then, every time they'd been out, especially in see-and-be-seen restaurants like this one, people stared and whispered. She'd thought it was because Robin was so gorgeous, but now it seemed more personal. They knew her name. What did everyone but she know about Robin? *I could ask, I suppose, but it might make Robin angry. I don't want to fight with her.*

"Lily?" Robin's gentle question pulled her from her reverie. "Where did you go?"

She looked up. "I…" She took a breath. "Who are you, Robin?"

"What do you mean?"

"It's not a trick question, sweetie. On our first date at the River Café, a photographer took our picture, and you said it might have appeared in the gossip column if Tanya hadn't taken the card from the camera. You're known at the two expensive restaurants you've taken me to. And people are always staring at us, like now. You're not just the owner of a small tech company, are you? Are you famous? If I'm going to carry your babies, don't you think I should know who you are?"

"You're serious about the babies, aren't you?"

"If things work out, yes. But don't change the subject."

Robin waited while the waiter placed their appetizers in front of them and walked away. She cleared her throat. "I've been planning to tell you, but I wanted to get to know you before I said anything." Her grip on Lily's hand tightened. "The night we first saw each other at Shazarak, I was celebrating taking my business, DiLuca Cooper Technologies International, public. As a result, my partner Katie and I became billionaires and many of our employees became millionaires or multimillionaires."

The color drained from Lily's face. "A billionaire?" She tried to withdraw her hand, but Robin held on.

Robin nodded. "Maybe it's because my partner and I are relatively young or maybe because I'm an out lesbian, the media has taken great interest. We've been featured on multiple TV shows and our pictures have appeared in all the newspapers and gossip magazines, so now I'm recognized wherever I go."

"I need to rethink this, Robin. I'm not sure I can—"

"I was afraid of that." Robin looked miserable. "At first, I was afraid you might be interested in the money and not me, but after getting to know you, I was afraid the money would drive you away. I'm sorry."

Lily looked down at the lovely salad on the plate in front of her and felt a wave of nausea. "I can't do this, Robin, I need to leave." She pushed her chair back.

"Let me ask them to pack our dinners to go, then I'll take you home. All right?"

Lily nodded.

Robin got up to confer with the waiter and pay the bill. Lily sipped her wine while they waited for the food to be ready, not speaking, not looking at Robin, though she could feel Robin's eyes on her.

The silence continued in the taxi, then in the elevator up to Lily's apartment. When they reached the door, Robin placed the package with their dinners on the floor, wrapped her arms around Lily and pulled her close. "I can't just walk away and leave this hanging between us. Let me come in, to talk."

Lily sighed, then retrieved her keys from her bag and opened the door. "Come in."

Robin picked up their dinners and followed her into the foyer, then into the living room. Lily tensed as Robin examined the room. The caramel-colored sofa and loveseat facing a wall of windows overlooking Central Park, the multicolor kilim rug, the cushions of various sizes and colors piled on the furniture and on the floor and the colorful paintings and cloth wall hangings—all melded together into an environment she hoped was warm and welcoming, one that invited guests to relax and stay a while.

"Nothing like the elegant designer apartments you're used to, I guess?" Lily flinched at the disdain evident in her voice. She hadn't intended to be so offensive, but maybe it would keep Robin from sensing how vulnerable she felt.

Robin stared at her for a few seconds and Lily steeled herself for an angry reply. "It's as I imaged it would be—warm, homey, comfortable and lovely. A place I would love to spend time in with you."

"Right." Lily turned away. She hadn't meant to be sarcastic. *How can Robin be so nice when I'm being so mean?*

Uncomfortable with the silence behind her, Lily looked back. Robin was staring at her, a puzzled look on her face. She opened her mouth as if to say something, then seemed to change her mind. As usual, Lily's inclination was to pretend everything was fine, but she hesitated, and Robin spoke. "Um, I'm starving. Could we eat and talk?"

"I'm not in a fussing mood. Does it have to be heated?"

"No. I asked them to make us sandwiches."

"Ah, the difficult life of a billionaire. Pay for an expensive dinner and end up getting sandwiches to take home." The punishing sarcasm in her voice surprised even her. *Just what am I doing?*

A flash of anger crossed Robin's face. Two quick steps and she was in front of Lily. She put one hand on Lily's shoulder and used the other to raise her face so she could look into her eyes. "You know, Lily, I want to talk through your concerns, but I won't apologize for being successful. I had nothing and I built a company that made not only me and my partners but all of our three hundred plus employees wealthy. That's the American dream, isn't it?"

Tears stung Lily's eyes. She hadn't meant to hurt Robin. "I'm sorry. It's just that you caught me off guard. I didn't mean to imply there was something wrong with you. But money complicates things."

"It doesn't have to complicate anything." She waved a hand around. "And you're not exactly living in poverty here in a three-bedroom apartment overlooking Central Park." Robin stroked Lily's face. "Can we eat facing your fabulous view, then talk?"

"That's where I eat when I'm alone." Lily took Robin's hand and kissed her palm. "You're right. I'm more than comfortable. Actually, it's four bedrooms, but the bank owns it, not me. My Chicago apartment was a present from my moms and it had appreciated a lot over the years. The money from the sale of that combined with a large bump in book sales gave me a hefty down payment. But the plan was for two salaries to cover the mortgage, so I'm house poor as they say."

Lily arranged their drinks, the sandwiches and napkins on the coffee table in front of the sofa, then turned off all the lights except a small lamp. She sat next to Robin, close enough to feel her heat and hear her breathing. Robin was perfect. Why did she have to be a billionaire? On the other hand, why did it bother her so much?

Lily took a deep breath, taking in air filled with the spiciness of the dressing on the sandwiches, the sweetness of Robin's cologne and the mustiness of her own sweat. As she slowly released the air, she relaxed and was surprised to find she was hungry. They ate in silence, staring at the lights across Central Park. When they had eaten, Robin took her hand and spoke. "Why do you think money complicates things?"

"It's not money per se, it's so much money. And how it changes the way people see you. Since one of my literary novels was made into a not-so-great movie, sales of my other novels increased. I make a decent living from my writing, but I'm far from rich. Yet I've been burned by women who perceived fame and fortune that I didn't have. One woman dropped me when she realized I wasn't rich and another woman walked away when she got that I didn't really have a Hollywood connection. Those interactions made it difficult to trust myself and I didn't date for a long time. Until Micki. And that experience confirmed that I can't trust my ability to read people. You *seem* honest and trustworthy, but…

"When you have that much money everyone wants a piece of you or something from you, like those models and other beautiful women hanging on you that first night. How do you trust anyone is interested in you? How can you trust that I want you, not your money or your status? You said earlier that you thought initially I might be after your money. Maybe I am. Can you trust me? What kind of life is it, always wondering if it's you or your billions?"

She looked around her apartment. "Lifestyle is the other thing. I like nice things, but I'm not into conspicuous consumption or living a high society life. I enjoy cooking and reading and seeing a movie with a friend. You seem to enjoy partying with lots of people and eating in fancy restaurants. For me a hot dog or a burger at a neighborhood restaurant can be as wonderful as a meal at One by Land. It seems to me that too much money can drain reality out of your life. Everything becomes appearances and seeing and being seen and who has the biggest and best or the most."

She brushed away the tears. "I don't want to live that way. I already don't trust my ability to read people. I don't want to go through life wondering if it's me or your money that draws people to me and our children."

"I hear you." Robin kissed Lily's knuckles. "I earned a very good living from my business before going public, so it's not like I had nothing and suddenly had a billion dollars thrust into my hands like some winners of the lottery. It's true that I can feel the difference in how people look at me and react to me, but I haven't changed, and if I start to get a big head, my friends will make sure I stay grounded. I know who I am and I understand how lucky I am. And you'll have to trust that I do know what or, should I say who, is real. That's why I'm here with you, Lily, and not one of the models or actresses I usually date."

She caressed Lily's face. "We both live comfortably on what we've earned from the work we love. Being this wealthy is very new, but I assure you I plan to use the money to help people. I'm not sure what I want to do yet, but I already have a team putting together some ideas. Katie and I will probably fund some things together. We just need time. I need you to be patient, to give me a chance to prove that I'm worthy of you."

"Oh, Robin." Lily shifted to face her. "I didn't mean to imply that you're unworthy. You're kind and sweet and thoughtful, I see how nice you are to people, and I respect your work ethic and your success. It's more about my insecurities than about you. My image of a billionaire is someone who ruthlessly takes what he or she wants and doesn't care about hurting people. You seem more genuine than that but...I'm not sure I can trust my judgment. Also, I'm serious about us having kids someday and if I misjudge you, you could take them from me and they could turn out to be rich and shallow. Do you see why I'm scared the money will come between us?"

"It doesn't have to come between us if you don't let it. I enjoy being with you and since neither of us has committed to an," she made quote marks with her fingers, "'us,' can't we just hang out, have fun and get to know each other better? See how it goes?"

Lily wanted to believe and so far Robin hadn't given her any reason to doubt her honesty and her willingness to play by her rules. She brought Robin's hand to her face. "All right." She kissed Robin's palm. "But I'm feeling a little off kilter, not quite in the mood to make love tonight. I need time to wrap my mind around this. Would it upset you if we wait a little longer?"

"I'd like to kiss you, then I'll leave, I promise."

"Um."

Twenty minutes later, Robin pulled away. "Time to go, I think."

Reluctantly, Lily stood. "Thank you for understanding."

"Waiting isn't easy, but I don't want you to have any regrets. I want you to want to have sex with me as much as I want it." Robin held Lily's face between her hands and kissed her nose. "Katie and I are flying to London the day after tomorrow to open an office. It'll be mostly business, but I'd love to have you along for the week."

"Thanks, but I'd rather go when it's just the two of us. Will I see you before you leave?"

"Now I've seen your apartment so it's only fair I show you mine. And just to prove I enjoy being at home with friends, I'd like to invite you, Annie and my friend Emma, who is staying with me, to dinner tomorrow night."

"Do you think they might hit it off?"

"They're both passionate about their work and though Emma is a professor of Middle Eastern history, the history and the archeology complement each other. They also have a similar sense of humor. Could be a match made in heaven. Or they might hate each other. Who knows, but it's worth a shot."

"Will you cook?"

"No. This is where money comes in handy. I'll hire a chef. Is that a terrible thing?"

"Just a little more terrible than bringing in takeout. Let's do it."

CHAPTER FOURTEEN

Robin's Dinner Party

The car Robin sent for Lily and Annie dropped them in front of a high-end but not ostentatious building in Battery Park City. Checking their names against a list, the doorman pointed to the left. "Ms. DiLuca is expecting you. Take that elevator to Penthouse A."

Robin greeted them at the door with a huge grin and two glasses of wine, red for Lily, white for Annie. "Welcome." She kissed them both on the cheek and waved them in. "Enter."

Lily's eye was drawn to the oversized windows, the circular white sofa and the complementary club chairs focused on the view of New Jersey across the sparkling Hudson River. "Oh my God, that's spectacular."

Robin beamed like a mother showing her infant for the first time.

"Look at the kitchen." Annie squealed. "It's gorgeous. I would kill for those floor-to-ceiling cabinets and the bluish marble countertops are striking. And look at that stove and refrigerator. All that's missing is a chef."

"Did someone call?" A woman dressed in white entered the kitchen from a door at the rear of the room. "Sorry, I stepped out to set the table."

"Lily, Annie, this is Tammie, our chef for this evening." She turned back to the living room. "And over there, standing in the corner where you can't see her, is sneaky Emma Whitfield, Middle Eastern historian *extraordinaire*. Emma, come meet Lily Alexander, writer, and Annie Newman, archeologist *extraordinaire*."

Lily put her free hand on her hip. "So how come I don't get *extraordinaire* after my name?"

"Because you, my love, are *fantastique* and *extraordinaire* and it's too much to say in one breath."

"Hey, wait a minute, Robin. You mean Emma and I are just—"

"Now, now, Annie, you know Lily is special because I'm trying to get her into bed."

Emma laughed. "Some things never change." She punched Robin's arm.

Emma and Robin seemed so comfortable with each other, Lily wondered if they'd ever been a couple.

"Come, let me show you around the apartment. It's not that big so it will only take a couple of minutes. Then we can enjoy the view and munch on the hors d'oeuvres Tammie whipped up for us."

She's right, thought Lily. *It's not that big but everything about it is just...spectacular.* The master and guest bedrooms both had their own bathrooms and water views, as did the office with a built-in rosewood desk and cabinets and two walls of books. Every room was beautifully decorated. "It's beautiful, Robin. Did you use an interior decorator?"

"No. Katie and Jan and one of our other Harvard roommates, the artist Mei Lin, all contributed ideas and helped me actualize my vision of the space I wanted to live in. Light, airy and comfortable. Like it?"

"Love it." She was relieved it wasn't ostentatious or vulgar, but she should have known, should have trusted. So why didn't she trust Robin to be the person she seemed to be?

Annie ran her hand over the desk, her eyes on the windows. "Wow. Robin. It's breathtaking. What a wonderful place to live and work."

Lily examined the books. "Your taste in books is quite eclectic."

Emma spoke from the doorway. "Robin has never met a book she doesn't love. She used to steal our textbooks in college and grad school and read them. It didn't matter to her what the subject was." She laughed. "The first few weeks of her freshman year we'd all be running around yelling, has anybody seen my blah-blah textbook? It took the five genius Harvard students a month to figure it out, but after we got it, we'd go straight into Robin's room to retrieve whatever was missing."

"Emma. What will these ladies think of me, stealing textbooks?"

Emma walked in and hugged Robin. "It wasn't just the textbooks that she inhaled. We nicknamed her Dr. Spock because it felt like she did a mind meld with each of us every night to absorb everything we'd learned that day. The funny thing was, all our grades went up because we worked harder to understand the material so we could answer her questions."

Robin tugged on Emma's ear lobe. "You're not supposed to tell tales out of school, Em."

"Ouch. Just telling the truth, genius girl."

"Yeah, yeah, let's go back to the living room."

Robin pulled Lily down on the sofa next to her. The other two sat near them, across from each other. Lily studied Emma. A blue-eyed blonde with a sophisticated, jaw-length haircut and perfect makeup, she was about the same size as Annie's five-foot-five inches. But while Emma was pale-skinned and slender, Annie was tanned and muscular from working on digs. Her red hair was short and shaggy for ease of care and her makeup light—just some lipstick and mascara to highlight her lovely hazel eyes. They would look nice together, Lily decided.

The first ten minutes were focused on teasing Robin, the common denominator, then Emma gazed at Lily. "Robin says you're a writer. What do you write?"

She hated this question, but this was how people got to know one another, so she spoke about her books. It turned out Emma was a fan of her mysteries and her standalones but had not read the romances. Before Lily could switch the focus back, Emma turned to Annie. "And you're a professor of archeology? Robin told me about your recent dig. Where do you teach?"

"Columbia. And where do you teach Middle Eastern history?" Annie deftly turned the spotlight on Emma.

Emma smiled. "I've been teaching at the University of Chicago, but I'm in the process of moving to New York City. I'll also be teaching at Columbia."

Annie leaned forward. "If you're going to live in faculty housing, we'll be neighbors."

"We will be, but the apartment won't be ready for a few weeks so I'm staying with Robin." She glanced at Lily. "I was one of Robin's suitemates at Harvard, and we also lived together at Stanford." She leaned over and patted Robin's leg. "The baby genius helped me pass the horrible mathematic requirements and discussions, and debates with her in grad school helped me develop the brilliant ideas that became the basis for my dissertation. She insists they were my ideas, but I'm sure they were hers."

Lily relaxed. Emma seemed to be signaling they were never lovers.

"And speaking of genius," Emma looked at Annie then Lily, "did Robin happen to mention that she was invited to speak at the World Economic Forum in Davos, Switzerland, this January?"

Lily felt Robin stiffen and when she swiveled to see her face, it was bright red. "That's fabulous, Robin, what an honor. Why didn't you tell me?"

"Because big mouth Emma told you before I could. I got the call a little while before you got here, and I was on the phone with Katie when the doorman rang up." She stood and walked to the windows.

Lily stiffened. Her place in the pecking order was clear. Second. "Why aren't you jumping up and down and running around screaming?"

"Because I'm fucking freaking out. What could I say that would interest all those high-powered executives?"

"You are a fucking genius, so just talk about your management philosophy and building a multibillion dollar business from nothing." Emma raised her glass. "To Robin, the only one amongst us who could possibly change the world with her ideas." Lily and Annie joined in the toast.

Robin turned to Lily. "Will this make a difference? Is it like having a billion dollars? Or is it okay because Professor Cordelia Alexander is also on the agenda?"

Lily joined her at the window and pulled her into a deep kiss.

Emma and Annie hooted. Emma turned to Annie with a frown on her face. "What do a billion dollars and Professor Alexander have to do with it?"

Lily leaned back to look in Robin's eyes. "No, sweet Robin, it's not the same. This is recognition of who you are. And no doubt the world would be a better place if your ideas were adopted by others." She kissed her again. "How nice you'll be on the same agenda as mama Cordy."

"You know, as best as I could tell over the phone, she might have recommended me. Have you told—"

"Not a word. But clearly she thinks you have something to say to those high-powered executives, of which, I believe you would be considered one."

Emma waved her arms trying to get their attention. "Hello. Am I the only one in the dark here? Billion dollars? Lily's mother? What the fuck?"

The other three women laughed. Robin was about to explain when Tammie appeared. "Dinner is ready, so please move out to the terrace and I'll begin to serve."

Emma whispered to Tammie as they filed out into the warm evening air.

Annie's eyes widened. She rushed to the wall at the edge of the terrace. "I don't know how you live here, Robin. I'd probably have a nervous breakdown trying to decide whether to work at the desk in the office or in the living room or on this terrace. Actually, even soaking in a tub with a water view in one of those bathrooms would be an option."

Robin grinned. "I spend most of my days in the office on Wall Street, so feel free to come soak anytime."

"And most of her nights wining and dining stick-thin models and actresses of the see and be seen persuasion." Damn, did she really say that out loud?

Emma looked puzzled. "Do I detect some resentment, Lily?"

Lily blushed. "Uh, no, I, um. Maybe a little jealousy if truth be told."

Robin grinned. "Oh, jealousy. I like that. Please sit here, Lily." She patted a chair to her left. "Emma sit across from Lily, and, Annie, sit there." She indicated the chair facing her.

Tammie walked onto the terrace with a bottle of champagne and popped the cork. "Compliments of Emma." She poured for them. "First course in a few minutes." She started back to the kitchen.

"Tammie, wait. Would you take some pictures of us?" Robin extracted a small camera from her pocket. They stood and posed.

Annie lifted her glass. "To Robin. Congratulations on a well-deserved honor. You have nothing to be nervous about. Just be your wonderful self."

The others raised their glasses and Tammie snapped a picture. She took a couple more while they drank, then a couple of them sitting at the beautifully set table.

"Thanks. It's nice to be appreciated." Robin's thumb drew circles on Lily's wrist. "How did you get the champagne, Emma?"

"I asked Tammie where I could order it and she had it delivered." Emma stuck her tongue out. "Don't worry, I paid. Which reminds me. Billionaire? Is somebody going to answer my questions?"

Robin and Annie turned to Lily. "I'm afraid that Robin being a billionaire will cause problems for us—"

"Really? Why?"

Robin tossed her napkin at Emma. "You wanted to know, so let her talk."

She tossed the napkin back. "Sorry."

Lily cringed at Emma's dismissive tone. "I've been trying to figure that out since Robin told me last night, and I'm still not sure I understand why it freaks me out. I believe money and power attract people who want some of either or both. I've been hurt by women who thought I had money or influence then dumped me when they realized I didn't. That includes Micki, the woman I almost married."

Lily glanced at Robin. As usual, she was attentive. Lily's eyes shifted to Emma who looked skeptical and then to Annie, who nodded and smiled, encouraging her.

"Anyway, this morning I suddenly remembered something from my childhood that I must have repressed. I was ten, I think, when I met Belinda in ballet class. We took a lot of classes together and became best friends though she went to private school and I to public. We hung out after class sometimes with my mama or the woman I thought was her mama, taking us for ice cream or to the park to run and play. Usually she came to my house for play dates but one Saturday Del and Cordy were busy so we went to Belinda's house. It turned out her family was seriously wealthy and she lived in a huge mansion with servants.

"We had had a great time playing with all her dolls and were eating lunch in the kitchen, when this strange woman dressed in fancy clothes and smelling like a perfume store arrived. She glared at me. 'Who is this?' The anger in her voice frightened me. It also seemed to frighten Belinda's mother. 'Lily is Belinda's friend from dance class, they like to play together.' The fancy woman stared down at me. 'Who are your parents, Lily?' Belinda tried to intervene. 'Mother, she's my friend.' Her mother smiled at her. 'Yes, darling, but I need to know who her people are if you're going to socialize with her.' She turned to me. I was shaking, but I'd been taught to respect adults so I answered. 'My mamas are Delphine Boudreaux Alexander and Cordelia Carlyle Alexander.'

"She shook her head, then turned on the woman I'd thought was Belinda's mama with a vehemence. 'Cajuns and lesbians.' She spat the words out. 'You know Belinda is not allowed to socialize with low-class people like this. And what the hell was she doing in ballet class? Only a Cajun would be stupid enough to think a fat girl like her could ever be a ballerina.'

"The woman tried to explain. 'But Belinda—'

"'Belinda is too young to understand that spending time with those beneath us can ruin our social standing.' She walked up to the terrorized woman and raised a fist as if she was going to hit her. 'I trusted you with my daughter, now get out and take that, that girl with you.' By this time Belinda was sobbing, but I was frozen. Belinda's mother's face was so ugly she looked like some evil monster. I'd never heard anyone use that vile tone of voice, and I didn't understand what Cajun and lesbian had to do with her anger, but I knew she hated me.' I was crying and cowering when the nanny took me home and explained what happened."

Lily took a deep breath. "I'd never seen my mamas so angry. It frightened me because at first I thought they were angry at me. Del was ranting and raving and talking about killing the bitch, her face looked ugly to me, and I was afraid she wouldn't love me anymore. Mama Del went to see the bitch and, I gathered from overhearing her describing it to Cordy, gave her a piece of her mind."

Lily smiled. "I guess I was traumatized because I'd forgotten this whole thing. The next morning my mamas sat with me and explained that what Belinda's mother said, was about her, not about us. That having too much money can change people. Not all, but some think wealth makes them socially superior, and they look down on anyone who has less money or who, for some reason, they decide is socially inferior. Sometimes the very wealthy are so self-involved they become cruel and careless of others feelings and it's best to avoid having anything to do with people like that. When the incident floated into my consciousness this morning, I was surprised to feel the hurt and the terror again after all these years."

They were silent for a second, then Emma jumped in. "So you think that encounter with a wealthy witch triggered your response to Robin's being a billionaire?"

Lily sipped her champagne, then looked Emma in the eye. "I think that's a good part but not all of it. It's hard to unravel. But wherever the feelings come from I know that life in a bubble like that, focused on things and appearances, is not the life I want for myself or for my children."

"You have children?"

"Geez, Emma, let her talk."

"No children yet. But I want them, and if Robin and I ever get serious, I would want to have at least two." She squeezed Robin's hand. "To answer your other question, Mama Cordy is Professor Cordelia Alexander of Stanford University."

"Oh my God, Robin, you had such a crush on her. You idolized her. Did you know when you met Lily that—"

"Of course not. Actually, I saw Lily across the room at the Shazarak and was attracted immediately."

"And romantic that she is, she threw a kiss and told me she loved me before we ever said a word." Lily kissed Robin's cheek.

"I'm trying to convince her that a mere billion won't change me and that I intend to be a good billionaire, using the money to improve the world. As soon as I figure out what that means."

"Didn't the money you gave to that soup kitchen she took you to convince her of your good intentions?"

"What?" Lily choked on the champagne.

"Oops, open mouth, insert foot. I guess you didn't tell her?"

"No, I didn't." Robin's voice was so deep it was almost a growl. "Better start thinking before you speak, Emma. It's a long way down to the ground from here. Oh good, here comes our melon and prosciutto." She waited for Tammie to serve before turning to Lily.

"I'm sorry I didn't tell you. After we worked there, I thought a lot about the people in need and the volunteers trying to help them, and it seemed to me that it shouldn't be such a struggle to deliver such an important service, filling a basic human need." She cleared her throat. "I didn't tell you because I didn't want you to know I had so much money or to think I was trying to buy your affection. Please don't be upset with me."

Lily's fingers caressed the nape of Robin's neck. "I'm surprised, not upset. I knew about the million dollars they got, but it never occurred to me that you were the anonymous donor. Of course, that was before I knew you were a billionaire." She hugged Robin. "That was generous. And doing it anonymously makes it seem genuine. It's what I would expect of you."

"So all's well that ends well?"

"You're pushing it, Emma. Why don't you entertain us with scintillating conversation that has nothing to do with me? Tell us about your latest book."

"Ah, yes. *Women in the Middle East: Past, Present, and Future* will be out in two weeks. I have a few copies with me if anyone would like one. Actually, Annie, you may be interested in the chapters on ancient women, common and royal."

The conversation was fascinating. The two academics argued some finer points and found agreement on many others. Robin, of course, had already read Emma's book and many others on Middle Eastern history and held her own with them.

Lily was most interested in the oppression of the women and how they would fare in the future. "So if women aren't allowed to be educated and face the threat of death for exercising the simplest right, can anything change?"

Emma opened her mouth, glanced at Robin and closed it.

Robin cleared her throat. "Actually, Katie and I have been discussing using some of our money to help that change along. And Emma has been really helpful with identifying the issues. But can we move this discussion into something a little lighter?"

Everyone laughed. Annie asked if anybody had seen any good movies and they shifted gears. They ended up laughing their way through the typical Italian meal of several small courses: after the melon, pasta con cacio e pepe (cheese and pepper), then grilled fresh sardines with string beans, fresh fruit and espresso.

Lily ate the last bite of pineapple and pushed the plate away. "Dinner was delicious. Am I the only one stuffed?" Judging by the groans, she wasn't. "Can we take a walk?"

"Sure. We can go down to the esplanade." They all stood. Robin threw her arm over Lily's shoulder while the two academics still deep in conversation faced each other. "Just let me talk to…oh, Tammie."

Tammie snapped a couple of quick pictures, then handed the camera to Robin.

"Thanks. Everything was great, as usual. We're going to take a walk and if you're ready to leave before we get back just pull the door shut. Do you want cash or would you rather bill me?"

"Bill. You or DCTI?"

"Me. And thanks again for a delicious meal."

As they were getting ready to leave the apartment, Robin pulled Lily into her arms. "Are we okay about the money?"

Lily sighed. "I'm working on it. I think maybe it can be managed. Give me a little time."

They exited the building and as they walked arm and arm to the esplanade along the Hudson River, Robin glanced back at their two friends who were deep in conversation. "They seem to be hitting it off, don't you think?"

"I do think. They're both positively glowing. I believe you hit the jackpot, Ms. DiLuca."

Robin nuzzled Lily's neck. "There's only one jackpot that interests me at this moment, Ms. Alexander. Can you guess?"

"Hmm. What could it be?"

"By the way, I know it's only weeks after our week in Paris for New Year's Eve but will you do me the honor of going to Davos with me in January? After all, your mama will be there to chaperone."

Right, Paris. "Yes. If we're still…yes, I'd love to." She'd almost said if they were still seeing each other.

Robin leaned over and brought their lips together.

Emma giggled. "Hey, no smooching in front of the kids."

Robin looked up. "Try it, I think you'll like it. We won't look."

Lily glanced over her shoulder at the giggling and rustling coming from behind them. It seemed their friends had taken Robin's advice and were in a clinch. Robin opened her mouth, but Lily put her finger on her lips. "Leave them be, sweetie."

They walked a while longer before Robin texted the car service to pick them up in front of her building. While they waited, Lily said, "Next date is my choice again. So how about a week from Saturday?"

"Terrific. The soup kitchen again?"

It was time to see whether another date that didn't include an expensive restaurant and nightlife would turn Robin off. "No, I'll do that this week so we can have a fun date. My treat all day and evening. Wear comfortable shoes and clothes. We'll start with breakfast at my favorite place at ten, then walk around Manhattan and do some sightseeing. Would you would enjoy that?"

"It sounds like fun." Robin was grinning like a ten-year-old. "I haven't done anything like that since Katie and I moved here from California. Can we eat hot dogs and pastrami sandwiches and pizza?"

"Only if you're good." She put her hand over Robin's eyes. "No wiggling of eyebrows, please. Is Katie an ex-lover?"

Robin suddenly became serious. "Katie was…is…my best friend and my family and my business partner and so much more, but we've never been lovers. She's straight."

She knew why she feared commitment, but she'd wondered about Robin's reason. Maybe it was unrequited love. "It sounds like she's important to you. I'd love to hear more about her and your relationship. Unless, of course, you think I'm being intrusive."

Robin opened her arms wide. "I'm an open book, Lily Alexander. There's nothing I want to hide from you, but let's wait until we meet again. Maybe I can tell you on one of our walks."

CHAPTER FIFTEEN

Robin in London

When the cat's away, inevitably she'll play. The thought popped into her mind as she stared at the pictures of Robin on the gossip page in the *New York Post* Annie had brought over.

"It was open to this page when I sat down at Starbucks and Robin's face jumped out at me. I know you don't read trashy newspapers or watch TV news, but I didn't want you to see it by accident or worse have someone call you about it."

In glorious color, Robin's beautiful face did jump off the page. Lily nodded and read the article.

Technology Billionaire Robin DiLuca Celebrates in London

There was no shortage of beautiful women hanging onto to every word uttered by Robin DiLuca, the world's most eligible lesbian bachelorette, who was in London celebrating the opening of a new office for DiLuca Cooper Technologies International. Word on the street is that DiLuca spends nights drinking and dancing, then takes one or more of the models and actresses home to play. Page Six previously reported that DiLuca has been seen about New York with someone she's serious about, someone she's been keeping off the radar. Has that romance gone poof?

Aware of Annie watching her, she studied the pictures again—one of the grinning Robin being kissed on each cheek by two gorgeous women; another of Robin kissing a redhead whose face was not visible; another of her holding up a glass for a toast while surrounded by women. What did she expect, being seductive, reeling Robin in, then not making sex a priority? Lily tried not to care, but tears stung her eyes. She put the paper down, picked up her cup of coffee and looked at Annie. "I guess you were right."

"About her finding someone else? I'm not so sure. I think you're the one she's serious about. Besides, it's a gossip column, for cripes sake. For example, we know she doesn't drink." Annie patted Lily's hand. "She's unique. A gorgeous, self-made lesbian billionaire business owner. Oh, and did I mention hot? Of course she's a celebrity. It's probably good publicity for the company."

Lily stared into her cup. "I don't know what to do, Annie. I think I'm falling in love with her and I know I'm crazy attracted to her, but I'm afraid that once we make love I'm going to lose her."

"You're still letting Micki fuck with your head and you need to get past her. You are an extremely desirable woman and you damn well know that Robin thinks so."

Lily nodded. "I want to believe. But then I think, if I'm so desirable why did Micki just toss me aside like a dirty tissue?"

"It seems to me you want Robin to prove you're desirable. But you need to deal with your feelings of inadequacy, rid yourself of Micki's poison, or you'll be trapped between want and fear forever. And probably lose Robin. I strongly suggest you consider therapy. If you're interested, I know a good therapist." She pulled a notebook out of her bag and wrote the name and telephone number. She tore the page out and handed it to Lily. "I'm having dinner with Emma tonight. Do you want me to pump her for information?"

Lily thought about it, then shook her head. "No. I'll talk about it with Robin when she gets back. If we still have a date, that is."

Annie stood. "You're overreacting to the article, but I do think you should make an appointment with the therapist. And, now, I must go prep for my noon class."

Lily stared at the pictures for a little longer, reread the article, especially the line about someone she's serious about, then folded the paper and walked it to the incinerator room in the hall. She rinsed the coffee cups, put them in the dishwasher, then, shaking her head at her silliness, she retrieved the newspaper from the incinerator room and carried it and the therapist's information into her office.

She sat at her desk a long time, staring at the pictures of Robin cavorting with the gang of fawning women. Annie was right. She was letting Micki's selfishness, Micki's careless abuse of her feelings and Micki's heartless public abandonment of her keep her from trusting that the person she was falling in love with could love her. She took a deep breath and keyed in the number Annie had given her for Hillary Martieri.

Feeling calmer once she'd made the appointment, she turned on her computer and reread what she'd written yesterday to bring herself back into the story she was writing. When her landline rang, she let the answering machine pick it up since anybody close to her knew she didn't take calls during her workday. Then, suddenly aware it was Robin's voice leaving the message, she grabbed the phone. "Hi."

"Hey. I know you don't like interruptions when you're working, but I thought you might pick up the landline if you heard me leaving a message. I've been missing you and I wanted to hear your sexy voice."

She was breathless with excitement at hearing from Robin. "I bet you say that to all the girls." She hesitated. "I saw in this morning's paper you're having a grand old time drinking and dancing. And taking girls home to play." Damn, she didn't want to push her away.

She heard a quick intake of breath. "Well, I cannot tell a lie. I *have* been dancing up a storm, fast ones only, but you know I don't drink and the only girl I want to play with is in New York. Dare I hope you're jealous?"

"Maybe. If you were here, I could explain it better."

"Hmm. Is telephone sex allowed while dating?"

She closed her eyes and imagined touching herself while Robin… "Maybe after we've made love for real but not for the first time."

"But I don't have to account to you what I do when I'm alone with my thoughts of you, do I?"

She was having difficulty breathing. "No talking about sex. Tell me about London."

Robin took a deep breath. "We've been working all day into the evening, hiring staff and getting things set up here, then I've been hitting the clubs at eleven or twelve. Needless to say, I'm exhausted. Katie says I'm getting in the way. She insists she and the five employees we brought over to stay and train can do what needs to be done."

"Too much partying?"

"Actually, the partying is because I haven't adjusted to the time difference and I need to burn off energy. But my mind seems to be back in New York."

Was Robin's mind on her? Or was she talking about the business? "I guess it's hard to leave the New York office to run itself."

"Not really. Between Jan and the senior staff, everything is under control. It's...other things. Uh, so I'm leaving tomorrow morning. And I was hoping we could spend Thursday afternoon and evening together, even though we're already committed to our Saturday date."

"That would be nice." Robin was coming home to her. Lily wanted to shout it, but she managed to maintain her cool.

"I think you'll like what I have planned. I'll pick you up at noon. Wear shorts or anything comfortable and sandals or other comfortable shoes."

Lily put the phone down, did a little happy dance, then picked up her cell and texted Annie. She couldn't stop grinning.

CHAPTER SIXTEEN

Coney Island

Prompt as usual, Robin was leaning against the doorframe when Lily opened the door. The green tank top she was wearing over dark green shorts made her green eyes pop. Her smile was blinding. Suddenly Lily felt shy. What had she done to deserve the attention of this gorgeous creature? They kissed, but when she felt them heating up, she turned to lock the door.

In the elevator, Robin cleared her throat. "I know you prefer public transportation, but I'm still tired from the trip and the time change, so I hope it's okay that Tanya will be driving us."

"Of course." Lily touched her face. "Where are we going?"

Robin put an arm over Lily's shoulder. "Have you ever been to Coney Island?"

Lily's eyes widened. "I've been wanting to go there."

"I thought we'd have hot dogs at Nathan's, then walk over to the Aquarium. If we're up for it, we can do some rides or just walk on the beach. Okay?"

"Super."

As Lily chatted with Tanya, Robin slumped against her. She turned. Robin had fallen asleep and her head was bouncing against the seat back because of the rough highway. She put her arm around Robin, cradled her head on her breast, then kissed her forehead. She looked up and met Tanya's eyes in the rearview mirror. They smiled and drove the rest of the trip in silence.

When they turned off the highway, Robin woke and nuzzled Lily's neck. "Umm. I'll bet if you'd come to London with me, I would have slept."

Lily raised her eyebrows. "Really?" She whispered into Robin's ear. "You think we would have slept?"

"Oh, God, Lily, don't do that to me in my weakened state. You keep whispering sweet nothings in my ear, I might have an orgasm in the car."

Lily kissed her ear and whispered. "Okay, sweetie."

Robin groaned.

The car stopped. "Nathan's." Tanya shifted to face them. "What time should I pick you up?"

"I'll text you when we're ready. Give your aunt my regards." They slid out of the car. Robin took Lily's hand. "So do you do that naturally or are you just a tease?"

Lily flushed. She tried to drop Robin's hand, but Robin held tight.

"Being near you makes me feel sexy and that stuff just pops out. It seems the universe is doing everything possible to keep us from making love."

Robin put her arms around her and turned her so they were face to face. "All I think about is having sex with you. I think the lack of sleep is making me sensitive and cranky. I've been looking forward to seeing you today and hopefully having a night of hot and heavy sex."

Lily nodded. "I don't mean to tease. I'm desperate to make love with you." It didn't escape Lily that they were still using different terms; she talked about making love, Robin about sex. And there was something in Robin's tone of voice when she said "hot and heavy" that made Lily uncomfortable.

"It's damn hard wanting you like this." She tilted Lily's face and kissed her nose. "But let's get to the important stuff. What do you like on your hot dog?"

True to form, Robin asked a passerby to take a picture of them eating their hot dogs, then they strolled over to the Aquarium.

It turned out that Robin, the Florida girl, had never been to an aquarium and took great delight in every exhibit. Like a child, she was wide-eyed to be able to experience the antics of the seals and the scariness of the sharks up close. She studied each exhibit with care, almost as if she was memorizing the information provided, but she seemed to know so much more than shown on the posters near the tanks. When she had a question about the sharks, she asked to see the Aquarium employee responsible for them and engaged her in a fifteen-minute conversation that was so far over Lily's head that she wandered away to a nearby bench to wait for her. It occurred to Lily that Robin knew a lot about a lot of things and could hold her own in discussions with professionals like Annie and Emma and someone who specialized in sharks. She'd been impressed by the range and the scope of the books in Robin's apartment and now, remembering what Emma said about Robin reading her suitemates' textbooks and trying to absorb everything they learned, she wondered where Robin fell on the genius scale. *Not too intimidating!*

The Cyclone was another story. Not surprising, Robin had never ridden a roller coaster, and now looking up at the huge wooden monster, she hesitated. "It doesn't look very safe." She pulled her phone out. "Maybe we should see how many people die here every year?"

"Well, sweetie, the Cyclone is a classic. I assume it would be shut down if it wasn't safe. Let's do it so you can cross it off your lifetime list of things to do. It's fun to be scared. We can hug and hold onto each other and scream together. What's not to like?"

"Golly, I know a way to hug and hold onto each other and scream together that's a lot safer than that thing looks."

Lily patted Robin's cheek. "Well, sweetie, since we aren't going to do that here, we might as well do this."

"I take it you've ridden this thing before?"

"Not this one but I ride the roller coaster every chance I get. I even made Mic…" She stopped short, not wanting to bring Micki between them. She was already too present.

"It's okay, Lily, I know you had a Micki in your life. But tell me, did she jilt you because you made her go on a roller coaster with you? Or was it because you teased too much?"

She seemed to be joking. Then again anger veiled as humor seemed more likely for someone as kind as Robin than full-out rage. The comment felt like a knife in the gut in any case. She wondered where it was coming from, this sudden anger. It wasn't her fault that things kept coming up. Was it? She closed her eyes and took a deep breath, then squeezed Robin's arm. "Not funny."

"Well, I don't find the thought of riding this monstrosity funny, but let's give it a go."

Robin's body stiffened as the attendant locked them into their car, her creamy skin drained of color and she gripped the bar in front of them with white-knuckled hands. Lily wrapped her arm around Robin's waist to comfort her and felt Robin's heart pounding. Would she panic? But after the third rise and fast drop, the look on Robin's face went from white with fear to pure exhilaration. They screamed and hugged until the car slowed and stopped. Then Robin insisted they ride it again. And again. On the third trip, Robin was sufficiently relaxed to take two or three selfies of them with her phone.

After the fourth trip, Robin cornered one of the people running the thing and shot questions at him until Lily dragged her away to walk on the beach. But Robin couldn't stop talking about the wooden roller coaster.

Lily listened attentively but herded Robin toward the beach.

At the edge of the hot, dry sand, they removed their shoes and walked hand in hand, enjoying the feel of the cold water lapping at their feet. Occasionally Robin ran ahead, leaping like an antelope, at first singing "Zip-a-Dee-Do-Dah," then making up happy songs about the thrill of the roller coaster and of being with the beautiful Lily. Had she misread Robin? Maybe she wasn't angry.

By dusk, Robin had won Lily an elephant on the midway and was starting to droop. She texted Tanya. While they waited for their ride, they discussed names for the elephant but couldn't seem to agree on one.

Lily bumped Robin gently. "If we can't agree on a name for a stuffed animal, how will we name our children?"

Robin's face darkened. "Maybe it's a sign that we're not meant to have children."

Lily studied Robin for a moment before responding. "Having second thoughts?"

"Just saying." She blinked. "I mean, we agreed that there is no us, so it seems silly, childish even, to talk about children if we aren't in a committed relationship."

Lily nodded. "Does this mean you want a committed relationship or you don't want children?"

Robin looked away. "I'm not—"

Tanya sounded the car horn as she pulled in front of them. Robin quickly reached for the door, helped Lily in, then slid in next to her. Instead of continuing their conversation as Lily expected, Robin changed the subject. "We have reservations at an Italian restaurant, Al di la Trattoria, in Park Slope, but we could go somewhere else, if you prefer."

"Italian is always good for me."

On the half-hour drive to Park Slope, Robin asked Tanya about her afternoon.

"I took my aunt to lunch at a Russian restaurant, then we hung out in her condo until you called."

Robin gave her a blow-by-blow description of riding the roller coaster, walking on the beach and winning the unnamed elephant. Clearly, she wanted to talk about anything but their relationship or non-relationship.

Mel was waiting when they walked into the restaurant. Lily was surprised. "How did Mel get here?"

"Didn't you see Tanya make a call after we confirmed we were coming here? I guess she took the subway from work." Robin cleared her throat. "Should we ask Tanya and Mel to join us tonight rather than sit at a separate table?"

"It's up to you."

They seemed surprised to be invited, but they were interesting women, both former military, both widely traveled, and not at all obsequious as Lily had anticipated. But she found her mind wandering back to the discussion she and Robin had started, the one that Robin now was avoiding. She'd thought they were moving toward each other, toward committing, but now she wasn't so sure. After all, Robin had made it clear up front that she just wanted to have fun, that she didn't do commitment or relationships.

After dinner, Robin dozed in the car and then, pleading exhaustion, she dropped Lily in front of her building with a quick kiss good night.

CHAPTER SEVENTEEN

Riverside Park

Robin couldn't stop smiling. Lily was adorable, excited, high energy and bubbly like a little kid going on an outing, but also very much an adult, drop dead gorgeous in her shorts and tank. She considered trying to get her into bed before they went out to breakfast. *Might not be that hard*, she thought. But this was Lily's day, and she didn't want to spoil it. *Wait a minute. Since when would sex spoil a date?* The unease she felt the other day burbled up. Her feelings for Lily were starting to feel like commitment. And she didn't do commitment.

Lily pulled her along. "Just another block. Here we are. Edgar's Cafe."

She stared at the huge painting of Edgar Allen Poe hanging on one wall of the small restaurant and wondered if she could actually eat with that face staring down at her. Lily's taste in restaurant décor left a lot to be desired. But the waitress and the owner greeted Lily like a long-lost relative, and she responded with her usual Southern charm.

"It's a beautiful day. You okay with sitting outside, Robin?"

Robin eyed the minuscule outside area, typical of a small neighborhood restaurant. "Sounds like a terrific idea." Much better than having Poe glaring at them.

After they had ordered, Lily smiled across the tiny table. "Thank you for humoring me. I often come here with my computer to write. Some days I have breakfast, then I get into working and suddenly it's lunchtime, so I order lunch. Nobody rushes me. I love it."

"Well, my smoked salmon, cream cheese and scallion scramble was truly delicious and the people seem very nice."

Lily's face lit up. "I told you." She slapped Robin's hand away when she reached for the check. "My treat today. Remember?"

Outside, Lily took her hand. "Come. We'll walk west on Ninety-first Street. There's an entrance to Riverside Park there. That way we'll see the flower gardens, then walk down to the Hudson River. Annie says it's beautiful."

The park was teeming with people jogging, biking, skating, reading or walking with and without children and with and without dogs. A woman with a cat on a leash and a man with a parrot on his shoulders were sitting near the flower gardens, which were not the neat, regimented rows or circles of similar plants she'd expected but an assortment of different plants of varying heights and colors enclosed in two large fenced-in areas. The gardens seemed untamed, bursting with energy and color, beautiful and free. They circled the two plots hand in hand in the bright sunlight, pointing flowers out to each other, then they strolled through the park, walked down a steep hill, through a short tunnel and onto a path along the Hudson River. Behind them was the George Washington Bridge, which seemed to hang over the water. To their right was New Jersey, which looked close enough to swim to, and before them was a marina with boats bobbing in the sparkling water.

Robin pulled Lily into a hug. "Annie was right. It is beautiful." Their eyes met. "But not as beautiful as you."

Lily brushed Robin's lips. "Shall we sit for a while?"

"Tired already, my little Southern belle?"

"No, I want to feel your body next to mine, and I don't think it would be a good idea to lie down on the path."

"Well, in that case, let's sit." She led Lily to one of the benches facing the water, put her arm over her shoulders and pulled her in close. "Does this do it for you?" Lily's head was on Robin's shoulder, her breath warm on Robin's neck.

Lily's voice was husky. "For now."

The words ignited a flame that burned through Robin. She knew sex with Lily would be fantastic, and she hoped there would be no interruptions tonight. She ran her hand up and down Lily's arm.

Lily shivered. "If you keep doing that, I might lose control out here in public."

"Hmm." Robin smiled. That made two of them.

"Distract me. Tell me about Katie."

"It's a long story."

"I'm yours for today and I'm all ears. Well, not all ears, most of me is nerve endings that are popping all over the place. Unless it's painful and you'd really rather not, please tell me."

"You may have popping nerve endings, but I find it impossible to think about anyone but you and anything but sex, with you breathing on me."

Lily shifted to face the water. Robin took a deep breath. *Where to start? What to say? How much to reveal?* They'd said they'd be honest with each other about their history, and she was sure it hadn't been easy for Lily to tell her about being jilted. So far nothing she'd revealed was as close to the bone as that. So she should do it or stop this…what? *Flirting with Lily? Romancing Lily? Trying to maneuver Lily into bed? All of the above?* She blew out her breath.

"The August after I graduated high school I turned fourteen, and a couple of weeks later, I left Florida for Harvard on full scholarship."

"Wow, that's young. You must have been scared?"

"I was terrified. My sixth grade teacher, Barbara, who was the first to recognize my intelligence, got me on the fast track and guided me to a full scholarship to Harvard. She was my guardian angel and I wanted her to take me there to help me get settled, but she and her partner had long-standing vacation plans, plus she thought it might help me bond with my dad if he went with me. I barely ever spoke to my dad, but she got him to commit to fly to Boston and help me get settled in the dorm. She gave him a list of clothing I would need and he promised he'd take me shopping in Boston.

"At the last minute he changed his mind. He said Barbara had arranged all of this and she should be the one inconvenienced. I knew Barbara was away with her lover until after Labor Day, so I said, 'Forget it, I'll fly to Boston on my own.' He was a drunk, so he didn't question it, nor, actually, did he care. Thankfully, Barbara had arranged for an old friend of hers who lived outside of Boston to meet us at the airport and drive us to the campus."

"Laura was surprised I was alone with just one small suitcase, but she drove me to the dorm. She wanted to come to my room, but I didn't want her to see how petrified I was, so I insisted I was okay. She put her hand on my shoulder, which almost undid me, and asked if I was sure. I nodded and smiled so she dropped me off and drove away. When I found my room, I closed the door and started to shake, then sob. That was when Katie appeared. She was a sophomore, but she'd spent two years in the Peace Corps before starting Harvard so she was older. She sat next to me on the bed, pulled me into her arms and let me sob. I'd had very little physical contact in my life and I wanted to curl up inside Katie and purr. But being so close to her, smelling her, feeling her breasts against me also awakened a yearning, which I later realized was sexual feelings. I wanted more but didn't know how to ask. So once I stopped sobbing, I responded to Katie's not inconsiderable physical charms by groping her. But she grabbed my roving hands, tilted my face so I was looking at her, then kissed my forehead. 'No, sweetie. I believe you need comfort more than you need sex. Let's just be friends for a while?' I was shocked. 'Sex?'

"Because I was so young, the dean had assigned me to Katie's suite and had given her a small stipend to look after me. And that's what she did. That day she helped me unpack and make my bed, then introduced me to our four suitemates, Mei, Emma, Nicole and Winnie. She and I had singles, but the others shared two rooms. When she realized I hadn't had lunch, she took me out to eat, gave me a tour of the campus, then accompanied me to the freshman orientation sessions. Afterward, we had dinner in the dining hall. It says something about my life up to then that I had never felt so cared for."

Robin glanced at Lily and was surprised to see tears streaming down her face. "What's wrong?" Lily used the bottom of her tank top to dry the tears. "I'm crying for that poor fourteen-year-old girl."

Robin added empathy to the list of qualities she admired in Lily. "I survived and thrived. Katie made sure of that. It turned out we had two classes together, but she walked me to all my classes every day until I felt comfortable on my own. We studied together every night, either in the suite or in the library, and ate all our meals together. She was like an older sister, really a mother, very protective, very nurturing. And I learned from her that it was okay to be physically affectionate. I hadn't realized how unhappy I was until I felt real happiness with Katie.

"My father never wrote, never called, never sent any money, and if I'd had to depend on the small stipend that came with my scholarship, I probably would have frozen to death that first winter. But when it started to get cooler, Katie noticed this Florida girl's wardrobe consisted of a couple of pairs of shorts, a pair of jeans, sweat pants, a few T-shirts and sandals; no warm clothes, no winter coat, no shoes, no boots, nothing. My father's promise to take me shopping in Boston was forgotten in his drunken haze and, of course, he hadn't given me any money when I left.

"Katie took me out and bought me socks, underwear, sweaters and pants and shirts and shoes and everything I would need to get through the fall and winter in fine style. She spent the entire semester's stipend she'd received from the dean, plus her allowance for the semester. Nicole, Mei and Winnie were all on scholarship too so they didn't have anything to spare, but Emma contributed a nice chunk of her allowance. And Katie's parents gave her money to buy me leather boots, snow boots, hiking boots, a hat, a scarf, gloves, and a heavy winter jacket, then deposited more money into her allowance account. I had never had so many and such nice clothes. Infant that I was, I took so much kindness for granted."

"And your teacher Barbara didn't help?"

Robin looked out over the Hudson, then took a breath. "Not long after I settled in at Harvard, Barbara's friend, the one who had picked me up at the airport, came by to tell me that Barbara and her partner were killed in a car crash coming back from that vacation."

Lily hugged her. "Oh, sweetie, you had so many losses at such a young age."

"Yes. But luckily I had Katie. And our other four roommates. I was like a chick in the hen house and they all took me under their wings and looked after me. Other than the first Thanksgiving when I went home with Nicole, I spent holidays and vacations with Katie and her family, but sometimes I went home with one of the others for a weekend. Katie found us summer jobs on Cape Cod, and we lived and worked together. I never went home again. I don't know how I got so lucky, but since then I've been trying to repay her, the others too, but I don't think it's possible."

"Was it ever sexual with Katie?"

"She's straight. I tried a couple of times, but she convinced me it would be better to stay friends and that's what we did."

"Are you in love with her?"

Robin laughed. "I had a crush on her for a long time a long time ago. I love her like a sister or maybe like a mother. I don't know because I can't compare it to anything. But I'm not in love with her. She's also my business partner."

Lily squeezed Robin. "That's a lovely story. No wonder she's so important to you."

Robin squeezed back. "Okay, enough serious stuff. I thought this was going to be a play day. What's next?

* * *

Lily moved out of Robin's embrace. "Have you ever kayaked?"

"Not for a long time."

"Can you swim?"

"Yes."

"Let's go. It's not far." She pinched Robin and took off, laughing.

Robin dashed after her. "Oh, no you don't, cheater." With her longer legs, she caught Lily right away and wrapped her arms around her. "You are so bad."

Lily leaned into her. "Are you going to punish me?" She breathed into Robin's ear.

Robin's arms tightened. "Tease. Keep this up and I'll—"

"You'll what? Tie me up and torture me with your tongue?" She laughed and grabbed Robin's hand, dragging her along the river until they came to the kayaks. "The kayaks are free. You get twenty minutes. It'll be fun."

She could see on Robin's face that she'd gone too far with the sexual teasing. When had she become the person who plays with other people's feelings? Was it a power trip? Or was it because she was scared shitless of getting close?

Lily took Robin's hand and pulled her out of the line to an empty bench nearby. Robin's body was rigid, her hand lifeless in Lily's, her jaw tense. Her eyes refused to connect. Lily knelt in front of her, touched her face, and kissed the palm of her hand. "I owe y'all an apology. I am so attracted to you. Being with you, no matter what we do, is a turn on. Making love with you is constantly on my mind which is why those teasing comments pop out."

She kissed Robin's palm and held it to her face. Robin's gaze remained on the river. "I admit I haven't gone out of my way to actually make love with you. I could have let Dawn stay at my apartment and spent the night at yours and the same thing when my mama showed up. I'm a big girl and I should have been able to tell her I'd see her in the morning. But I'm still raw and uncertain and pained by what Micki did. I can't go through that again. It would kill me. And I'm afraid if we make love, you'll go away. I've gone into therapy to try to get past it so I can be with you the way I want, the way I think you want." She looked up into Robin's eyes. "I don't want to hurt you. I would understand—"

Robin pulled her up onto the bench next to her. "I understand you're hurting, Lily, and I've been trying to let you take the lead, but the teasing makes me feel you're playing with me. Or holding out for a c—"

She took a deep breath. "Apology accepted. Let's enjoy the day." She grinned. "Now how about I beat your ass at a kayak race?"

Holding out for what? A commitment? Was that what she was doing? Didn't Robin have a pony in this race? Why was it totally her responsibility? And now Robin was shoving this discussion aside again in favor of having fun in the moment. That was good for the moment, but not so good for working out their issues. Well, she'd said up front she wanted to have fun and play, that she wasn't into pain and tears. And for her a good part of having fun was sex. Was she right that once Robin had taken her to bed, she would dump her? Well, tonight was the night, so she'd know soon enough. Lily hugged her.

"You really think you can beat me? Let's go."

The race was a draw, but they were both soaked so they lay on the grass in the sun, drying out, then went for a beer and a snack at Pier 1, the outdoor restaurant a little beyond the kayaks. Afterwards, Lily led them to the subway, and they went downtown to walk the High Line. She was curious about the park, thirty feet above the street on a former elevated railway that had once carried trains along Manhattan's West Side. They held hands and laughed and joked as they strolled the one-and-a-half-mile-long park, admiring the wildflowers and grasses, the art installations and views of the Hudson River. From time to time they stopped to rest on a bench. Lily leaned into Robin's arms. As they silently people watched, she kissed Robin's palm, then shifted to kiss her lightly on the lips. Lily felt close to Robin and sensed sadness and tenderness that hadn't been there before.

For dinner, they took the subway uptown to One-hundred-twenty-fifth Street and Broadway to Pisticci, an Italian restaurant on nearby LaSalle Avenue.

"So, my Southern belle," Robin teased, "do you only eat in restaurants in basements?"

Lily blushed. "I go where the food is good and the prices are right. Glitz and glamour don't do it for me."

"Do you know that when you get excited or upset you sound more Southern?"

"I go to some childhood place inside and it just comes out that way. Does it bother you?"

Robin rubbed her thumb over Lily's hand. "I like it."

CHAPTER EIGHTEEN

Breaking Up Is Hard To Do

Dinner was delicious and romantic. But the low-level anxiety Robin had been feeling most of the day had gone sky high after she'd had a fantasy about them getting married—Lily in a white gown, she in a tux. It happened while Lily was in the ladies room. Robin was hyperventilating as Lily approached the table again, so she stood, held the napkin in front of her mouth as if she was dabbing her lips, muttered "bathroom" and dashed away. Since this wasn't the first time she'd hyperventilated, she knew what to do. After five minutes breathing deeply she was back to normal. Happily, Lily didn't question her story of a sudden urge to pee.

As they stepped out of the restaurant into a beautiful evening, Robin took Lily's hand. "Want to walk to your apartment?"

Lily seemed uneasy. "I'd love it. But are you up for another two miles?"

Had she sensed Robin's anxiety?

Robin smiled. "You bet."

Robin's mind was racing as she threw an arm over Lily's shoulder and pulled her close, relishing the way their bodies fit together. Lily was smart and playful and fun to be with. Robin loved the time they spent together and desired her more than any woman she'd ever dated. But when had she lost sight of her original plan—have sex with the sensual blonde across the room and move on? Seeing Lily was starting to feel like a commitment. She knew she didn't want a committed relationship, she knew she didn't want children and she knew she'd stop seeing Lily after they'd had sex a couple of times. Lily was already fragile from Micki's heartless treatment. Walking away would hurt Lily. Maybe ending it now before they had sex and things got more involved would be kinder.

Lily stopped walking. "You're so quiet. Is everything all right?"

"Just enjoying the evening." And now she was lying. To protect Lily? Or herself?

She sought Robin's eyes. "Did you enjoy today?"

"I did. It was fun." *And I was hoping we'd end up in bed tonight, but a quick break would probably be the easiest.*

They were down at Eighty-ninth Street when they noticed the huge trailers and the lights and the crowd. Lily pointed out the familiar actress from *Law and Order SVU*. "They're always shooting the show around here."

While they watched, another actress moved into the scene from the sidelines, there was an exchange of dialogue, a struggle, she was cuffed, then escorted toward a police car off camera. As the cuffs were being removed, she looked their way, smiled and waved. Robin waved back.

"One of your many admirers, I presume?"

Robin smiled down at her. "As a matter of fact. Her name is Donna Darnly."

"Well, Donna wants to talk to you." Lily couldn't keep the annoyance—or was it jealousy—out of her voice.

"What?" Robin turned toward the woman who was waving her over, then turned back to Lily. "Excuse me. I'll just be a minute." She didn't think Donna would want to have anything to do with her after being dumped.

Aware of Lily's eyes following her as she approached Donna, she resolved to be careful of Lily's feelings. But as they talked, Donna trailed her hand up and down the bare skin of her arm, then did the same on her thigh, below her shorts. She shivered.

She turned to see whether Lily had noticed. Apparently, she had, because she quickly looked away, but not before Robin saw that her eyes were wide and her smile uncertain. Donna gently touched her chin and turned her face back to her. "I've missed you, Robin. Meet me later." Her hand slipped under Robin's T-shirt and caressed her stomach. "I'll show you a good time. You won't regret it."

After spending the whole day with Lily, her body was so ready that a lamppost could probably spark her, but, unfortunately, neither Lily nor the lamppost would be available sexually tonight.

"Remember, no commitment. Give me your address." She handed her the small black notebook and pen she always carried, looked at what she wrote and pocketed the book and pen. Donna ran her fingers around Robin's jaw and was about to lean in for a kiss. *Lily.* Her breath caught. "Go." She pushed Donna toward her trailer. "See you later."

She took a deep breath trying to steady her heart, then walked back to Lily who looked at her curiously but didn't ask.

"She invited me to a party at her apartment later." Another lie. Yes, this was definitely getting too involved.

Lily glanced at her phone. "It's almost eleven. How much later could it be?"

"She said about twelve thirty. These acting people keep weird hours." She took Lily's arm. "Shall we continue walking?"

At Lily's door, their tender kisses deepened as usual, but tonight sadness and regret were mixed with the passion Robin felt. She was dying to take Lily to bed, and she had no doubt Lily wanted her, wanted her to come in, wanted to let her in. But she cared about Lily, knew that having sex and then dumping her would be worse than just walking away. Finally, she stepped back, kissed her tenderly once more and looked into her eyes. "Lily, I—"

"Don't." She put two fingers on Robin's lips. "Just go. It's okay." She took Robin's face in her hands and kissed her gently. Her eyes glistened. "Really, it's okay." Her voice was soft, her smile tender.

Robin blinked back her own tears. She hadn't expected to feel so bad. She stared into Lily's eyes, nodded, then walked to the elevator. She didn't look back.

CHAPTER NINETEEN

Lily's Lament

Lily opened the door to Annie and fell into her arms, sobbing. Annie held her and pulled the door closed behind her. "What's wrong?" In between sobs, Lily murmured something into her shoulder, but Annie didn't understand a word of what she said. After a couple of minutes, Lily's sobs subsided. She looked up through swollen eyes and offered an apologetic shrug. "Sorry, Annie, why don't y'all come in?"

"Are your mamas all right?" Annie followed her into the living room and sat next to her on the sofa. She picked up Lily's hand. "What's wrong?"

"I let Robin go last night."

Annie swiveled to face Lily. "What do you mean, let her go?"

Lily shifted away from Annie. "She was up front about no commitment, that she didn't do relationships. And the clearer I got about wanting a commitment, the more I sensed her pulling away. So I said it was okay for her to go. Remember I promised to not make a scene if we broke up?" A sob escaped.

"I'm sorry you're in such pain, but I have to tell you I'm relieved to see you cry. I worried about you after Micki. You didn't cry at all, at least not that I saw, and I wondered what you did with all the feelings. But you've been dating Robin for what, a month? *You* decided to let her go and *you're* devastated?"

Lily nodded. "That's just it. There were no feelings after Micki. Well, I was pissed and embarrassed but no regrets, no sadness, no sense of loss. Just relief at realizing my true feelings and happiness about being on my own. Losing Robin feels different." She blew her nose. "I know it sounds stupid, but from the minute our eyes found each other that first time in Shazarak I felt an intense connection. I thought I didn't want commitment either. But I was lying to myself and to her."

"If it's any consolation, Robin hung out with you longer than she usually does."

Lily pulled away from Annie. "What does that mean?"

Annie stood. "Shit. I didn't mean to say that."

"Well, you did say it, so you'd better tell me what you meant."

Annie walked to the window, keeping her back to Lily. She stared down at Central Park for a minute, then turned back. "I overheard two women talking about her in the ladies room at Shazarak the other night. After they stopped drooling over her, the women discussed the fact that she's commitment phobic, that she dates lots of women but rarely goes out with anyone more than three times."

"We went out way more than three times and I thought she was feeling the same connection as me."

"Tell me again why you let her go?"

"I'm not sure I really had a choice, but I felt her drifting away and I thought it would hurt less if *I* did it. Besides, I did give her that damned contract." She burst into tears again.

"Dammit, Lily, do you hear yourself?" Annie had her hands on her hips. "Dumping her so she wouldn't have the pain of dumping you. What about *you*? What about *your* pain? And if it's so painful to let her go, why aren't you fighting for her?"

"I'm not fighting for her because she doesn't want me. She just wants sex. And because she hates hurting people so it's hard for her to break up."

"Hello. This is the twenty-first century. Assuming the sex is good, what's wrong with having a sexual relationship and seeing where it goes?"

Lily blushed and looked away. "There was no…we didn't have…
you know I don't trust my feelings."

Annie opened her mouth but no words came. She stared at Lily.
"You never?"

Lily shook her head. "I think I was afraid she would dump me
after we had sex."

"So you dumped her *before* you had sex. I don't understand."

"At first, she was talking about having sex and I was thinking
making love. She was clear she wanted to get me into bed but I—
call me old-fashioned or scared—decided we had to date and get
to know each other first. I was trying to be in control, I guess. After
a few dates, I was ready but things kept getting in the way. She was
tired, we were tired, her business, people staying at my apartment.
Of course, I just rolled passively with it instead of fighting to make
the time."

"And Robin was okay with that?"

"She seemed to be. We were both really turned on. Do you
think that's why she drifted away?"

"I don't know, Lily, you two seemed really into each other the
two times I spent time with you, but when we had dinner at her
apartment I did notice you sort of sneak attacking her about the
models she dated before you and also making a big deal about her
money. Maybe she thought *you* weren't really interested."

Annie crossed to the sofa and took hold of Lily's hands. "Listen
my friend, you are funny, intelligent, kind, personable, gentle, self-
effacing and so caring you actually broke up with Robin to protect
her from the pain of doing it." Annie looked directly into Lily's
eyes. "I'd better stop. I think I'm falling in love with you."

"You're not." Lily's face and her voice registered her shock.

"Just joking." Annie laughed. "It's too soon to know for sure, but
I think Emma could be the one for me." She squeezed Lily's hands.
"You have so much going for you, Lily, yet you constantly doubt
and second-guess yourself. Why?"

Lily pulled away. "I'm a big baby, aren't I?" She smiled through
her tears. "My agent would tell me to suck it up and put all these
feelings in a new romance."

"I don't think you're a big baby and I don't think that all you
want from life is fodder for your writing. I only have Micki and
Robin to compare but you agreed to marry Micki, who you didn't

love, and dumped Robin, who it sounds like you might love." Annie took her hand. "Are you sure you're in touch with your true feelings now or are these rebound feelings?"

"I need coffee." Annie followed Lily into the kitchen and watched her spoon coffee into the pot, fill it water, then set cups and milk and sugar on a tray. When the coffee was ready, they went back into the living room. Annie sat on the sofa, Lily put the tray on the coffee table, handed her a cup, then sat next to her. "I really think I'm done with Micki." Lily stirred her coffee, then took a sip. "My feelings for Robin aren't rebound feelings but I think you're right, I am doubting and second guessing myself."

"You need to figure out the source of your low self-esteem and work on building your self-confidence before you can have a relationship with Robin—or anyone for that matter."

Lily chewed her lip as she stared out the window. "I know what it is." She put her coffee down, stood and faced Annie. "It's this." She swept her hands in front of her, indicating her body.

Annie frowned. "What?"

"My body, I'm fat and—"

"Holy bat shit, Lily, you can't..." She stood, put her hands on Lily's shoulders, and tried to look into Lily's eyes but red-faced, Lily stared over Annie's shoulder. Annie pulled her into a tight hug. Lily's arms hung loose for a few seconds, then she wrapped them around Annie. A soft sob escaped Lily.

"Oh, Lily. How can you not know you're gorgeous? I would kill for a body like yours." Annie pulled her head back so they were eye to eye. "Your body is exactly like your mama Del's—"

"Yes, Del is, um, voluptuous, but I'm just fat and you don't notice it because I usually wear big shirts and things to cover myself."

"Uh-uh, I'll say it again. You are gorgeous and apparently you're the only one who doesn't see it." Annie laughed and shook her head. "Haven't you noticed that when we're out women fall all over themselves to talk to you and dance with you. I'm your best friend and your best friend wouldn't lie to you. Right?"

Lily hesitated, then nodded. "That's my cleavage. Everybody likes breasts."

"True. But. You. Are. Not. Fat. And I would wager Robin's billion if I had it, that Robin definitely doesn't think you're fat. In fact, Emma was surprised at how into you Robin was."

"Surprised that I'm not anything like the beautiful thin models and actresses in Robin's stable of admirers?"

"No. Surprised at how happy Robin seemed with you, at how much she wanted your approval, at how her face lit up when you walked into the room."

Lily paced, thinking. "I do feel she cares for me, but I'm sure she was about to dump me. Why would she do that?"

"Maybe she's scared like you. Maybe she thinks she's not good enough for you. Maybe she thinks you prefer poor, unattractive, dull-witted women."

Lily stopped short. "Oh."

Annie smiled. "You care for her. Why did you dump her?"

"You think she might be afraid? Should I call her? Lily began to pace again. "What if she moves on?"

"If you don't get your shit together, it won't matter if she's moved on or not." Annie plopped down on the sofa and picked up her coffee. "I can't tell you what to do, but if it were me I'd do therapy three times a week to figure out the trust and body image issues. Once you've replaced your self-doubt with self-confidence, you can call Robin, if you're still interested, and get her to commit. You're strong, Lily. You can do it."

"What have I done, Annie? The thought that I've lost her scares me to death. Robin is so alive. She's vibrant and sexy and beautiful inside and out, plus kind and generous and fun to be with. Not only that, she's brilliant and challenges me intellectually like no one ever has. Just looking at her fires up my body, kissing her reduces me to a bowl of Jello and her touch electrifies me. I feel like I want to lose myself in her, to take her to bed and never get out, to spend forever with her."

"Wow. Could this be love?"

"If it is, it's a lot harder than I thought it would be."

CHAPTER TWENTY

If This Is Love

Robin reread the pink telephone message Jan had deposited on her desk a while ago. Donna had called, as she had at least once every day since that night six weeks ago. *What a bust.* Donna enjoyed it, got what she wanted and didn't even notice that Robin's body was there but her mind and heart were…elsewhere. A taker, for sure, willing to put up with a shell as long as it came with money and serviced her on demand. Damn, she didn't like being so mean-spirited, but the difference between someone like Donna and someone like Lily was…

"Be careful," Jan had warned this morning. "Donna insisted you would want to talk to her after the hot night you'd spent together and she's probably going to be stalking you outside the office one of these days." Robin sighed. Why was it so difficult for some women to understand about no commitment? Lily understood.

Robin idly crosshatched the circles, squares and triangles she'd drawn on the pink slip, then added a few arrows and question marks to her doodles. Was she in love? How much time does it take to fall in love? Some believe in love at first sight. Is that what happened? Had she already fallen in love when she mouthed "I love you" to

Lily that first night? Others talk about hours or days or weeks or months or even years before they knew. She swiveled her chair and stared out the window. The Statue of Liberty usually calmed her, helped her focus, but not lately.

She'd not heard a word from Lily. On the other hand, she hadn't taken the initiative to call, though she'd thought about Lily every minute of every day in these six long weeks. She wondered what Lily was doing, wondered how she was feeling, wondered whether she thought about her. Did she feel abandoned by Robin, or was she relieved, as she had been when Micki dumped her? Her heart clutched. *Selfish bitch.* Because Lily had honored her promise and let her go without crying and begging, she'd pretended Lily wasn't in pain.

Her office door opened and someone plopped down in one of the chairs facing her desk. Only Jan or Katie would come in unannounced. She guessed Katie, since Jan had already spent days probing to find out what the hell was going on. Katie tended to let her be so she could solve it for herself and only intervened when it was clear that wasn't happening.

"Want to talk about it?"

She swiveled to face Katie. She shrugged. "I'm not sure I know how to."

"Let's go out for dinner, some place private where we can talk." She stood and made a shooing motion with her hands. "Up. Get a move on."

Downstairs, Katie flagged a cab. "Any ideas about where we can eat and talk?"

Robin leaned forward and spoke to the driver. "LaSalle and Broadway, please."

Katie raised her eyebrows.

"Italian. I assure you we won't meet anyone we know there. It's One hundred twenty-fourth Street, I think."

When they were seated in a quiet corner, Katie ordered a glass of chianti and Robin her usual seltzer and lime, and they both ordered salads and pasta. Katie looked around. "Reminds me of when we were students."

"Good guess. Columbia University and Barnard are just down Broadway."

"How did you—?" The look on Robin's face answered her question. "Lily brought you here."

"She did." Robin fiddled with her silverware. Their dinner had been romantic, intimate, and it was then she caught herself in a fantasy about marrying Lily. Scared the shit out of her.

"So what happened with Lily? You seemed so happy dating her I thought she was the one. Then, all of a sudden, you stopped seeing her."

"It's hard to explain."

"As long as it takes." Katie grinned. "I told Michael I might sleep at your place tonight." She lifted her wine glass. "To friendship. And sharing."

The waitress arrived with their pastas, got refills on their drinks, then left them to it.

"So tell me?" Robin looked ready to run, so Katie automatically shifted to the process she'd worked out to help Robin deal with her issues. "Okay. I'll start. The night of the IPO you spotted this sexy blonde across the room and fell into lust." She looked up.

Robin nodded.

"And even though she left before you could seduce her with your sexy green eyes, lovely body, I-only-want-to-have-fun attitude and the billion dollars in your wallet, you managed to find her. Am I right so far?"

Robin grinned. "So far so good."

"Emma said she had dinner with you, Lily and Lily's friend Annie, who she's now dating, and she thought Lily was definitely enamored."

"I thought so too. Go on."

"You have to finish the story, Rob. You've always succeeded at getting what you want so I can't imagine what went wrong."

Robin twirled pasta on her fork and put it in her mouth. She chewed slowly, thinking. "After the night I first saw her, I couldn't get her out of mind or my dreams, so I went back to Shazarak every night the following week. I couldn't admit to myself that I was desperate to find her, so most nights I went with my usual going-out crowd and the intention of finding someone to go home with. No one seemed attractive, and I went home alone every night. The night I found her I'd gone after working late and I was alone."

"Jan told me you'd ditched your entourage once you found Lily. Interesting."

Robin didn't comment on that comment. "She was even more sexy up close and her voice...Anyway, she told me she'd been looking for me too. When I tried my seductive powers on her she said what would we tell our children if we jumped right into bed."

Katie laughed. "Your children?"

"Yeah, that was my reaction too, but she said she wanted to carry my babies, two of them. I actually had a nightmare about murdering babies that night. It's the kind of thing you'd think would turn me off, right? But it had the exact opposite effect. I was ready to throw her on the floor and have sex right there in the middle of Shazarak. "

"But you didn't, I assume?"

"No. She said no making love until we dated and got to know each other. Notice that I said sex, she said making love. And it wasn't just using different words. I was befuddled by her, but I was sure I'd get my way sooner rather than later, so we talked and danced until the club closed, then she wouldn't let me in her apartment so we necked in her hallway until I was weak in the knees."

The waitress removed their pasta dishes, brought their salads and refilled their glasses.

Katie eyed her. "Necking in hallways? Was the sex worth it?"

"That's just it. There was no sex."

"You dated her what, a month? And no sex. Is that why you split?"

"Yes. No. Sort of."

"Really?"

"Actually, she agreed to have sex after our second or third date, but somehow things got in the way: her friend needed a place to stay, her mother was in town for a few days, we were tired after volunteering at a soup kitchen, I was exhausted after London. She admitted she could have been more aggressive about making time, but she was jilted last December and has trust issues and a problem committing."

"Sounds perfect since you're not into commitment." Katie frowned. "I don't understand."

"I'm not sure I do either. For her, having sex means making love, means commitment. It was just sex to me—seduce her, have fun, then move on. But then I got to know her and care about her and though I was, and am, still ready to toss her into bed, I worried I would hurt her if we had sex and I walked away. I think I scared myself because I started thinking it wasn't just about sex and if it wasn't just sex, then it meant commitment. I don't do commitment. The clincher was the night we had dinner here and I had a fantasy about us getting married."

"And you ran?"

Robin nodded. "That other woman didn't show up at the church on their wedding day and left her to clean up the mess. I can't. I wouldn't. She's wonderful. Christ, Katie, she's brilliant and sensual and fun and honest and loving and down to earth and she doesn't give a damn about my money. We haven't gotten near a bed and yet I know it will be off the charts. And," her voice broke, "she says she wants to have my babies."

Katie reached for Robin's hand. "Oh, Rob honey, you have it bad. I do believe you're in love."

Robin's head jerked. "In love? Then why do I feel so bad?"

CHAPTER TWENTY-ONE

Let the Wooing Begin

Annie and Lily were eating take out Thai when Lily's intercom buzzed. "Delivery coming up, Ms. Alexander."

"It must be a mistake, Lewis. We already received the food we were expecting." But her doorbell was already ringing. She opened the door to a man struggling with a humongous flower arrangement. She pointed to the hall table, then tipped him.

"Wow. Who sent it?" Annie walked over to watch her read the card.

"It says 'Missing you, Robin.'"

Annie raised a fist in the air. "Yes. It's taken almost seven weeks, but she's come through. Are you going to call her to thank her?"

Lily stared at the obviously expensive flowers. "Let's eat."

"Let's eat?" Annie's voice went up an octave. "You've been mooning around wanting to see Robin and suddenly you don't care?" She followed Lily to the dinning room table, grabbed her chopsticks and plucked a shrimp from her pad thai. As she chewed, she watched Lily pick at her drunken noodles.

"Those flowers are generic; they're not for me. I'll bet she told her assistant to send them, and this is the standard arrangement any woman would get. And the note is typed, not personal. I want her to see *me*, Annie. I thought she got me, but maybe I've been wrong, maybe I really was just another conquest for her."

"So what are you going to do?"

"Nothing." She glanced at the card she was still holding. "Actually, I'm sending them back."

"To the florist?"

She walked to the hall, replaced the card in the flowers, then sat at the table again. "To her office." She googled the address, then called the messenger service she used for deliveries to her agent.

"Are you going to attach a note explaining?"

"Nope. Either she gets me or she doesn't."

Annie frowned. "Maybe you should talk this over with Hillary before you do anything."

Lily narrowed her eyes. "You know therapists listen, they don't talk. Hillary wouldn't give her opinion."

"I don't know, Lily. As you asked, Emma and I haven't discussed you and Robin since you stopped seeing each other, but from the little she said before that and based on what you've said and what I saw Robin was really into you. Maybe she wanted to give you the space to find yourself. Or maybe she needed to find herself. Whatever. She sent a peace offering. You should call her."

"Thanks to therapy, I trust myself again. But I'm not sure I trust Robin. Trust that she really sees Lily, the person, not the body, and that she really cares about the person, not just the sex. I'm in love with her and it's up to her to show me she's ready to commit. I am."

* * *

Jan and Katie watched Robin finger the huge arrangement of flowers standing in the middle of the conference table in her office. "Was there a note?"

Jan shook her head. "The envelope was torn so she obviously read the card, but then it was scotch taped and sent here to you."

Robin sat with her elbows on the table holding her head in her hands. "Shit."

"Based on what you've told us," Katie said, "I would bet she's in love with you too. Don't you think so, Jan?"

"I agree."

"So I think it's just a matter of getting it right." Katie put her hands on Robin's shoulders. "Don't get depressed. Let's analyze this. Is there something about these particular flowers she might hate?"

Robin looked up at the gigantic arrangement and thought about Lily. "Jan, is this the standard bouquet you send when I want to say I'm sorry?"

"Yes. That's what you said you needed."

Robin smiled. "I bet she hated it."

Jan frowned. "But how would she know it was the same arrangement you've sent other women?"

Robin paced around the table, looking at the flowers from all angles. "Well, she's a romance writer for one, so she knows about these things. Also, from the first time we met, she got that I was a player with lots of women. And, third, she would hate something so showy and impersonal."

Jan thought for a minute. "You think she'd like a smaller arrangement?"

"That's good, more personal, right, Katie?"

"I really don't know her. It's worth a try."

Jan nodded. "I'll have it delivered tonight."

* * *

Maybe this was a waste of everybody's time and Robin's money. Lily shook her head as she read the card enclosed with the smaller arrangement of flowers.

Missing you, Robin.

The flowers were beautiful and the sentiment sweet. But the card was typed again, and the flowers were still a generic arrangement, so it didn't feel at all personal. Clearly, Robin didn't get her.

At eight the next morning she called the florist to find out whether Robin had ordered the flowers herself. She hung up, then called the messenger service.

* * *

Later that morning, Katie and Jan followed Robin into her office. When she spotted the flower arrangement on her desk, she turned. "Lily's?"

The two women nodded, then Katie said, "Tell her, Jan."

"The florist said he got a call first thing this morning from Lily. She said she didn't know who sent the flowers, were they by chance from DiLuca Technology? When he said yes, she said 'oh, from Jan, I don't remember her name,' and he said 'yes, Jan Haskell.' He was very apologetic about revealing my name."

Robin rubbed her face. "Now what?"

"We can—"

"No." Katie cut Jan off. "Clearly, this is about you and Lily. The gifts or whatever have to be something you think she'll appreciate, something personal to the two of you, something that shows you understand her. Jan and I have to step back."

"But I don't know—"

"Don't whine, Rob." Katie jumped in again. "You are a very romantic woman and you're really into Lily. I suggest you think about her and come up with something romantic and personal, then *you*, not Jan, make it happen. *Capiche?*" She turned to Jan. "You and I need to stay out of it. Let's go to work."

"Hey, can I at least have one of Jan's assistants bring me coffee and a muffin so I can eat while I ponder this issue?"

Robin sat with her feet up on her desk, sipping her coffee and nibbling her corn muffin. Lily liked simple things. A small bouquet of colorful flowers should do it. She started to pick up the phone, but remembering Katie's instructions she stood and strolled out of the office. "Be back in a little while."

She headed for the fancy florist that DCTI used but changed her mind. Using her phone she looked up florists on the Upper West Side, then took a taxi to a small shop on West Seventy-second Street. The woman who took the order suggested a colorful selection of mixed flowers. Robin paid with her personal American Express and wrote a card.

Would love to see you and talk, Robin.

Whistling, she strolled downtown and hopped on the subway to her office.

* * *

Lily smiled. This was more like it. The lovely bouquet of flowers was from a local Upper West Side florist and the card was in Robin's handwriting. She was getting warm. Should she call her? Too soon. It could be a fluke. She'd call the florist tomorrow just to be sure.

* * *

When the flowers hadn't arrived at her office by noon, Robin called the florist to ask if they'd been delivered. The woman checked. "About six last night," she said, "and the young lady called this morning to say how lovely they were. She said she wasn't sure about the card. She described you and asked if you had come in to order the flowers. I hope you don't mind, I confirmed it."

"No, that's fine. Did she say anything else?"

"Just 'thank you.'"

She kept them. But now what? Something else? Chocolate. Lily loved the chocolate dessert at the River Café. And chocolates from a Belgian chocolates place on Madison Avenue usually were a hit when she sent them. Jan usually took care of it but not this time. She took a taxi uptown and selected an assortment, not the usual humungous one, a human-sized one, and wrote a note.

Sweets for the sweetest Southern girl I know. Would love to talk,
Robin.

She paid to have it delivered and went back to work.

Robin was puzzled to find the candy on her desk the next morning. Why wouldn't she like chocolate? Come to think of it, Lily rarely ate dessert so maybe she watched her weight. Or perhaps sending chocolate was too run-of-the-mill for her, too generic. What did Lily want from her? Was she supposed to jump through hoops just to get her attention? *Damn her. No, don't damn her.* At the River Café she'd surprised Lily with the chocolate Brooklyn Bridge dessert that was their specialty and she'd loved it. She thought about that evening and Lily's delight in the dessert and realized it was the whimsy of it, not that it was chocolate.

Lily was testing her, maybe wanting to see how far she'd go to get back together. Well, she didn't build a multibillion-dollar business by waiting for something to happen. Lily didn't know whom she was dealing with. She'd really think about the next step, try to get it right and not send anything until she'd broken the code. A couple of things she was sure of, Lily was playful, unpretentious and didn't care about her billion dollars.

She taxied over to the River Café, ordered the Brooklyn Bridge dessert, paid for it and delivery and wrote yet another note.

Walking the bridge was romantic, wasn't it? Chew on the Brooklyn Bridge and think about me, about us, Robin.

Jan and Katie watched her do a victory dance the next morning when she walked into her office.

Jan couldn't contain her curiosity. "Why so happy this morning?"

"She kept the Brooklyn Bridge."

Jaws dropped. Jan and Katie exchanged a glance, then spoke simultaneously. "You bought her the Brooklyn Bridge?"

Robin stopped dancing, looked at the two most important women in her life standing there with their mouths open, then doubled over with laughter.

Jan frowned. "What's so funny, wise guy?"

Robin wiped the tears from her eyes. "I sent her the dessert from the River Café that looks like the Brooklyn Bridge."

Katie punched Robin's arm. "Christ, Robin, do you realize that you're so crazy about this woman that we believed you'd bought the bridge for her?" All three of them fell into fits of laughter.

"Okay, get out of my office, I have to figure out what to send next."

At the door, Katie turned. "Other than nonverbally, has she responded to you yet?"

"Just nonverbal. She's making me jump through hoops, but I'm starting to enjoy the game."

Katie smiled. "Ah. Young love." She closed the door and left Robin to her planning.

Robin glanced at her watch, then called Pisticci. She couldn't place a delivery order until they opened for the evening, so she settled in to do some work. At four thirty, she appeared at the restaurant and selected a salad, an appetizer and a pasta dish for delivery: fresh shaved fennel and greens with aged parmigiano and extra virgin oil, Vegetable Ceci-grilled squash medallions capped with *mozzarella di bufala* and a warm chickpea purée, Maltagliati-lamb ragu over flat pasta with fresh spinach and a dollop of creamy ricotta. She asked them to enclose the note she'd written before leaving the office.

Dear Lily,
    Dessert last night and dinner tonight. Ass backward as usual but sent with love. Did I just say love? Enjoy and think of me. Remember how we felt at dinner that night. Before I screwed up. Love again, Robin

She stopped at the liquor store near Lily's apartment and had a bottle of full-bodied, bold red wine delivered with a note.

    Enjoy this bold, full-bodied red. I'll be thinking of a certain bold, full-bodied woman tonight. Love, Robin

* * *

Annie sat at the table. "Thanks for inviting me, Lily, but maybe you should have asked Robin to share the dinner she sent you. She did, after all, say 'love' twice in the note. And 'love' again in the note with the wine." She sipped her wine. "Um, the woman has good taste."

Lily tasted the wine. "She definitely knows how to please in the wine department."

Annie grinned. "I'll bet she knows how to please in a lot of departments."

"Don't leer. It's unbecoming." Lily smirked. "Anyway, I need more proof she gets me. And I'm enjoying the game. I'll know when it's over."

"You remember she's a billionaire, right?"

"Her money doesn't interest me. I don't need someone to take care of me or to wine and dine me. I'm happy she's a success doing what she loves and the fact that she built a multibillion-dollar business that cares about its employees shows what kind of person she is. I love that she's brilliant and kind and playful and giving and fun. I love who she is. Maybe because I have some money of my own, hers isn't important to me."

* * *

Lily's jaw dropped when she opened the door to accept the UPS delivery. "What in the world is that?"

The UPS man muscled the box into the foyer of her apartment, then stepped back. "Sign here." He handed her an electronic thingy to sign. "Got a picture of a boat on the box," he said, as she returned the thingy.

She tipped him and closed the door. *Thingy?* She should know the name of that...thingy. She studied the box. Giggled. A kayak. At least she didn't send two. She looked again. It was a tandem, a kayak for two. No note, unless she managed to get someone at LL Bean to open the box and put one in. Well, it was too large to struggle with now. Maybe in the morning.

She went online to LL Bean's website to check it out. It could be used as a tandem or converted to a solo. She should have expected that Robin would have thought of everything. Later that afternoon two paddles for the kayak were delivered and that evening a small bouquet of white lilies with a single rose in the middle arrived from the local florist. She opened the note.

> *Thoughts of you surround me and I'm flooded with feelings I never expected to feel. All I think about is spending the rest of my life paddling with you. Love, your Rosaria*

She'd called Annie when the kayak arrived and they'd made plans to meet at Fred's for a burger. After they ordered, she handed Annie the note.

"Damn, she's romantic. But what's with the 'Rosaria'?"

"A private joke."

"So are you going to call her? This sounds like a marriage proposal. What more do you want?"

"Just a few more days."

Two days later, she opened the door to a messenger bearing what looked like a book wrapped in paper with hearts on it. She signed and brought it into the apartment, then sat and stared at it. Robin had been doing so well. What if this package proved Robin didn't really get her? She thought about calling for reinforcements, but Annie was teaching an all-day seminar; she was on her own.

After circling it most of the day, she poured a glass of wine, sat on the sofa and, holding her breath, tore the wrapping paper. The cover was a picture of them, one of the selfies Robin had taken on the roller coaster. Big smiles, really happy to be together. She let out the breath and relaxed. The first picture in the album was blurry but clearly her, looking at someone or something behind her. She recognized the dress as the one she'd worn the night they first saw each other. Underneath in Robin's neat handwriting it said:

I saw you across a crowded room and I knew we were meant for each other.

Next was the picture the paparazzi photographer had snapped at the River Café, which showed her hand on Robin's face, their eyes locked.

Look at us. Our second date and already in love?

She was right. How had it happened so fast? She paged through the photos Robin had taken, creating her history and chronicling their relationship. On many of them Robin had commented about how happy and how into each other they looked. At the end, after the last picture, Robin had written:

Dear Lily,
These pictures were taken to help me build a history for myself. Now, more than anything in the world, I want to build a future with you. And our children. Please talk to me, my sweet Southern girl.
Love, Robin

Robin loved her; that meant all of her. First she cried, then she called Hillary to schedule a special session the next day. She wanted to be sure she was ready to deal with Robin, ready to trust her totally, ready to risk showing her love—and her body.

The next afternoon the florist delivered one white lily and one red rose in a lovely cut-glass vase. A small box wrapped in what looked like Tiffany paper was attached. Lily's heart fell. *Tiffany? So she doesn't really get me at all.* She slowly unwrapped it and smiled when she saw Bette Midler's CD, *It's the Girls*, and the least expensive iPod, a purple Shuffle, with "No one but you" engraved on it and "Be My Baby" loaded. She played the song over and over. Then, grinning, she went down to the Apple Store on Broadway and Sixty-seventh Street, purchased a silver iPod Shuffle and had it engraved. She took it home and loaded two songs on it, wrapped the fountain pen she'd spotted in an antique store and bought for Robin weeks ago when she wasn't even sure she'd ever see her again, then went out again, this time to the florist on West Seventy-second Street.

* * *

Katie and Jan pounced on Robin as soon as she walked into the office the next morning. "You had a delivery this morning."

Her good mood vanished. "Damn, I was sure she'd love what I sent. I think I should give up." She slouched into her chair behind the desk and stared at the red lily and white rose in a pretty silver vase and the small packages next to it.

"What is it?" As usual, Jan couldn't contain her curiosity.

Robin stared at the flowers. "Wait a second. I sent a white lily and a red rose with one package containing the Bette Midler CD and an iPod. This is a red lily and a white rose with two small packages." She tore the wrapping paper from the long, round package and held the beautiful antique pen up to the light.

Katie reached for it. "That's gorgeous. Damn, I wish I'd found it for you."

Robin grinned, then opened the small package. A silver iPod. She read the engraving and tears streamed down her face.

"What is it, Rob?" Katie ran to her.

She swiped at the tears and handed the iPod to her. Katie read the inscription aloud.

No one but you.

She laughed. "You did it, Rob. You got the girl. Oh, wait, there are two songs loaded on the iPod." She passed it back to Robin.

Robin selected the first song—"Be My Baby"—and then the second. "Will You Still Love Me Tomorrow?"

"Oh, God. I can't believe this. I think I'm getting married."

Katie and Jan pulled her into a three-way hug.

Katie kissed her cheek. "Don't you think we should meet her so we can approve?"

"I'll let you know when. But I'm going to download a song and then I'm going to her apartment." She turned on her computer and downloaded the song to her new iPod.

The doorman at Lily's building was reluctant to play, but Robin promised him a hundred dollars if Lily was mad, so he buzzed her apartment to say she had a telegram. Who can resist a telegram? Robin went up.

She rang the bell and the door opened immediately. Lily seemed puzzled to see Robin standing there.

"Telegram." Robin played the song she'd loaded to her IPod, "Get Me to the Church on Time." A smile lit Lily's face and she pulled her into the apartment. They kissed for a long time. Then Robin got down on one knee. "Lily Boudreaux Carlyle Alexander, will you marry me?"

"Oh, God, yes. Yes. But you've got to meet my mamas first."

"And you've got to meet my…family, Katie and Jan. Can we take a walk and talk now, or do you need to keep writing?"

As they strolled past the doorman, hand in hand, Robin slipped him the hundred dollars anyway. Without discussing it, they crossed the street and walked into Central Park. They strolled around Strawberry Fields, then wandered aimlessly along the paths before sitting by the lake, the excitement and connection between them palpable.

Robin shifted on the bench to face Lily. "I want you to know you can tease as much as you like. I'll wait forever for you to be ready as long as we can be together."

"I'm ready." She took Robin's hands in hers and kissed one palm, then the other. "I needed to know you wanted me, not just a quick romp in the hay, fun as that would have been. Now we don't have to be quick."

Robin kissed Lily's nose. "There you go again, teasing. But you know what, I love it, I love you and I'm ready whenever you are. Should we call your mamas?"

"I'd rather tell them in person. Are you willing to fly to California?"

"I already know Dr. Alexander."

"But not as her future daughter-in-law. Besides, Del is in charge of the emotional stuff so she needs to approve. When are you available? I'd like to go as soon as possible."

"Can you coordinate with Jan? She has my schedule and can make arrangements for us. But factor in a couple of days so I can get you a ring before we go."

"I don't want an engagement ring, just a wedding band. What about you?"

"The same." She pulled Lily up. "Let's walk. I'm too excited to sit."

Holding hands and stopping to kiss frequently, they randomly followed paths, enjoying the warmth of the late afternoon sun, the smell of new-mown grass, and the songs of the musicians they encountered. They sang along with the guitarist singing "You Are Always on My Mind." Much later they stopped to listen to a small combo playing and singing "I Will Always Love You" and walked away singing. In both instances, Robin dropped twenties into the open guitar cases. "Gotta support working artists."

"That's nice of you, sweet Robin." Lily touched Robin's face. "I missed you so much. I was petrified I would lose you if I didn't deal with what Micki did and with my own stupidity."

"Hey, I'm here."

"Right. But it took seeing Hillary, my therapist, three times a week to understand what was going on and then change my thinking."

"At least you got help so you could get what you wanted." Robin pulled her closer. "I was miserable and moped around. I did a lot of walking and thinking about my life, trying to figure out why I was so unhappy and why I walked away from you, but I withdrew from everyone." She laughed. "At least I tried. Jan can't stand it when I'm unhappy, so she kept trying to get it out of me. Then, when I got too sulky and irritable, Katie took me out to dinner and helped me figure out I was in love with you and wanted to be with you forever. That was when I told Jan to send the first flower arrangement."

Lily buried her face in Robin's neck. "Don't think I didn't appreciate them, but I needed to know that you see who I am and how I see the world."

"I see you." Robin kissed the top of Lily's head. "It took a little while, but I got it. I guess I did all right."

"You did."

"Are you hungry? The Boathouse restaurant is in the park. Shall we have dinner?"

"Sure, it's a beautiful evening, the food is good and I always enjoy eating by the water."

Later, as they walked to Lily's apartment, they were quiet, enjoying the connection and the night. Lily was trying to figure out what to do. She was beyond ready to make love with Robin. She could invite her in tonight, but she wanted their first time to be special.

Robin tightened her arm around Lily. "Let's go away tomorrow for a couple of days. It's the beach, so casual dress and bathing suits. We can sleep in separate bedrooms if you want."

"I want to be alone with you."

"Tanya will drop us off, but then we'll be alone. Pick you up at noon."

CHAPTER TWENTY-TWO

Fire Island

The one-and-a-half-hour drive was pleasant. Tanya was in the front seat, but this time the glass separating the driver and passengers was raised, and it was opaque, not clear like in taxis.

"Is the glass so you can make out back here in privacy?" Lily was half teasing, half curious.

Robin flushed. "I sometimes use the car with clients."

"Uh-huh. And the other times?"

"Dates, friends." She looked at Lily. "I won't say it hasn't happened." Her eyes traveled from Lily's face to her breasts and over the rest of her body, then she smiled. A wolfish smile. "Want to try it out?"

Lily certainly didn't want their first time to be in the backseat of a car like two horny teenagers, not even the back seat of a luxury car. She smiled. They *were* two horny adults.

"What are you smiling about?"

"Making out sounds nice, but I'm more interested in finding a way for you to hold me but still keep our seatbelts on. Can we do that?"

"Lean forward." Robin moved her legs to the middle, then swung her right leg up and over Lily. Now between Robin's legs,

Lily scooted back into her arms, then snapped on the middle seatbelt. Robin wrapped her arms around Lily, pulled her closer, then kissed her neck. "Comfy?"

"Um. So where are we going?" Not that she really cared. She could stay like this forever, basking in the heat of Robin, the caress of her sweet breath on her neck, and feeling the thrum of her heartbeat.

"Fire Island. The Pines. Ever been there?"

"No. It's a gay town on the beach, right? Are there tons of paparazzi?"

"Not usually. But, in any case, I thought we'd avoid the social scene. The house will be stocked, so we can eat in and enjoy the beach and each other."

"That sounds wonderful."

Robin tightened her hold on Lily and rested her chin on Lily's head. "My thoughts exactly."

They were quiet, enjoying the sound of classical music drifting from the front of the car and the physical connection. Then Lily broke the silence. "Do you own this house or rent it?"

"Own it. Katie and I bought it together after the sales of our first software package took off. We both love the beach. In fact, Katie met Michael out here."

"I thought it was all gay?"

"It's a lot gay, but Michael's family has a house in a nearby town. He and a group of friends came to dance at the gay bar and Katie was with our group. Somehow they found each other in the sea of lesbians and gay men."

"It sounds like she's pretty relaxed around lesbians."

"She's strong and independent and focused on friends and work, not on capturing a man to take care of her, so she fits in better with lesbians than she does with a lot of straight women her age. Most of her friends are lesbians. That was true in college and grad school as well."

"How does Michael deal with that?"

"He's a pretty open guy and he likes and respects Katie for who she is. As I understand it, Katie is a lot like his mother, so he knows what he's getting. They're great together. When he gets back from Europe, the four of us will have dinner."

"I'd like that. Tell me about Jan."

"What about her?"

"Well, I take it she's not one of your Harvard or Stanford friends, but it's obvious she's important to you. When and how did she come into the picture?"

"When we first came to New York City, Katie and I rented an apartment on Twelfth Street and Avenue A in the East Village. We lived and worked there. I had already developed an early version of our first software product while we were at Stanford, and Katie was trying to sell it and get us some venture capital while I added features." She nuzzled Lily's neck. "Are you sure you're interested?"

"Everything about your life interests me, sweet Robin." She twisted and kissed her. "Go on."

"Anyway, this kid with black and purple hair, black lipstick, weird black eye makeup and tattoos panhandled on the corner near our apartment. Usually I'd give her some money, or I'd take her in the deli and buy her a sandwich. But this one day in October it was freezing and she was shivering so badly she couldn't even ask for money. So I took her to lunch with me. Genius that I am, I had figured out she was a runaway, but she deflected any questions about her age or where she was from or anything personal. It took me a while but then I realized she was afraid I would try to send her home. So I told her my story and assured her I understood about wanting to get away from your family. After another few cups of coffee she trusted me enough to confide that she was sixteen, had run away from an abusive father six months before, lived on the street and didn't have any warm clothes. Obviously, I couldn't let her go back on the street and freeze, so I bought her a warm coat, gloves, a hat and boots and took her home with me. By that time Katie was there, and we agreed she could sleep in our living room in exchange for some work." She smiled at the memory. "And Jan being Jan, she didn't just jump at the chance, she bargained and got us to pay her something as well."

"Gutsy, huh?"

"That she was and is. Anyway, it didn't take long for us to figure out that she was really smart and ambitious. She spent hours learning the system on her own, and when we sold it to a couple of small banks, we cleaned her up and she helped us train the users. After that, we insisted she get a high school degree and we paid for her to go to college. As the company grew, we wanted her to help run it, but she decided she'd rather be the assistant to the two of us so she could run everything. She's an integral part of the company and our lives. She's also a multimillionaire by the way."

"Is she a lesbian?"

Robin laughed. "Depends on the day."

The car stopped. Tanya tapped on the window, then lowered it. "We're at the ferry."

"That was fast." Lily unbuckled her seat belt and sat up. Robin did the same.

Tanya opened the door for Lily and helped her out. Robin got out on her side. Tanya retrieved their bags from the trunk, then addressed Robin. "Call when you're ready to be picked up."

"You bet. Thanks."

Tanya smiled at them "Have a good time." She got into the car, then drove away. They walked to the window and bought tickets for the next ferry.

It was a bright sunny July day with nary a cloud in the sky, so Robin headed to the shaded area of the ferry. Lily beamed. "This is so beautiful. I didn't realize we had to take a boat to get there. Is this the Atlantic?"

"No, the Great South Bay, but the house is on the Atlantic side of the island."

The ferry took about forty minutes, and the walk to the ocean side of the island was just a few minutes. Lily's breath caught. The house was right on the beach. The Atlantic Ocean, which she'd never seen before, was right there, waves crashing wildly. A beautiful sight. She turned and kissed Robin. "This is fabulous."

"We think so. Let's go in."

The house was large, with two bedrooms and two baths, an open kitchen and dining room and a spacious living room with a fireplace on the ground floor and three bedrooms and three baths upstairs. The decor was appropriate for the beach, casual but comfortable and tasteful. Outside, a deck wrapped around three sides.

"Come on. Our rooms are upstairs. I'll show you to yours so you can wash up and change, and then we'll have lunch on the deck."

Upstairs Robin ushered her into a bedroom and placed her bag on the bed. "I think you'll be comfortable here." She picked up her own bag. "Come downstairs whenever you're ready." She closed the door gently.

Hands on her hips, Lily stared after Robin. *So separate bedrooms as promised but not for long if things go as I expect.* She stretched. She could be comfortable here. The bedroom was lovely, filled with light and a breeze from the ocean visible through the sheer white curtains billowing on the wall of windows and the French doors to the deck. It was decorated in shades of blue, had a queen-sized bed with a night table and lamp on each side, a chaise with a lamp and table next to it and a small desk. As Lily washed up in her private bathroom, then changed into shorts and a T-shirt, her body tingled with thoughts of making love later.

Lily opened the sliding door, stepped onto the deck and gazed at the ocean, mesmerized by the sound and the smell and the sight of the waves battering the shore. It seemed much more violent than the Pacific. Alerted by the sound of another sliding door opening, she wasn't surprised to feel Robin's arms circle her waist from behind. Robin's chin rested on her shoulder. "Gorgeous, isn't it?"

"It is." Robin swiveled to face her, then kissed her, slowly and deeply. Lust surged through Lily as her senses filled with Robin, the scent of her light cologne and sweat, the taste of the sea on her lips, the silkiness of her hair and the sweetness and warmth of her breath. Robin pulled back. In the sunlight, her black hair gleamed like a raven's feathers, her sparkling green eyes surpassed the beauty of the sparkling sea and her smile was sexy and inviting. Lily's heart filled with love. Why wait?

"Let's eat."

Lily blinked. She wasn't thinking about eating but once Robin mentioned it, she realized she was hungry. So, fingers entwined with Robin's, she followed her downstairs to the table set on the deck off the kitchen.

Lily's attention shifted to the table. One hunger at a time. They had as much time as they wanted today.

The food was glorious: avocado stuffed with shrimp salad, quinoa salad, beet salad with peaches, a mixed green salad, cantaloupe and cherries and honeydew, prosciutto and provolone cheese and rolls. They helped themselves. Robin offered beer or wine or lemonade and Lily chose lemonade.

"This food is delicious. Where did it come from?"

"I ordered it from a restaurant in Sayville, where we got the ferry, and it was sent this morning. The woman we pay to take care of the house met the early ferry and put everything in the fridge."

Robin moved her chair so they were sitting next to each other, facing the ocean. She took Lily's hand and held it to her heart. Lily kissed Robin's temple, then raised their clasped hands in the air. "As much as I love this, sweetie, I can't eat with my left hand."

Robin kissed the hand she was holding and then placed it in Lily's lap. "Sorry." They ate and chatted and when they finished, they cleaned up together, stopping often for kisses and touches. "Shall we walk on the beach? Since this is a weekday it shouldn't be too crowded."

"I'd love it. Let me get my things." Lily ran up the stairs and returned with her hat and sunglasses. "I'm ready."

They left their sandals on the deck and stepped into the hot sand, then dashed to the water's edge to keep their feet from burning. Holding hands, they walked in the wet sand, occasionally dashing away from the aftermath of a strong wave.

After a half hour, they turned back toward the house. Robin pulled Lily into an embrace. She lifted Lily's sunglasses and looked into her eyes. "Have you given the wedding any thought?"

She kissed Robin's palm. "Are you absolutely sure?"

Robin kissed her nose. "I'm nervous, but I'm positive. What about you?"

"Scared but sure. I want it to be small, just my family and a couple of friends on my side. What about you?"

"Katie and Jan, Emma and our other roommates plus some other friends from Harvard and Stanford, but I guess I pictured something big and wonderful that would include clients."

She felt Lily tense. "I understand your reluctance, Lily, but I would never hurt you like that. Never. It took me a while to get it, but I want to be with you forever." Lily started walking and Robin followed. "Can we compromise? A very small ceremony and dinner with just our nearest and dearest, then after a wonderful, sex-filled…" Robin wiggled her eyebrows "…honeymoon, we have a huge reception, call it a party, to celebrate. What do you think?"

Lily put her arm around Robin's waist. "I still think this wiggling of eyebrows needs to stop. I also think a separate reception after the fact is a great idea."

"Really?" Robin ran circles around Lily and started singing. "We're getting married in the…" she skidded to a stop, "when?"

"Soon, but let's wait until we see my mamas to decide, just to be sure they can be here. Is that okay?"

"Yes. Is your family religious? Who will marry us? City Hall doesn't sound too romantic to me. And I want it to be special. A classmate of mine clerked for Justice Ruth Bader Ginsburg. Maybe we could get her to officiate."

"Justice Ginsburg is a media draw and her presence could turn the wedding into a circus." She was silent for a few seconds. "Unless she's willing to keep it low key, not let anyone know until we're on our honeymoon. We could talk to Cordy about it."

"Dr. Alexander knows her?"

"Between them, my mamas know everybody. When we get back to the city, I'll call them to find out when they're available for us to see them in California."

"Great." Robin kissed her. They started walking again. "Hey, want to join me for a swim when we get back to the house?"

"As long as there's no dunking."

"If kissing is allowed, there'll be no dunking. Let's change." Robin grabbed her hand and they raced to the house. "First one on the deck in a bathing suit wins."

"Wins what?"

"If I'm first, you have to kiss me, and if you're first, I have to kiss you."

"Sounds fair."

As she changed, Lily worried anew about Robin's reaction to her body. The women she usually went with were models and actresses whose livelihood depended on them being thin. And she was far from thin, with her full breasts and not-flat stomach and hips. Maybe she should say she changed her mind. She pulled the tank top on again and headed for the door. With her hand on the doorknob, she hesitated, thinking about all the work she'd done with her therapist on this subject. *Might as well know now.* If Robin was repulsed by her body, they should find out before they made too many plans and involved too many people. She shivered at the thought of another public rejection.

She pulled her tank over her head, slipped her shorts off, then vacillated between the bikini and the full suit. She bit her lip. She stared at herself in the mirror. Intellectually she got that she wasn't fat, and if she looked objectively she could see that her body was like Del's, lush and sexy. But it was a struggle to keep from reverting to her old self-image as she had just done. *The bikini it is.* She threw a big shirt over the skimpy black suit and went out to the deck where long-legged, small-breasted, slender Robin was waiting in her bikini to collect her kiss.

Robin immediately sensed the change in her mood. "What's wrong?"

Lily snuggled into Robin, enjoying the feel of her hands moving over her body. She heard her therapist's voice encouraging her to be honest, encouraging her to remember she either loves you or she doesn't, but it doesn't negate who you are. *Robin loves me.* She took a deep breath. "I'm afraid you'll be repulsed by my body."

Robin kissed her tenderly. "Are you kidding? It was your body swaying to the music that first captivated me at Shazarak. I thought you were the sexiest woman I'd ever seen and I couldn't keep my eyes away from you. Then, when our eyes met, all I could think of was you, making love to you. I love your body, I love you."

"But you prefer thin women?"

"They were mostly decoration and they pursued me. None of them ever aroused me the way you do."

"But you made love with them."

"No, Lily. I had sex with a few of them, not that many." She flushed. "And mostly it was about them, about me servicing them, not a mutual thing at all." She caressed Lily's face. "You are the most beautiful, sexy, sensual woman I have ever known, and I think all the time about kissing every inch of your gorgeous body." She kissed Lily again. "I'm really looking forward to making love to you." She cleared her throat. "You're the only woman whose body I've ever fantasized about."

"I love you, Robin."

"I love you." She unbuttoned Lily's shirt and threw it on a nearby chair. "All of you." She kissed the swell of Lily's breasts peeking over the skimpy bikini bra. "I adore your breasts." She got on her knees and kissed the small bulge of her belly. "And your sweet belly, and this hip, and this hip, and this thigh, and this thigh, and this calf and this calf." She turned her around. "And last but not least, these butt cheeks. I don't want to hear you say anything negative about your body ever again."

Lily pulled her to her feet. "Thank you." She dashed off the deck. "Last one in the water is a loser."

CHAPTER TWENTY-THREE

Love in the Pines

The ocean was colder than she expected, but Lily warmed quickly as they rode the waves, splashed and played, then swam, then splashed and played and kissed and touched and rubbed. Finally, exhausted by the sun and water and all the activity, they showered and sat on the deck, Lily with a glass of sauvignon blanc and Robin with her usual seltzer and lime.

"Do you have a drinking problem, Robin? Is that why you avoid alcohol?"

Robin shifted her gaze to the breaking waves in front of them and didn't respond. Lily felt bad for asking.

"No. I don't have a problem. But I'm afraid I could. My father was, and if he's alive, probably still is, a drunk. I remember almost nothing of my childhood, but I have a shadowy memory of a crazy woman who smelled of booze, so I think my mom might have also been a drinker."

"Why don't you remember? Did something traumatic happen?" Lily flashed to her own childhood with her loving mamas, her Boudreaux and Carlyle grandparents, aunts, uncles and cousins. She had so many happy memories. Still, she *had* forgotten the incident with Belinda's mother. But forgetting your entire childhood seemed weird. Was it because both her parents were alcoholic and the memories were unpleasant? Or was Robin damaged in some way? And, if she was, what, if anything, did it have to do with their future?

Robin shrugged. "I don't think so but if I knew the answer to that, I would probably remember."

"Did you ever talk to your brothers about it?"

She shrugged again. "Both my brothers are older and were out of the house before I left Florida, so I never had the chance." Robin swallowed and turned her gaze to the pounding ocean. She rubbed the back of her hands over her eyes.

"Oh, sweetie, I'm sorry. I didn't mean to upset you." Lily got out of her chair and cradled Robin's head to her chest.

"It's all right. It's just, sometimes I wonder why he hated me so much that he never even called to see if I'd made it to Boston."

"Alcohol does strange things to people, love."

"That's why you needed to know about it. If we're going to have children, maybe we should skip my egg and just do two of yours."

Lily held her at arms length. "No way. I can't think of anything more wonderful than having a little Robin running around. As a matter of fact, you'll go first."

"Do you want to have the children right away?"

"I think we should have some time by ourselves to travel, have fun and be free to do anything we want before we have a baby. What do you think?"

Robin smiled. "Have I told you I love you?"

"Not often enough. And I might ask you to prove it later."

Robin stood. "Whoa. You mean—"

Lily's smile was mischievous. "How about I see what's available to make us dinner?"

Robin grabbed her and kissed her deeply. "You're a tease, you know that?"

"So you've said. What do we have for dinner?"

"I'll barbecue some steaks and veggies, you make a salad. Deal?"

* * *

After they ate and cleaned up, Robin sprawled in a chaise on the deck and pulled Lily down on top of her. They talked and kissed. Gentle kisses deepened to passion, tentative exploration of bodies became more insistent, breaths came in gasps, hearts pounded. Lily broke away. "Time for bed, sweet Robin." Her voice was rough and deeper than usual.

Robin groaned and held her tight for a moment, then followed.

CHAPTER TWENTY-FOUR

Ah, Sweet Love

They went to their separate bedrooms. After brushing her teeth and changing into pajama pants and a T-shirt, Robin went to Lily's room to say goodnight. Lily was propped up on pillows with a book in her hand. She put the book down and opened her arms. Robin crawled onto the bed and Lily pulled her close.

Robin snuggled. "Does this mean…?"

Lily ran her fingers through Robin's hair. "It means I love being close to you. It means I like talking and getting to know you better. It means…let's see what happens."

Accompanied by the clap of the breaking waves, the fishy ocean smell and a gentle breeze, they talked late into the night. There was still so much they didn't know about each other and stripping away the layers brought them closer. They fell asleep holding each other.

A too-close flash of lightning followed by the crash of thunder directly overhead woke Lily with a start. Robin pulled her closer as if to protect her from the elements. It was pitch black outside and in. Lily rolled on top of Robin and kissed her softly, and even with the constant rumble above them, the waves crashing and the wind and rain whipping against the house, she heard Robin's soft gasp of pleasure. Lightening illuminated Robin's face. With each strike, the glittering emerald eyes, the soft smile and the look of pure love flashed as if they were under a disco ball.

Feeling Robin's body under her, the friction of their breasts rubbing, the tautness of their nipples and their mutual heat, Lily knew exactly what she wanted to do. As the storm raged around them, she touched Robin's face, tracing her features in the flickering light. Robin raised her head and met her lips. The sweet kisses turned passionate and the storm inside matched the one outside as desire replaced Lily's fear and uncertainty. When Robin's hand moved to her breast, she broke the connection. "Be still, I'm going to make love to you."

Robin tried to sit up and roll on top of her. "I'd rather—"

Lily pushed her back. There was another boom and the whites of Robin's eyes flashed in the darkness. Her breathing was rapid and she seemed to be having trouble getting enough air. Lily waited for the next flash and stared into her eyes. "I didn't like hearing that you mostly serviced the women you had sex with. I know you're used to being in control, sweetie, but we won't work if you're the only one giving. If it gets too intense, raise your hand and I'll stop."

Robin's hand shot up.

She laughed. "No stopping before we start. Trust me, my sweet Robin, please trust me."

* * *

She stared at Lily. She did trust her. But it was true she was usually the one in charge, the one giving. She'd rarely let anyone make love to her except a few times in grad school and even then she'd faked orgasms. She'd never been able to tolerate being touched so intimately, and she didn't know if she could now, even by Lily.

How could Lily know? None of the women had ever questioned Robin when she said she didn't need anything, that making love to her was enough. But Lily saw her. Really saw her. Saw through her. She'd been focused on her need to touch Lily, to make love to her, and she hadn't considered Lily's needs. She should have known Lily wouldn't go for one-sided lovemaking. But she knew now that if she denied her, any chance of a relationship would evaporate. She could do this. Couldn't she?

Lily straddled her. "It'll be more fun if y'all try not to think of it as torture." She went back to kissing.

This she could handle. Robin relaxed as their tongues met again, fanning the fire that was never far off when Lily was near. She gasped when Lily's hand brushed her breast, caught between the desire for more and the need to throw Lily aside and run to the beach.

Lily pulled away. She ran her hand gently over Robin's face, then placed it on a hardened nipple that obviously had no qualms about being touched. "Easy, sweet Robin, I'm going to get us both naked, then I'm going to kiss you and touch you. Stay with me. Okay?"

Robin nodded. She was determined to try. Lily pulled Robin's T-shirt over her head, then tugged Robin's pajama bottoms down. Her fingers grazed Robin's pubic hair and the insides of her thighs. Robin shivered and kicked the pajamas off her ankles.

Lily knelt on the bed and pulled her own tank top off. Holding her breath, Robin extended her hands and cupped her breasts. Lily pushed her hands away. "Down, girl." She rose and slipped her pajama bottoms off. Robin's eyes widened as a lightning flash washed over Lily. She reached for the lamp. Her eyes raked the voluptuous body from the full breasts to the slightly rounded belly and the curly blond hair, the lovely hips and the long slender legs. How could Lily think she would be repulsed?

Lily's grin was mischievous. "Maybe if you think about making love to me, you'll get into it."

She could do that. She'd been doing nothing but thinking about making love to her since the first time she saw her in the bar. As Lily straddled her, Robin's hands meandered over the curves of her body, touching the glorious softness of her breasts, her belly, her hips, her thighs. She sighed.

Lily smiled and stretched out on top of Robin, her skin hot even in the refreshing ocean breeze and the cool rain blowing in. Once again, she returned to kissing but now her hands were busy touching, exploring, running featherlike over Robin's body, replacing thoughts and anxiety with a pleasurable lightness. She seemed to intuit the exact moment for her lips and tongue to burn their own path from head to toes, then toes to head. Stopping to kiss behind Robin's knees and her inner thighs, Lily then buried her face in the crinkly black hair. When Robin tensed, she continued on to her breasts. Robin moaned when Lily took a breast in her mouth and instinctively pushed her breasts forward at the same time as her hand gripped Lily's shoulder to push her away. Lily took advantage of the distraction to slip between Robin's legs and slide two fingers inside. Robin gasped, her hips pushed up and the hand pushing Lily away relaxed as her body responded to Lily's rapidly increasing stroking and thrusting. Lily panted. "That's my sweet Robin."

Robin locked on to her eyes. "Lily." She pushed against Lily's hand, her breathing quickening, the pressure mounting. Then she exploded. And burst into tears. Lily held her tightly as she came down, kissing her eyes and forehead, stroking her hair, caressing her neck and rubbing her back while she sobbed.

Neither spoke for a long while, then Robin raised herself on one elbow to stare down at Lily. "Sorry. I've never been emotional during sex before."

She reached up and brushed Robin's hair back. "No apology necessary, sweetie. Maybe it's because we're not having sex, we're making love. Being emotional is good where love-making is concerned. I'm glad we were able to touch an untouched place."

"You made me feel…" Her voice broke. "I've never had an orgasm with anyone before."

"My sweet Robin." Lily brushed the tears from Robin's cheeks with her fingers. "I've loved you since the first night we saw each other. And I love you even more now for making yourself vulnerable, for trusting me and opening your body and your heart." They dozed.

* * *

When Lily opened her eyes again Robin was watching her with a sweet smile, holding Lily's hand to her heart. Seeing she was awake, she brought Lily's hand to her lips, kissed her palm and took a finger into her mouth. The storm outside had subsided and the sky was aglow with shards of pink and orange, the breeze was gentle and fresh and the sound of the waves muted. But the storm inside Lily was mounting quickly. Who knew a finger could be so sensitive.

Lily moved to meet Robin's lips. As their kisses deepened, her desire flamed. She needed those lips everywhere. Now. Breathless, she pulled away and whispered into the air between them. "My breasts."

Robin pulled her head back to stare into Lily's eyes. She grinned. "Yes, ma'am."

As instructed, Robin started with her breasts, then slowly made her way down, seeming to savor all the places Lily thought she would hate, until Lily squirmed and moaned with pleasure at the kisses—the licks and touches as delicate as the flutter of the wings of a butterfly.

Long before Robin buried her head between Lily's thighs, she was wet and welcoming. Using her teeth and tongue and fingers, Robin teased Lily's already flaming passion higher and higher until she screamed Robin's name, tensed and arched. Robin held her tight, kissing her, murmuring her love.

When her heart and pulse slowed to normal, Lily smiled sweetly. "Y'all are a great lover, Robin, but then it was me I doubted, not you." In bed Robin was just the right balance of tender and generous and masterful, totally attentive to Lily's body and focused on pleasuring her. She ran a hand over Robin's body, thanking the universe for the awful things that had paved the way for her to meet Robin— the unfortunate relationship with Micki that brought her to New York City and the unfortunate dinner date with Glory that brought her to Shazarak where she and Robin had, it seemed, fallen in love. Feeling Robin's nipples harden in reaction to her touch, Lily took it as an invitation to make love to her again.

* * *

They spent that day and night in bed, dozing, eating and making love. The next morning they went for a walk on the beach, then had breakfast on the deck.

"So, my sweets, how old were you when you had sex for the first time?"

"Sixteen. My senior year at Harvard. Until then, Katie kept me on a really tight leash. Other than time in class, we were together studying in the library or in our suite and when we did go out to lectures and concerts, movies and dinner, it was just us and our suitemates."

"She took her responsibility seriously."

"She did. In fact, when I turned sixteen my suitemates had a birthday party for me and I learned she had threatened Emma and Nicole, our two lesbian roommates, with beheading if they so much as kissed me. And she got them all to pledge to keep an eye on me. But after the party she said I was mature enough to start dating and she loosened up. Though roommates were still off-limits, they coached me on how to date and what to do sexually." She grinned. "I managed to find plenty of willing participants. What about you?"

"I kissed and fooled around a little in high school, but freshman year at college I met someone and we were a couple for a little while."

"Do you believe in happily ever after?"

"I do. I believe my mamas have found it. I hope we will. Do you have doubts?"

Robin looked out at the ocean. "I'd like to believe in it. I don't know about my life before Harvard, but my life since then has been magical. And now there's you." She reached over and traced Lily's jawline. "I think a part of me was afraid of committing because giving yourself to someone means they can hurt you by leaving." She tried a smile that didn't quite convince. "And deep inside I feel like there's a little dark cloud floating around out there just waiting to cast a shadow on me."

Lily caught Robin's hand on her jaw and held it to her cheek. "I think everyone is afraid, at least a little bit, that something bad will happen and ruin their happy ever after. We don't know what the future holds so let's enjoy our happy ever after while we have it." She leaned in and kissed Robin.

Robin pulled her close, then tickled her. "Well, I sure am enjoying my happy ever after right now. I'm sorry to say we have clients coming in from Wisconsin to look at the software tomorrow afternoon, and I have to be there to make the presentation."

"That's fine. The deadline on my mystery is coming up fast."

"I think Michael is still in Europe doing a big deal for his company, but will you have time to have dinner with Katie and Jan?"

"Only if you promise to come home with me after."

"Well…if I have to."

"So do y'all want to go to bed and explore our happy ever after while we still have time?"

"Umm."

CHAPTER TWENTY-FIVE

Celebration

As they walked into the dining room of Shazarak, Robin reassured Lily for the tenth time at least that Katie and Jan would love her, yet she still felt apprehensive. After all, Katie was the most important person in Robin's life. What if Katie hated her or she hated Katie? What then? Somehow the thought of Jan wasn't as scary as the woman who'd nurtured Robin from a skinny, needy, nerdy fourteen-year-old to the wonderful woman she was in love with.

Robin steered her to a table where two women stood with huge smiles. "Relax, they don't bite, besides you're cutting off the blood supply to my hand."

"Oh, sorry."

Then they were there. The shorter one, with wavy, streaked light-brown hair cascading down her back and sparkling blue eyes, a generous mouth and a huge grin, pulled Lily into a crushing hug. "I'm Katie. I've heard so much about you and I am so happy to finally meet you."

"I'm happy to meet you too," Lily whispered. "But I fear y'all hate me for making Robin pursue me."

Katie laughed and whispered back. "Not at all. If you hadn't made the little beastie confront her feelings, she would have bedded you and moved on without letting herself know she was in love."

"Hey, what's all that whispering? Are you ganging up on me already?"

The full-figured, dark-haired, dark-eyed woman sporting tattoos on her arms and a ring through one eyebrow moved in and touched Katie's shoulder. "Yeah, break it up so I can say hello too."

Katie stepped back.

"You must be Jan." Lily hugged her. "I hope y'all didn't mind that I sent your flowers back?"

"Nah. Robin's a little tone deaf, but your message came through loud and clear. Welcome to our little family." She kissed Lily's cheek.

Robin threw an arm over Lily's shoulder. "Don't believe a word they say about me."

Lily smiled and hugged her. "What makes y'all think we're talking about you?" This was how family should be— loving, happy, teasing. Robin's women would fit right in with her own family.

"Do I hear the South in your voice, Lily?" Katie asked.

Robin fidgeted, clearly worried they wouldn't like each other. Katie touched Robin's face and locked eyes with her. The affection in that touch and in her eyes moved Lily and seemed to calm Robin.

"Yes, you do. I lived in Alabama until we moved to California when I was sixteen. She flushed. "My accent is most pronounced when I'm emotional—nervous or happy or angry, it doesn't matter. I know how important you and Jan are to Robin, so I've been nervous about meeting you, afraid maybe we won't like each other."

Katie took her hands and looked her in the eye. "I can't imagine that Robin would be in love with someone I wouldn't like. Now, whether you like me is another story." She kissed Lily's cheek. "I hope we'll be great friends."

Lily felt Robin tense and, following her gaze, saw Annie and Emma walking toward the table, holding hands.

"I know it was presumptuous to assume I know what you want and I should have asked first, but I invited Annie and Emma to join our celebration."

Lily caressed Robin's face. "That was a loving thing to do, sweetie."

"I wanted my other suitemate, Nicole, and her lover, Nora, to meet you, but they're both doctors so they'll come later. Is that okay?"

Lily leaned in to kiss Robin without thinking about it. When they came up for air, the other four were watching them with huge smiles on their faces. Lily blushed. "Sorry, y'all, it's impossible to resist her."

Annie wrapped her arms around the two of them. "Congratulations. I'm thrilled for you both." Emma wormed her way into the huddle. "Congratulations. Lily, you're the best thing that's happened to Robin since she met Katie and me at Harvard. Take care of her."

"I intend to, Emma. Thanks."

Robin flushed. "Let's sit before Emma goes off on one of her rants. Besides, I was too busy to eat lunch and I'm starving."

"Oh, oh, this must really be love if you forgot to eat." Emma eyed them. "Hey, it looks like you two finally got around to doing the deed."

"Emma." Robin raised her voice and her hand, but Emma dashed to the other side of the table before Robin could whack her.

Lily looked from Emma to Annie. "Yeah, we did all right. And I notice you and Annie looking flushed and leaning into each other."

"Got us." Emma kissed Annie.

Katie turned to Jan. "Think we can survive all the pheromones floating around us?"

Robin grinned. "As long as you don't flash a tat, you'll be safe from Jan."

Jan bumped hips with Robin. "Smart ass."

Once they were settled, the waitress arrived with champagne and glasses, which she filled and placed in front of each of them. Katie stood and clinked her knife against her water glass. The room went silent. She raised her glass. "Everyone, please stand and join me in toasting our friends Robin and Lily on their engagement."

Lily looked around. Every table was standing, everyone holding a flute of champagne.

With tears in her eyes, Katie lifted her glass and spoke to them. "Wishing you, Robin and Lily, happiness, health and love forever." She drank and everyone in the room did the same, then cheered. Katie waved the waitress over. "In honor of Robin and Lily, I'm picking up the check for everyone seated now, please let them know."

It was a fun night. The trepidation she'd felt about meeting Katie and Jan melted away. And when Nicole and Nora arrived a little later she felt an instant connection to them. Basking in the warmth of the group, she marveled at the obvious love and bond between Robin, Katie, Emma and Nicole, who, with Jan, were Robin's family. The eight of them joked and chatted and, unlike she had with Micki's friends, she felt accepted, appreciated, and included. She and Robin held hands under the table. And throughout the meal there was a steady stream of people stopping by to congratulate them and thank Katie for the treat.

They danced and sang and celebrated until the place closed, then everyone went home. As promised, Robin accompanied Lily. Happily, the next day was Saturday.

They both groaned when Lily's cell played a happy tune at eleven the next morning. "It's Del." She kissed Robin. "Go back to sleep. I'll take it in the living room."

Robin rolled onto her. "No, don't leave me."

"Okay, just let me have a little space." She pushed Robin off her. "Hey, Mama, I was going to call you this morning. I'm thinking of coming to visit. There's someone, Robin is her name, I want y'all to meet." Robin's lips were on her neck and a hand was trailing down her body, making it difficult to breathe. She batted Robin's hands away.

"Why, Lily honey, y'all sound absolutely breathless. You must really be smitten by this Robin."

"Smitten? Yes, I am, Mama." She captured Robin's hand. "When you meet her you'll understand. She's sexy and brilliant and fun and—"

"Well, that should be sooner than you think. President Obama asked Cordy to lead some hifallutin' commission and she said she would. Then out of nowhere Columbia University offered her the most prestigious chair in her mathematics universe and she accepted that. We're comin' to New York City Thursday so Cordy can finalize everything and we can check out the apartment they're giving us. They're putting us up in a hotel so we won't be staying with you, but plan on you and your gal spendin' lots of time with us, starting with dinner Thursday. Just a second, Cordy wants to say hello."

Cordy was less effusive than Del, more formal. "A new gal, that's great news, honey. Did we meet her at your...at the...in December?"

"You can say it, Mama, ill-fated wedding. No, I didn't know her then. But I'm sure you're going to love her."

"That's nice, but you're the one that counts. Do you love her? And are you sure? I don't want you getting hurt again."

Time to change the subject. "When will you begin teaching?" She wanted to wait until they met face to face to surprise Cordy with Robin. Since she'd recommended Robin to speak at Davos, she surely remembered her and thought highly of her.

"I'll probably start mid-August so we'll be moving sometime early August."

"I can't wait to see you both." She hung up, turned to Robin and tickled her until they were both breathless.

"So what's the story with the mamas?"

"They'll be in New York Thursday for a few days. Cordy is going to be teaching at Columbia so they'll move here permanently in early August."

"Fantastic. Call them later and get their flight information. I'll have Tanya pick them up."

"Y'all are so sweet."

"You dropped into Southern speak. Are you nervous about me meeting them?"

"No. Um, yes. Mama mentioning Micki made me anxious that you might—"

"Don't." Robin wrapped her arms around Lily. "Now that I have you, I'll never let you go."

CHAPTER TWENTY-SIX

The Mamas

The maître d' smiled. "Ms. DiLuca, so nice to see you again. Your guests just arrived a few minutes ago." She picked up menus. "This way, please."

White-faced, Robin ran her fingers through her hair, then smoothed her jacket. "Do I look all right?"

Lily smiled. Robin knew she must have asked her that a hundred times since they'd dressed, but she couldn't help being nervous.

Lily adjusted the collar of Robin's shirt "You look terrific."

"Are you sure they won't hate me?"

"Absolutely." Lily took Robin's hand and tugged her forward. "They're going to adore y'all just like I do."

Robin stopped short. "You're nervous too, my Southern beauty."

"Yes. I'm afraid y'all won't like them."

"No worries there. I already adore Dr. Alexander."

"A teacher is different than a mother-in-law and Del can be a mite overbearing."

Robin blanched. "Now you tell—"

The maître d' cleared her throat.

Lily smiled. "Oh, sorry." She squeezed Robin's hand. "Come."

As they approached, the mamas stood. Robin felt more anxious and unsure than she'd ever felt giving a presentation in front of hundreds of people; even her TED talk hadn't been as scary. Lily's hand on her back propelled her forward, but when they got closer the blood drained from her face. Again. Dr. Alexander was glaring at her.

She looked from one mama to another waiting for Lily to break the silence and introduce them. Then Dr. Alexander grinned and pulled her into her arms. "Dr. DiLuca, what a wonderful surprise. I never expected Lily's Robin would be one of my most brilliant and challenging students." She cleared her throat. "And I suppose it's all right to say now, one of my all-time favorites."

Robin blushed. Over Dr. Alexander's shoulder, she watched Del and Lily grin, high-five each other, then hug. "Since Cordy seems to know her, Del, let me introduce Robin DiLuca."

"Cordy darlin', let me at this gorgeous Robin our daughter has found. She must be somethin' if y'all are huggin' her and looking like y'all won the lottery."

Del spun Robin around and hugged her. "So nice to meet you, Robin, especially now that you have the Cordy seal of approval." Robin didn't think she could get redder, but she felt another surge of blood to her face.

Lily hugged Cordy. "Shall we sit?"

The maître d' appeared immediately and handed Robin the wine list. She cleared her throat and looked at Lily, moved her eyes to Del, then Cordy. "Champagne?"

"What's the occasion?" The mamas spoke in unison.

Lily and Robin locked eyes. Robin cleared her throat. "Maybe proposing champagne was somewhat presumptuous." She took Lily's proffered hand. "I'm in love with Lily and I've asked her to marry me. She said yes, but I would like your permission."

The mamas exchanged a glance. Robin had never understood the meaning of the expression "the silence was deafening" until now. The mamas stared at the two of them. "Lily, are you sure? It's so soon." Cordy's eyes went to Robin. "Nothing against you, Dr. DiLuca. Do you know…did Lily tell you about—?"

All fear gone now, Robin went into protective mode. "Yes, Dr. Alexander. I know all about it and I know that she worked hard to figure it out. I leave it to Lily to discuss her own feelings, but let me reassure you both, I am totally, helplessly in love with her, and while I don't know what the future will bring, I'll never intentionally do anything to hurt Lily and I would certainly never do anything as despicable and cowardly as that woman did."

The mamas exchanged another glance. "Lily?" This time it was Del who spoke.

"I understand y'all are worried that I'll make another mistake, but I'm sure this time. Really sure." She kissed Robin's hand. "I never told y'all I went into therapy to figure out what happened with Micki. I know you never took to her."

Del looked at Cordy. "Oh, darlin', we thought we hid it so well. Maybe if we'd been honest we could have saved you from—"

"No. Del, I'd convinced myself I was in love with her. But I've come to understand she was drawn to my perceived fame and fortune. I believe she loved the chase, not me. For months, I puzzled over why she waited so long to break it off. She was always bragging about me being a successful writer so maybe she thought that was enough reason to marry me. Or perhaps it was the money she thought I made as a successful writer." She shrugged. "I'll probably never know why she waited to dump me, but once I got over being embarrassed, I realized she'd saved me from a huge mistake."

She smiled at Robin and kissed her hand again. "Robin is also persistent and persuasive, but she loves me, respects that I'm a successful writer, but, for sure, she isn't after my money. I'm sure she's the one for me, forever."

Del nodded, but she glared at Robin. "How can you be sure about the money?"

Cordy laughed. "Do you remember the article I read you about students of mine who became billionaires?"

"Yes, of course." Her eyes widened. "Robin?"

"Yes, ma'am. And my friend Katie Cooper. We built a technology firm after we graduated from Stanford and took it public a few months ago." She stared into Del's eyes, then switched to Cordy. "I love Lily and I want us to be married, something I never imagined for myself, but if you're against it I'll do my best to convince you we're right for each other. I'm willing to wait until you approve. She's worth waiting for."

"Mama—"

Cordy held up her hand. "Just a minute, Lily, you dropped this on us from out of nowhere. You admit you almost made a huge mistake eight months ago and now you're telling us this time is for real and we're supposed to jump up and down and cheer. I know you don't really need our permission to get married, but can we four spend time together while we're in New York so we can get to know Dr. DiLuca before giving our blessings? I must say I'm favorably disposed."

Lily opened her mouth, but Robin put her finger on her lips to still her. "Only if you call me Robin."

Cordy grinned. "Only if you call us Del and Cordy."

"It's a deal. Should we seal it with champagne or would you prefer something else?"

"Champagne is fine for us." Del was the one who answered.

* * *

Lily and Robin spent as much time as possible with Del and Cordy in the next four days, going out for meals, walking in Central or Riverside Park or on the High Line. They talked and laughed a great deal. Conversations ranged from hot dogs to mathematical theories to New York City apartments to politics to business to whatever interested one of them.

Robin orchestrated dinner at Shazarak Saturday night so the mamas could meet their friends. Robin made the introductions. "Cordy and Del I'd like you to meet Dr. Katie Cooper, my best friend and business partner, and her fiancé, Dr. Michael Stein. Across the table is Jan Haskel, my other business partner, Dr. Nicole Summerfield and her partner Dr. Nora Tannen, and last but not least, Dr. Emma Novick. Dr. Annie MacDonald you already know."

Cordy lifted her glass. "Good to see you again, Dr. Cooper, Dr. Summerfield and Dr. Novick. And, you of course, Annie."

Del surveyed the table. "It looks like Lily, Jan and I are in the low-brow minority. This is an impressive group. All PhDs, Robin?"

They all laughed. "No, ma'am. Katie, Michael, Emma and Annie are PhDs. Nicole is a neonatal specialist and Nora is an ER doctor. Katie, Emma and Nicole were my suitemates at Harvard and Stanford."

The dinner conversation was lively and varied, Michael joining right in with the women.

They stayed to dance, and it was clear that Lily got her love of dancing from her mamas. Once the music started, neither Del nor Cordy sat. They danced with each other and everyone else. Robin couldn't believe that she was actually dancing with Dr. Cordelia Alexander, the professor she had worshiped when she was at Stanford. Jan fell in love with Del and couldn't get enough of dancing with her.

At brunch with everyone the next day, Del cleared her throat and stood to speak. "Cordy and I would like to thank all of y'all for a wonderful weekend. Cordy knew some of you, but I'd like to say we're both thrilled to see our Lily surrounded by such a loving group of friends. One of the best things about these last few days is seeing how in love Lily and Robin are and hearing from each of you why you think they belong together. Robin, sweetheart, Cordy and I have fallen in love with you. We couldn't ask for a more perfect daughter-in-law." She picked up her champagne. "Please join me in wishing Lily and Robin the happiest of marriages."

Robin and Lily locked eyes across the table, then Robin raised her glass. "I know it's not politically correct to love your mothers-in-law, but I'm the luckiest woman alive because by marrying the woman I adore, I get to share her mamas, two women that I have grown to love in a really short time. Thank you." She sipped her seltzer as the others drank their champagne. Lots of tears were swiped away.

"Is Labor Day weekend okay for all of y'all?" Hearing agreement, Lily turned to the mamas. "I'll call Belle and Ben to make sure they're available. And let's do the same with our other friends, Robin. Once we confirm the day we can start to plan the wedding."

CHAPTER TWENTY-SEVEN

The Wedding

No church, no organ music, no people she didn't know. Lily was adamant. Robin happily agreed. So the celebration on this brilliantly sunny day early in September was for them and their nearest and dearest—Del and Cordy, Ben and Bella, Lily's brother and sister, Katie and Michael, Jan, Irene, her agent, Annie, Emma, Mei and her boyfriend, Nicole and Nora, and Winnie, Robin's fifth Harvard roommate, and her date. Since Cornelius Carlyle was Lily's uncle as well as her sperm donor, he'd been invited but was unable to make it. Not knowing about Robin's wealth, he'd sent them two open tickets to Hong Kong so they could visit.

Tomorrow evening Robin and Lily would fly to Greece and spend ten days on a yacht in the Mediterranean with a female captain and crew. The Saturday after returning from their honeymoon, they would host a huge formal wedding reception for Robin's business associates, her many friends from Harvard and Stanford and Lily's friends from Chicago, Iowa, Alabama and California. On Sunday, they planned a more intimate brunch for friends who had attended the reception.

At the moment, though, everyone was on the terrace of Robin's apartment sipping champagne and eating hors d'oeuvres in advance of the ceremony, which would be followed by a sit-down dinner under an awning on the terrace.

Lily stood in the doorway to the terrace watching Robin, her black hair glistening in the sunlight, her eyes flashing and her smile broad and contagious, as she hugged and kissed everyone. She circulated, but seemed to gravitate to Del and Cordy, who had opened their arms and their hearts to her.

A hand on Lily's shoulder, then a voice in her ear. "You're not changing your mind, are you, Lily?'

"Not a chance, Katie. Just admiring her and congratulating myself on my good luck."

"That's good, because she's totally yours and that comes with responsibility."

"She's precious and fragile, I know." She turned and hugged Katie. "You did a wonderful job with her."

"I can't take all the credit. Emma, Mei, Nicole, and Winnie were there for her too."

"Well, y'all are wonderful. I promise I will never hurt her."

"Well, then, I think you should get married today." She put her arm through Lily's and escorted her onto the terrace. "Here comes the bride."

All eyes turned. Lily blushed.

Robin was at her side instantly and took her in her arms. "You look gorgeous." They'd decided that Lily would wear a traditional white wedding gown at the big reception and Robin would wear a tux but that today would be informal. So Lily was wearing a filmy white dress in the style that Robin loved on her, a wrap-around showing lots of cleavage, and Robin was wearing white pants and a white peasant shirt.

In keeping with wanting a low-key celebration, they'd dropped the idea of asking Supreme Court Justice Ruth Bader Ginsburg to marry them, and Cordy had volunteered to become certified as a Universal Life Minister so she could officiate. At one o'clock, the time they'd set for the ceremony, Cordy cleared her throat. "Everyone, please sit so we can begin." She waved to the chairs, facing the river, under a canopy erected to protect them from the sun. Lily and Robin stood just inside the apartment with Annie and

Katie, while everyone settled. Then Bella started the song they'd selected to walk down the aisle together—Bette Midler singing "Be My Baby"—and the four of them boogied down the aisle to stand in front of Cordy, who waited with her back to the river. If anyone doubted that Dr. Cordelia Alexander approved of Lily marrying one of her all-time favorite students, they just had to look at her. Her normally reserved face seemed lit from within today.

She waited for the music to stop, cleared her throat and smiled at Robin and Lily. "I'm thrilled that you, Lily and Robin, asked that I be the one to marry you, but before I proceed I want to be clear. To me and Delphine," she smiled at her wife sitting in the front row, "marriage is a forever commitment and we feel it's important that our children find spouses who believe that as well. Robin, in the short time we have known you as our daughter-in-law-to-be, we have learned to love you, and we trust that by marrying Lily you are making a forever commitment to her and to our family."

Robin squeezed Lily's hand. "I am."

Cordy smiled. "In that case, let's begin." She put on her glasses and opened the book she was holding.

CHAPTER TWENTY-EIGHT

Two Years Later

Five days ago they'd returned from three weeks in Mongolia, and last night they'd celebrated their second anniversary with the mamas and their closest friends. Now still in bed, they were enjoying Sunday morning in their new, larger Battery Park City apartment, Robin reading a mathematics book that Cordy had given her as a present at their anniversary dinner last night, and Lily updating her travel journal and pasting the pictures Robin had printed for her in their travel photo album.

Humming, Lily thumbed to the beginning of the album and smiled at the pictures they'd taken on their honeymoon in Greece, then New Year's in Paris the December after they married. How audacious she'd been, making the reservations for the two of them that July, not knowing whether they'd even be dating in December. Robin had turned it into a family celebration, so instead of the week alone in Paris that Lily had imagined when she made the reservation, everyone was there. It had been wonderful. And despite the crowd, as romantic as she'd imagined.

She turned to their trip to Davos. Robin and Cordy had both delivered impressive speeches and once again it turned into a family outing with Del and Ben and Bella, Katie and Michael, Jan and a boyfriend that trip, Annie and Emma and Nicole and Nora. Winnie and her husband came from Spain, where they were living, and Mei flew in from China, where she was working on a huge architectural project.

She flipped through the rest of the book—Hong Kong, China, Nepal, Japan, Vietnam, South Korea, Thailand, Spain, France, Italy, England, Germany, Israel, Hawaii, Tahiti. They'd done the traveling they'd dreamed of doing, done wonderful things and seen wonderful places. Now she was feeling the urge to settle down. She glanced at Robin. Was she ready?

She put the album down and picked up the Book Review section of the *New York Times*, but as usual when she had something on her mind, she found it hard to concentrate. She lowered her paper and studied her wife.

"We just celebrated our second anniversary, sweet Robin, and I'm hankering to make a baby. Are y'all ready?"

Robin peered over her book. "Does this have anything to do with Katie deciding to get pregnant?"

"Of course. Wouldn't it be nice if our kids were the same age and could play together? Besides, we've been married two years, we've traveled the world like we wanted and done a lot of exciting things. It's time to settle down."

"I kind of like the idea of our kids getting together. Members of families usually have kids around the same time, right?" She leaned over and kissed Lily. "You know it's not fair that straight people just have to have sex to have a baby, and we have to harvest eggs and grow them in a glass dish in a lab."

"I don't know. Why not think of it as we can make love as often as we want without worrying about getting pregnant?"

"Hmm. I like your attitude." She put her book aside. "Will we be able to make love when you're pregnant or will we have to do without for nine months?"

"I believe we'll be able to, but just in case..." She dropped the newspaper on the floor and rolled onto Robin. Later, as Lily stroked Robin's hair and watched her doze, she felt a surge of love, love that had grown rather than diminished over their two years of marriage.

Robin opened her eyes. "Will you call Dr. Stafford tomorrow or should I?"

"Why don't you? I can be free anytime, but you have to do most of the startup work to get us an egg to make a baby and your schedule is usually filled."

"Have you given any thought to the…to a sperm donor?"

"Cordy thinks one of her former students would be perfect. He was a year behind you and, she says, nearly as brilliant."

"Well, I'm glad she said, nearly. I wouldn't want my genes to be overwhelmed by someone as insignificant as the sperm donor. "Do you have a name?"

"Lucien Arceneaux. He's Cajun but not related to Delphine. At least not for generations. His family lives a little ways outside of New Orleans."

"Ah, yes. Lucien. We called him Lucky. I had classes with him and we worked on several projects together. I found his warmth and upbeat attitude attractive. Actually, now that I think of it, he was a lot like you. Yes, he would be perfect."

"What else do you remember about him?"

Robin thought for a moment. "He's brilliant but not nerdy." She sat up. "He played the cello and the guitar, had a decent voice and, I think, he was into photography. Where is he? Does Cordy think he'd be willing?"

"He's married, has three daughters, and is a tenured astrophysics professor at the University of Hawaii. She thought you should contact him and casually mention her name, then she would follow up if necessary."

"Do we have a telephone number?"

"But of course."

* * *

Money, it turned out, couldn't buy everything. Who knew that even though they'd been recommended by Nicole, one of the most respected and sought after neonatal physicians in New York City, they'd have to complete an extensive questionnaire, then wait eleven weeks for their first appointment with the certified reproductive endocrinologist, she had highly recommended?

Finally, the week before Thanksgiving, they were in her office, anxious to meet Dr. Erika Stafford and discuss making a baby. Forcing herself to sit still, Robin glanced at Lily and received a shy smile in return, confirming her suspicion that Lily was nervous too but covering it better. They'd done extensive research, so they knew what they were doing was called reciprocal, or partner, in vitro fertilization or IVF. Robin's eggs would be harvested, put in a Petri dish with their donor's sperm to be fertilized, then implanted in Lily's uterus where it would, hopefully, grow into a baby Robin.

Dr. Stafford greeted them with a warm smile and they introduced themselves. She shook their hands. "I'm happy to meet you in person after reading about you in the materials you provided." She led them into her office. Instead of sitting behind her desk, she took a club chair and waved them to the sofa. "I'm sure you've read the brochures and done your research so forgive me if I bore you, but I have to review the process with you. The IVF process for lesbians is almost identical to that for heterosexuals except usually the woman who will bear the child hasn't had a problem conceiving or carrying a child. Lily, you'll be carrying the baby?"

Lily nodded.

"And you're both clear that since Robin will provide the eggs, she will have a genetic link with the child and that although Lily will carry the baby her link with the child will be gestational not genetic?"

They spoke simultaneously. "We're clear." They smiled at each other.

"A big difference from the heterosexual procedure is that your insurance company will most likely not cover the costs because it's not medically necessary. That is, as far as we know, Lily could get pregnant the usual way or with a turkey baster."

They laughed.

"And the cost is not trivial. Each attempt to get pregnant can run fifteen thousand or more dollars, and there's no way to know how many times we'll have to repeat the process. Only twenty-eight to thirty-five percent of the women who try IVF get pregnant. I assume the money is no problem for you?"

Robin smiled. "Whatever it takes."

This was one of those times that being the wife of a billionaire came in handy, Lily thought.

Dr. Stafford nodded. "Have you selected a sperm donor?"

Robin and Lily exchanged a glance. Robin answered. Lucien Arceneaux had been honored to be asked and, after discussing it with his wife, readily agreed. "We have. And an attorney who specializes in third-party parenting is drawing up the necessary papers—for this child and any future children we decide to have with him as the donor."

"Good. And I assume he's willing to undergo the donor eligibility testing required by FDA regulations?"

Robin answered again. "He is. And he'll arrange for the frozen sperm to be here by the time we're ready for it."

"Okay. Here's how it will go. We'll start by giving you both oral contraceptives to synchronize your menstrual cycles. This can take anywhere from six to nine weeks. We'll also give Robin medications to stimulate the maturation of the multiple eggs needed. Lily will take medications to help prepare her uterus for implantation." She looked at each of them. "Are you with me?"

"Yes." They each answered.

"When your cycles are synchronized, we'll sedate Robin and retrieve her eggs. Under ultrasound guidance, we insert a needle through your vagina into your ovary to remove your eggs. The fluid obtained is examined under a microscope, and if we are certain eggs are present, it will be placed in a Petri dish with active sperm from your donor." She smiled at them. "We let them play around for somewhat more than three days, then we check to see whether the eggs have been fertilized. Several days later, if the fertilized eggs are beginning to grow as embryos, we'll transfer *some* of them to Lily's uterus through her cervix with a slender catheter. Thus the possibility of multiple births and a horde of little Robins.

"Lily, you will receive hormones to encourage the embryos to attach to the wall of your uterus and grow. Once we do the transfer, we wait. Your job, Lily, will be to stay quiet for a few hours, then take things easy for about two weeks. We will monitor you. When the embryo is attached and growing, your pregnancy test will be positive and prenatal care begins. If not, we start over.

"So, ladies, are you ready to start on the path to motherhood?"

Lily leaned over and brushed Robin's lips with hers. "Bring on the horde of little Robins, I say."

Robin grinned. "What Lily said."

CHAPTER TWENTY-NINE

The Pregnancy

As she entered the hospital room, Nicole smiled at them. They'd asked Robin's Harvard roommate to deliver their baby because they both trusted her, but now that there seemed to be a problem, it was comforting to know she was a highly respected obstetric specialist who could handle anything that came up.

"The baby looks fine, but I'm concerned about your ability to carry for the full term, Lily. You're at twenty-one weeks, and while there are a couple of instances of survival, for all intents and purposes, if he or she were born today, your fetus wouldn't be viable."

Robin stiffened. Lily gasped. "Oh my God. Are we going to lose the baby?" She locked Robin's hand in a death grip. Robin didn't seem to notice.

"Is Lily at risk?" Robin avoided looking at Lily. "Because if she is, let's abort and start over."

"What?" Lily pulled her hand away. "Don't go there, Robin, if I abort naturally so be it, but I will not choose to abort."

The anger in the voice of her usually easy-going wife shocked Robin. "I can't lose—"

Nicole put a hand on each of her friends. "Lily is not in danger, Rob. And as I said, the baby looks fine. I just can't guarantee it will go to full term." Her voice was gentle, her calm reassuring to Lily. "But every additional week of gestation increases the probability of a survival. Another two weeks and there's a seventeen percent chance of survival, three weeks and it increases to thirty-nine percent and four weeks the survival rate goes to fifty percent. If you hold out for six more weeks, the percentages go to ninety or ninety-five."

Robin was agitated. "You talk about survival, Nicole. What about healthy? Aren't premature babies usually impaired in some way?"

"Yes, Rob, they can be severely impaired but not all are."

"Isn't there something we can do? Whatever it costs, do it."

"The only thing we know to recommend is complete bed rest, but we're not even sure that really works. If the baby is very premature and we have some warning, we can increase its chances of surviving by treating Lily with steroids before the birth. The steroids can make a difference in whether or not the baby is able to breathe outside the womb. Once the baby is born, this hospital has an advanced neonatal unit with the highest rating for dealing with premature babies." She squeezed their hands. "You know I'll do everything humanly possible to save my niece or nephew."

Robin was pale. Lily brought Robin's hand to her lips. "Bed rest is a small price to pay for the life of our baby, and our Jess has your genes so I'm sure she'll fight to hang on."

Nicole frowned. "Jess? Did someone in my office slip about the baby's sex?"

Lily shook her head. "Everybody has been discreet. But we got tired of being abstract so whatever the sex, Jess is the name. I have a few questions about the bed rest, Nicole."

Nicole smiled. "Why am I not surprised? Fire away."

"Do I have to stay in bed all the time, or can I get up to shower or use the bathroom? On my back or side, or can I alternate? Can I write if I feel inspired? What about sex?"

"I'd like you to stay off your feet as much as possible. Showering and using the bathroom are fine, but no cooking or laundry or cleaning or lifting. No strolls in the park, but when you get up to use the bathroom, stroll around the apartment for a few minutes to reduce the chances of a blood clot. Alternate your position. If you're on your side, place a pillow between your legs and bend your knees. On your back, elevate your head and shoulders. Write if you can find a comfortable position but, sorry, no sex. Any other questions?"

"When can I go home?"

"I've done the paper work to release you. Call me immediately if you have more contractions or more bleeding." She rubbed Robin's shoulder. "She'll be fine, Rob. Try to relax or I'll have to put you on bed rest too. By the way, my mom and dad send their regards. Mom asked whether she should send the chitlins recipe to Lily."

Robin laughed. "She's never going to let me forget, is she?"

Nicole grinned. "She loves to tease you." Her phone beeped. She read the screen. "Sorry, I have a delivery. The nurse should be in shortly to officially discharge you. Take care. Both of you." She dashed out the door.

"What was that about chitlins?"

"A family joke. My freshman year Katie was committed to spend the Thanksgiving weekend at a Peace Corps training for new volunteers, so I went home with Nicole. All weekend I waited for her mom to serve chitlins and collard greens and fried chicken, you know stereotypical African-American foods, but we had a big turkey dinner with all the trimmings on Thanksgiving, lasagna one night, and grilled salmon another. Finally, I asked, 'Aren't we going to have chitlins?'" Robin smiled with the memory.

"Nicole's mom and dad laughed so hard, they were practically rolling on the floor. My fourteen-year-old self was mortified and totally confused. Seeing I was close to tears, Nicole hugged me. Then her parents pulled themselves together, took turns hugging me, and apologized. Although they are black, Nicole's mom and dad had never tasted chitlins, actually weren't even sure what they were. They grew up in New York, but their roots were in Barbados, not the South. It was a good lesson for me about stereotypes. And it's been a running joke between the four of us ever since."

Lily was pleased that remembering helped Robin relax. *Probably Nicole's intention.*

Robin helped Lily dress. About a half-hour later the nurse arrived with instructions and a wheelchair to transport her to the lobby, and Robin wheeled her down.

Lily blessed Tanya for bringing the luxury town car, which would cushion her on the badly potholed roads through the park. As usual, Tanya got out to assist Lily, but Robin practically shoved her out of the way. When they had settled in, Lily met Tanya's eyes in the rearview mirror. "Thanks for bringing the town car. As you can see, we're a little stressed. We'll be better when we get home."

Tanya nodded. "The baby is okay?"

"Yes. I'll be on bed rest for a while, but we'll be fine." She rubbed Robin's back then kissed her temple. "Really, Robin, don't worry, we'll be okay."

"Go easy, Tanya, we have precious cargo here." She put a hand on Lily's belly. "I'd feel better if I could wrap the two of you in bubble wrap and foam rubber for the next couple of months."

Lily saw Tanya's smile in the mirror. "Hmm, that might not be as comfortable as lying in bed and reading or working." She lifted Robin's hand and kissed her palm. "Besides, you wouldn't be able to hold my hand or kiss me."

Tanya stopped in front of their building. "Need help, Robin?"

"I can handle her, thanks." She got out of the car and went around to Lily's side. The doorman had rushed forward to help, but she put her hand up. "If you bring the building's wheelchair to the curb, I'll assist her from the car."

Tanya got out of the car and came around. "Backup." She watched but didn't try to intervene as Robin helped Lily to the sidewalk and into the wheelchair. Before they walked into the building, Tanya kissed their cheeks. "Take care. Call if you need anything, even a drug store run or food delivery."

Robin wheeled her into the bedroom, helped her sit on the bed, slowly undressed her, then pulled her nightgown over her head. She kissed her gently.

Lily held Robin's face between her hands. "Having you undress me doesn't exactly make me feel calm. But thank you, sweet Robin."

"What do you need? Pillows, water, a book, your computer? Name it."

"I'll start on my back, so get me more pillows from the closet in the guest room."

Robin retrieved the pillows and helped her prop herself up.

"Now, book, water and computer, then I'll take a nap and you can go back to work."

"No way. I'll be working from home until you deliver or are allowed out of bed."

"Oh, sweetie, we're looking at three months or more. I'll bet Del will come over to work here during the day, and Annie or Emma will come when they're not teaching. Or if it makes you feel better, we can hire a nurse for when you're at work."

Robin crossed her arms and stared down at her. "Nope. I'm not leaving you. I'll work from home, and if I do have to go to the office for a sales presentation or something unusual, then we can arrange for someone else to stay with you for a few hours."

Robin had decided and Lily knew better than to argue. Robin was afraid she was going to lose her and the baby and felt she needed to be there to protect them. If their roles were reversed, she knew she'd feel the same way. She patted the bed. "Come take a nap with me."

Robin grinned. "That's more like it." She slipped her shoes off, climbed on the bed and threw her arm over Lily. "Are you sure she said no sex?"

Lily pinched her. "Nap, you bad girl."

CHAPTER THIRTY

The Delivery

Lily glanced at the clock. Three eleven a.m. She'd been cramping for what seemed like hours. Neither praying nor using Robin's steady breathing to calm herself helped. Twenty-four weeks and five days wasn't nearly enough time. She needed to hold on for Jess. *Shit*. What was that? She dipped her finger into the liquid that had spurted from between her legs and sniffed. Blood. She'd hoped the cramps would pass, but the blood worried her. She touched Robin's shoulder. "Robin." She spoke softly, not wanting to frighten her.

Robin was instantly alert. "Are you okay?" She rolled over and wrapped an arm around her. "Jeez, you're covered in sweat and the sheets are soaked." She brushed Lily's hair away from her face. "Is it Jess?" She turned on her bedside lamp. "Oh shit, you're bleeding."

"I need to go to the hospital. Call Nicole, then bring me some towels so I can clean up a little before dressing."

"I'm calling an ambulance before I do anything."

"No, no, just get a taxi." She tried to sit up.

"Absolutely not."

She recoiled. Robin never spoke to her in that commanding voice.

"Sorry. I'm worried." She sat on the bed next to Lily and took her hand. "Please, let me take care of you." She entwined their fingers, then keyed 9-1-1 into her phone. "My wife is a little under twenty-five weeks pregnant and she's bleeding. We need an ambulance immediately." She gave the address, then selected Nicole's emergency number on her cell. "This is Robin DiLuca, I'm taking my wife to the hospital in an ambulance, and we need Dr. Summerfield to meet us there." Finally, she called down to let the doorman know to send the EMTs right up.

Lily winced as the ambulance sped through the night, seeming to hit every pothole twice. "Where's the bubble wrap and foam rubber when you need it?"

Robin wiped Lily's forehead with the gauze the EMT had provided to keep the sweat from dripping into her eyes. "You should have mentioned it before we left home. It's hidden in my closet, but in the rush to get out, I forgot."

Lily clutched Robin's hand to her heart. Robin was pale, probably as terrified as she was, but her steady presence was comforting.

Nicole was waiting at the emergency entrance when the ambulance arrived at the hospital. She rushed Lily to a delivery room and had her hooked up to a monitor as she was examining her.

"Your contractions are coming every two minutes, and I see the top of the head of a very aggressive baby trying to escape, so we're going to have to prep you for delivery. It's earlier than any of us would like, but I'll do my best." She glanced over her shoulder. "Someone help Robin scrub in." She turned to the staff of nurses waiting for orders. "Let's get Lily prepped." She hugged Robin and moved her to the door. "You couldn't be in a better place for this kind of birth." She closed the door behind Robin and walked back to Lily. "How are you doing, Lily?"

She grunted in pain. "Worried about Jess and Robin. Will Jess survive, Nicole?"

Nicole sat on the bed, took Lily's hand, then used a gauze pad to dab at the sweat running down her face. "I'm not God, Lily, so no guarantees. But you know I'll do everything possible to help Jess survive and grow into a healthy baby." She hugged Lily and kissed her cheek. "The rest will be up to Jess. But if he or she is anything like Rob, I believe we'll have a happy ending." Nicole stood. "I need to wash up, then we'll welcome baby Jess." At the door, she turned. "Oh, Lily, because Jess is so early everyone in the room including you and Robin will be wearing masks, hair covering, gowns and gloves to protect her. And, just a reminder, since this is a teaching hospital there will be several residents observing and assisting."

The nurses took care of covering Lily. When Robin entered Lily recognized her worried green eyes above the mask and reached for her hand as she sat in the chair near her head.

"I called the mamas, Annie and Katie to let them know what's happening. They're all coming to the hospital as soon as they can get dressed. I figured I could call everyone else later."

"Thank you, sweet Robin. I'm glad you'll have some support when we're done."

Robin kissed her knuckles. "Okay, breathe." She started the routine they'd learned in their birthing class.

When Nicole entered, all conversation ceased and everyone focused on her. She smiled at Lily and Robin. "Ready?"

Lily met Nicole's eyes over the masks they were both wearing and took a deep breath. "When you are." She was anxious to start so she could know the ending.

"Okay. Just so you know. Jess is arriving so early that he or she will be extremely small and unable to regulate his or her body temperature. Once I clamp and cut the umbilical cord you're going to see us moving very quickly. Within five seconds of removing him or her from your uterus, we will wrap Jess's body in plastic wrap, connect a pulse oximeter and place him or her immediately on the radiant warmer," she pointed, "over there. We'll do a quick exam then remove him or her to the NICU, that's the neonatal intensive care unit. As long as Jess's heart rate is good, we're good." She moved toward Lily's feet and sat on a stool between Lily's legs. "I'm sorry, my friends, but Jess will be too small for you to hold."

Lily swallowed. "Don't worry about us. Do what you need to do for Jess."

Robin stood. "Wait, Nicole. Why the oximeter and the plastic wrap?"

"The oximeter measures the oxygen level in the blood and helps us determine the correct amount of oxygen to administer. The plastic wrap conducts heat and allows radiant heat from the warmer to cross through, but it stops evaporative temperature losses."

Robin nodded.

"Remember we'll be moving fast so stay out of our way, Rob. Once Jess is born I'll stay with him or her and Dr. Radswill," the younger woman standing next to Nicole raised her hand, "will finish up with you, Lily." Nicole moved in front of the screen. "Do you want to cut the cord, Robin?"

Lily squeezed her hand. "Go, Dad."

Robin smiled. "Of course." She handed her camera to one of the residents.

"So stand right at the screen and be ready to move fast. Someone hand Robin the scissors and, when we're ready, show her where to cut." She waited for Robin to move into place. "And Sandy, stand behind me on the right so we can be sure you get good pictures of Jess's debut."

"Okay, Lily, push. Hold it. Relax." She placed her hands to catch the baby. "Push again. Keep pushing. That's it. Relax." She lifted her head to smile at Lily and Robin over the drape. "You're doing great. Jess definitely takes after you, Rob. He or she is in a big hurry to get here. It won't be long now. Another push or two should do it. That's it, that's it, keep pushing." Nicole's excitement encouraged Lily to push harder. "I have a…girl. Jess is a girl. Quick suction the mucus." A whimper followed rather than the lusty cry they'd expected.

"Clamping."

A nurse pushed Robin forward and showed her where to put the scissors. The intern quickly snapped pictures as she cut. Nicole elbowed Robin out of the way. "Good work, Rob. And here we go."

As Nicole had described, she and the nurses moved quickly to the warming table. Lily couldn't see from her position, but Robin moaned. "Shit." She backed away, looking like she wanted to throw up.

Nicole glanced at Robin. "Don't get nervous, Rob. She's not fully developed yet. She'll do the rest of her growing in the incubator, which is where we're taking her now. See you both later."

Robin was vibrating. Lily grabbed her hand and pulled her close. "Calm down, love."

Robin sat in the chair. She was pale. They were alone except for Dr. Radswill and a nurse. Everyone else had followed Nicole to the NICU with Jess. She crushed Lily's hand. "Did you see her?"

"No. What did she—?"

Her eyes were wide. "I've never…I didn't expect…she doesn't look human. She's no bigger than my hand," she held her hand out, "and covered with black fur. She looks battered. Her head is big and her arms and legs spindly, like a large spider or a crab or an alien with translucent skin that shows all her veins and arteries."

"Don't worry. That's normal for a baby born so early." Dr. Radswill looked up from dealing with the after-birth. "It will be a while before she looks like a typical newborn." Her smile was reassuring. "I'm almost finished here, then we'll take you to your room."

When the nurse came in, Lily asked how Jess was doing. "I don't have any details. Dr. Summerfield will talk to you both later, but I can tell you she's one pound three ounces."

As they rolled down the hall, she could see mothers holding their newborns on their chests in some rooms and at their breasts in others. She quickly dried the tears in her eyes when they turned into her room.

When they were alone, Robin took her hand and stroked her hair. "She's horrible, Lily. I know it's an awful thing to say, but I feel like I could throw up. What should we tell everyone?"

She took Robin's face between her hands and turned so they were looking at each other. "You heard the doctor. It's normal for premature babies to look like Jess. You tell everyone she's almost four months premature and not fully developed, so she's in the NICU getting the best possible care. Ask everyone to pray she makes it. Can you do that?"

"Yes."

"So kiss me and go talk to my mamas."

Lily was dozing when Robin returned with the mamas and Katie and Annie. The visitors were encouraging, but she could see that Robin was really working at being positive, so she claimed exhaustion and asked if she and Robin could be left alone. Her mamas kissed her, promised to return tomorrow, and asked Robin to walk out with them. Annie gave her a hug and followed.

Katie hugged her, then plucked a tissue out of the box on the bed and dried Lily's tears. "I'm so sorry, honey. You know Nicole will do everything possible. If she's anything like her biological mother, Jess will fight hard to thrive and grow in the NICU, but the next few months will be hard for all three of you. You and Robin need to take care of each other."

Lily couldn't keep the tears from spilling. "Robin is freaked because Jess doesn't look human."

"I'll do my best to be there for her, but you know as well as I do she goes into lockdown when she's scared. Maybe between the two of us…" She kissed Lily's forehead. "Try to rest and let us know if you need anything. I'm sure Jan will come by in the morning, and I know Michael will want to see you both, but I'll hold him off a day or so."

A few minutes after Katie left, Robin came in looking like she was carrying the world on her shoulders. "Nicole will be in shortly to talk to us."

"Get on the bed with me, sweet Robin. Hold me."

CHAPTER THIRTY-ONE

The Premature Baby

They were kissing when Nicole arrived with her usual entourage of residents and fellows. She rapped on the door. "Hey, you two, no sex in the hospital."

They separated like two teenagers caught necking. Lily blushed. "Are you sure?"

Nicole smiled. "I'll check the rules, but I'm almost certain." Her smile drifted away. "In any case, we need to talk about Jess."

Robin sat up. "Is this when we get the bad news?" Her voice was taut, filled with as much anger as she ever let herself express.

"Not news, my friend." Nicole moved close to the bed, placed one hand on Robin's shoulder, and grasped Robin's hand with the other. "Information, so you know what to expect going forward."

Lily grasped Robin's other hand.

"We never know for sure, of course, but we've made so many advances in caring for low-birth-weight babies that there's at least a forty percent chance Jess will survive. The good news is that, as a rule girls do better than boys and single births like Jess do better than multiple births."

"She's just over a pound. If she survives, will she live or will she just exist?" The underlying anger was still there in Robin's voice.

"Unfortunately, we can't predict a good or bad outcome based on the length of time in the womb. However, at only twenty-four weeks and five days gestation, Jess was born before she was physically ready to leave the womb and most of her body's systems are underdeveloped. If she survives, she's at risk for serious disabilities such as cerebral palsy and she may be blind, deaf, mentally impaired and/or have other life-long health problems. We have her on respiratory support and since the coordination she needs to suck and swallow won't kick in for another eight to ten weeks, we've inserted a feeding tube through which we'll feed her Lily's milk to give her an extra immune-system boost." She focused on Lily. "If you're willing to pump, we'll need you to start right away so we have a supply of breast milk. If you're not willing, we'll feed her a special formula."

"Of course I'll pump."

"Also, the combination of a lack of body fat and a larger skin-to-body-weight ratio means Jess is susceptible to hypothermia, which is why we immediately wrapped her in plastic wrap and placed her on the warmer. We'll keep her in a warming device in the NICU until she can regulate her temperature on her own. I'm so sorry, but this means you won't be able to hold her yet."

They clung to each other. Lily took a deep breath. "Is it a foregone conclusion that she'll be impaired in some way?"

"Some babies come through it with no problems. There are even a couple born much earlier who survived without long-term issues. We'll have to wait and see."

"Why is she covered in fur?"

Nicole smiled. "That's not fur, Rob. It's fine hair, called lanugo. It's usually shed before a full-term birth. It will disappear by itself."

"When you see her later in the NICU, she'll be connected to various machines and IVs, but that's all standard for a premature baby. She'll be closely monitored, but right now her heart is good and we see no problems."

"What can we do besides pumping?"

"Jess is likely to be in the NICU for three or four months while her body continues to develop as if she were in the womb.

Although you can't hold her initially, you'll be able to spend as much time with her as you want, talking or reading to her. Some parents sing." She squeezed Robin's shoulder. "I suggest you leave the singing to Lily."

Robin glared at her, then her shoulders relaxed. "You're right."

"You'll be able to touch Jess in the incubator, and once she can regulate her own body temperature you can do what we call 'kangaroo care,' which is holding the baby skin-to-skin for an hour or two. The next few months will be grueling and stressful, and it's just as important you take care of each other as be here for Jess."

Lily rested her head on Robin's shoulder. "When can I see her?"

"As soon as you're able to walk to the NICU. Rest up for a bit, then see how you feel." She looked directly at both her friends. "I'm sorry I can't give you a definitive answer about Jess's future, but as I've said, anything that can be done will be done. We'll be seeing a lot of each other in the next few weeks, but now I have to catch a couple of hours of sleep before rounds." She kissed their cheeks, hugged Robin, then left with her entourage.

They sat in silence for a while. "We can do this, Robin. She's your daughter, she's strong, she'll make it."

"I'm sorry I was such a wimp earlier, but seeing her like that was a shock. She's ours, Lily, and though I want her to be okay, we'll love her no matter the problems."

Lily smiled. "I never thought I'd be happy to be married to a billionaire. We'll be able to take care of her, whatever her needs. Take me to see her, Robin."

"Nicole said to rest for a few hours. Are you sure you're up to it?"

"I won't rest until I've seen her. What if something happens to her before I…"

"Okay."

Lily swiped at her eyes. "Sorry, I guess I'm emotional. Give me a hand getting up, I'm a little sore."

They asked the nurse for directions, and arm and arm they headed down the hall, Robin slowing her pace and supporting Lily. When they reached the double doors, they rang the bell and waited. A nurse opened the door, checked their wristbands and escorted them in. The bubbling, bleeping, binging from all the equipment, the crying of the babies and the bustle of the conversations of parents, nurses, doctors and other medical staff moving around the room hit them like a bucket of cold water. It was far from the hushed atmosphere they'd anticipated.

"The first time is always a shock. You'll get used to it. Come this way so I can get you into gowns and show you how to scrub in." The nurse smiled. "I'm Connie, by the way."

After a lesson on how to scrub their hands and arms for a full three minutes, they put on the gowns and the nurse led them through the room, explaining what they were seeing. "Once babies are stabilized, they're transferred to one of these large plexiglass boxes, called isolettes or incubators, to protect them from temperature fluctuations in the room."

As they walked, Lily realized Jess was not the only baby needing help. There was box after box with babies so tiny they looked like they couldn't possibly be real, and every one of them was hooked up to machines with wires and tubes and IVs. Some of the incubators were decorated and all of them had blankets draped over the top. "Who decorated these? And why are they covered?"

"As the babies become more aware, some families decorate, others don't. We cover them to protect their eyes from the lights."

At last they reached a box that said Jess DiLuca, Lily swayed but couldn't take her eyes off this tiny creature that was her daughter. Robin's arms tightened around her. No wonder Robin was freaked out. Connected to machines and monitors, their fragile girl looked like a tiny animal in a laboratory experiment. As Robin had described, her veins showed through translucent skin. She really could pass for an alien or a spider with her long legs and arms. Maybe she would be tall, like Robin. Her eyes were sealed and the hair did look like fur.

"Jess," she whispered, "your mamas are here. Everything is going to be all right, baby girl. You concentrate on growing. We'll do the worrying."

Robin helped Lily into the chair the nurse brought over. She pointed to the isolette. "What are those two holes for?"

"That's so we can reach the babies for treatments and diaper changes and whatever we need to do to them. If we need total access to the baby, we can unhinge that wall." She indicated the far wall of Jess's isolette. "You know you can't hold her yet, right?"

Lily nodded. "How long before we can?"

"That's up to her, but it will happen. Until then, get a small soft toy and sleep with it a few nights, then we'll put it in the isolette with her to familiarize her with your smell. Your husband can do the same."

"Wife, not husband. Robin is her other mother."

She smiled at Robin. "You too, then. It will comfort her. And while you're here talk to her or if you're so inclined sing, but no belting allowed." She grinned.

"Can we touch her?"

"Yes. Let me show you how. Place your hands like this and use a firm touch. Her skin is very thin, so don't rub, it will hurt."

Lily put her hand through the portal and placed it on Jess's tiny legs. She felt a surge of love followed by a flash of terror as the reality of her fragility hit home. This was her daughter. She'd lived in her body more than five months and she would love her no matter what, if only she lived. A sob escaped. Robin put her arms around her.

"It's hard, I know," the nurse said. "I'm sure your dreams about having her didn't include any of this," she waved a hand at the NICU, "but we're going to do our best for her and hopefully in a few months, she'll be at home with her two moms. Come, Robin, touch her like this." She guided Robin's hands into the box, then withdrew hers. "Some babies like to be rocked." She showed them how to gently rock the incubator. "Stop if she cries or seems uncomfortable. You can stay as long as you like, but remember, you're here for the long haul so get some rest."

They stayed about an hour talking softly to Jess, then Robin could see Lily fading and she insisted they go back to her room. Robin stretched out next to Lily and they talked quietly, dozing off and on. Nurses bustled in from time to time to check Lily's vitals, help her pump and escort her to the bathroom. Every couple of hours they visited Jess for an hour. In between they had lunch and dinner and napped.

It was getting late, and Lily encouraged Robin to go home and get some sleep.

Robin wanted to stay. "I don't know if I can sleep without you in bed."

"Try. You'll sleep better at home. We're going to need our strength."

Finally, Robin stood and stretched. "Okay, you get some sleep too. I'll be back early." She kissed Lily. "Sleep well."

CHAPTER THIRTY-TWO

One Hundred Five Days

When the nurse woke her at four in the morning so she could pump her breasts, Lily bolted up, fear clenching her heart and making it difficult to breathe. "Has something happened to my baby?"

"What?" The nurse seemed confused. "No. I'm here to help you pump. She needs your milk."

Now she was anxious and needed to see her daughter. "Can you help me to the NICU so I can see my baby?"

The nurse hesitated. "I'm not sure if you should—"

"Please." Her eyes filled with tears. "I really need to be there for her."

"Let's pump your breasts, then I'll see." Once again the little milk that came out hardly seemed worth the effort, but the nurse seem satisfied. "Don't worry, it takes some time to start flowing. Give me a second." She left the room with the milk.

It took a few minutes, but she came back smiling. "I'll take you and leave you there, and when you're ready to come back, you can ask one of the nurses to call the desk, and someone will come get you." She helped Lily swing her legs to the side of the bed, then stand. She hadn't expected to still feel so exhausted. Jess was so small so she hadn't needed stitches, but she was sorer now than earlier and it hurt to walk. The nurse noticed her grimace as she stood.

"Are you sure you don't want to rest a little more?"

"Definitely."

Lily took the arm the nurse offered.

It felt this time like they were on a five-mile hike, but she pushed on despite the discomfort until the nurse stopped. "I know you're anxious to get there, but you're going to wear yourself out. Let's slow down." After that, they inched along until they were outside the NICU. The nurse pressed the buzzer.

It was only a minute or two before a NICU nurse let her in. The noise slammed her again. There was no sense here that it was the middle of the night. The nurse introduced herself as Tina and took her arm. "Did anyone show you how to wash?" She led her to the sinks.

"Yes, earlier."

Tina watched her wash and nodded her approval before handing her a gown and walking with her to Jess's incubator. "Has anyone showed you how to touch her?"

"Yes."

"Good. You know you can't hold her yet, right?"

Lily nodded.

She patted Lily's shoulder. "I'll be sure to keep an eye on Jess for you. I need to check my other babies now, but let me know when you want to go back to your room." Tina pulled a chair close to Jess, helped Lily sit and then left them alone.

The urge to hold her daughter was overwhelming, but touching her would have to do for now, so she put her hand on Jess's leg and began to talk. She told Jess about her other mom, her grandmas, her aunt and uncle through blood and her honorary aunts and uncles through love and friendship. She talked until her throat was raspy.

She sat back and closed her eyes to rest for a minute. A kiss on the forehead woke her. She opened her eyes and smiled at Robin standing over her. She was surprised to find herself reclining. It took a few seconds to remember where she was, and her eyes shot over to Jess who seemed to be sleeping, then back to Robin.

"She's fine, Lily. The nurse, Tina, said your touch seemed to calm Jess so it was good you sat with her. She also told me you've been here since about four and when you fell asleep, she pushed the chair into the reclining position. Are you okay?"

"A little groggy. How did you sleep, Robin?"

"I missed you in bed." She rubbed her eyes. "And I had weird dreams about babies."

"I know." She waved an arm indicating all the boxes. "It feels a little like being in a science fiction movie, doesn't it?" She yawned. "What time is it?"

"Six. Come on, they want you back in your room to wash, eat, and pump. We'll come back after breakfast."

"Did my touch really calm her?" Her eyes filled with tears. "I'm not much good at this mothering thing. So far there's only a few drops of milk when I pump. The nurses keep telling me it's normal, but I feel like a failure."

Robin helped her up and held her. "I noticed yesterday, so I asked Nicole about it and she said not to worry. It takes four or five days to get going. She said even a few drops are helpful for the baby. Try not to stress, Lily, that will make it harder."

They spent most of the day with Jess, getting familiar with the workings of the NICU, touching and talking to their daughter. Robin had bought some children's books so they read her stories. Robin talked about her life at Harvard and Stanford and Lily told stories from her childhood. In between, they walked the halls and hung out in Lily's room. They talked to other mothers and fathers in the NICU during the day and again in the evening. One mother suggested Lily keep a journal describing her feelings and what was happening so she asked Robin to bring her a notebook and some colored pens and pencils.

The evening nurse reminded them about bringing small soft toys to put in the isolette so Robin went down to the gift shop and came back with a stuffed animal for each of them to sleep with, two journals, and a variety of pens and colored pencils. At ten that night, Lily sent Robin home, tucked the soft toy between her breasts, then went back to the NICU to sit beside Jess and tell her again about her family and friends. She chatted with another mother who said she'd read a suggestion to take a picture every day to record the baby's progress visually, so she called Robin and asked her to bring her small camera in the morning.

Later she picked up one of the notebooks to begin recording Jess's history so she'd know about her early life even though she wouldn't remember it.

Day One

Your birthday, Jess, and your moms were thrilled to see you even though you showed up more than three months early. You were quite a sight at one pound three ounces.

Lily described their first day in the NICU in detail, wanting Jess to understand how happy they were to have her.

Day Two

At four a.m. this morning I got a nurse to bring me here, because I missed you and didn't want you to be lonely.

My poor baby alone in the incubator hooked up to so many machines, I wanted so badly to hold you and comfort you but you are too fragile for that right now. So I had to be content with touching you through the portal of the incubator. I hope you enjoy it as much as I do. Dad (Robin) and I spent the day with you today, reading from the storybooks she bought for you and telling you about your family. We are so happy you are with us. We love you and pray you fight hard to grow and get strong.

Nicole released Lily from the hospital the next morning.

Day Three

Well, Jess, Mama Lily is no longer a patient in this hospital like you but dad (Robin) and I have decided to not leave you alone while you're here, so we'll be sleeping in a room near your incubator and one of us can be with you almost twenty-four hours every day to read to you and talk to you. The nurses promise we might be able to change your diaper soon.

Day Five

The noise in the NICU is enough to make a person crazy. And you babies have this little trick you play on parents and NICU staff. When one of your alarms goes off to signal a problem like a heart stopped, one at a time all your alarms go off until the entire room is filled with ringing alarms. That just enhances the terror your mamas face every single day that our Jess might not make it, that we'll be the parents crying over you, dead before you even had a chance to live. Mamas become experts on all the medical conditions that might kill you and all the terrible things that can be wrong with you if you live. But we are hopeful because you are a fighter.

Day Nine

It's just you and me babe. Mama Robin was unable to sleep in the hospital , so I insisted she go home about ten p.m. and come back at seven or eight in the morning to spend the day with us. I don't know that she's sleeping so well at home either, but it's easier for her to be restless at home than in our small room here in hospital. She worries about you as I do. You haven't had any serious problems this week and for that we're thankful, but it is stressful sitting here watching you and trying to communicate with you while you mostly sleep. At least we think you're sleeping, but your eyes aren't open yet so we can only guess by your reaction to things. We touch you a lot and we think you smell us on your stuffed animals. We feel good because we think you react to our voices.

Day Eleven

The incessant noise, the banging and clanging and ringing and the crying of mothers whose babies have died, these things alone are enough to make a mother feel crazy. Add to it the constant fear that you won't survive, Jess, and life in the NICU is excruciatingly stressful. Every day I wake up not knowing what to expect. A routine morning like this one changes quickly into a terror-filled day, filled with emergency surgery and blood transfusions.

Thank God Robin was with us this morning when the alarms on your incubator started ringing and suddenly there was blood all over everything. You looked like you'd been shot. I was screaming, Robin was calling for help. The nurse and other medical staff responded immediately and somehow your aunt Nicole was there in an instant. She rushed you into surgery and fixed the blood-vessel tumor, known as a hemangioma, which had exploded and caused you to lose 20% of your blood. When you returned to your incubator, you were pale and had extra IVs stuck in your tiny arms. I don't know how they even find those minute veins. Auntie Nicole says not to worry, you are a fighter and you'll get past this. Oh, God, I wish I could take your place my sweet baby. Love, Mama Lily.

Day Fifteen

You are doing well, your color is back and you have gained a little weight. I can't wait for you to open your eyes so I can see if they are green like dad's. I have a feeling you are going to be beautiful like her. You jerk and twitch a lot but other than that you don't move much.

I must be getting used to this place because I barely notice the noise any more and it feels like home. Well, not quite, but I'm comfortable and I know all the wonderful nurses and they know me and I enjoy talking to you. I wonder if you'll have any memory of any of this.

Day Twenty-Seven

You are doing well and continue to gain weight. You now have the loveliest eyebrows and eyelashes and occasionally blink and open your eyes but I don't think you can focus yet. Alas it's still too early to tell whether you have your dad's eyes.

Happily your heart is good and your aunt Nicole says you are doing really well.

CHAPTER THIRTY-THREE

Robin's Nightmares

Robin paced the living room. Another nightmare. They seemed to be coming more frequently. At first they were sporadic. Now the minute she dropped off to sleep, she slipped into a version of the same nightmare. And this evening in the NICU, an image from the nightmare flashed through her mind, and she'd staggered back, afraid of what she might do. Lily hadn't noticed but had been her usual loving self and encouraged her to go home when she claimed to be tired.

Hoping to exhaust herself enough to sleep without dreaming, she'd walked the seven miles from the hospital. Well, that plan was a bust. She had fallen right to sleep, but the nightmare came, as usual, soon after. She shivered. Her T-shirt and pajama bottoms were soaked with sweat. A hot shower would relax her.

Under the steaming water, the image that had flashed in the NICU flashed again, taking her breath away. The debilitating fear she'd experienced in the NICU as she imagined herself picking up Jess hit her again and weakened her knees. She shivered, braced herself against the shower wall and sobbed. Her tears mixed with the water streaming over her. Twice in one day her nightmare images had come into her mind while she was awake. What if she acted on them?

Filled with fear and guilt, she dragged herself from the shower and dried off. A normal person wouldn't have these terrible thoughts of hurting her child. And herself. Or was it Lily? It was hard to tell. She flushed with shame.

Maybe it was because Jess was still so small and the NICU was such a scary place. Maybe as she grew into a regular baby the dreams would stop. Maybe once they were home she would be able to relax and enjoy their child. But the impulse to follow through on that fantasy was so strong that she'd had to pull herself away from the isolette. For now, she didn't trust herself and she would avoid the NICU.

Every night she considered confiding in Lily or Katie or Nicole. But the thought of seeing fear and loathing in their eyes scared her. If they saw her as the monster she was, she would lose everything and everybody that made her life worth living. She would kill herself before hurting Lily or Jess.

She collapsed on the bathroom floor, wrapped her arms around herself and rocked. Was she having a breakdown? She had no memory of her childhood. Had she done some terrible thing as a child? Had she been one of those child murderers? Was she crazy?

CHAPTER THIRTY-FOUR

NICU

As the weeks passed, they maintained the same schedule. Robin going home at ten to sleep, then returning at seven in the morning with clean clothes for Lily. They would eat breakfast and lunch in the cafeteria except when Robin had something special sent in, but Robin insisted they go out for dinner each night. Twice during that time Robin convinced her to come home to sleep, but between waking up to pump and calling the NICU a couple of times during the night to check on Jess, she didn't get any more rest than she did at the hospital. And neither did Robin. Whenever Lily opened her eyes, Robin was either awake in the living room reading or out for a walk, no matter the time. As they neared the end of their fifth week in the NICU, Robin looked exhausted and seemed jumpy and anxious. Whenever Lily asked, she got the same answer. "I'm worried about Jess and you." She wondered if her not sleeping at home was making Robin nervous. "Would it be better if I came home to sleep every night?"

"No. I miss you, but I want you to stay with Jess."

"You look like you haven't slept in days." She rubbed Robin's arm. "Maybe you should go back to work. The noise in this place is enough to make anyone bonkers and just sitting around is not your strong suit. How about you work during the day, have dinner with me, hang out for an hour or two, then go home to sleep? No need for both of us to keep watch and I can call you immediately if there's any change."

"You'd be okay with that? I don't want you to feel like I'm abandoning you…and her."

Day Thirty-Seven

You're getting bigger and stronger everyday my beautiful little girl. You are still small but you are starting to look like a baby.

We started skin-to-skin care today for the first time. Although we could only do it for a couple of minutes today, it is so wonderful to feel you on my chest, feel you breathe, have your perfect little hand with your perfect little nails grasp my finger. The joy of it is hard to describe. Grandma Del was here again today and Grandma Cordy will come tomorrow for her visit as usual. Soon your grandmas will be able to do skin-to-skin care with you and they are so excited. Keep up the good work sweetie.

Day Fifty-Six

You are moving and stretching more than jerking or twitching and they tell me it means your muscle tone is getting better. And you are starting to be more alert. In fact, we think you wake up and are attentive when you hear my voice.

Today was exciting because you turned when I touched your cheek. Auntie Nicole says they call this the rooting reflex and it might mean you'll be ready to breast-feed soon.

Jess continued to do well, gaining weight, looking more like a human baby, responding to touch and sound. But the new schedule didn't seem to make a difference for Robin. She continued to lose weight and the deep dark circles under her eyes telegraphed the fact that she wasn't sleeping. Though Robin picked Lily up for dinner, she pled exhaustion to avoid coming up to the NICU. On the rare occasion she did visit the NICU, she refused skin-to-skin time, which had gone from less than a minute to hours at a time, and she rarely even looked at Jess. Robin insisted there would be plenty of time for her to get acquainted with Jess later, when she came home. Lily was seriously worried about her not bonding with their daughter. She called Katie and asked her to come to the hospital for lunch.

Katie came that same day. She spent a half hour in the NICU with Lily and Jess, and then they went out to lunch. After they ordered, Lily looked across the table. "I'm worried about Robin. She's not eating, she's not sleeping, she rarely comes to the NICU and when she does she avoids looking at Jess and refuses to hold or touch her. I thought it was because I wasn't home with her, but on the nights I do sleep at home she's withdrawn, has no interest in making love and either wakes up screaming from a nightmare or sits up all night watching TV. She won't talk about what's bothering her, and I'm scared to death I'm losing her." She burst into tears.

Katie reached across the table for Lily's hands. "Jan and I have noticed the changes, but we assumed she was spending a lot of time in the NICU and that the changes were due to the stress. She won't talk to either of us about what's bothering her. She's rarely in the office a full day. Mostly she comes in for a few hours at night when no one but the support people are around. She does keep up with work, but she leaves notes for everyone and doesn't answer her cell, even for me. If she's not here with you, what do you suppose she's doing?"

"I was hoping she'd confided in you."

"Do you think she's having an affair?"

Lily shook her head. "Absolutely not. She's suffering. She seems troubled. She wakes up screaming and crying, dripping in sweat. I'm afraid she's having a breakdown of some sort. Do you know if there is any kind of mental illness in her family?"

"She's never mentioned it, but she knows very little about her family."

Lily pushed her lunch aside. "I've suggested she see a therapist to discuss what's bothering her, but she says it's nothing, she's fine. She's always been able to talk to you, Katie. Could you try to help her? Or at least get her into therapy?"

Day Sixty-Six

Aunt Katie came to visit today and she says you look wonderful. I agree. She's carrying your cousin who is scheduled to be born in about four months. We talked about how nice it will be when you two can play together.

Day Seventy-Two
Our first day of breastfeeding, Jess. I hope it was as wonderful for you as it was for your mama Lily.

Day Ninety-Eight
One more ounce, my darling daughter, and you'll be able to come home with me, away from the noise and the alarms and the hospital. I look forward to having you home with me and Dad so you two can get to know each other better.

Because you are still small and have issues and we have to be careful that you don't get sick, we'll have a full-time nurse there with us, but at least all these machines and the incessant sound will be gone. Eat lots, my love.

Day One Hundred Four
Sleep well tonight. Tomorrow we go home. You made it, my brave, strong baby, and tomorrow we begin a new phase of your life and ours as the family we envisioned when we decided we wanted you. I can't wait.

CHAPTER THIRTY-FIVE

The Breakup

What did it say about their relationship that they'd learned to yell? In whispers. As Robin made her escape, Lily listened to the soft click of the front door, followed by keys turning in the two locks, the rattle of the elevator doors sliding shut, then silence. No screaming, no tears, no dramatic slamming of doors.

She regretted asking Robin to feed Jess, trying to force a connection that should be natural. She put down the bottle Robin had pushed into her hand before fleeing, unbuttoned her shirt and offered Jess her breast. As she rocked, Jess found her rhythm. The relationship was killing Robin. Well, not their relationship. Lily knew Robin loved her, cherished her even. It was her relationship with the baby or rather the lack of relationship.

Jess had been home a month and Robin was still struggling. She wouldn't look at the fragile baby, wouldn't hold or even touch her and was being torn apart by her overwhelming guilt about it. Everything Lily loved about Robin—her playfulness, her spontaneity, her love of adventure and fun and laughter—was being squeezed out of her by the internal battle she was fighting.

Occasionally at night in bed her sexy, loving, playful Robin was present, but most nights Lily was so exhausted she dropped off to sleep the minute she put her head down. Actually, Robin was rarely in bed, often spending the night in the office. Working, she said.

The tears ran freely as she nursed, tears for what she knew was coming, for the loss of the love of her life. Robin wouldn't ask her to choose, but she loved her too much to watch her suffer. Like a bird trapped in a glass house, Robin would only survive if she set her free.

She changed Jess and put her in the crib, then climbed into bed where she finally succumbed to the sobs that had been threatening since Robin stormed out. She cried herself to sleep.

* * *

Robin strode out of the building, her face red with shame, barely able to hold back the sobs until she was alone on the walkway along the river. What a fucking coward. She couldn't give up her Lily, but the nightmares and the images that constantly popped into her mind whenever she let her guard down petrified her. Was she going crazy? She wished she could talk to Katie. But if Katie saw her as the monster she was, she might lose her, and the loss of both Lily and Katie would surely kill her.

If she stayed, she might harm their little girl, but even if she continued to control herself, Lily would be caught in the middle between her and the baby and would end up hating her. The thought of gentle, loving Lily hating her brought bile to her mouth. She couldn't do that to Lily or herself. Besides, what kind of a mother could she be, unable to even look at, much less hold her daughter? Even selfish Robin DiLuca wouldn't subject a child to live with that. She had to be the strong one and leave her soul mate and the baby—for their own safety.

She turned and started walking with no destination in mind, just to keep moving, to give herself time to think it through, to gather her strength.

* * *

The digital clock read five-seventeen a.m. when Robin slipped into bed. Lily rolled over on top of her and kissed her. Robin's cheeks were wet, her body convulsed as a sob escaped.

Robin wrapped her arms around Lily. "I can't do this, Lily," she whispered, through her sobs. "I love you so much, but I feel like I'm dying."

"I know, sweetheart. Talk to me, please." Her kiss ignited their passion, and they made love, first wild and desperate and later tender.

In the morning, Robin dressed for work and came into the kitchen. Lily poured her a cup of coffee. Robin thanked her but couldn't meet her eyes.

Lily wrapped her arms around Robin from behind. "I'd like to understand. Can we talk about what's wrong?"

Swiping at her tears, Robin shook her head.

Lily knew she was going to have to be the brave one. She turned Robin and pulled her into a tight embrace. "It's all right, love. We'll work it out tonight." She kissed her temple.

Robin's arms tightened. "I love you." She separated from Lily, took a deep breath and headed for the door. "See you later. I hope…" she glanced at the baby carrier on the table, "she's okay today." And she was gone again.

Lily sighed. Robin couldn't even say Jess's name. *Poor baby. We promised you two adoring moms and now you're stuck with just me, an exhausted, about to be single, broken-hearted woman.* She blew her nose, dabbed her tears, then grabbed a pen and a pad and sat at the table with her coffee to make a list.

In the early afternoon, Robin texted Lily to tell her not to bother with dinner, she would pick up something.

They sat in silence, their tear-filled eyes meeting over the table, neither eating much. Lily was having a hard time swallowing and pushed her plate aside. Robin moved behind Lily and put her arms around her. "You have to eat, hon, for you and for the baby. I can't leave if I have to worry about you."

Lily leaned back. "I promise not to be a drama queen, but I'm really not hungry now."

Robin laughed, a beautiful sound Lily hadn't heard for months. "Good. I'd hate to think you were going to compete with me for the drama queen role, my beauty." She kissed the top of Lily's head.

"Flatterer. Stringy hair, dripping breasts and leftover baby fat a beauty do not make."

Robin sat again. Her eyes met Lily's. "You always look beautiful to me." Her voice broke. She looked down. "I don't know if I can do this."

Lily reached across the table and patted Robin's hand. "Let's talk." She pulled a sheet of paper out of her pocket and smoothed it on the table. "I made a list." She cleared her throat.

Robin put a hand up. "Let me start. I'll continue to support you and, and, um, the baby. I'll deposit money in our joint checking account every month, so you'll only have to ask if anything unusual comes up." She held Lily's gaze. "This is one promise I can keep, and it's not up for discussion."

Lily nodded. Their medical expenses were astronomical. Not that she doubted Robin would do anything different.

"Second, you stay here in the Battery Park City apartment, with the nurse, the housekeeper, use of Tanya and the car and whatever else you need, and I'll find another apartment. Third, no divorce."

"No divorce? I thought—"

"I can't promise I won't sleep with anyone and I won't ask you to promise either, but you're my wife until you say different or I feel different. Okay?"

Lily nodded through her tears. "I love you so much, Robin." She kissed Robin's palm.

Robin sniffed. "Those are things I thought of. Even if I can't be here, I want to take care of you." She swiped at her tears. "What have you got?"

Lily looked down at her list. "I'm comfortable caring for Jess myself now. But I'd like to have a nurse available some days or parts of days so I can focus on writing."

"You know whatever you want or need is fine with me. Arrange it with the service and include the cost in your estimated monthly expenses."

"Right. One of the benefits of being married to a billionaire." Their long-running joke. She raised her eyes and smiled at Robin. "This apartment will be too big for just me and Jess. My tenants are leaving in two months, and I'd rather go back to my apartment on Central Park West. You can stay here."

Robin squeezed the bridge of her nose, thinking. "It's too big for me too. I'll move into a hotel while I look for something smaller and sell it after you move out." She swiped at her eyes. "Anything else?"

"Do you have the contract?"

"You know I always carry it with me."

"Can I have it for a minute?"

Robin opened her wallet, removed the creased paper and handed it to Lily, a questioning look on her face.

Lily smoothed the paper. And read it. She picked up her pen and added a short sentence just above her signature.

> *I, Lily Boudreaux Carlyle Alexander, promise that should Robin DiLuca and I decide at any time for any reason to terminate our relationship whatever it's nature and no matter how long we've been together, I will let her go without screaming and crying and accusations and hurtful language. I also promise that I will cherish whatever time we do have together, strive to make it fun and mentally and physically fulfilling and that forever after I will remain her friend.*
> *No one but you, forever*
> *Lily*

Lily handed the contract back to Robin and she read aloud. "No one but you, forever." She folded the paper and returned it to her wallet, then covered Lily's hand. "Me, too, Lily. I promise I will work this out and come back to you."

Lily took a deep breath. "This is the hardest Robin, but I think we need to make a clean break, not see each other for at least a year, maybe more."

Robin gasped and pulled away.

"It's not punishment, Robin. I don't think I could bear to be with you and then watch you walk out of my life again and again. I need to separate so I can get on with my life and Jess's. If you want to see Jess on some kind of schedule we can ask the mamas to be the intermediary."

Robin jumped up and began to pace. "No, no. I can't."

"You really don't want to see your daughter?" She knew she was pushing it, but she wanted Robin to think about what she was losing by leaving.

"You're the one I have to see, Lily."

"It would be too painful for me."

Robin took Lily in her arms. "I'll try to stay away." She inhaled. Even mixed with the smell of baby powder and milky breasts, Lily's fragrance was tantalizing. She looked at the baby in the carrier on the table, her daughter whether she liked it or not.

Lily followed her gaze. "She's your daughter, more than mine. Remember, you're her dad."

"No, I don't want to see her. That's the point." Robin broke down. "I'm so sorry, Lily, so sorry."

"Why?" Part of her wanted to comfort Robin, the other part wanted to smack her. "Please tell me why you can't see her? She's just an innocent baby. Is it because she might be impaired in some way?"

"No. No. Not that. I just can't. Someday you'll understand."

"Why can't you tell me now?"

Robin shook her head. "Maybe when she's older. Will you tell her about her dad?"

"I don't know, Robin."

"It's not important. You're who's important to me."

"Apparently not so important that you'll tell me what's going on, why you're abandoning us." The anger in her voice shocked Lily, and Robin recoiled as if she'd struck her. She was trying to honor the contract she'd written the night they met, but she was hurt and scared. She took a breath. "Sorry. The last item on my list is telling people. I'd like for us to tell the mamas together, if that's all right with you. And shouldn't we do the same for our closest friends?"

Robin looked miserable, but she nodded. "I agree. We owe it to the mamas. And our nearest and dearest friends." She thought a moment. "Then maybe we could have a brunch and invite the rest of our friends, let them know too."

They began to put the plan in motion. The next day Lily spoke to her tenants and found they would be happy to get out of their lease a month early, so they put their apartment up for sale and Robin began to look for an apartment of her own.

Three days later the mamas came over for dinner. They planned to wait until after they'd eaten to talk, but Lily and Robin were so nervous that Del handed the baby to Cordy, put an arm around each of them and asked gently. "What's wrong?"

Clinging to Del and each other, they cried. When they calmed down, Del led them into the living room. They clung together and collapsed on the sofa. Del and Cordy sat facing them.

Robin looked at Lily, then at the mamas. "I'm leaving Lily." A sob escaped. "I have...issues. But I hope to come back."

There was a stunned silence, then Cordy cleared her throat. "Is there someone else?"

"No. I'm in love with Lily. There's no one else."

Cordy turned her attention to Lily. "And you?"

"No one else. I'm in love with Robin." She kissed Robin's temple.

"Then why?"

Robin wiped her eyes. "I can't be with Lily and," her eyes went to Jess snuggled in Cordy's arms, "the baby right now. I have issues I need to work out."

"What issues? Can we help?"

"I can't talk about it." She sniffed. "You can help by," she broke down, "by not abandoning me. I need you both to love me even if you don't understand."

Cordy stood and handed Jess to Lily, then pulled Robin up into her arms. Del wrapped her arms around Lily and Jess. As Robin sobbed, Cordy rubbed her back. "We love you like a daughter, so there's no abandoning you. But I don't understand why you need to separate while you work it out."

"It's what we have to do, Mama. And we need the separation to be complete. So we're asking you and all of our friends to not mention Robin to me or me or Jess to Robin. I know it's hard to understand, but please trust it's what we need."

Robin cleared her throat. "One more thing, when I visit, would you put away all pictures of us and the baby?"

Cordy let go of Robin and stepped back. "I don't like this at all, Robin. We trusted you. What happened to your promise to never do to Lily what Micki did? And whatever happened to your promise of commitment forever to Lily?"

Cordy rarely got angry, so it was intimidating to watch her pace furiously, hands fisted at her side, her voice hard and loud.

Robin swallowed. "I love Lily and I am committed to her forever. I just can't be with her now."

Cordy stood face to face with Robin. "So what? Is she supposed to put her life on hold while you go off and do God knows what?" Her voice was getting louder.

Lily stood with Jess in her arms and moved between them. "Please calm down, Mama. Robin and I have worked this out. Getting angry with her won't change anything."

Cordy turned to Del. "I'm not very hungry. Let's go."

"Just a minute, Cordy." Del stood and wrapped her arms around Lily. "Do you want us to stay, Lily?"

"No, Mama, we're good."

Del turned, hugged Robin, then kissed her forehead. She had tears in her eyes. "I wish I understood, but we're here whenever you're ready to talk."

Lily walked the mamas to the door, then sat next to Robin on the sofa. Robin swiped at her tears. "That went well. Or as well as could be expected, I guess."

"It's a shock. I expected Del to blow up, not Cordy. But she loves and respects you and I think she must feel betrayed in a way."

They'd thought speaking to their closest friends would be easier than the mamas but, in some ways, it was harder.

Katie burst into tears. "Talk to me, Rob. Let me help you through this. Don't run away." She sobbed. Michael put his arm around her.

Emma leapt out of her chair and circled Robin, smacking her shoulder with every word. "Dammit, Robin, talk to us. How can you do this to Lily and Jess?" Her voice broke on a sob. "And us."

Jan sat in stunned silence, tears creating black streaks on her face.

Annie held Lily's hand. "I'm so sorry." She said it so softly only Lily heard.

"Is it Jess? It looks to me like she's going to be fine, but we'll…" Nichole indicated her soon-to-be wife Nora and the others in the room, "help you through whatever happens. Don't do this, Rob."

White-faced, Robin stood stoically, letting them express the anger and the hurt. She didn't speak until they had exhausted their pleas and huddled together dispiritedly. "I know it's a shock. And I'm sorry I can't explain it. I love Lily," she looked at her friends, "and all of you, but I have to be alone for a while."

In the end, they agreed to abide by the rules that Robin and Lily had set down.

The third round of telling was easier. Their closest friends came to support them at the brunch to announce their breakup to the others in their circle.

After everyone had eaten and they were socializing, Lily and Robin stood and Lily clinked a knife on a glass. The chatter stopped. "Robin and I have something to share with you." Lily took a deep breath. "We're separating." She waited, giving their friends time to absorb what she'd said. "It's amicable and a mutual decision. We don't want you to feel you have to take sides, but we do ask you to avoid inviting us to the same events and to avoid talking to Robin about me and Jess or talking to me about Robin for at least a year."

The shocked silence was followed by expressions of sorrow, but no one pressed for reasons. Within fifteen minutes, Lily and Robin were alone except for the two women hired to serve and cleanup the brunch. Lily sat in the rocker in the bedroom feeding Jess and Robin went for a walk.

It took another month for them to finally separate. Lily and Jess moved into her large sunny apartment in the building overlooking Central Park. Robin rented a loft in Tribeca, and there was a buyers' bidding war for their apartment in Battery Park City. All the financial arrangements were in place. Jan agreed to act as the intermediary so they wouldn't have to talk to each other.

And that was that.

CHAPTER THIRTY-SIX

Separation

Breaking up is easy. But if you're still deeply in love with each other surviving the breakup is hard. Lily felt as if Robin had died. But she hadn't. She'd chosen to leave. The emptiness of life without Robin was unimaginable. Although Robin's playful and fun side had been in short supply during the stress and turmoil of the last few months, her love and gentleness had always wrapped Lily in a warm blanket of security. Without that comfort, Lily drifted in a fog of grief and longing, unable to write or focus on anything. Other than responding to Jess's demands to be fed, she left her care to the live-in nurse. She lay on the sofa and watched reruns of programs like *Castle, Bones* and *Law and Order*. She tried to forget. But though her heart was broken, her mind was whole and cluttered with memories it wanted to share.

They let her wallow in her pain for ten days, then strong hands pulled her into a sitting position and shook her. She assumed it was the nurse, who had been manhandling her, shoving Jess into her arms and pulling Jess away from her, annoying the hell out of her. But when she forced her eyes open it wasn't the nurse but Cordy on her knees and Del hovering just behind, their eyes filled with compassion. And pain. She struggled to come back from the memories she'd been watching in rerun. From a distance she felt Del brush the hair off her forehead. "Come, Lily baby, time for you to take a shower."

Her sweatpants, actually Robin's, were too long, and she tripped as her mamas led her into the bathroom. Cordy braced her as Del stripped off her sweatpants and T-shirt, then Cordy helped her into the shower. Under the hot water, with Cordy's hands on her waist, she struggled to emerge from the haze. After fifteen minutes she felt able to stand on her own. She peeled Cordy's hands off. "I can be on my own, Mama. I'm going to wash and then shampoo my hair. I'll be out in a while."

Cordy stepped back but remained in the bathroom, watching.

Lily sniffed. How pathetic. She smelled. Squeezing gel on her body, she methodically cleaned herself, then applied shampoo and did the same with her hair. She kept her back to Cordy so she wouldn't see her tears. Robin loved this rosemary shampoo and used to bury her face in Lily's hair and inhale. Frequently, it ended in their making love. The tears flowed as she massaged in the rosemary conditioner. They'd made love often in their last few weeks together. It had been tender and loving and sad.

"Time to finish up, Lily."

She should have known she couldn't fool Cordy. "Coming."

Cordy wrapped her in a towel and held her close. She whispered. "Be brave for Jess, my sweet girl. Your pain won't go away, but it will get better. Jess has only one mama now and she needs you to be present."

Lily used the towel to dry her tears. "I'll try, Mama. It's just…I feel so alone without Robin."

"You're not alone, Lily. It's not the same, but you're surrounded by love. Your mamas and your friends are here. We want to take care of you. Don't leave us and Jess."

The pain in Cordy's face shocked Lily. Cordy was the rational one, the one who rarely showed a lot of emotion. Lily stroked Cordy's face. "I'll try, Mama. I swear I'll try."

For the next two months, Lily was not alone. Her mamas discharged the nurse and moved in with her so she had company day and night, and if one of them couldn't be there during the day, Annie or Emma or Nicole or another friend was recruited. They helped her with Jess, held her when she cried, hugged her when she was down and soothed her when she was agitated. Initially, Lily felt like a fish in an aquarium, separated from everyone by a glass wall that only she knew was there, a wall that prevented them from seeing and hearing the memories on continuous play in the background of her mind.

Only Jess penetrated the wall. Her beautiful green eyes so like Robin's followed Lily's every move and whether she was nursing or eating or sitting quietly, she demanded Lily's full attention. And though she couldn't actually speak, she looked Lily in the eye and chatted constantly, obviously trying to talk.

Her first word came one evening when Lily was reading her a bedtime story. The mamas and Lily stared wide-eyed at each other. When Lily laughed and hugged her, Jess giggled, wriggled her fanny, waved her arms and repeated the word. "Book, book, book." The "k" wasn't quite there yet, but there was no doubt she was saying "book."

It seemed like a miracle. In the five and a half months since Jess had been home from the hospital she had been tested for everything they could possibly test for, including deafness, blindness and neurological problems, and they had found no indicators of serious deficits. But this early speech seemed to indicate that not only had she been spared but that she was exceptional. Like her mother. Enchanted, Lily increased her reading time. The more she read, the more excited Jess got when she saw the books come out. Soon Jess was pushing books away when they didn't interest her and nodding her approval at others.

But the mamas were concerned that Lily showed little interest in anything other than Jess, and they gently encouraged her to get back to work. Del, of course, was more direct than Cordy. "I don't care what it is, darlin', write what you're feeling, start a novel or a short story or an essay, just put your butt in the chair and write. I'll entertain Jess. Or should I say, she'll entertain me?"

She tried. Every day for almost three weeks she went into her office, turned on the computer and sat in front of a blank screen, unable to think, unable to find words, any words. Then one day her mind wandered to how like Robin Jess appeared to be, and suddenly she felt an overwhelming urge to share Jess's phenomenal intellectual growth with Robin. Not only was Jess's vocabulary increasing exponentially every day, but she was putting words together into sentences. She couldn't see or talk to Robin right now, but writing about Jess would give Robin and Jess a history of Jess's early childhood.

She opened a new folder, labeled it JESS HISTORY and started to write. Several hours later she stood, stretched and walked to the window. She blinked. How was it that she hadn't noticed the vibrant reds and yellows and oranges of the leaves in Central Park? She shook her head. Her relationship was dead. Not her. And certainly not Jess. Whatever the problem, Lily knew Robin wouldn't want her to stop living, that she would want her to take care of herself and Jess.

She breathed deeply, did a few yoga stretches and went back to her computer, feeling lighter than she had for a while. She selected the folder for *In a Lonely Place*, the almost-complete literary novel she'd been working on before Jess was born, opened the file and began to read what she had written.

She walked out of the office with a huge grin, brimming with ideas for changes and for the remaining chapters. The glass wall had cracked and the fog had lifted. For the first time since Robin left, she felt almost like herself.

In the living room, she stopped to watch Cordy and Jess reading on the sofa.

Jess pointed. "Mama is here."

Lily grinned. "Hey, baby girl, you reading with grandma Cordy?"

Cordy glanced up at her as Del came out of the kitchen. The relief on both their faces at seeing her looking relaxed and happy brought home again how lucky she was to have such loving parents.

"Reading 'bout stars, Mama."

Robin had bought glow-in-the-dark stars and planets for the ceiling in Jess's room but never installed them. When they'd moved into this apartment, Cordy found them in a box and pasted them up to replicate the solar system. Thrilled that Jess was showing an interest in science, especially space and stars, Cordy had been buying books for her. "I have free books."

Cordy's eyebrows shot up. She pointed to the two books Jess was holding, then lifted the one she'd been reading from.

Three. Three books. Her daughter was counting. "Did you teach her to count, Cordy?"

"Not me." Cordy turned to Del. "You?"

Del's eyes were huge. "Not me. I didn't think she…no."

Lily swooped Jess off the sofa. "My wonderful, sweet, genius baby. I love you." She twirled around.

Jess screamed with delight. "Fun, Mama."

The next day Lily needed no prodding to go into the office. Now that the dam had broken, words were flowing and she had no problem getting back into the novel. A week later the mamas went back to their own apartment. Lily wanted to spend as much time as she could with Jess and still have time to write. Cordy recommended a few Columbia graduate students as sitters, and Lily scheduled them for two-hour slots around Jess's naptimes in the morning and afternoon.

With the ache for Robin constantly thrumming in the background, Lily immersed herself in Jess and her writing. But she didn't go back to the solitary life she'd led before Robin. Enamored of their grandchild, the mamas, and sometimes Annie and Emma, came for dinner two or three times a week. She had lunch or dinner almost every week with Katie and Michael or Jan or all three. Nicole and Nora had tough schedules but stopped by for coffee or a meal when they were able. And Mei and Winnie stopped by with their spouses when they were in town. Jess charmed them all, and a part of Lily was sure they only came to spend time with the baby.

All her visitors scrupulously avoided mentioning Robin. As worried as she was about Robin and as difficult as not knowing was, Lily fought the inclination to ask, but from the rare fragment of information she picked up, she gathered Robin had pulled away from everyone, including Katie, and rarely saw anyone outside of work. Her heart ached for her love, alone and in pain.

With a few weeks of concentrated effort, she'd finished *In a Lonely Place*. Her publisher loved it and rushed to bring it out for the holidays.

They'd been living apart seven months at this point. She tried to control herself, but she couldn't and read the business news, the gossip columns and the gay press in the papers and online every day. Initially, the only mention of Robin was an article about her living in Milan due to a problem in the DCTI office there. Toward the end of the year Robin's picture began appearing, usually with a beautiful woman on her arm. A different woman every time, Lily was happy to see.

When her book hit the bestseller list, Robin sent flowers and a note congratulating her on the great reviews. More surprising, she also sent Lily and year-old Jess tickets for a vacation at LezBeach, a lesbian resort, the first two weeks of February.

CHAPTER THIRTY-SEVEN

Robin to Milan

Robin swiveled her chair toward her office door when she heard it open. Her heart stuttered at the sight of Katie with baby Mikie curled up in a sling on her chest. Curled up on Katie, safe and sound, seemed like a good place to be. If only.

Katie rubbed Mikie's back. "We have a problem."

She sounded stressed. Robin racked her brain trying to work out what she'd done to upset her. "I—"

"The Milan office is in trouble. Giancarlo was seriously injured in a car accident last night, and we have no one there capable of running the office. I've reviewed the senior staff twenty times trying to figure out whom to send, but I haven't come up with anyone I'd trust to recruit and train his replacement. Any suggestions?"

Robin twirled her favorite fountain pen, the one Lily had sent when they were courting, and studied Katie. She'd distanced herself from Katie and everyone else to avoid the questions and their concern, but she hated the tension between them. Jan was the only friend who hadn't allowed herself to be pushed away. Laidback, she made no demands, seemed to understand Robin's need for silence and treated her, as always, with loving, irreverent humor. They chatted and had dinner once in a while, but she knew Jan's ultimate aim was to get her to talk and that made her uneasy. Katie rocked gently from side to side. "Well?"

Mikie was as close to a nephew as she'd likely ever have and she'd never even held him. Had hardly looked at him. It hurt Katie. She wished she could tell Katie it was for his protection. After all who knew how dangerous she was. Maybe it wasn't just her daughter she wanted to murder.

"Robin, are you still a part of this business? How about some help here?"

"I'll go." It just popped out of her mouth, but actually it was a great solution. An eight-hour plane ride away from Lily and Jess should keep them safe from her.

"What the f—?"

"It's the perfect solution. We both know I haven't been much good around here lately. A change of scenery might straighten out my head. I can Skype or FaceTime into the morning meetings, though it will be afternoon in Milan, and handle any issues that come up that way. You and I are the most qualified to recruit and train staff at that level. It makes sense."

Katie eased herself into the chair facing Robin's desk. "Are you sure, Rob? You'll be all alone in Italy."

She hoped her sadness didn't show through the smile she offered. "Not much different from here, wouldn't you say?"

"True. But it's a choice here and some of us..." She lifted her chin. "You know I'm available any time of the day or night whenever you're ready to talk."

Robin pushed her fingers through her hair. "Maybe it's better that I go away for a while. It's hard with Lily so close. Did she tell you I called twice? The contact was too painful for her. She cried and begged me to abide by our agreement and not call again." She lifted her shoulders. "So what do you think about Milan?"

Katie patted Mikie's behind. "You know I'm here for you, don't you?"

"I do, Katie, and I...I love you. Someday I'll explain." She turned away from Katie in case the tears prickling her eyes started to flow. "So are we agreed?" Her voice was almost a whisper.

Katie hugged her from behind, Mikie a lump between them, almost as big as the lump in Robin's throat. "I love you too, Rob."

She kissed the top of her head. "Go. Take care of business. Take care of yourself. And come back to me soon. I miss you. Besides, Mikie is going to need a playmate before too long."

Her office door opened. "I'll ask Jan to make the arrangements." The door closed softly, then opened again. "Call me from Milan anytime you want to talk." Katie closed the door again, leaving Robin alone with her sadness.

* * *

After visiting Giancarlo in the hospital and meeting with his wife and doctors, it was clear to Robin his traumatic brain injury meant he'd be unable to work for a long time, if ever. Human Resources assured her the firm's insurance would cover all costs and the disability policy would kick in when he'd exhausted his sick leave. She turned to recruiting.

It took a month to find her, but she recruited a terrific Italian woman currently running a smaller operation for a German company in Berlin who wanted to come home to Italy. In addition to Italian and German, Carla spoke English. Experience-, language- and personality-wise, she was perfect to run DCTI's Milan office. Three weeks after she arrived, they hired a second-in-command so DCTI wouldn't face this problem in the future.

Aside from training the new staff, conferencing with the New York staff and an occasional dinner with Carla and other Milan staffers, Robin was alone. She walked for hours, ate good Italian food, visited the sights and museums of Milan and read. One morning she woke feeling rested. It wasn't until she was in the shower that she realized she'd not only slept through the night, but she hadn't had a nightmare. In fact, thinking about it as she dried off, she hadn't had any daytime terrors in weeks. Could it be?

At the office, she went through the overnight pouch Jan sent everyday from New York. Sipping her espresso and munching on a croissant, she read the mail, newspapers and the few reports that were not electronic, then moved on to the articles Jan clipped about DCTI and other items of interest. A sheet of paper with a note in Jan's large scrawl was clipped to a stack of the articles.

Danger: these articles are about Lily. Proceed at your own risk. Nothing bad, though. Love ya, miss ya.

The articles were a mix of rave reviews for Lily's new novel, *In a Lonely Place*, and interviews with Lily. She made herself another cup of espresso, then read through each of the interviews twice, searching for some hint of how Lily was doing, studying the professional headshots that accompanied the stories for clues to how she was feeling.

The only thing she learned was that Lily had nearly finished the book when Jess was born, had put it aside to be with her in the NICU, and then took several months to get back to it. Flooded with shame and guilt and sadness, Robin rushed from the office with a curt nod to the receptionist. And walked. And thought.

Lily interviewed well. She'd shut down an interviewer trying to poke into their relationship with a statement. "As most of the world knows, we're taking some space." Then she'd brought the interviewer back to the novel. "Do you have any other questions about *In a Lonely Place?*"

"Taking some space." True. But Robin wanted to know how Lily was feeling, whether she was thinking about her, about getting back together. Could she do that now that the nightmares had stopped? Was it safe for her to be around Jess? She had to be sure before she went back.

After walking an hour, she returned to the office and reread the reviews and the interviews. She was happy for Lily. This book was a big deal and Hollywood was bidding for the movie rights. She had to do something. Flowers were safe. She would send flowers. The number for their favorite florist on Seventy-second Street was in her phone and it was early enough in New York to call.

"A simple bouquet of colorful cut flowers. You know what we like. I'm out of the country so I'll have to dictate the note I want you to enclose."

I'm sorry this isn't a personal note but I'm in Milan and I want to congratulate you on *In a Lonely Place* hitting number one on the *New York Times* Bestseller list. And on the great reviews. Thinking of you as always. No one but you.
Robin

After the woman read it back to her, Robin hung up. She hoped she'd done the right thing by contacting Lily. Though she hadn't admitted it to herself, she also hoped that Lily would respond to the flowers. But after a week without a note, text or email, she knew she wouldn't hear from her. She had, after all, asked for absolutely no contact for at least a year. But now she couldn't get Lily out of her mind. She needed to do something. It was an advertisement in one of the gay newspapers that Jan sent that gave her the idea. She booked two weeks in a two-bedroom casita at the LezBeach Resort in Mexico and two first-class plane tickets and sent them with a note wishing Lily happy holidays.

The almost five months in Milan had dragged and sped by at the same time. As she settled into her first-class seat for the flight home, she was in better shape than when she left, both physically and emotionally. But now she felt anxious about being back in New York.

CHAPTER THIRTY-EIGHT

LezBeach Resort

With some trepidation about traveling with a year-old infant, Lily packed up Jess and off they went to the beach resort. They had a fabulous time. Because she was so intellectually advanced, Jess was quickly upgraded from the infants group and got to run and play and terrorize the three-to-four-year-olds while Lily got some quality alone time to write or lie in the sun. She hired a sitter in the evenings and socialized with women she met on the beach or at the pool or the bar. She danced and laughed and chatted, met interesting and attractive women and even felt strong sexual vibes with one or two. But the few she kissed left her cold, and the thought of sex with any of them incited memories of Robin, her scent, her touch, her love, and she couldn't.

When they got back, the first thing she did after settling in with Jess was call Hillary, her old therapist, to make an appointment. Later that night, she wrote a note thanking Robin for the vacation and telling her what a great time they'd had. She enclosed a picture of her and Jess on the beach but asked Jan, her go-between with Robin, to tear it up if Robin didn't want to see it.

Two days later, while Jess was at nursery school, Lily stepped into Hillary's familiar and comfortable office and settled into the chair facing her old therapist. The hum of the noise machine was comforting.

"It's nice to see you, Lily." Hillary's voice conveyed caring and intimacy and confidence.

She'd been a little nervous about seeing her again, but she relaxed, realizing she'd made the right decision to talk about her feelings to a disinterested, no, to an objective person, who she felt cared about her but would not condemn Robin.

"It's nice to see y'all too, though I wish I didn't feel the need."

Hillary smiled but didn't respond. Lily knew it was up to her and though she'd thought about this discussion a lot since she'd decided she needed to talk to Hillary, she was flummoxed about starting. "I'm not sure where to begin."

"The beginning?"

Lily chewed the cuticle of her thumb as she considered the beginning. "I sent you an announcement so y'all know Robin and I got married about three and a half years ago. But you might not be aware that a little over a year ago we had a baby, a girl, Jess, who was almost four months premature."

"That must have been stressful."

"Extremely. She was only one pound three ounces at birth so we spent over a hundred days in the neonatal intensive care unit.

"It sounds awful."

"It was." She took a deep breath. "Anyway, for the first couple of weeks we were with her twenty-four seven, taking turns sleeping in a room the hospital provided for us, but then I noticed the dark bags under Robin's eyes and her air of exhaustion and I realized she was barely sleeping or eating. So thinking she might sleep better at home, I suggested she go home at night and return in the mornings. But it didn't work. She lost weight and seemed on edge all the time, so I tried spending a few nights at home with her—"

"All this while worrying about Jess?"

"Yes. Robin was suffering and I wanted to help her. But my sleeping at home didn't help because she barely slept. We'd get into bed together and I'd wake up an hour later and she'd be sitting in the living room staring out the window or I'd find a note that she'd gone out for a walk or, the worst thing, she'd wake up screaming and crying. She couldn't or wouldn't say what was wrong. All she'd say was she was worried about me and Jess. Finally, I suggested she go back to work and come to the hospital in the evening to have dinner with me, then hang out with Jess for a few hours." She blew her nose and dried her eyes.

"And did she?"

She nodded. "But it didn't really help because when she came to the NICU with me after dinner she wouldn't look at Jess, didn't want to touch her and refused skin-to-skin care. Feeling your baby on your chest is one of the most wonderful things you can imagine when you've only been able to touch her with your hand and I was devastated for the two of them. Then, she refused to come to the NICU at all. But even that didn't seem to relieve the problem."

"And this went on for how long?"

"Jess came home after one hundred and five days. I thought it would be better once we were all home together and could get into a family routine. But it was worse. She wouldn't be alone with Jess and wouldn't say her name or acknowledge her. I was hoping if she could get started, just hold Jess, she'd fall in love with her. So one night I handed her a bottle of milk I'd pumped and asked her to feed the baby. She couldn't do it. She stormed out of the house in tears. I couldn't bear to see her suffer, so the next morning I let her go." Lily broke down.

Hillary let her cry until she grabbed a tissue from the box on the table next to her. "You said it's a little more than a year. What brings you here now?"

Lily smiled. "You said start at the beginning." She shifted her position in the chair, gazed out the window, then looked at Hillary. "My latest book made the bestseller list and Robin sent a gift to congratulate me, tickets for me and Jess to spend two weeks at the LezBeach resort in Mexico. We just got back the day before yesterday and we both had a great time. I thought enough time had passed, thought maybe I'd have a fling, you know not necessarily anything serious but put a toe in the water, have some fun." Her eyes went to the window again.

"And did you? Have fun?"

Lily shrugged. "I did. But while I enjoyed dancing and flirting with the women I met and while I was attracted to a couple of them, as soon as things got sexual all I could think about was Robin."

"Are you still in love with her?"

"Absolutely."

"And she?"

"It was never about us not loving each other."

"What was it about then?"

"Robin never could articulate it, but I think it was her inability to deal with the possibility of Jess being less than perfect. But she knows absolutely nothing about Jess because she asked her friends never to mention her. And since I said I couldn't tolerate seeing her if we split, she doesn't come by the apartment so she hasn't seen Jess since she left."

"Is Jess your biological child?"

"No. Robin's fertilized egg was implanted in me."

"So you carried Robin's baby, which I assume you both wanted."

Lily nodded.

"And when she was born, Robin left you to deal with her alone in the NICU for more than three months?"

"Yes, but—"

"And in the middle of this high-stress situation with her child, you felt Robin needed you to take care of her?"

"Robin is my wife, and Jess is as much my child as Robin's."

Hillary held her hand up to keep Lily from defending Robin. "And when you finally left the high-stress situation, Robin abandoned you and her baby?"

"It wasn't like that."

"What do you feel for Robin now."

"I love her. I miss her. That's why I'm here."

"And has she made any move to come back or to see her baby?"

"No."

"Do you think you might be a little angry at her?"

Lily was confused. "Angry? No, of course not."

Hillary stood. "Time is up. We'll continue Thursday."

CHAPTER THIRTY-NINE

Robin Therapy

Without asking, Jan cut Jess out and gave Robin the picture of Lily. Robin had seen pictures of Lily in the newspapers as her novel lingered for months on the bestseller list, but seeing her in a bikini looking relaxed and happy and more beautiful than ever hit her hard and she sat at her desk and cried. She was still in love with Lily and couldn't bear to think they'd never be together again. That afternoon, she called Olivia, the therapist Katie had recommended months ago, and scheduled to see her the next afternoon.

Robin was in a state of high anxiety as she sat in the waiting room. To her, needing therapy was a sign of weakness, and she'd never been able to admit she needed help from anyone except Katie and her other roommates. At one time or another during the past year, each of them had gently encouraged her to try therapy.

When the door to the inner office opened, Robin sprang up. The blondish, sixtyish woman waved her in. "Robin, I presume? I'm Olivia Cummings. Please sit."

Robin assessed the situation. A couch and an easy chair facing what was obviously the therapist's chair. She considered taking control and sitting in Olivia's chair but then took the easy chair.

"Well, Robin, I'm glad I don't have to fight you for my chair."

She flushed. "Busted."

They laughed, and Robin decided she might like Dr. Cummings, but she couldn't keep herself from fidgeting.

"Tell me a little about yourself, Dr. DiLuca."

"If you know I have a PhD, then you already know something about me, Dr. Cummings. By the way, I prefer Robin."

"And I prefer Olivia, unless it makes you feel more secure to call me doctor." She smiled.

Yes, Robin definitely liked this woman. She seemed warm and welcoming. "Olivia it is." She thought for a second. "You may know then that I'm the Chief Executive Officer of a technology company and you may have seen my picture in the gossip pages at events sponsored by my company."

Olivia nodded. "Is this your first time in therapy?"

"Yes. I've always felt it was…a weakness to need help from a professional."

"So what brings you here now?"

"I have issues with my child that are keeping me from my wife." Robin shifted uneasily in her chair; her gaze flew to the windows as the color crept up.

Olivia waited, but Robin didn't know where to go from here. How to say it? She cleared her throat and shifted again, glancing at Olivia.

"Ordinarily I wouldn't intervene with questions. I would wait for you to tell me what's on your mind, but since today is your first session and your first time in therapy, I'm going to help you a bit. After today you are in charge of what we talk about in each session. Do you understand, Robin?"

"Yes. It's just hard to know where to begin. And please don't tell me to begin at the beginning because I don't know where the beginning is."

"I find how you framed the issue interesting. Are you living together and having problems because of your child, or are you separated and the child is keeping you apart? Tell me about your marriage. What is your wife's name?"

"Lily. We've been married about three and a half years. Our daughter, Jess, is just over a year old. We've been living apart since she was a month or so old. I left because of Jess." Waves of shame and guilt and sadness washed over her. She started to stand, then fought the need to run and sat, her eyes on the window again.

Olivia was silent, but Robin was aware she was observing her. "What are you feeling right now?"

Robin shrugged.

"Can you elaborate?"

Robin shook her head.

"I see. Perhaps you could talk about why, if this has been going on over a year, you came in today?"

Robin nodded. "Lily had a book on the best seller list for two months so I sent her a gift—two weeks at an all-inclusive lesbian resort plus airline tickets for her and Jess. When she got back this week, she sent a thank-you note and enclosed a picture of…her on the beach. Seeing the photo threw me, made me realize how much I miss her, how much I love her. And I want to fix things between us. Katie had given me your number when this first happened, but I wasn't ready until yesterday to call."

Olivia considered what Robin said. "So you and Lily are in regular contact and you send her gifts and she takes them and sends you notes, but something about Jess is keeping you apart? Am I close?"

"No. Lily and I are not in contact. When I left, she said it would be easier for her to not see me than to have to watch me leave time and time again. I called her twice in the beginning, but she asked me to stop. When I saw her picture in the paper after the success of her book, I was proud and happy for her and I wanted to do something for her, so I sent flowers and later the tickets with a note. It appears she decided to accept the gift."

Olivia scratched her head and smiled. "I noticed you hesitated when you said Lily had enclosed a picture. Was it just her or was Jess in it?"

The flush was back. "Um, I think Jess was in it, but Jan, my assistant, cut her out and just gave me Lily."

"Why would your assistant decide that you shouldn't see your daughter's picture?"

"Because when I left Lily and Jess, I told all our friends and family, and Jan is both, that I didn't want to hear about Jess or see her." Her eyes bounced around the room, then settled on Olivia.

Olivia raised an eyebrow. "I see. Or at least I think I'm getting clearer." She smiled. "One or two more questions, then we'll stop. How do you feel about our session today?"

"I don't have anything to compare it to."

"Does that mean you don't have any feelings about it? Was it hard, or easy? Did you hate it? Do you hate me or do you think we can work together?"

"I feel scared. I don't want to talk about the things I came to talk about, but I feel comfortable with you and I think we can work together. I'd like to."

Olivia stood. "All right, then. I'll see you again tomorrow, then Friday, and next week we'll go to Monday, Wednesday and Friday. Is that still what you want?"

Robin stood and looked down at her. "Yes. I'll see you tomorrow, same time."

CHAPTER FORTY

Lily Therapy

Lily was disturbed and maybe a little angry when she sat in the chair in Hillary's office. Hillary smiled.

"I am pissed, Hillary. I didn't like what y'all said about Robin. I came to talk to y'all cause I thought you could be objective. Instead y'all attacked Robin for no reason."

"So you're angry at me but not at Robin?"

"Yes."

"So if you don't want to talk about your anger with Robin, what do you want to talk about?"

"There you go again. I'm not angry with Robin. I want to talk about why I can't have sex with other women, why I can't forget about Robin."

"Why do you think?"

She shrugged. "Maybe because I'm in love with her? But don't you think I should be able to have casual sex with other women?"

"Do you think that?"

"I do. But I can't and that's what I need you to help me with."

"It's not going to be fast. But let's go back to the beginning. Talk to me about Robin, what's so special about her that you still love her after all…after all this time. We have a lot to do, so get started, Lily."

CHAPTER FORTY-ONE

Robin Therapy 2

As Robin took her seat for her third session, she grinned. "Okay, Olivia. I get it. My last session was a bust, and I will never again waste fifty minutes sitting in silence staring at you." She took a breath. "Katie says I should talk about my family. I don't—"

"What do *you* want to talk about, Robin?"

Three weeks later, they settled in facing each other, and Robin began to talk about something that happened when she was in graduate school in Stanford. After about twenty minutes, Olivia leaned forward. "How many sessions have we had, Robin?"

She thought for a minute. "This is the twelfth."

Olivia nodded. "How do you feel about where we are?"

"Okay, I think. I've told you a lot about myself and my friends and—"

"You've covered a lot of ground, it's true, but when I ask about your feelings you talk in generalities and if I ask about your family, you skitter away. You are a beautiful, brilliant and successful woman, Robin, and an interesting conversationalist. Now, there are therapists who would be happy to sit and listen to you chat about your life, but I'm not one of them. My goal is to help you to work through the issues that you feel are problems, that keep you from living a happy, fulfilled and productive life."

"But—"

Olivia put her hand up. "Let me finish, please. If I remember correctly, you came into therapy to deal with a problem that involved your daughter Jess. Yet you've managed to avoid even mentioning her name."

Robin paled.

Olivia studied her. "I know I said I would let you lead, but I feel you're wasting your time and money and my time by avoiding the problem you said you wanted help with, that Jess was keeping you from Lily. You've mentioned Lily, but it seems to me that Jess is the elephant in the room. She's just a year old. Why are you so afraid of her?"

Robin tried to hold back the tears, but they flowed. She doubled over in her chair and covered her face with her hands as she sobbed. It was more than fifteen minutes before she looked up, embarrassed.

Her faced filled with compassion, Olivia was watching but she didn't speak.

"I'm sorry, I didn't mean to do that." She glanced at her watch.

Olivia smiled gently. "I have no doubt you didn't mean to do it. Don't worry about the time. I felt it was important to confront you today, so I've left the next session free in case you want to begin to delve into Jess today. If you don't, we can stop at our usual time."

Robin's instinct was to run, to get away from Olivia, but her gut told her it was now or never. She took a few deep breaths. "I'd like to stay and talk about Jess."

Olivia nodded. "Good. Clearly, you're really troubled by her."

"I don't know if I told you, but Jess was almost four months premature and I freaked when I saw her. She only weighed a pound and three ounces and she didn't look human. My friend Nicole, the neonatal specialist who delivered her, reassured me she was normal for a baby born so early. It took me a couple of days, but I got past the shock and, with Lily's help, started to see her as our little girl. We knew she might die, we knew if she survived she might have serious mental and physical problems, but she was our daughter and we would love her and take care of her."

She rubbed her forehead. "I'm not sure exactly when it started, but one night I had this dream, nightmare really, that I…" She started to hyperventilate.

"Hold your breath for a second, Robin, then take a deep breath through your nose, fill your belly and let the air out slowly through your closed lips. Do it until you feel in control." She watched Robin follow her instructions and relax. "Can you continue or do you want to stop?"

"I want to get it out." She took another deep breath. "I dreamed I picked up the baby by her feet and smashed her head on the incubator." Tears streamed down her face. "It scared me, and I thought it would upset Lily so I didn't say anything. But after that night, anytime I closed my eyes, I had some version of the dream. Sometimes it was a table, sometimes the wall, sometimes the floor, but always I held her by her feet and swung her and smashed her head. Her brains splashed over me. After a while, the nightmare included Lily in the room watching me and after I smashed the baby, I said, 'It's your fault' and I put a gun in my mouth and killed myself." She began sobbing again.

"Did you tell Lily or Katie or anyone?"

"No, because by then it was no longer just a nightmare. Anytime I was near Jess I saw myself grabbing her feet and smashing her head. I wanted to kill my own daughter in the most horrendous manner. How could I tell anyone?" Her voice was anguished; the pain slashed through her gut, the sobs racked her body.

Olivia's voice was gentle. "I'm honored that you trust me enough to share this, Robin. I understand how painful it is to admit to these feelings, but I want to remind you that they are just feelings, that you removed yourself from the situation before you could do any harm. Talking about it is the first step to changing. You've done good work today. It's probably best if you don't talk about it outside this room for now, but I suggest that you spend the evening with someone you trust, someone who makes you feel safe. Who would that be?"

"Katie." Robin thought for a second or two. "No, Michael is away. I can't be around baby Mikie. Emma and Annie feel safer."

"Call and arrange to have dinner with them and, if possible, sleep at their place. Are you still having these nightmares or the fantasy?"

"Not for a few months."

"You've gotten into something very deep this afternoon. I'd like to schedule another extra session tomorrow morning. I'm booked from eight in the morning until about nine tomorrow evening but I could meet you at seven a.m. before I start my day, if you're willing."

"I'd like that."

"The nightmare might return tonight, so be sure you're in a place you feel safe." Olivia stood. "I know you have trouble asking for help, but call me, day or night, if you need me."

CHAPTER FORTY-TWO

Robin Therapy 3

Ever since that pivotal session two months ago, Robin had been working hard to figure out what had triggered the nightmare and the fantasy with no luck. Olivia didn't think it had come out of nowhere, but so far they hadn't been able to get to the source.

Robin was excited today. She felt she'd had a sort of breakthrough and brought two lattes to this afternoon's session. Before she sat, she handed one to Olivia. "I hope you like lattes?"

"I do, but what's the occasion?" Olivia sipped, then smiled.

"I dreamed about my mother last night. It's strange, because I don't have any memories of her and I don't remember if I've ever seen a picture of her. I didn't really get a good look at her in the dream, but it was her."

"Tell me the dream."

"We were alone in a house which could have been our real house, but I'm not sure, and she was angry at me for something. I was afraid of her. She was cooking and I was sitting on a stool or steps watching her when she pointed this big knife at me and said, 'You can't be my daughter, you're not a real girl,' then she came toward me waving the knife and I ran up the stairs and hid…in a closet, I think, and waited for her to come for me. Then I woke up."

"What did you feel in the dream?"

Robin stared out the window. "I was afraid, but I wasn't terrified. It felt familiar."

"How old were you?"

She closed her eyes. "Four or five maybe."

"Have you ever dreamed about her before?"

"Not that I remember. Maybe the work we've been doing trying to get me to remember my childhood brought it up."

Olivia was silent, and Robin could see her thinking through something. In their four months working together she'd learned to wait until Olivia formed her thought.

"I have a couple of ideas that I think will help your therapy, Robin. I hope you're open to them, though they may be scary." She met Robin's eyes.

"I'm listening."

"First, I think it's time you visited your family to learn more about your childhood, about how your mother died, maybe get some pictures to jog your memories. What do you think?"

She'd never considered this. Really, it was as if they were dead. In fact, they were dead to her and, she imagined, she was dead to them. "What if they won't see me?"

"I can see why you'd think your dad wouldn't want to see you, but why would your brothers object?"

She shrugged. "I guess because they've never tried to contact me."

"Have you tried to contact them? And do they even know where you are?"

"It's really scary. Suppose I find out something I don't want to know, like maybe I killed my mother or something like that?"

"If you know, you can deal with it. But I don't want to convince you. It's just a suggestion. Think about it."

"Could I bring Katie with me?"

"That would be up to you."

"All right, I'll do it. What's the other thing?"

"Would you consider volunteering in the children's ward of a hospital? It would give you the opportunity to gauge your reaction to children, some with serious mental and physical problems, and put to rest your fears about being around Jess. Or if you have a problem, we'll know there's more work to be done. I've spoken to a friend who works at the hospital, and she's willing to introduce you and keep an eye on you in the beginning to be sure you're okay."

"Do you think it's safe? That I'm not a danger to the children?"

"I'm confident, but you can leave at the first sign of a problem." Olivia stood.

Robin hesitated, then got out of the chair and tossed her empty cup into the trash. "Does your calendar say this is scare-the-shit-out-of-Robin day?" At the door, she turned.

"I'll give both a try."

CHAPTER FORTY-THREE

Robin and Ted

Things had gotten better. Since she told Olivia about her nightmares and fantasies and her fears, she'd been more relaxed and hopeful. More like her old self. Katie and Jan and her other close friends had welcomed her back with open arms though she hadn't discussed her therapy with any of them. She'd even been to see the mamas to let them know she was actively working on her issues. They'd been happy to see her and happy she was getting help, but she sensed they were wary. She understood. She'd hurt their daughter and their granddaughter.

She discussed her plan to go to Florida with Katie and Jan and asked Jan to find a private detective to track down her brothers and her father. Ever resourceful, Jan went online and found telephone numbers for her brothers in Florida. Tonight, she was having dinner with Jan and Katie at Katie's house, so they could be with her when she called Ted, her older brother, about coming down to visit. She decided she'd enjoy dinner more if she called first.

They sat around the table in the small conference room Katie had set up in her brownstone for when she worked at home. Using the conference phone would allow the three of them to hear the conversation. Katie squeezed her hand. Robin took a deep breath, then dialed. It rang six times, then a girl answered. "Hello."

"Hello. I'm calling to speak to Ted DiLuca. Is he at home?"

"Um, who's calling?"

"Robin DiLuca, his sister."

"Really?" The girl didn't attempt to contain her excitement. "Dad, Dad, pick up the phone. It's her, it's your sister Robin."

Jan high-fived Robin. Robin grinned.

They could hear the girl breathing heavily over the phone. Katie put the phone on mute. "Well, someone is happy to hear from you." She took the phone off mute.

"Robin, is it really you?" His voice was deep and rich, and clearly he too was happy to hear from her.

"It's really me. How are you? And I gather you have a daughter?"

"Two actually and a son and a wife as well. What about you?"

Her eyes went to Jan and Katie, then back at the phone. "Um, I have a wife and a daughter too."

"That's great. I am so happy to hear from you. Geez, it's been too long."

She didn't know what she'd expected, but her brother was so obviously glad to hear from her that she kicked herself for waiting so long to contact him. She could do this, go to Florida and reclaim her past. "I'd love to come to Florida to see you and get to know your family, if that's okay?"

"It's more than okay. It's wonderful. My girls have been dying to meet you, and they'd kill me if I let you go without a commitment. So when?"

She glanced at Katie and Jan again. "Is Friday evening too soon?"

"Just a second." They heard him talking to someone in the background. "It's great. Ellen, that's my wife, says you're welcome to stay with us, but, in any case, plan on coming here for dinner. Can you be here by six thirty?"

"No problem, but I think it would be easier for me to stay in a hotel for our first visit. How's Paul?"

"Paul is okay. I can arrange for you to see him sometime over the weekend if you'd like. Do you want to see Dad?"

Robin took a breath. "Do you think he'd want to see me?"

Ted cleared his throat. "I'm not sure, Robin. He's a drunk, so you never know. And if you look the way I remember, maybe not."

"How do you think I look?"

"You had black hair and green eyes like Mom. I imagine now that you're older you must be a dead ringer for her. My girls both look like her and he won't see them, but he's okay with my son."

"Well. Let's play that by ear, depending on how I feel when I'm there. Give me your address and I'll see you Friday."

They exchanged information and hung up. Katie and Jan hugged her. She couldn't stop grinning. "Let's eat, I'm starving."

Jan remained seated when the other two stood. "You guys pull the food together. Let me make your plane and hotel reservations, then I'll join you. You going, Katie?"

Katie looked at Robin. "Do you still want me along?"

"It's up to you. He was pretty excited about seeing me, so I'm okay going alone."

"Easier if I stay home."

"Okay, Jan, just me. Make it for the early afternoon Friday with the return on Sunday night." She stood. "I'm going to call Olivia now. I guess the food is up to you and Michael, Katie."

CHAPTER FORTY-FOUR

Robin Goes to Florida

She followed the GPS to the driveway of a sprawling one-story home hidden behind shrubs and palm trees in an older development of similar homes in Boca Raton. She sat for a minute steeling herself, then the front door was thrown open and a girl dashed out, followed by a younger girl and a boy, followed by a tall fellow who must be her brother. She got out of the car and had about a second before he pulled her into his arms. They embraced for a long moment. She closed her eyes, feeling a confusing mixture of sadness and happiness as she hugged this strange, yet familiar brother. She opened her eyes and over his shoulder spotted a woman in the doorway, most likely her sister-in-law, Ellen. Three very excited children surrounded them. The girls reminded her of…oh, they looked like her.

Ted released her and held her at arms length. "Wow. You look great all grown up."

She laughed. "So do you. And who are these people?"

"Ah, yes, your nieces and nephew." He put an arm around the oldest girl. "Sara is thirteen, Victoria is seven and," he tapped the boy on the head, "Teddie here is ten." He draped an arm over her shoulder. "Come, let me introduce you to Ellen."

Ellen hugged her. "I'm so happy to meet you finally."

They moved inside. She was feeling overwhelmed. She hadn't thought about her family much over the years, but she never expected this warm and loving welcome. Ellen seemed to sense her need for a little space. "Dinner will be ready in about twenty minutes. Let's give our guest some breathing room. Ted, give Robin a tour of the house and show her where she can freshen up. Make sure you give her a clean towel. You three," she signaled the kids to follow her, "come set the table."

She liked the house a lot. It was nicely decorated but comfortable and, with three kids, clearly lived in. Besides the large kitchen, dining room and living room, there were four bedrooms and four baths, plus a screened-in Florida room overlooking the pool. The kids caught up with their tour and each proudly showed her their bedroom. Watching the girls, she wondered for the first time whether Jess looked like her. By the time they sat down at the dining room table, Robin felt back in control and in the moment. The two girls claimed the chairs next to her. Teddie sat next to his mom. "We saw you on TV," Sara blurted out, "all the time, and in the newspapers."

Ah, so they knew she was a billionaire. And a lesbian. She looked at Ted. "Once you learned I was in New York, why didn't you contact me?" Was it because she was a lesbian?

Ted and Ellen exchanged a look. It was Ellen who responded. "We thought about it. Up until your company went public and you were all over the newspapers and television, we had no idea where you were living or what you were doing. Years ago we'd discussed hiring a private detective to find you. But then, and more recently when we saw you, we decided if you were interested in reconnecting, you knew where to find us."

She hesitated. "It didn't have anything to do with…my lifestyle?" She wasn't sure about using the word "lesbian" in front of the younger children.

"Your being a lesbian is a non-issue for us. If you hadn't become a billionaire, I might have called." Ted met her eyes. "But I didn't want you to think the money was the reason."

Lily was right. Money does complicate some things. Like Lily, Ted and Ellen were interested in her, not her money. Lily would like them. Lily. If only…She caught herself drifting down a path she didn't want to go now and forced her attention back to

Ted. "I understand. And you're right. I knew how to find you. It's complicated, though," she cleared her throat, "so, uh, maybe we could go into it later?"

Ellen picked up her discomfort. "Of course. But we're all so curious about you, would you mind telling us about what you've been doing?"

All eyes on her, she gave them the short version. Harvard, Stanford, New York City and DiLuca Cooper Technologies International. She omitted Lily and Jess.

Sara, sitting on her right, leaned into her, hanging on every word. She was almost levitating with excitement. "I'm dying to live in New York City. What's it like?"

Robin thought for a minute, then described her loft in Tribeca and her office on Wall Street with a view of the Statue of Liberty. She tried to convey the excitement of the city, the crowds, Broadway shows, the ballet, the opera, concerts in the park, the museums. But it was Coney Island—the Cyclone, the aquarium, the midway, walking the high line and kayaking in the Hudson, all the things she'd done with Lily, that fascinated them.

After they'd eaten dessert, Ellen took pity on her. "Okay, kids. You'll get to spend all day tomorrow with your Aunt Robin. It's time to do the dishes, then go to your rooms, as usual, to do your homework, read and wind down."

They moaned but went to work. She was happy they hadn't asked about her family. She would tell Ted sometime over the weekend, but she had many questions for him and she didn't want to get sidetracked. Once the kids were settled in their rooms, the three adults moved into the Florida room with coffee.

Ted took what she assumed was his chair, the recliner, and watched her and Ellen settle on the sofa. "I can't tell you how happy I am to have you here. Why did you decide to come home now?"

Home. She repeated the word in her mind. Was Florida home? She'd never thought so, but she felt comfortable sitting here with her older brother and his wife. "To be frank, my therapist suggested that it was time that I reconnect with my family. I have no memories of my early years, of our mother, nothing actually before I was a little younger than Sara." She took a deep breath. "Lately, I've been having disturbing dreams that Olivia, my therapist, thinks might be memories."

Ellen's quick intake of breath and the look she exchanged with Ted made Robin feel she had hit a nerve. But she'd come to learn about her family so she pushed on. "I'd love to hear about our childhood, about what our mother died of and when, and anything else you can tell me."

Ted cleared his throat. "Funny, I've always thought it was the memories that kept you away."

Robin tensed. "No. I…there didn't seem to be anything or anyone here for me. Dad let me take a plane to Harvard alone at fourteen, with a few dollars and nothing but some shorts, T-shirts, a pair of jeans and sandals. He never called to see if I made it or if I needed anything, like winter clothes or a coat or a hat or boots. I figured he didn't care. You and Paul were away and not in contact. Frankly, I didn't think you cared either."

She looked down at her hands. "The only one I knew cared was Barbara, the teacher who mentored me and helped me get into Harvard, and she died shortly after I started at Harvard. But she'd made sure I was taken care of. Since I had just turned fourteen, she pressured the dean of students at Harvard to arrange for an older student to look after me. And Katie and the other four roommates in our suite took good care of me. Katie is only eight years older than me, but she's the closest thing I've had to a mother in my life. At least a mother I remember. She's also my business partner."

He looked pained, as if he wanted to cry. "I'm sorry I wasn't there for you, Robin. I spent a lot of time in therapy dealing with that, but I was a teenager, involved in my own things."

"I didn't come here to make you feel guilty, Ted. You're not that much older than I am and whatever you did, I'm sure it was more than he did." She walked to the recliner, placed her hands on the arms and leaned toward him. She locked onto his eyes, trying to connect, to make him understand. "You know my history, Ted, and I need you to share it with me. All of it, even if it's bad or I did a terrible thing." He touched her face. "I understand."

Robin returned to the sofa and leaned forward with her hands clasped between her knees. "What was I like as a kid?"

He sat back and sipped his coffee. She'd noticed there was no alcohol at dinner, so he was aware of the danger. "Actually, you were very much like our two girls. I'm sure you notice they look exactly like you, same hair, same eyes, same lanky body, but what you can't see by looking is they have the same raw intellect, the same extremely high IQ. Like you, they both taught themselves to read, but you were well under a year and they were closer to two.

"You're only six years older than me. How can you remember when I started to read?"

"Our mom had baby books for each of us. I'll give you yours later. Unfortunately she didn't make any entries for you after you were about nine months, but she did note that you started reading around six months and the last entry was about you starting to write." He sipped his coffee.

"Do you remember that you used to steal books from me and Paul? You read any book you could get your hands on—textbooks, fiction, history, picture books, anything. You asked for books on subjects that interested you, which was almost everything, and I got them out of the library. Our three are the same. They gobble up every book in sight and are interested in everything."

She laughed. "I lived in a suite with five roommates at Harvard and for the first month they'd wander around the suite yelling 'Has anybody seen my, you name it, textbook?' They quickly learned that it probably was in my room. Where do the kids go to school?"

"Right now to the neighborhood public school, but we've been putting money away so we can send them to this really good school for special kids like them. Hopefully, we'll be able to afford to send Sara next term. Vicki and Teddie will have to wait. But you did all right without a special school."

"It's true, but I might have had an easier time in a special school."

"You didn't even go to school until you were seven or eight."

"Really? Why?"

"She never enrolled you, so you weren't on anyone's radar. Paul and I were too young to think about things like that. And Dad never paid much attention to you and didn't notice. The woman he paid to cook and clean after Mom died thought you were retarded because you hid in your room most of the time and hardly spoke. But then you got sick and she had to take you to the pediatrician and I think it was someone in his office who figured it out and got the authorities involved."

"Why did I hide? Didn't I speak to you?"

They exchanged that look again.

"I can see there's something you two are hiding. You might as well just tell me."

Ellen touched Ted's arm. "She needs to know, hon."

He got up, walked to the window and stood half-turned away from her. "When you were six, our mom killed our sister and herself in front of you." He spoke quickly as if he wanted to get it over with.

Her blood drained to her feet. The image of the swinging baby and the gunshot to the mouth filled her mind. Her heart raced. She breathed quickly, but she couldn't take in air fast enough. She started to stand but fell back. Ellen moved next to her and put an arm over her shoulder. "Try to relax, Robin." She put a hand on Robin's chest and raised Robin's chin with her other hand. "Keep your chin up to clear your airway. Breathe. That's it."

It took a minute, but she calmed down. A sister. She massaged her temples. "I didn't know we had a sister."

She watched Ted sort through his words before speaking. "Rosaria." He smiled. "By the way, that was supposed to be your name, but Dad was drunk and couldn't remember the name Mom had selected so the nurse asked me if I knew. I remembered Ann was the middle name, then I decided you were like a little bird, so I said Robin. Dad of course didn't remember and took the heat when she found out."

Robin grinned. "Thank you for that, big brother." She walked over and high-fived him.

He put his arm around Robin. "Rosaria was three months premature, but our mother insisted on bringing her home from the hospital against doctor's orders. Dad, of course, supported anything she wanted. Anyway, the baby was so small she carried her on a pillow and wouldn't put her down. She stopped cooking or doing anything other than holding the baby and trying to feed her. The baby cried, actually sort of mewled like a kitten, constantly. One day she took the baby by the feet and—"

"Swung her and smashed her head on the table, then put a gun in her mouth and killed herself."

"You remember?"

"No. Or yes, I guess. That was the nightmare I was having, over and over again. And the image I would see whenever I let my guard down." She went limp with relief, and Ted helped her to the sofa before continuing.

"Mom was scary. Paul and I would do anything to stay out of the house, so it was late that day when we got home from after-school activities—about six—and found you sitting next to her in the dark kitchen holding her hand. You weren't crying. You were covered in blood and brains."

"In my dream she says, 'You made me do it' just before she put the gun in her mouth. I guess Olivia was right. It was a memory."

Ted nodded. "They said she died between eight and ten in the morning, probably not long after we left for school. The coroner's report said you must have been standing close because you had the baby's tissue and her tissue on your face, in your hair and on your clothing. It also said she was drunk and had taken some pills. The police report concluded that you'd sat with her all day until we got home. You were withdrawn and sad after that, as one might expect."

"Why did she hate me so much that she said it was my fault, then killed herself in front of me? Who does that to a six-year-old?"

He shrugged. "Paul and I got the best of her. She was a fun and loving mom, she'd laugh and play and sing most of the time, but even then, from time to time she'd suddenly get moody and distant. As I understand it, she was warned not to have any more children after Paul, but she wanted a girl and Dad gave in to her like he did on everything. I think she had serious psychological issues that were exacerbated by giving birth to you. After you were born, the good mom disappeared. Paul and I learned quickly to stay out of her way as she walked around the house cursing and mumbling, but she was indifferent to us. All her rage and frustration and nastiness were focused on you."

He sat next to Robin and took her hand. "She was mentally ill. It's not unusual for one child to become the focus of parental craziness. Though I was only six when you were born, her behavior toward you was so erratic, almost violent, that I have clear memories of it and I understood even then that you weren't the cute little girl she wanted. Don't get me wrong, as you'll see when we look at pictures, you were a beautiful kid, but you were tall and gangly for your age, you had a mind of your own, you refused to wear dresses and you insisted on short hair." He smiled. "In fact, you cut it yourself with scissors or even a knife if that's all you had when you decided it was too long. She criticized everything you did, called you a freak, neither a girl nor a boy, and said you were ugly and stupid. I wish I had stopped her, but I guess a part of me was happy it was you and not me."

"You were a baby yourself, Ted, what could you have done against your mother? But what about him?"

"She could do no wrong in his eyes. Even today, when he's sober enough to talk, he'll make excuses for her murdering her child. He can't stand to see my girls and will probably reject you. You all look like her."

"I had no idea. I don't remember ever seeing a picture of her."

"Except for your height, you're the spitting image of her. I thought you might want some family pictures so I had copies made for you. The kids are making an album for you to take with you. It should be ready before you leave."

"Thank you, I would love to have some pictures for my…You were talking about how she treated me."

"Right. Until the baby came, it was almost a game for you. Maybe even negative attention was better than being ignored, but you seemed to enjoy provoking her. Sometimes she chased you with a kitchen knife. You would get close, then when she tried to grab you, you would run away, laughing, and hide in one of the many secret places you'd found. Once the baby was in the house, you stayed just out of her reach but watched her constantly."

"Do you think I killed the baby?"

"No. I have all the reports and I had copies of everything made for you. I'll give them to you when you leave later and you can read them whenever you feel like, but it's very clear from the angles, etc., that she did it. I think you were fascinated by the baby and maybe a little jealous."

Bombarded with feelings that she needed to process, Robin stood. "I need some time to absorb all of this, so I'm going back to the hotel. But we're spending the day together tomorrow, right? I'd love for all of you to join me for breakfast at the hotel around ten."

Ted turned to Ellen. She smiled. "We'd love to have breakfast. The kids are willing to get up early to be with their newly found auntie. I'll bring bathing suits and things so we can sit on the beach while you two get some alone time. Are you all right to drive, Robin?"

"Don't worry. It will be a while before I fall asleep."

CHAPTER FORTY-FIVE

Florida

Rather than go up to her room, she handed the doorman her car keys and set out along the nearly deserted beach, enjoying the pleasant night air and the soothing sound of the ocean, trying to absorb all she'd heard tonight. After walking an hour, she sat on a bench facing the water and called Katie. With Jan conferenced in, she told them about the kids, Ellen and Ted, the visit and the photo album that would give her some of her missing family history. She left out the gruesome details. It was Olivia she wanted to share that with. And Lily. She selected Lily's name from her contact list, wanting to call her, wanting to hear her voice, to tell her she wasn't crazy and wasn't going to kill their daughter. But she knew in her heart that she still had work to do with Olivia before she could be with her wife and daughter. If they would have her.

The next morning, when she met Ted and his family at the entrance to the hotel's restaurant, Paul, a thinner version of Ted, was with them. They eyed each other nervously for a few seconds, then moved into an awkward hug. "Thanks for coming, Paul. I've been anxious to meet you."

"Yeah, me too. It's been too long. Sorry I never tried to contact you."

"Hey, we're all guilty of that, so let's just go from here."

They were seated at a large round table with a lot of shuffling so the two girls could sit on either side of their auntie. Teddie, her nephew, eyed her across the table—too cool at ten to fight his sisters just to sit next to his exotic aunt. She made a mental note to give him some special attention.

They studied their menus and ordered. When she looked up from her menu, Paul was staring at her. She flushed. He looked away.

There was an awkward silence, then Ellen spoke. "Since you called on Wednesday, the children have been working on making a family album for you."

She noticed that Ellen always included Teddie, but Ted focused mainly on the girls. Was that because he wanted to share how much like her they were? Or guilt for not being there for his little sister? Or pride because of their brilliance, though it seemed Teddie was no slouch in the brains department?

"That sounds wonderful. I can't wait to see it. And I'd love to know how you three are dividing the work amongst you. Let's start with Teddie. What are you doing?" With that they were off and running, taking turns talking about what they were doing. Ellen met her eyes across the table and smiled.

When they'd eaten, the kids were anxious to get to the beach, and Robin gave Ellen the key to her suite so they could change into bathing suits. Robin and her brothers went for a walk.

After a few minutes, Paul broke the silence. "You look exactly like her. I know I was staring, but looking at you brings back feelings, bad feelings. She terrified me. I remember feeling relieved when she focused her craziness totally on you, but then as I got older, I also felt guilty."

Robin spread her hands. "I'm sorry, Paul. I hope with time you'll see me, not her."

He nodded. "To this day I have nightmares about finding you with her that afternoon, the baby's head split open like a broken doll, our mother's face half-gone, you sitting next to her, holding her hand and cradling the remains of her head in your lap."

She stopped walking. "I had her head in my lap?"

Her brothers both nodded.

She tried to imagine what her six-year-old self felt, holding her dead mother's hand and staring at her half-face all day, but she could only dredge up deep sadness and a sense of loss. Even more devastating was the irony that, according to Ted, her mother seemed to hate her. But as he said, negative attention must have been better than not being seen at all. Her heart ached for that child. Oh, God, was she doing the same to Jess?

They walked on, one on either side of her, not speaking, feeling the shared sadness and the horror. "Did we get any counseling to help us deal with what we'd seen?"

"No." Ted was the one who answered her. "Things were different back then. They thought if no one mentioned it, we'd forget."

"No one noticed I was catatonic? And you two must have acted out in some way after."

"Our dad was barely around, and when he was the liquor made him more catatonic than any of us. I don't think he even saw us." Paul's laugh was harsh. "And the woman he paid to clean and cook and supposedly take care of us was a drunk too so forget her noticing anything."

"I'm sorry to bring these memories back for you two, but I really need to know."

Paul touched her shoulder. "It's not like I ever forgot, Robin. Her suicide sent me on a downward spiral that I'm just climbing out of now. I became a problem at school and was suspended so many times I lost count. After a while, they stopped calling him in because they figured out he didn't care, and the goal became to pass me onto the next school."

He wiped a tear away. "I got caught stealing a car at sixteen and they threw me out of high school. The detective who worked her murder and suicide intervened and convinced the judge to let me live with him and his family until I was old enough to enlist in the Navy. Of course, our father had no objection." He blew his nose.

Maybe remembering was worse than forgetting. She put a hand on Paul's arm. "How long were you in the Navy?"

"Ten years. It was good. I got my GED, began to take college classes and started to get my head turned around a little. Right after I left the Navy, I went into therapy. With the support of Eric, the detective, and Ted, I was able to finish my bachelor's degree in math and get accepted into the PhD program in physics at Miami U. Luckily, the few professors still there who recognized the DiLuca name, seem to remember his brilliance, not his drinking." He smiled. "I'm starting to feel a glimmer of hope."

"Oh, Paul, I'm so sorry. Maybe I was lucky that I didn't remember. What about you, Ted?"

"I was twelve when Mom died, and I guess I was better able to handle it. I'd been trying to take care of you two while she was alive but not feeding us or doing laundry. After she died and he totally abandoned us, I felt even more responsible for you two, and that's where my energy went until I got the scholarship for college and left home. The experience drove me to want to understand her and him and why they were the way they were, and I think it was the reason I became a psychiatrist."

They were silent as they walked. The bright sunlight, the soothing ebb and flow of the turquoise ocean and her happiness at connecting with her brothers battled with the life-shattering memories of their shared childhood. Both she and Paul had lost years to the pain, he in remembering, she in not remembering. And because she didn't remember, she'd walked away from the only woman she would ever love. And her child.

After a while, Ted took her hand. It wasn't until they were headed back to gather the troops for lunch that Paul took her other hand. Tears filled her eyes. Paul brushed something out of his eyes. *Tears too*, she thought.

Ted treated everyone to lunch at the beach, and they hung out and talked for most of the afternoon. She invited them all to dinner and let the kids decide where to go. As they separated to shower, change and relax a bit, she asked Paul to invite his girlfriend along.

By unspoken agreement, they didn't talk about the past at all over dinner and it turned out to be a lot of fun. Everyone was in good spirits; there was lots of joking and playfulness. At some point during the evening, Robin looked around and smiled. Her family. She felt comfortable and happy with them. She wished her other family—Katie and Jan and especially Lily and Jess—was here. But this wasn't the last time, she knew. Now that she'd found them she wasn't letting them go. At the end of the evening, Ellen invited them all to brunch the next day so they could spend time together before her evening flight.

The memories the next day came from the photos included in the album: of her parents as children, then as a young couple, and their wedding pictures. She really did look exactly like her mom, who in these pictures was smiling and happy. Later pictures included Ted and Paul and her as an infant. She was surprised to see pictures of her growing up, the last at twelve when Ted left for college. Apparently, Ted was a budding photographer, and he, rather than either of her parents, had captured their childhood.

With tears in her eyes she strode across the room and kissed him. "Thank you, Ted, I can't tell you how wonderful it is to get my past back through your pictures. And thank you, Sara, Victoria and Teddie, for the effort you put into creating such a beautiful album. I especially love the pictures you drew and the poems and stories you wrote. It's one of the loveliest gifts I've ever received." She didn't attempt to stem the tears as she moved around the room and kissed each person. "I'm so lucky to have found you all again."

Ted pulled her into a hug. "There are many more photos. We didn't give you all of them, so you'd have to come back soon to see them."

"Don't worry about that. I'll be back."

During the afternoon, Ted, Ellen, Paul and his girlfriend were sitting around talking when Ellen asked the question she'd been dreading. "We haven't heard a single thing about your wife and daughter. Do you have pictures and when can we meet them?"

She flushed, cleared her throat and spoke. "We're separated at the moment." She gazed at the expectant faces. "I'm hoping we'll get back together. It had to do with Jess, our daughter. She was premature, and her birth brought on violent nightmares, which turned to daytime fantasies. I didn't realize they were memories. I thought my subconscious was trying to get me to kill my baby. I left them so I wouldn't harm her." She took a deep breath. "That's the first time I've been able to say that to anyone other than my therapist."

Ellen moved next to her and hugged her. "Thank you for trusting us."

She thought about it for a second. "I do trust you. I'm hoping Lily will take me back, but I need to do some more work in therapy before I approach her."

"How old is Jess?"

"Twenty months."

"Well, if there's any way we can help, call us." Ted was the one who spoke, but the others echoed his offer.

Before she left for the airport, she pulled Ellen and Ted aside. "I'd like to do something for you and I hope you'll accept the gift—"

Ted stood straighter. "You don't need to give us anything, Robin."

"Wait, just let me finish. I'd like to set up an educational trust for my nieces and nephew so they can all go to the best private schools you can find for them. You know I made a lot of money when we went public and I'd love to do this for the kids. You don't have to answer now. Think about it and call me." She handed each of them her card. "You have my cell, but you can also contact me at the office."

Ted opened his mouth to speak, but Ellen put a hand on his arm to stop him. "That's a very generous offer. But this would be a multi-year commitment. Are you aware of how much tuition is at these schools?"

"I assure you, money is not a problem."

CHAPTER FORTY-SIX

Lily Terminates Therapy

The minute she sat facing Hillary, Lily launched into the story of her expedition to Shazarak the night before.

"It happened again. I met this woman and we danced and laughed and even did some kissing. At the end of the night, I invited her back to my apartment and somehow without the music and the excitement of the bar, it felt flat. Then she kissed me again and started to heat up, but I could have been kissing the mirror for all the excitement I felt. Initially I was bored, then I was downright turned off, so I claimed exhaustion and sent her on her way. I feel bad 'cause I don't like treating women that way, leading them on, then not delivering."

She looked at Hillary. "What do you think?"

"What did this woman look like?"

"What? Oh, tall, short black hair, blue eyes, on the butch side."

"Remind you of anyone?"

"Yes. I've been seeing you once a week for almost three months, and nothing has changed. Y'all were able to help me get over Micki, why not this?"

"What was the issue with Micki?"

"Because of her dumping me, I was feeling unlovable and afraid to trust my feelings. But you helped me learn to tune into myself, to get to my real feelings."

"And what are your feelings telling you now? About Robin? About other women?"

"Why are you making me repeat this? You know that I'm still in love with Robin, and I want her back. I don't want anyone else."

"Listen to yourself, Lily. What did you just say about Robin?'

"That I love her and don't want anyone else."

Hillary didn't speak, and after a minute Lily's eyebrows shot up. "I don't feel turned on because I only want Robin?"

"Trust your feelings, Lily. Until you get over Robin, you'll remain in limbo. Are you angry at Robin for abandoning you and Jess?"

"I. Am. Not. Angry. At. Robin. She loves me but had to leave for some reason."

"Then there's nothing for us to do. I think it's time you terminated therapy."

"You're kicking me out? Aren't you obligated to help me?"

"I'm here to help when you're ready, Lily."

CHAPTER FORTY-SEVEN

The Third Year

At Christmas, two plane tickets and vouchers for the first two weeks of February at the LezBeach resort were delivered to Lily with a handwritten note from Robin.

You both had such a good time last year. Enjoy. I miss you.

I miss you too, Lily thought. Last year's trip was a gift to celebrate her book hitting the bestseller list, but this was just a…gift. A reminder. Was she keeping Robin front and center by accepting it? Was she picking at a scab, never letting the wound heal? Should she send it back?

Who was she kidding? Robin was never far from her thoughts and the wound was so deep she felt it would never heal. It would be fun to get away again. Jess loved the beach, and while she'd accepted she'd probably never have another relationship, maybe she'd be ready to have casual sex this year. At the very least, she could relax and get some writing done. What the hell?

Unfortunately, she was sick the week before they were supposed to go, so she rescheduled the plane and the hotel for a week later.

Two-year-old Jess had flowered into a miniature Robin, precocious and beautiful, with Robin's sparkling green eyes, high cheekbones, glistening black hair and exuberant personality. She tested high on the genius scale and talked non-stop with a vocabulary and conceptual ability way beyond her chronological age.

Jess didn't remember last year's trip, but Lily showed her pictures and she was excited. "Will my dad be there?" she asked in her raspy voice, a leftover from the tubes in her throat in the NICU.

Lily rolled her eyes. Most of the other kids in the nursery school had dads and she had come home one day asking for her dad. Like Robin, she was relentless when she wanted something and she didn't give up inquiring about her dad. In desperation, Lily showed her a picture from their wedding reception, she in a white gown, Robin in a tux. She pointed to Robin. "That's your dad."

Jess grabbed the picture out of her hands and studied it. "Does she look like me?"

"Yes, she's beautiful, like you."

Jess kissed the picture and placed it carefully on the night table next to her bed. "Will my dad be at the beach?"

Lily was watching her from the doorway. "No, honey, your dad won't be there, but we'll have fun anyway."

Jess started crying. "Mommy, I need my dad. She has to be at the beach."

Oh God, what had she done? She picked up Jess and sat on the bed with her. "I want her too. We'll see her when we come back from the beach, okay?"

"Promise?"

"I promise." Now all she had to do was convince Robin to see her, but she'd deal with that when she got back. There was a slim chance Jess would forget. Very slim.

Jess got upset again when the eight-by-ten wedding picture wouldn't fit in the small purse Annie had given her for her birthday, so Lily dug out one of the wallet-sized versions for her. "Thank you, Mommy." She kissed the picture, then tucked it into the purse with her other valuable possessions. That purse went everywhere with her.

A week later than scheduled, they arrived at the LezBeach resort. Jess got right into the swing of things. The counselors put her in the two-to-four-year-old group, but she was so much more advanced than the other children she was moved to the five-to-eight-year-old group after two days. Lily alternated time at the beach with time writing at the casita. At night, she bathed Jess, sat with her while she ate, then put her to bed. She left Jess with a sitter, then went to dinner with new friends, hung out in the bar and danced.

It was the only time of the year, she permitted herself to go out to dinner and dancing every night, and she loved it. It would be perfect if she met someone she liked enough to have sex with, but, even if she didn't, she was having a great time and so was Jess. The first week flew.

CHAPTER FORTY-EIGHT

Robin Therapy

The last therapy session. Bittersweet. Sweet because she'd accomplished what she'd come for. Bitter because it meant leaving Olivia. As she looked around the room, imprinting it in her memory, her eyes met Olivia's. She'd felt safe here, safe with Olivia. She would miss her.

"The door is always open, you know." Olivia smiled. "You're leaving tomorrow?"

"Yes. Lily and Jess will be flying home while I'm flying there."

"Have you written the letter yet?"

"Partially. I'll finish it and put it in the mail before I leave." Robin leaned forward. "Are you sure it's all right to mail it and then leave for two weeks?"

Olivia sipped the latte Robin had brought for her. "You're dropping this on her out of nowhere, so she'll likely need some time to absorb it. Just include a number where she can reach you if she wants to talk to you before you get back." She smiled at Robin. "You've worked very hard and come a long way in the year we've been together. How are you feeling?"

"Thanks to you, I've confronted my fears, found my family and learned who I am and what's important to me. I feel happy and hopeful for the future. My only fear now is that Lily won't take me back and won't let me be a part of Jess's life."

"You're pretty persuasive so I have faith. But I'm always here if you need me." Olivia stood and walked Robin to the door.

"I don't know if this is allowed, but I've wanted to do this for a long time now." Robin pulled Olivia into a hug. "Thanks, Olivia."

Olivia smiled and returned the hug. "Good luck, Robin."

* * *

Robin put down the pen and stared out the window of her loft, considering whether there was anything else she wanted to say. She thought she'd nailed it, but reread it before signing.

Dear Lily,

I hope I'm not too late to come home to you and Jess. I owe you both apologies. That I love you has never been in doubt, but I would like the opportunity to meet my daughter, and to love her, no matter her condition. A little late, I know, but, nevertheless, true. I still want to be her dad though I no longer see that as just dropping in to play and have fun. Rather, I'd like to be a full-fledged parent with all the responsibilities that come with the title.

I'm sure your eyebrows are pretty high by now. It's taken me almost two years of wandering in the desert of life without you and a year of that time in intensive therapy to work through my problems. I know you thought I was having difficulty with Jess and the likelihood of future problems, but that was far from the truth. In reality, the problem was my screwed up past and my fear that I'd hurt Jess if I stayed.

To be certain that I was not a danger to Jess or other children, my therapist encouraged me to volunteer to work with children, including those born prematurely, who have various diseases and afflictions. I've learned a lot about love and loving. I won't make excuses for being a coward, but I can say with pride, I've grown up and the feelings I was struggling with are no longer a problem.

As I write this, you and Jess are getting ready to fly back from the LezBeach resort and I hope you both enjoyed it as much as you did last year. I'll be flying there this afternoon for my own two-week vacation so we'll be passing in the air.

You probably think that it's the old cowardly me sending this then fleeing the country, but I discussed it with Olivia, my therapist, and concluded that it might be best to give you time to think about all this while I'm away. Please feel free to call me if you have any desire to talk before I get back. You have my cell and Jan knows how to get in touch with me at LezBeach.

Please know whatever you decide that I love you dearly and regret every day leaving you and our baby. I pray (yes, pray) that you will let me back into your lives so I can spend the rest of my life making it up to both of you.

No one but you, forever.
All my love,
Robin

She sealed the letter in the envelope she'd prepared, picked up her suitcase and on the way to the elevator dropped it in the mail chute in the hallway. She glanced at her watch and hurried down to the waiting limo.

After takeoff, Robin told Brenda, a friend from her graduate school days and her guest for the next two weeks, that she wanted to nap. But when she dozed off, her dreams revolved around losing things by doing too little too late.

Brenda touched her shoulder gently to wake her. "We're landing, Robin."

She shook off her anxiety and sat up, happy to see the bright sun out on the tarmac.

CHAPTER FORTY-NINE

LezBeach Resort

Robin spent the first afternoon and evening sitting on the patio of her three-bedroom casita enjoying the sun, the sound of the ocean and the ocean breezes. Not in the mood to socialize, she encouraged Brenda to go to the dining room alone, then had dinner delivered to the casita and ate by herself on the patio. After a walk on the beach, she wrote in her journal, read for a while, then went to bed.

The next morning they ate breakfast on the patio, then settled into two chaise lounges under a palm canopy on the beach. Brenda talked nonstop about the fun she'd had at the bar last night, but Robin was distracted. All she could think about was Lily. When would she receive the letter? Would she be happy about it or angry? Would she consider taking her back? Should she call her later this week or wait? Finally, restless as hell, she left Brenda and strolled down the beach. She stopped when she saw a group of six- or seven-year-old children with a couple of counselors staring at something in the sand. It turned out to be a dead shark.

Working with children at the hospital had put Robin in touch with how much she enjoyed children, their unselfconsciousness, their playfulness, their inquisitiveness and their joy in the world.

She lingered, watching and listening. The intelligent rapid-fire questions of a gravelly voiced little girl wearing a floppy green hat impressed her particularly. Stumped by one of the questions, the counselors rolled their eyes at each other over the kid's head.

"Maybe I can help," Robin said and answered the question in detail.

As she spoke, the children spun to look at her, then all but the little girl turned back to the fish. She couldn't see the girl's face under the hat, but she felt the intensity of her scrutiny. The girl edged closer. "Are you my dad?" Robin loved her gravelly voice. It took a few seconds for her question to sink in, and even then she wasn't sure she'd heard it right.

"I'm sorry. What did you say?"

"I said," she practically shouted, "are you my dad?"

There was a titter of nervous laughter from the group of kids.

"Um, I don't think so. What's your name?"

"If you were my dad, you would know my name." The girl skipped back to the group, which had started making its way down the beach.

Robin laughed. Impertinent little thing. She watched her run and skip and jump down the beach. Something about that kid was familiar. *Could it be?* She shook her head. *Get a grip, Robin. Not only are Lily and Jess back in New York City, but that girl is three or four years older than Jess.* She turned and continued her walk, going in the opposite direction from the children.

Later, after lunch at the casita, she was reading in her lounge chair under the palm umbrella when she became aware that the group of children was back. Her eyes lit on the green hat, and she watched the girl getting the other children to chase her, fearlessly running into the water, forcing the counselor to drag her out, and building sand castles, then laughing as she stomped on them. She was so vibrant, so full of life, the kind of child she'd thought she would have. She knew now she'd love Jess no matter what, but she'd seen enough preemie babies in the hospital to know the kinds of problems she could expect Jess to have. Most likely she would be very different than Little Miss Green Hat.

When the counselors settled the group down to rest, drink water and have an afternoon snack, Robin wandered over to them. "How old are the kids?"

"They're five to seven."

"The one in the green hat is a handful."

The counselor laughed. "She sure is. What an instigator. Actually, she's younger than the others, but she's tall for her age and so precocious and mature that we had to move her up from the two-to-four group."

As if she sensed they were talking about her, the girl turned to stare at Robin. "How old is she?"

"Around two, I think." She studied Robin. "You know, she looks like you. Are you related?"

Robin's heart started to tap dance. *Could it be?* "What's her name?"

"Jess DiLuca."

Robin felt faint. "Thanks." She staggered back to her lounge chair.

Brenda looked up. "You look like you've seen a ghost. Are you okay?"

"I just saw my daughter."

"What? I thought they were supposed to leave on Sunday."

"Yeah, I don't know what happened, but the girl over there in the green hat is Jess."

"And that means Lily is around somewhere. What are you going to do?"

"Shit, you're right, Lily must still be here too. I don't want the counselor to think I'm a pervert, so I won't do anything for now. Look, they're going in the water and she's taken her hat off. Could you walk over and see what she looks like?"

Brenda strolled along the beach, stopped to watch the kids frolic in the water for a few minutes, then turned back. "She's a miniature you, same coloring, same hair and same eyes."

"She asked this morning if I was her dad. When Lily was pregnant, I used to tease her and say I don't want to be just another mommy, I want to be the dad. But how could Jess know that? Would Lily have told her?"

"Nah, she probably asks every black-haired, green-eyed butch she meets. You look like you need a drink."

"I don't think seltzer and lime is going to help much. I'm going back to the casita to take a shower and think about what to do. See you later."

* * *

Jess was chattering a mile a minute as Lily washed her, but Lily was distracted thinking about the chapter she was struggling with. "What did you say, Jess?"

"You're not listening, Mommy. I said I thought I saw my dad today, but she didn't know my name so it wasn't her."

"Stand up, please, so I can lift you out of the tub." She wrapped the girl in a towel, hauled her out and began to dry her. "You're not asking everyone on the beach if she's your dad, are you, sweetie?"

"Of course not, Mommy, just the one who looked like my dad, but she wasn't."

She nuzzled Jess, kissing her neck and her face and her belly. Giggling, Jess pulled away, then tickled her. Lily tickled her back and soon they were rolling on the floor, laughing. "I love you, Jess."

"I love you too, Mommy."

As usual, Jess protested having to wear a diaper to bed.

"We agreed you wouldn't have to wear a diaper during the day, but you would wear one at night, remember?"

"Yes, Mommy, but I'm really big now, and I only wet myself once this week, so I don't need a diaper."

Lily tossed her on the bed and deftly secured the diaper. "When you go four weeks in a row without wetting the bed at night, you won't have to wear a diaper. Show me four fingers."

"I know what four is, silly."

While Jess was distracted, Lily quickly pulled her pajamas on her and rolled her under the light blanket.

"I'll ask my dad what she thinks when I meet her, okay?"

Relentless, just like your dad. "Sure, baby." Lily read to her until she fell asleep. She dressed and, when the sitter arrived, went to meet Lindsay for dinner. As she related the story of Jess running up to some stranger asking if she was her dad, she noticed Lindsay resembled Robin—tall, slightly androgynous with dark hair, but blue, rather than startling green eyes like Jess and Robin. She also realized that she was really full of herself and not as smart or attractive or sexy or funny as Robin. She sighed. She'd thought she'd have a fling this year, but clearly she wasn't ready yet. Well, it didn't mean they couldn't dance and have a good time after dinner. She'd just be clear up front to avoid problems at the end of the night.

CHAPTER FIFTY

Robin and Jess

Robin needed to be alone, so she encouraged Brenda to go out for dinner and dancing again. After dinner alone on the patio, she stretched out on the chaise lounge, reading. She was dozing when something tickled her face. She brushed it away, but it didn't stop, so she opened her eyes and stared into the greenest eyes she'd ever seen, other than in the mirror. She jerked to a sitting position. "Jess, what are you doing here?" She glanced at her phone. "It's after midnight."

The little girl smiled. "You know my name. I knew you were my dad. Were you fooling this morning?"

Robin opened her mouth, but she didn't know what to say.

The girl put down the diaper she was carrying. "I came to show you the picture in case you forgot about me." She opened the little purse she was holding and held up a photo. "See, there you are with Mommy. She told me you were my dad. I didn't know."

Seeing the picture of her and Lily at their wedding reception, a tsunami of loss hit Robin. They'd created this beautiful child out of their love for each other. And now Jess thought she'd been forgotten. "I didn't forget about you. I didn't know it was you under that big hat." Tears stung Robin's eyes, and she pulled the girl onto her lap, breathed in her smell and kissed the top of her head. "Jess, your mommy will be worried about you. Do you know the number of your casita?"

"Of course, silly. It's two two two."

"Was your mommy asleep?"

"No, silly. My sitter Mary Ann and her friend Merry were wrestling on the sofa so I came to show you the picture." She held up the diaper. "You need to change me."

"How did you know where to find me?"

"I heard your friend tell the waiter your number when he brought her drink." She yawned and turned to wrap her arms around Robin's neck. "I'm glad I found you, Dad."

Robin held her close, savoring the feeling of her little body, cursing herself for missing two years of her daughter's life. She felt Jess go slack and she lay back with her on her chest. She didn't know how Lily would react, so she'd enjoy her daughter for just a few more minutes before taking her back.

"Robin, wake up. It's two o'clock." Brenda was shaking her shoulder, another woman behind her.

She opened her eyes. Oh, shit, she'd fallen asleep with Jess. Lily must be frantic.

"What are you doing with the child, Robin? Did you kidnap her?"

"No, she just showed up." She sat up, waking Jess.

The girl smiled. "Dad." Robin's heart melted.

Brenda's eyebrows went up. Her friend grinned.

Robin kissed Jess's forehead. "It's very late, Jess, and your mommy will be worried. I'm going to change your diaper, then take you home." Luckily, she'd learned to change diapers as a volunteer in the children's ward at the hospital. She put a towel on the bed, then removed Jess's pajamas and the wet diaper, washed and dried her, then put on the clean diaper. Her pajamas were soaked.

Brenda watched, a big smile on her face. "Nice work, 'Dad.' Who knew DiLuca was so domesticated?"

Robin looked over her shoulder. "Make yourself useful, Bren, and hand me one of my T-shirts, please?"

Jess smiled when she slipped the T-shirt on her. Her eyelids were drooping again and within seconds of Robin lifting her to her shoulder, she became dead weight, snoring lightly. Robin was overcome with sadness over the lost years, but she'd learned enough in therapy to know to focus on the future. *Regretting the past helps no one.*

"Um, Robin, this is Greta. Um, do you need me to come with you?"

"Thanks, Bren, I think I'd better go alone." She grinned. "Don't feel you have to wait up for me, ladies." She set off to find Lily's casita.

As she walked along the sand, she realized Jess had traveled a long way to get to her. The beach was unlit and the paths dim; most kids her age would have been frightened. Her kid was fearless and determined. She kissed Jess's head. Lily must be beside herself. Finally, she reached the two hundred-numbered casitas. She'd expected to hear people calling for Jess, but it was quiet. As she approached two twenty-two, Lily was standing in the doorway, embracing a woman. Apparently, she hadn't noticed Jess was missing.

When she was close enough to hear, she realized Lily was actually fending off the woman. As often as she'd thought about Lily, dreamed about her, imagined them together, with the golden light of the casita behind her, she was even more lovely, more sensual than she remembered. Her body reacted to her as it always did, with a burst of desire. And Lily's voice, even angry as it was now, still traveled through her body like warm chocolate.

"What about 'no' don't y'all understand, Lindsay? I told y'all upfront, just dinner, a couple of drinks and dancing, no necking, no sleeping together. Save yourself some embarrassment and leave now." She turned to go inside.

"Want to sleep with the great Lily Alexander." The woman grabbed Lily from behind. She shrieked, pivoted, pushed the drunk away and stood over her lying in the sand. "Don't you dare touch me. Ever. Now run along and sober up. Y'all can apologize tomorrow." She turned to go back into the casita.

Robin cleared her throat. "Um, Lily, I have something of yours."

"Robin?" Lily spun around. She grabbed the doorframe to steady herself. "What are y'all doing...how did you get Jess?" She looked like she might pass out. Her voice was higher than usual. Robin couldn't tell if she was frightened or angry or going into shock. One thing was clear. She didn't look happy to see Jess in her arms.

"She came looking for me." Robin glanced at the drunk who was trying to stand. "Shall we go inside and talk?"

Lily stared at her as if not quite believing she was real. She blinked, extended her hand to touch Robin's face, hesitated, then touched Jess instead. Their eyes locked over their daughter. She blinked again and her eyes flicked from Robin's face to the lump draped over her shoulder and back. She shook her head, then waved Robin into the casita. Lily was so close behind that Robin could hear her breathing, almost gasping for air, and smell her favorite rosemary shampoo. Overwhelmed by her nearness, Robin stepped aside so Lily could lead the way and she could breath. They exchanged a glance at the sight of the babysitter asleep on the couch. Lily snorted and muttered something Robin didn't understand, then stepped closer and prodded the girl. She yawned and sat up, her eyes darting between them, then she stood quickly. "Sorry, I must have dozed. Um, why is Jess out of bed?"

"Just what I was going to ask you." Now Lily's voice was sizzling hot with rage. "She was found wandering—where, Robin?"

"Over by the twelve hundred casitas."

"Do y'all know how far that is? Do you know she's not quite two and she's been wandering around in the dark all the way over to the twelve hundred casitas? What the fuck were you doing while she walked past you and out the door?"

"I, uh, fell asleep?"

Robin shifted Jess to her other shoulder. "According to Jess, you and your friend were playing on the couch and didn't hear her when she asked you to change her diaper."

Lily's face was almost purple. "You are in deep shit. You know you're not allowed to have someone with you when you babysit unless you get permission first. Get out. I'll deal with this tomorrow."

The girl grabbed her bag and scurried out the door without a backward glance.

Lily leaned over, hands on her knees, trying to catch her breath.

Robin had never seen Lily so angry. Was it her fear for Jess? Or was it anger that should have been directed at her? Or maybe some of both. She would take whatever Lily dished out.

When Lily straightened she seemed calmer. "Let's get her to bed." She ushered Robin into the smaller bedroom.

Robin put Jess into her bed and pulled the blanket over her. They stood watching her sleep for a minute. "She looks like an angel. I never expected she would be so beautiful and funny and smart."

"Is that your T-shirt she's wearing?"

"She was soaking wet. She had a clean diaper, but her pajamas were wet too, so I figured a T-shirt would be better than nothing."

Shaking her head, Lily turned and Robin followed her to the living room. Robin sat on the sofa, Lily on the chair facing her. They hadn't been this close since the day they moved into their separate apartments. She controlled the desire to take Lily in her arms, knowing they needed time to get to know each other again. "You're as beautiful as ever, Lily. I've missed you."

Lily looked away. "I'm going to kill Mary Ann. It sounds like she and Merry were having sex and not paying attention to Jess. I mean she had to walk right by them to get out of the casita." She blew out a breath. "Sorry. When I think Jess could have decided to go in the water or do whatever, I..." She covered her face, her shoulders shook.

Robin fought the urge to get up and comfort her.

"She could have died or been hurt." Lily looked up and dried her eyes. "Sorry."

"But she's okay. I couldn't believe she walked so far to get to me. In the dark." She reached a hand toward Lily, then dropped it. "You've done a wonderful job with her. I'm amazed. She seems too grown up to be not even two."

"She has turned out well, hasn't she? I would attribute a lot of that to your genes, Robin. She's exactly like you—the good parts and the maddening parts, like getting up in the middle of the night and wandering around in the dark."

"Has she ever done that in the city?"

"No. I think this was her need to find her dad. She's been driving me crazy for a couple of weeks wanting to see her dad. In desperation, I showed her your picture right before we left to come here. I never dreamed you'd be here at the same time."

"I'm not sure what happened. I tried to time the reservations so you and Jess would be back in the city by the time we arrived."

She laughed. "I screwed that up. I was sick so I rescheduled to come a week later."

"Lily, I—"

Lily put her hand up. "Don't. Seeing you is hard enough."

"Would you consider getting back together?"

"I can't think about it like this, Robin. You drop into our lives out of the blue, and I don't know, I don't know."

"Would it be all right for me to spend time with Jess? Here and when we get home?"

"I guess she's perfect enough now for you to love her, huh?"

Robin recoiled. It felt as if she'd been stabbed. "I deserve that. And more for leaving you with a sick infant. But it was never about her not being perfect." She blinked back the tears that sprang into her eyes.

"Well, it sure the fuck would be nice to know what it was about." Her face was getting red again.

"I'd like to talk to you about it. Maybe after we've had some sleep."

Lily stared at Robin, then looked away. "Jess needs you. I won't keep you from seeing her." She looked down. "But please don't try to steal her away from me."

"Oh, God, Lily, I'm sorry I've hurt you so much." She took Lily's hand. "I would never take her from you. I just want to be a part of her life. And yours if you'll let me." She stood. "Maybe I could babysit while you go out, so we don't have a repeat of tonight."

"What about your social life?"

"I come for the sun and the relaxation. I don't socialize. I usually eat in the casita and hang out with friends or work or read."

"You said 'we,' before. You're here with someone?"

"Yes. Brenda came along to keep me company."

"Is she...are you—"

"There hasn't been anyone else, Lily. Not for me." She stood. "Bren and I were friends at Stanford and we reconnected when she moved to New York City from California about a year ago. We're both single, so we hang out. That's it. Can we meet for lunch tomorrow and figure out when I can see Jess while you're here?"

"One o'clock, here, so I won't have to get a sitter while she naps."

"One it is." She leaned in to kiss Lily's cheek, but Lily's hand on her chest stopped her.

"Don't push your luck, Robin. I agreed to let you into Jess's life."

Robin nodded. "See you tomorrow."

* * *

Lily watched Robin walk into the night, a thousand thoughts racing through her mind. Robin here, as beautiful as ever, but more comfortable in herself. Robin here, saying there's never been anyone else. Robin here, wanting to spend time with Jess. Wanting to come back into their lives. She closed the door and sank onto the couch. She'd dreamed of this since the minute they'd separated. She was still in love with Robin, was weak in the knees at seeing her, wanting to kiss her and desperate to make love to her. Longing to have her back to complete her life. So why was she hesitating now? Because she wanted to hurt her. Because she was angry. Well, Hillary would be happy she was finally in touch with her anger.

She smiled as she got ready for bed. Angry or not, she was thrilled that Jess had taken things into her own hands and brought her dad home.

CHAPTER FIFTY-ONE

Lily and Jess and Robin

Lily woke with a start, gasping for breath, then quickly wrapped her arms around Jess before she could get to her feet and pounce again. Looking into the eyes of her grinning green-eyed monster, Lily rolled her over and covered her with kisses while tickling her until she gave their signal to stop.

"Uncle, Mommy. Uncle."

She rolled again to pull Jess on top of her, both breathing heavily. "You're getting too big to jump on me like that."

"But it's fun, isn't it, Mommy?" She straddled Lily. "I found my dad last night. I thought I dreamed it but look," she pulled Robin's T-shirt away from her chest. "Did my dad bring me home? Can I see her today? I miss her."

"Going out by yourself in the middle of the night was very bad, Jess."

"I know, Mommy, but you were out and Mary Ann and Merry were playing and didn't hear me when I said my diaper was wet so I went to find my dad to change me." Her gruff voice, her impeccable logic and her desire for her dad touched Lily's heart, but she needed to make sure Jess understood what she'd done wrong.

She pulled Jess into her arms and kissed her nose. "You are a brilliant two-year-old, that's why you're in the five-to-eight group, but you're still a little girl and you can't go wandering off in the middle of the night. Next time, wait for me and I'll take you to your dad. Understand?"

Jess rolled her eyes. *Damn. She rolls her eyes just like the dad she'd never met before yesterday.* Lily struggled to keep a straight face. "Jess?"

"Yes, Mommy, I understand but—"

"No buts about this, Jess. If you wake in the middle of the night, you wait for me to come."

"What if my dad is here and you're not? Can I go with her?"

"I...yes, of course, baby, you can go with your dad." Maybe having Robin in their lives would be a good thing, because she was going to need all the help she could get with this child as she grew.

"I thought my dad would be here this morning. Can I see her today?"

She sat up with Jess in her arms and swung her legs over the side of the bed. She brushed the hair off Jess's forehead and kissed her. "Dad is having lunch with us today. Time—"

"Like a family." She jumped off Lily's lap and started hopping around the room. "The mom, the dad and the little girl."

"Oh, sweetie, not yet, but maybe soon." She said it softly, not wanting Jess to hear. "Come on, you little scamp, time to get ready for camp." She carried her into the bathroom.

"You made a poem, Mommy."

Around noon, Robin texted to say she'd ordered lunch for them and to ask if she could pick Jess up from camp. Lily felt a stab of anger and her first instinct was to say no. She took a deep breath. Jess needed Robin, and if she was honest, she needed Robin and not only to help her manage their genius baby. She called the head camp counselor and arranged for Robin to pick up Jess, then texted pick-up time and location to Robin.

Her heart flipped as she watched them walk toward her, hand in hand, Robin leaning over and Jess looking up, intent on some discussion. She smiled and went into the casita for her camera. Time to start making memories for Jess. And Robin.

She was fast. She caught them still involved in their discussion, then when they paused, laughing and when Robin picked up

Jess and they stared into each other's eyes with the same funny expression on their faces. She snapped a few more pictures when they stepped onto the patio, tickling and teasing each other. She grinned as she put the camera down. She'd forgotten what it was like to be with Robin.

Lily watched in fascination as they continued to play during lunch. And Jess let Robin feed her, something that was usually verboten these days. At one point Robin met her eyes. "Is this okay? I don't want to—"

"It's fine. I'm enjoying watching you together." Her eyes filled with tears. "But we have nap time," she looked at her watch, "in ten minutes, Jess."

"No," Jess yelled. "I don't want to nap. I want to stay with my dad." She kicked the table.

"Hey, sweet cheeks." Robin pulled Jess close. "That's no voice to use with your mommy. Remember I told you that Mommy and I need to talk about when you and I can spend time together?" She dried Jess's tears. "Would you like to apologize?"

"I'm sorry, Mommy." She left Robin, crawled into Lily's lap and put her thumb in her mouth.

Lily ran her fingers through Jess's hair and spoke over her head. "A charmer. Remind you of anyone?"

Robin blushed. "Ya think?"

"I think." She didn't know which of them was more adorable. She kissed Jess's head. "Would you like your dad to change you and stay with you until you fall asleep?"

Jess took her thumb out of her mouth. "Would you, Dad?"

The look of joy on Robin's face touched Lily. It didn't matter if it was just because Jess was perfect—the important thing was Robin wanted to be with her daughter.

"I'd love to, sweet cheeks." She stood and opened her arms. As if she'd been doing it her whole life, Jess reached for her, then turned to kiss Lily. "Later alligator."

"Robin, did you teach her that?"

"Not me."

"Why do you call me sweet cheeks?"

Lily listened to their chatter as they walked into the house. Her heart was full as she went back to her writing. But she didn't write. She stared at the screen of her laptop, flooded with images of

Robin, of her with Robin and new images of Robin with Jess and of the three of them together.

A half-hour later, a heavy-lidded Robin appeared and sat next to Lily on the sofa.

"She was so chatty, I almost fell asleep first."

"That little head is chock full of information, thoughts, questions, ideas, you name it. I'm surprised she ever gets to sleep. So it looks like you and your daughter have bonded."

"Does it upset you? I know it must feel like I just barged in after the hard part is over and now I'm licking the cream off the top." She grinned. "That was a crappy metaphor, but you know what I mean."

"I do resent you dropping into our lives after all this time. But I'm also enchanted watching the two of you together. And I actually think the really hard part is yet to come. I was thinking this morning that it might be nice to have someone to share her teen years with."

Robin shifted closer on the sofa and took Lily's hand. "Do you mean that? It's okay for me to spend time with her?"

Lily extracted her hand. "I won't deny that I feel angry—my therapist has been trying to get me in touch with the anger since you left. But she needs you, Robin. She needs her dad. And I would never deny her that."

"I swear I'll make it up to her, Lily. And you, if you'll let me."

Lily shifted away from Robin. "So let's talk about how we handle the next four days."

"Would it be presumptuous to suggest that we have lunch like this every day? I pick her up, we eat, I put her to sleep?"

"I think the routine will be good so she knows she'll see you."

"And I'd love to have dinner with her and you if you don't have plans. Then I could hang out with her and put her to bed. What do you think?"

"Why don't we try it tonight? I have plans, but I'll cancel the sitter. I usually give her dinner, then I put her to bed before going out. So I'll be around while you're eating, but then it'll be just the two of you."

Robin reached for Lily's hand again, but Lily pulled away. "Uh-uh. If I'm going to have to fight you off, Robin, we'll have to rethink this."

Robin looked as if Lily had slapped her. She felt bad, but what did Robin expect? Open arms and an invitation to bed? Actually, part of her wanted to offer Robin just that, but she needed time to work through her anger. And hopefully, she would work through it, because she loved Robin and even being abandoned by her without an explanation hadn't changed that.

"Sorry. It won't happen again. You're being so much more generous than I deserve." She stood. "When we get back to New York, I'd like to spend some time with you and explain why I left."

The next morning, lying in bed before the daily attack, Lily realized she'd spent the entire evening thinking about Jess and Robin. And about Robin. Her date kept asking what was wrong. She kept lying, but she didn't feel good doing that to a perfectly nice woman. It would be better to cancel her plans for the evening and stay home with them. She braced herself when she heard Jess racing toward her room and just before the weight hit her she had a moment of clarity. *Who am I kidding? I want to be with Robin.*

After Robin put Jess down for her afternoon nap, she stopped to talk to Lily. "She was a little less manic today. Maybe she's getting used to me being around."

Lily laughed. "No way. Stay around and you'll discover that every day is a new adventure with your precocious daughter."

Robin shrugged. "I was afraid she was bored with me already." Lily knew her well enough to know she was pretending nonchalance.

She looked down at her computer to avoid Robin's eyes. "By the way, my plans have changed for this evening, so if you don't mind I'll stay home with you two."

Robin's face fell. "Oh, would you rather I—"

"It's up to you. I don't want to butt in on your bonding time."

"Thanks for asking. I'd love for the three of us to spend the evening together."

Dinner was fun. Lily watched them tickling and giggling and poking each other and remembered thinking when she was first pregnant that she was going to have two babies on her hands. But with all the playfulness, Robin got a lot of food into Jess and managed to teach her some things about the moon and the tides as well. So maybe not two babies.

"Mommy?" They were quietly enjoying their chocolate ice cream dessert.

"Yes, baby?"

"Why does my dad sleep in a different house? Amelia says her mommies sleep in the same bed. Are you diborced?"

Robin choked. Their eyes met briefly.

Lily cleared her throat. "It's a 'v' not a 'b,' Jess. Divorced." She waited while Jess repeated the word. "Dad and I are not divorced. We both love you and we love each other, but we have problems we have to fix before we can live together. Do you understand?"

"No." Jess shook her head vigorously. "I want us to be together like tonight. Why do we have to have another house?"

"You just found your dad, Jess. We need time to fix things, but we'll spend lots of time together like this. I promise."

"Will we all live in the same house?"

"Not right away, baby. We have to see if we can fix our problems."

"Hey, sweet cheeks, can we have a family hug?"

"What's that?"

Robin swept Jess into her arms. "Come on, Lily." Lily stood and the two of them hugged Jess. Their eyes met over their daughter's head and the connection was as strong as ever. Robin smiled. "How about I change your diaper and put on your pajamas and the three of us watch a movie?"

"Can we watch *Mary Poppins?*"

They snuggled on the sofa, one of them on either side of Jess. When Jess fell asleep with her head on Lily's shoulder, they were surprised to find that she was holding each of their hands.

"We need to tell her tomorrow that she and I are leaving in two days and you're not. She won't be happy."

"Neither will I." Robin stood. "I like Jess's idea of us being a family and living together." She gave a little salute. "See you tomorrow."

* * *

Lily looked up at the knock, surprised to see Robin at her casita in the middle of the morning, surprised by the flip-flop of her heart and surprised by the sudden stab of desire. "Hey, you're early this morning."

"I wanted to talk before I pick up Jess for lunch. A week is an awfully long time for a child and I don't think you two leaving without me would be good for Jess. I—"

"Not everything is about you, Robin. We've done just fine without you up to now." Angry tears filled Lily's eyes and she swiped at them. "And when did you, who couldn't even look at Jess, become the expert on her?"

Robin stumbled back. Her eyes widened, her left hand went to her cheek, as if she'd been slapped, her right hand went to her heart. She met Lily's eyes.

Lily felt like a crazy woman, vacillating between wanting to make love to her and wanting to hurt her. "I'm so sorry, Robin."

"It's all right. I deserve your anger, Lily. I hurt you and I can't change that. But more than anything in the world, I want to be there for you and Jess from now on." She extended her hands palms up. "I thought we could discuss options for leaving together so Jess—"

"What options?"

"I've come up with three. I could change my reservation and fly back with you tomorrow which is fine with me. Or if you don't have anything pressing at home, you and Jess could stay another week and we all fly home together. I checked this morning and the resort is booked solid so you'd have to move into my casita. It's three bedrooms, but Brenda has moved in with the woman she met the first night we were here, so it would be just the three of us." She took a deep breath. "I'm voting for number two, but you may like the third option: leave things as they are and I call you when I get home. Think about it. I'll see you for lunch and you can tell me then." She turned and walked away.

Lily dropped her head into her hands. Definitely not three. Maybe one, but if she was honest, she wanted option two. She could write here just as well, maybe better, than she could at home. In fact, with Robin back in her life, these past few days had been extremely productive. And, angry or not, there was no denying she was enjoying being with Robin and seeing her with Jess was a dream come true. Not to mention that Jess was ecstatic spending time with her dad. They'd have to deal with the real world when they got back, but another week would solidify Robin's bond with Jess and their bond as a family.

The only question was whether living in the same house she'd be able to hold herself back from making love with Robin. She reached for her cell to call Hillary to schedule a telephone therapy session to help her deal with the rage that kept bubbling up. She smiled, thinking again that Hillary would be a lot happier than she was about her getting in touch with her anger. And maybe Hillary could help her figure out whether she needed to resist Robin. She made an appointment for four o'clock.

They were holding hands and singing as they walked along the path to the casita, apparently a camp song that Jess had learned this morning. When Jess spotted her sitting on the patio, she dropped Robin's hand, ran to her and wrapped her arms around her neck. "Want to learn the new song, Mommy?"

"I do, sweetie, but you know we try to have quiet time at lunch so you can take a nap. How about when you wake up later you teach me?"

"But Dad won't be here then. We have to sing together."

She exchanged a look with Robin. "Well, what about before or after dinner? What do you think, Dad?"

Jess giggled. "You're silly, Mommy. She's not your dad."

"I think it's a great idea. Maybe we could take a walk on the beach after dinner so we can sing really loud."

Jess jumped up and down. "Walk on the beach, walk on the beach."

Robin swept her into her arms. "Quiet time, sweet cheeks. Let's wash up so we can eat lunch."

Robin tiptoed out of Jess's bedroom and sat opposite Lily, who was working on the patio. "So?"

Lily finished the sentence, then saved the document. "So."

Robin was leaning forward, waiting for the answer. Lily was tempted to drag it out, but she found it impossible to be cruel and cutting when she wasn't angry. "So, I choose option two if it's still on offer." Robin's smile reminded her again of how much brighter the world, and her life, was with Robin in it.

"You'll stay and move in with me? Now I know how Jess feels. I'm about to jump up and down and scream, 'Move in, move in.'"

Lily grinned. "Maybe you should save it for when we walk on the beach tonight. I'm sure your little shadow will have the same reaction."

Robin started toward her, then stopped. "I know you're really angry, but your willingness to let me in means a lot to me. Would it be all right for me to give you a thank-you kiss? I promise I won't be out of control if we share the house."

Lily pulled Robin into her arms, kissed her lightly and touched her face. "I'm not sure where we're headed, Robin, but I think this next week will be fun for all three of us."

Robin touched her lips and grinned. "I'll take care of all the arrangements for moving your things and for changing your flight home."

After dinner, they walked on the beach, one of them on either side of Jess, swinging her on demand. They sang the camp song loudly, then ran and splashed in the water. When Jess was tired, she asked Robin to carry her, then fell asleep in her arms.

"I gather you didn't want to tell Jess about staying and moving into my casita?"

"I realized she'd drive us crazy if she knew ahead of time. We'll tell her the day of."

They walked back in silence. Lily thought about her therapy session. Hillary had encouraged Lily to express her anger and talk to Robin about it and her hurt. Hillary had asked, "Do you love Robin, does she love you, do you want to be with her?" The answer to all three was an unequivocal yes.

Then Hillary had asked, "Do you trust that she won't leave again?" And she couldn't answer. She knew she wanted Robin back, but she wanted to be less angry and she wanted to be sure she could trust her to stay. She took Robin's hand and they smiled at each other.

CHAPTER FIFTY-TWO

Shared Casita

Lily woke to a loud oomph followed by a growl, "Christ, Jess," followed by "You said a bad word, Dad," followed by giggles and screams. It was their first morning in the casita and Jess had pounced on her dad instead of her. She examined her feelings for traces of jealousy, but it was happiness she felt. Jess was theirs, after all, and even if it was a long time in coming she liked sharing her with Robin. Jess had been flying high last night when they'd told her the three of them would be sharing the same house. And Robin hadn't been much better. She had been the calm one, but she felt it too, the joy of being a family.

Robin was crying "Uncle" over and over and Jess was paying no attention to her surrender, so Lily went to save her. Robin spotted her in the doorway. "Help me, please save me from the tickle monster." Lily moved to the bed intending to pull Jess off Robin, but Robin dragged her down and the two of them attacked her.

"We tricked her, Dad. Kiss her. We do tickles and kisses."

Their eyes met, and Robin's lips moved toward Lily's lips, but at the last second she followed Jess's lead and planted quick kisses on her face. Then she turned on Jess and she and Lily tickled and kissed her until she cried uncle. The three of them lay there for a second, then Jess rolled over and straddled the two of them. She grinned. "I like this, Mommy and Daddy."

Lily rolled over, taking Jess with her, and stood. "Time for breakfast. Who do you want to wash and dress you?" As if she didn't already know the answer.

"Dad, Dad, Dad."

She handed Jess to Robin. "I'll get breakfast."

Jess wanted to stay home with them, but Robin put her foot down. "You have to go to camp while Mommy and I work. No if, ands or buts, sweet cheeks, so get your cute butt in gear."

"Uh, oh, Mommy, Dad said another bad word." She reached for Robin's hand. "Can you carry me, Dad?"

Robin swung her up and onto her shoulders, and they jogged down the beach with Jess whooping and laughing. Lily shook her head. They were adorable together. When they were out of sight, she turned to her computer and her love story. Several hours later, Robin's voice penetrated her concentration, and she looked up, surprised to see her and Jess facing each other and having what looked like a serious conversation. Lunchtime already? She stretched and went out to see if there was a problem.

"Tell me again what Amelia said." Robin's voice was gentle.

They both looked up when she came onto the patio. Jess was crying and her thumb was in her mouth.

"Girls can't be dads, so you're not my dad."

Robin focused on Jess. "I'm sure Amelia is nice, Jess, but she's just a little girl and she doesn't know or understand everything." She took a deep breath. "Being a dad is a job, like being a teacher or being a doctor or being a mom." She gently dried Jess's dripping nose. "Do you understand?"

"Think so," Jess mumbled around her thumb.

"Mommy and I and all the mothers here are lesbians, which means we're all girls and while some of the children here have only one mommy, you and most of the other children have two mommies. So I'm your mommy just like Mommy Lily. You know that, right?"

Jess nodded.

"Dad is just a nickname. Do you know what a nickname is?"

"Yes."

"I think it's fun for you to call me Dad, but you can call me Mom, Mommy, Mama or even Robin as long as you're happy when you see me coming. Do you understand?"

"Yes."

"I'll take care of you like Mommy Lily but there are other things I think a Dad should do, that I wish my dad had done for me when I was your age. For example, I like to carry you on my shoulders and twirl you around and throw you in the air and do other things not all mommies do."

Jess bounced up and down. "And wrestle in the sand with me and splash water at me and have races and make funny faces."

"That's exactly the kind of thing."

Robin crossed her eyes and stuck out her tongue. "Lunch is here."

Jess giggled. "You're silly, Dad."

They were quiet watching the waitress move their lunch from the cart to the table. As the waitress walked away, Robin kissed Jess on the nose. "If you're still confused, sweet cheeks, your mommy might be able to make it clearer."

Lily shook her head. "Take some time to think about it, baby. Wash up for lunch now and we can talk about it after your nap if you want."

"Okay, Mommy." Jess slid off the chair. "Will you help me, Dad?"

Robin smiled at Lily and swept Jess up in her arms. "You bet."

Later that night, after Jess was in bed, they were sitting on the patio enjoying the evening. "Jess hasn't mentioned the dad thing again. Do you think she got it?"

Lily laughed. "Well, darlin', I do think she understands the basic idea, but you can be sure she's mulling it over in that busy little mind of hers, and it will pop up again when you least expect it. You might give some thought to round two."

"She really is exceptionally bright, isn't she?"

"She tests off the charts. Her vocabulary, her comprehension and her ability to grasp concepts are well beyond her actual age. She was just over five months when she started talking and not long after she was speaking in sentences and counting and writing. And one day I put her in front of my computer and I realized she wasn't just randomly pressing things, she was reading the options and making selections. She reads everything, not just children's books. And she keeps a journal. It's the red notebook by her bed. Open it and take a look sometime. She has a million questions, about everything. She's so like you, it's uncanny. It's wonderful and challenging at the same time. We'll need to fight like hell to make sure she has a normal childhood."

"What do you mean?"

"Look at camp. Intellectually she's way beyond her age group so they put her with the five-to eight-year-olds, but socially she's much younger. Her nursery school thinks she should be in regular school already."

"There must be special schools in New York City where she could be with other children like her. Do you want me to look into it?"

"Does that mean you're willing to do more than have fun, Dad?" She put her hand up. "Joking. It would be great if you'd take that on."

"I'll put together a list, then we can discuss the most promising and check them out when we get back."

"Sounds good. She must get this from you, Robin. I know you have no memory of your childhood, but I'll bet you were just like her as a child."

Robin hesitated, not sure she wanted to get into this now, but she realized she didn't have to go into the whole story now. "Actually, I went to Florida a few months ago to see my brothers. According to Ted, the older one, that's exactly how I was, but my parents didn't notice."

"How could they not notice?"

"Well, my father was and still is an alcoholic, and my mother was…I don't know what. An alcoholic, a pill addict and somewhat crazy, according to Ted. She apparently focused all her rage and hatred and craziness on me. And talk about being over your head socially, my whole world before I went to school was my two brothers and my mom or an alcoholic minder. I'd never had a friend."

Lily slid her chair closer and reached for Robin's hand but caught herself, and pulled back. "How terrible for you. What made you decide to find your family?"

Robin searched those warm gold-brown eyes and knew it was all right to talk about it. "Some issues came up in my therapy, and Olivia, my therapist, suggested I talk to my dad and brothers."

"That must have been hard."

"It was and it wasn't. I didn't see my dad, but Ted and Paul were both very welcoming and willing to talk about what I was like as a child. I learned some things that I'd repressed." She cleared her throat. She hadn't planned to do this now but *carpe diem*—"seize the day" as they say. "Something happened to me as a child that triggered my leaving you and Jess." She tried to sound casual, but her stomach clenched and her shoulders tensed, and she knew Lily would see and hear her distress.

Lily looked concerned. "You don't need to talk about this if you're not ready."

Was she ready? Would she ever be ready? Probably not. "Not talking is part of why I had to leave you. If I'd been smarter or braver or more trusting of the people who loved me," her voice broke, "and not so sure you all would abandon me in disgust, I would have talked about what was going on and spared us all, especially you and Jess, a lot of pain. What I'm going to tell you isn't an excuse, but it might help you understand…me. And why I did what I did. It's hanging over me so if you're willing to listen, I'd like to tell you now."

Lily put a little distance between them. "Tell me."

"I looked like her, green eyes, black hair, olive skin, but I was tall like my father. Like Jess. And I wasn't at all feminine. In fact, many people thought I was a boy. According to Ted, she never accepted me as her child and we fought constantly. Even before I was a year old, I refused to wear dresses and insisted on short hair. She ridiculed me and told me I was ugly and stupid, that I was a freak, that I wasn't a girl or a boy. Some time between the age of one and two, she stopped taking me out with her, left me home alone."

Lily was aghast. "Where was your dad?"

"As I said, he's an alcoholic. And he worshipped her. He refused to see anything she did in a negative light. Ted says he told him how she treated me during the day, but he ignored it. He hasn't changed, Ted says. Despite everything, he still refuses to believe she was crazy." She could hear the bitterness in her voice.

"I was six years old when my sister was born." She put a hand up to stop the question that was sure to follow the frown on Lily's face. "I know. I never mentioned a sister. But I didn't remember her. The baby, Rosaria, was three months premature."

Lily gasped. "Oh, God. The name intended for you? Do you need water or tea?"

"No, thanks." Robin rubbed her neck. "Ted remembers Mom pacing around the house muttering about the doctors keeping her from holding her little girl. He believes she took the baby home too soon, against doctor's orders, and he remembers the baby being horrible looking, skeletal, with veins showing and yellowish skin. I guess she was jaundiced. And she cried all the time, not a real cry, but like Jess sounded in the beginning." She grabbed a tissue and dried the sweat on her forehead.

"Mariana, my mother, acted as if nothing was wrong. She carried her on a pillow—never put her down, talked and sang to her constantly. She stopped even pretending to care about the rest of us, wouldn't leave the house to shop, or even if food was in the house, put the baby down to cook. Ted took care of Paul and me. With money our father gave him, Ted fed the three of us what twelve-year-old boys eat, peanut butter and jelly, American cheese, bologna, pizza and McDonald's burgers and fries. We ate upstairs in his bedroom because it was so scary being around her."

Robin's mouth felt as if she'd swallowed a tablespoon of sand, and she was finding it difficult to talk. "I do need water." She went to the cooler, handed a bottle to Lily, then drank half her bottle without stopping. She paced. "Ted says I was independent from a very young age, washing and dressing myself as best I could. I was talking by the time I was six months old and taught myself to read soon after. I devoured any book I got my hands on, including his and Paul's schoolbooks, which, it seems," she smiled, "I was always stealing. The boys got me library books about subjects that interested me, which was just about anything, and I read everything in my parents' library. My dad was the chair of the Physics Department at Miami U and my mom was the brilliant young student that he got pregnant, so they had lots of fiction, science, math, history philosophy books, and the *Encyclopedia Britannica*." She smiled at Lily. "So yes, I was a lot like Jess, but thankfully she's had you—"

"Don't." Lily jumped to her feet and embraced Robin. "Don't go there, Robin, please."

She leaned into Lily, feeling a gush of love. Inhaling her scent calmed her. Then Lily seemed to realize what she had done and disengaged. Robin took a swig of water.

"I don't know when my dad became a full-out alcoholic but according to Ted, his drinking got worse after I was born and he was almost always drunk. He must have sobered up to teach or maybe it was tenure, but he taught at Miami until he retired a couple of years ago. I don't know why Ted and Paul don't hate me since my birth seemed to trigger both of our parents disappearing." She stared into the distance, took another swig and thought for a minute before continuing.

"This next part came back to me in therapy. I thought I'd made it up until I talked to Ted and Paul. She never registered me for school and I didn't go out, so I was home all the time. At first, it was just me and my mother, but after Rosaria was born, it was the three of us. I was afraid of the baby, scared she'd jump up and attack me like on TV, but I was also fascinated. Ted told me I asked him why my mother loved her and not me who was big and strong."

Robin stopped to rub her temples but realized she needed the space and the comfort of pacing while she got this last part out. "I had fantasies of throwing Rosaria away or pulling her head off the way I'd broken every doll I'd been given or putting her in the oven as my mother often threatened to do to me." She cleared her throat.

"Mariana sometimes chased me with a knife or a wooden spoon or whatever was nearby when she deigned to acknowledge me, so I'd learned to keep my distance. Ted said I was always near but just out of reach, watching. Then one day, I was in the kitchen watching her try to feed the baby, who had been crying constantly and wouldn't take the breast or a bottle. She went from pacing and muttering to screaming and ranting. I was ready to run, but instead she grabbed the baby by her feet, swung her in the air and slammed her head on the table.

"Oh my God, Robin."

Hearing the shock in Lily's voice Robin drew back from the horror of the memory and focused on her, surprised to see tears streaming down her face. She wanted nothing more than to hold

Lily and to be held, but she forced herself to continue. She needed Lily to understand. She closed her eyes, shutting out the present.

"I remember the sound of that tiny head hitting the wood, seeing her brains splatter, feeling the wetness on my face and in my hair. And I remember the hate on my mother's face when she looked at me. 'See what you made me do. It should have been you, you freak.' She picked up a knife and came toward me. I ran up the stairs and hid, but she didn't follow. After a while, I snuck downstairs again and she was talking to herself and gesturing with a gun. When she saw me standing in the doorway she smiled. I hadn't seen that smile for a very long time and I edged closer to her, though I was still poised to run. When I stopped, she pointed the gun at me and said, 'This is your fault,' then she put the gun in her mouth…"

Robin shuddered, reliving the sound of the gun, the feeling of the wet spray, and seeing her mother drop to the floor. She took another bottle of water and, keeping her back to Lily, drank the whole thing.

"Oh, Robin."

Aware that Lily had stood up, she avoided looking at her and quashed her response to the sympathy and love she heard in Lily's voice. She was determined to tell her the whole story and didn't want to break down.

"I was a little over six years old. I remember the blood splashing me. I remember trying to wake her. Ted and Paul got home about six o'clock that night and found me covered in blood and brain tissue sitting by her body, holding her hand and cradling what was left of her head in my lap. I was in shock. The medical examiner estimated she'd died between nine and ten in the morning. The autopsy found that she was filled with drugs and alcohol. Apparently after Paul was born she suffered from depression, which got worse after I was born."

Suddenly she was in Lily's arms, and Lily was petting and kissing her. "My poor, Robin. I'm so sorry. So sorry, I didn't know. I would have made you stay."

"I didn't know myself, Lily. I repressed everything. Ted said my father and I acted as if it hadn't happened. He couldn't accept it and I guess my little brain couldn't handle it so I forgot it. Afterward, my father hired someone to cook and clean and be there in the day for us, but she was also an alcoholic and did the minimum. She thought I was retarded because I was withdrawn and didn't speak to her.

"My dad hadn't realized I wasn't in school but didn't do anything about it when he found out. Then, months later, I got sick and the family pediatrician realized I wasn't in school and he sent a social worker to register me. I started first grade the September after I turned eight. Because that was far from where I was intellectually, I became a problem student. My dad totally withdrew from us and pretty much ignored the school's complaints. I was promoted because it was clear I had mastered whatever they were supposed to be teaching, but no one ever paid much attention until Barbara Fielding took me under her wing."

Robin was close to collapsing, but she wanted to get it all out now that she'd started. Hopefully, it would help Lily understand. "Let's sit." She led Lily to the sofa.

"The night we met and you brought up us having babies, I had a violent nightmare about killing babies. From time to time after we discussed having a baby, I'd have a similar nightmare, though usually I didn't remember the details. But sometime after Jess was born, the nightmares became more and more frequent and more specific. I saw myself grabbing her feet and smashing her against the wall or a table, killing her, then shooting me or shooting you.

"As time went on, the nightmares came when I was awake—at first just in the NICU, then I'd be walking or eating or whatever and the images would flash in my mind. I was having flashbacks, but I didn't know that's what they were. I thought I was fantasizing about killing her and you. I thought if I didn't see her in the NICU, I would be okay. But the nightmares and the daytime images didn't stop. So when she came home, I was petrified I was going to hurt her. It's ironic that super-verbal me was unable to put what was going on into words. I just knew I had to go away before I hurt her. And one of us."

"Oh, sweet Robin, I had no idea. How horrible for you to go through that all alone." Lily rubbed the nape of Robin's neck, soothing her. "When did you go into therapy?"

"Not soon enough. A couple of months after I left you, when I was in Milan, the fantasies and nightmares became sporadic and then stopped. Then last year when you sent the picture from here, Jan cut Jess out and gave me the part with you. I wanted so badly to come home to you. I cried all that day. Then I called the therapist Katie had been encouraging me to see since we separated. I started the next afternoon."

"So you worked it through?"

"It took a month of seeing her three times a week before I was able to tell Olivia about the dreams and daytime images. After another couple of months, Olivia felt sure these thoughts didn't just come from nowhere and she suggested I find my family. Once I talked to Ted, I realized it was a memory, not a fantasy, and I stopped dreaming about it.

"The other thing Olivia had me do was volunteer on the children's ward at the hospital. Eventually Nicole got me in as a volunteer to work with families of premature babies—and, of course, with the babies. I've spent a great deal of time with children of all ages, many of them dealing with the problems I thought Jess might have. I learned that I love kids, healthy and not so healthy, so-called normal and afflicted. I wanted to be sure that I wanted to be with her and not just you. And I do."

"Oh, Robin. If only I'd known maybe we could have stayed together."

"If I've learned anything in therapy, and I learned a lot, it's that the past is the past and you can only change the future. You'll see when you read the letter I sent, which says that I was prepared, no, anxious, to come back to you both, no matter Jess's condition. I hope you'll take me back."

Lily leaned in and kissed Robin. "More than anything I want you back in our lives, but you're going to have to deal with my anger before we can get into bed together."

"I'll wait until the end of time, Lily."

They kissed. And kissed. And kissed. Finally, Robin spoke. She was breathless. "Isn't this where we started?"

Lily pulled back to look into her eyes. "Got a problem with that, big girl?"

Robin smiled. "No. No problem. None whatsoever."

They lay on the chaise on the patio, Robin holding Lily, neither speaking, both enjoying the contact. "How was it seeing your brothers after all these years?"

"It was wonderful. Paul has spent years struggling with what our mom did, but he's starting to get past it. He's dating someone who seems nice, but I gather he has a problem with commitment. Sound familiar? Ted is a psychiatrist. His wife, Ellen, is warm and smart and lovely. She teaches elementary school. I think you'll like her a lot. And I have two nieces and a nephew. The oldest girl, Sara, is thirteen. The youngest, Victoria, is seven. They both look like Jess and me. Teddie, the boy, is ten and looks like Ted. The kids made me a photo album so I'll be able to show you family pictures when we get back."

"Wow. Jess is going to be ecstatic that she has more cousins."

"In fact, the three of them are exceptional too. Ted and Ellen have been struggling financially to give them the kind of schooling they need, so I set up a fund for their education."

Lily turned and kissed Robin. "Why am I not surprised."

"It was great getting to know them and hearing stories about our family. I brought them all to New York for Christmas and we had a wonderful time. They're anxious to meet you and Jess. Maybe we'll take a trip to Florida or we'll bring them to New York again, once we're settled, so you can all get to know each other."

CHAPTER FIFTY-THREE

Getting Together

They fell into an easy rhythm, Robin taking Jess to day camp in the morning, then working or reading on the patio while Lily worked on her computer inside. Afternoons Robin picked up Jess and the three of them had lunch at the casita, then a nap for Jess and camp again for a few hours while Robin and Lily went back to work.

Jess loved for the three of them to be around the other children and their families, so some nights they went to family dinner in the dining room instead of eating on the patio. Afterward, they walked on the beach or watched a movie until Jess got sleepy.

With only two days remaining before their flight home, Robin worried that Lily would want them to go to their separate apartments. They had talked a lot about things, and Robin had stoically endured Lily's angry attacks. They were usually sniper attacks that seemed to come out of nowhere. It hurt, but of course she deserved it, and she worked to avoid getting defensive as she encouraged Lily to talk about the hurt behind the anger. She was in limbo. But afraid of receiving a negative answer, she didn't ask.

Walking to pick up Jess for dinner, she decided she was being a coward, and jogging back with Jess on her shoulders, she resolved to ask tonight once Jess was asleep.

After dinner in the family dining room, they walked on the beach, each of them holding Jess's hand, swinging her, singing the songs she loved to sing and, of course, chasing her and tossing her in the air. Feeling morose about not knowing how long they would be together as a family, Robin asked if she could bathe Jess when they got back to the casita. Lily eyed her but, as usual, agreed. True to her word she was giving Robin the time she needed to bond with her daughter.

* * *

Lily felt Robin's anxiety but was experiencing anxiety of her own. Did she or didn't she want Robin to move in with her? Although she understood why Robin felt she had to leave, she couldn't help feeling angry that maybe, just maybe, if Robin had trusted her enough to express her fears, they could have worked through them together or at least spent less time apart. She knew she would break if Robin walked out again. She could hear them giggling and splashing in the bathroom and couldn't keep from smiling. Could she deprive Jess of this, of more precious time with her dad? She loved seeing them together and they clearly loved being together. And she loved Robin, was in love with her still and loved being with her and Jess, being the family they were meant to be. Hillary helped her see there were no guarantees. She didn't doubt Robin's love for her or her love for Jess. She just—

It was awfully quiet in there. She listened. They were having a serious conversation. She walked down the hall and stood outside the bathroom, eavesdropping.

"Do you know Grandmama Cordy and Grandmama Del?"

"Yes."

"And Aunt Katie and Uncle Michael and Aunt Annie and Aunt Emma and Aunt—"

"I know them all, Jess, all of your aunts."

"Where did you go?"

Robin didn't answer.

"Where did you go, Dad?"

Robin coughed. "I heard you, sweet cheeks, I…I'm trying to remember."

"I missed you, Dad. Did you miss me?"

"I missed you so much it hurt."

"So why didn't you come? I didn't see you. Or did I forget?"

"No, my beautiful girl, you didn't forget. You didn't see me."

"Why?"

Lily listened, at war with herself. Part of her wanted to step in and save Robin. The other, angry part wanted her to have to deal with the hurt she'd done to her daughter. She remained still.

"I was lost, Jess, and far away, so far that I couldn't find the path back to you and Mommy. I was sad all the time I was away. And I was all alone because I didn't know how to ask for help to find the path. But I worked hard to find the way back, Jess, and now I'm here with you and Mommy."

"I need you, Dad. Promise you'll never go away again."

"I'll always be sorry that I missed a part of your life, sweet cheeks but, cross my heart," her voice cracked and Lily could hear her struggle, "I promise I will never ever leave you again. Come here, will you forgive me and give me a hug?"

There was a splash, then Jess giggled. "Uh-oh, you're being bad, getting your clothes wet, Dad."

"I love you, my beautiful girl."

"I love you too, Dad. I'm glad I found you."

"I'm glad you found me too. Come, time for pjs."

"Will you live with me when we go home?"

"I promise I will see you every day. Mom and I have to figure out the rest."

When she heard the swoosh of the water as Robin lifted Jess out, Lily went back to the living room.

Later that evening, after Jess was asleep, Robin brought Lily a glass of wine and sat next to her on the sofa. Lily expected her to talk about the conversation with Jess that she'd overheard, so she was surprised when Robin broached their leaving. "Have you given any thought to our living arrangements when we get back? I feel like I'm dangling in the wind."

"Like you left me dangling for two plus years?"

"I imagine what you felt was a lot more painful, but yes, like that."

As usual, Lily regretted what she'd said as soon as it popped out. She opened her mouth to apologize, but Robin stopped her with a finger on her lips. "Don't apologize, Lily. You feel what you feel and if you hold it in, it will only fester. I'm not the Robin who needed to run at the first sign of conflict. I'm a big girl now. I can take it."

Lily nodded and sipped her wine. They sat in silence for a while, then Lily stood. "I'm going to bed. Can we talk about this tomorrow after Jess goes to camp?"

"Sure. But before you go to bed, I want to give you something." She stood and removed her wallet from her pocket, then handed Lily the contract she'd written the first night they met. "I won't be needing this anymore because I will never leave you again, whether we get back together or not. I know for sure that there is no one but you for me. And though I don't think I will ever try to leave you and Jess again, if by some fluke I do, I hope you scream and yell and cry and throw yourself in my path. And get our family and friends to do the same."

Lily looked at the creased contract, and tears filled her eyes. "Good night, Robin."

CHAPTER FIFTY-FOUR

No One But You

Robin checked the clock. Three thirty. Three more hours until Jess pounced on her, four to five hours before she and Lily had a chance to sit and talk privately. One thing was clear in her mind. Whatever Lily decided tomorrow morning, she was not giving up. She would fight for Lily and Jess. She heard a noise, listened carefully to confirm that Jess wasn't sneaking around in the middle of the night. But all was quiet from her room. Must be someone returning from a late night walk on the beach.

Tonight's bathtub conversation with Jess had been very painful—hearing her struggle to understand why her dad hadn't been there for her, knowing how much she'd hurt her by not being in her life, wanting to throw herself down to beg her forgiveness but knowing she was too young to understand. She'd kept a diary after leaving them. Maybe one day when Jess was an adult, she'd let her read it. Perhaps it would help her understand that her leaving was her stupid ass way of protecting her. She would do everything in her power from now on to make Lily and Jess feel secure in her love. She hoped Lily understood the commitment she was making to them by giving her back the get-out-of-jail contract she'd written that magical night they'd met.

There it was again. Someone was moving around in the living room or the kitchen. She was about to get up and check on Jess when the door to her bedroom opened. The figure in the dim light of the doorway could only be Lily. She held her breath.

"Robin?"

"What's wrong?"

"Nothing. Can I get into bed with you?"

"Yes." She spoke softly. "Are you all right?"

Lily slipped under the sheet and lay on her side facing Robin, her hand on Robin's chest. "I…yes, more than. Is this okay?"

"Christ, Lily, you should know you're always welcome in my bed. I…um—"

Lily kissed her, a deep probing kiss, then pulled away. "Let me talk. You just listen."

"There's no one but you for me either. I love you as much as I did the day we married, maybe even more seeing you with Jess. I can't deny the anger is deep and I can't say it won't continue to pop out without warning, but I appreciate your willingness to deal with it, your willingness to acknowledge that I have a right to be angry. I hope one day it will dissipate and disappear." She took a deep breath.

"I overheard. No, actually, I eavesdropped on your conversation with Jess tonight. I'm sorry for being so sneaky, but I was proud of the way you didn't lie to her or flinch from the truth about not being there. Right now, she doesn't really understand it, I think, but there will be more questions, and I respect that you're willing to try to explain it in terms she can understand. I'm sure that won't change. She has known you for less than two weeks and she loves you and is connected to you. I attribute that to you and your wholehearted plunge into her life and her reality. I can see how much you love her."

A lump formed in Robin's chest. "More than I ever imagined."

"Shh." Lily put her fingers over Robin's lips. "I've been wrestling with the question of us living together again almost since Jess found you and brought you home to me. Something about wanting her dad and then going out and finding her touches me profoundly.

She is such an extraordinary child, determined and brave and sweet and kind, not to mention brilliant. Like her dad. She needs you in her life."

She kissed Robin again, lingering longer this time. "Every time I thought I was ready to ask you to move back in, I got angry and pulled back. With Hillary's help, I realized it was because I felt I couldn't trust you, couldn't trust that you wouldn't leave us again, even though I understand your fears and your memories. But tonight I realized that a lot of my anger was because you didn't trust *me*. I know you were terrified you would hurt Jess, but if you'd told me, perhaps I could have helped you deal with it, perhaps we could have dealt with it the way couples do. Instead you cut me out, abandoned me and Jess and ran. It's that running I've been afraid of, I think."

Robin tried to sit up, but Lily pushed her down. "Just listen, please. Hearing you promise Jess that you would never leave her again, your willingness to tear up the contract we made, your saying that if ever you tried to run, I should scream and cry and throw myself on you to stop you, eased that fear for me. I want us to live together as a family. I want us to be a family. Please move in with me and Jess." Her voice dropped to a whisper. "Please make love to me now."

Robin sucked in air. "You mean it. You'll take me back?"

"Jess needs her dad. And I need my Robin."

Robin pulled Lily on top of her. "Let the kissing begin."

They jumped apart as thunder crashed overhead, followed by lightning, then smiled and went back to kissing.

"Mommy, I'm afraid." Jess's cry parted them again.

Robin smiled tentatively. "Is it all right if I go?"

"Go, Dad." In between claps of thunder, Lily could hear the murmur of their voices, Jess questioning, Robin comforting. After a few minutes she got up to get a bottle of water, then peered into Jess's room to see what was happening. Her heart expanded at the sight of Robin seated on the bed with Jess in her arms explaining about thunder and lightening, answering Jess's questions. As Jess's voice became sleepier, Lily went back to bed to wait for Robin.

Robin woke her with kisses. "I believe we were starting something. Are you up to continuing or do you want a rain check?"

"That was a horrible pun. No rain check for me. I want what I want right now. Get naked." Lily pulled her tank top over her head and slipped her shorts down as Robin did the same, then tumbled Lily onto her back, covered her with her body, and buried her face in Lily's hair. She inhaled. "Oh, God, I've missed you Lily."

Accompanied by thunder and lightening, their lovemaking was gentle and sweet and intense, like the first time.

CHAPTER FIFTY-FIVE

Three Years Later

Lily lounged by the pool at the small but exclusive lesbian resort that Robin, Katie and Jan had purchased as an investment. This year they'd blacked out the first two weeks of February for their personal use; only their guests were allowed at the resort. It was easier that way because their families included men.

She smiled, watching Robin in the pool with all the little children. Jess, who was leading the others to attack her dad, hooted with joy every time Robin tossed her into the deep end of the pool. The younger ones screamed happily as Robin gently deposited them on their feet in the low end. Every once in a while, Robin glanced over and locked eyes with her. Those eyes, that connection, still did things to her that no married mother of two, soon to be four, had a right to feel. But lucky her, she never failed to experience the surge of warmth and the tingling in the groin.

Suddenly aware of her mamas settling in chairs, one on each side of hers, she shifted her attention away from Robin. And sex.

Del took her hand. "Are y'all comfortable, darlin'?"

Lily smiled and patted her large belly. "As comfortable as a beached whale can be, Mama."

"Only six weeks to go." Cordy took her other hand. "Will you stop after the twins are born?"

"If these two are mine, come as easily as Gabrielle did and have her temperament, who knows?" Her eyes went to Jess sailing through the air to the deep end of the pool. "But if either one or both are Robin's and are like Jess, we'll probably have to stop at four to manage them. Either way we'll be happy. Why do you ask?"

Del smiled. "Listening to Jess and Cordy discussing math problems last evening made me think about how wonderful and difficult having two more like Jess could be for you two."

"That's for sure. When we agreed to put both our eggs in the petri dish and let the universe decide whether we'd have another one of mine or another one of Robin's we failed to anticipate the fickleness of the universe." Lily patted her stomach. "Thus, twins of unknown genetic makeup."

"It's already a full-time grandma job keeping up with your two and Bella's Duncan, so even one more Jess will be difficult and wonderful." Cordy squeezed Lily's hand. "When I think about your twins and Bella and Mary's twins all arriving around the same time, I go into grandma overwhelm mode."

"I don't know, you don't look that upset to me, Cordy."

Cordy grinned. "At least we're two grandmas. It will be busy and tiring, but it'll also be fun. Actually we're both looking forward to it."

Lily felt a surge of love for her mamas. "And speaking of Bella and Mary, I haven't seen them around this morning. Everything okay?"

Cordy stood. "Bella is lying down. She's not feeling well, so Nicole is with her, making sure she and her twins are okay. And Mary is on the beach with Duncan. The little guy loves the water and I believe his Aunt Robin is going to start teaching him to swim tomorrow."

Del got to her feet. "Well, darlin', if y'all are good we're going to take a swim in the ocean, then play with Duncan so Mary can spend some quiet time with Bella. See you at lunch."

The mamas left and she picked up her book. Sometime later, Katie plopped down next to her. "Morning." She followed Lily's eyes. "The kids all adore her."

"Me too."

"And I...I'm so glad we did this. Everyone is enjoying themselves. Robin has gone from no family to building herself a wonderful extended family."

"She has, hasn't she? We need to do this every year, Katie. I love that all our kids are growing up with each other, but I also love that our families are getting connected, your brother and sister and their spouses and children, my brother and sister and their spouses and children, Robin's brothers and their families, and Nicole and Nora, Mei, Winnie, Emma and Annie and their families. It's wonderful."

"We've already blocked out the same two weeks next year. No guests here other than our friends and family and the college kids we hire as camp counselors to watch the children and plan programs for them. But speaking of extended families, how goes it with your two expected extensions?"

"Not many people get to have their obstetrician along on vacation, and Nicole says I'm fine and it's likely I'll carry them to term, which will be good for the twins."

"Robin is hoping for one of yours and one of hers. What about you?"

"I'll take two of anything as long as they're healthy. Another Jess would be fun, but two might do us in." She giggled. "Jess is fascinated by the twins. She talks to them and loves to feel them kicking. Now she's after Nicole to teach her everything about babies. Nicole said Jess is like a baby vampire, but it's not your blood she wants—it's all your knowledge she wants to suck out of you."

"It's true. I've heard her talking to Emma about Egyptian history and her Uncle Ted about the brain and emotions, and, you name it with anyone she can corner." Katie's eyes wandered back to Robin. "It's amazing how much alike they are. And just like her dad, Jess is more than willing to share what she knows. Earlier today, I went looking for Mikie and Janie and found them sitting under a tree on the beach with some of the other children. The camp counselors were nearby, but Jess was in charge, teaching them about the ocean and tides with pictures and charts. They were all mesmerized. Gaby was hanging on her big sister's every word."

"Jess is very good with Gaby and other children as long as she's in charge. Robin is working to make sure that she's aware of other children's needs, that she understands that not everyone is as brilliant as she is and that sometimes she has to let the others be the leader. Gaby is more laidback than Jess. But then, most people are. And while she adores Jess, she's no slouch in the brains department and when she has something to say she pushes back until Jess gives her space."

"It's eerie but watching Jess with Robin's nieces Sara and Victoria is like looking at one of those charts showing our progression from apes, only it's Robin in various stages of her life. I've talked to Ted and Paul and they said, despite how Robin's mother treated her, she was as exuberant as Jess before she watched her mom murder her sister and commit suicide. Seeing Sara, a brilliant but normal fifteen-year-old, makes me remember how fragile and withdrawn and wounded Robin was when she came to Harvard."

"You were only twenty-two. How did you have the...the strength, the will to take on a needy fourteen-year-old?"

Katie watched Robin frolicking in the pool. "In the Peace Corps in Africa, I worked in a refugee camp with children who had grown up in war-torn countries. They'd lost everything, including parents and siblings and had never known love. One of the first things I learned was I couldn't make it better, that if I got too involved they would suffer another loss when I left. When I met Robin, I realized she was a lot like those children, but I knew I could be there for her as long as she wanted me, so I went for it."

"You did a great job." Lily shifted, trying to sit up. "The kids are being called out of the pool. I guess it's lunchtime."

"I'd better go see that my two actually eat." Katie extended a hand, helped Lily sit, then kissed her cheek. "See you on the patio at the adults' lunch."

Lily watched as Robin lifted the younger children out of the pool, helped Gaby remove her water wings and headed over to her, a daughter holding each hand. As they got close, Gaby dropped Robin's hand and ran to her. "Mommy lap." She held her arms out. Lily laughed. "Mommy doesn't have a lap, Gaby. You have to stand next to me."

Lily helped the girl climb onto the chair with her and wrapped her arm around her, then covered her face with kisses. "Did you have a good time in the pool?"

Gaby giggled. "Dad fro me high."

"Not as high as me, Mommy." Jess stood next to the chair, wrapped her arms around Lily's neck and kissed her cheek. "Say 'throw', not 'fro' Gaby."

"Throw." Gaby stuck her tongue out at Jess. "I like fro better."

Jess frowned. "But—"

Lily put an arm around Jess. "I saw, Jess. Dad tossed you in the deep end of the pool. It's a good thing you're an excellent swimmer." She squeezed her green-eyed girl. "I heard a rumor that you taught a class this morning."

"Not a rumor, Mom." Jess beamed. "It was about the ocean. Dad and Sara and Victoria and Teddie helped me draw pictures for the class and this afternoon we're going to draw lightning and thunder and cloud pictures for tomorrow's class about weather and the atmosphere. And Gaby is going to help. Right, Gaby?"

"I like to hear Jess tell about the fishies."

"I'm glad you're learning from your big sister." Lily kissed Gaby, then looked at Jess. "You're not forcing the children to come, are you, Jess?"

"No, Mommy." Her raspy voice communicated extreme patience. "They like to learn."

A camp counselor appeared. "Excuse me, I'm supposed to bring Gaby and Jess to lunch."

Robin helped Gaby down. "Go to lunch with Amy, girls. We'll be along shortly." She sat next to Lily.

"You must be exhausted after all that playing in the sun and tossing children around in the water."

"It is kind of tiring." She wiggled her eyebrows. "Want to take a nap with me later?"

Lily laughed. "Yes. But no hanky panky." She caressed Robin's face. "Well, nothing too strenuous."

"Have I told you lately that I love you?"

"You might have said something like that when you left me in bed this morning." She took Robin's hand and kissed it. "Are you having a good time?"

"I am. I never dreamed I could feel so…loved, so full of love. It's a little overwhelming, having all the people I love in one place, a beautiful place like this, feeling the love in the air, watching connections being made and realizing that not only do I have you and the girls and the mamas but so much more. A loving community for our girls to grow up in."

Lily patted her stomach. "How can you be so sure the twins are girls? You know the odds are against that. Has Nicole slipped?"

"Not to me. Now if it was Emma, the world would know, but Nicole knows how to play it close to her chest. Anyway, just a gut feeling. Jess thinks so too."

"And have you and Jess discussed whether she'll be okay without a brother?"

"Only in so far as I've told her we take whatever we get. Ah, there's the gong for the adult lunch. Let me give you a hand." She took Lily's hands and pulled her up into a hug, nuzzling her neck. "I look forward to the day when we can be close together again."

Lily laughed. "But then we'll be too tired to do anything but sleep."

"I think we should get a nurse this time, and not just because I want to make love to you all the time, but it will help to be able to get away for a few hours now and then."

Lily kissed Robin's nose. "We'll see. Give me your arm and help me waddle to lunch."

As they made their way to the patio, Robin stopped and faced Lily. "You know, when you told me you wanted to carry my babies the night we met, I thought you were mad. But I would have agreed to anything to have my way with you. And here we are, more than seven years and almost four children later, and all I can think about is having my way with you. I love our life, I love our girls, I love all of our family and friends, but most of all, I love you because you are the source of all that is good in my life. "

Lily's eyes misted. She held Robin's face in her hands, stared into the green pools of love, then kissed her gently. "No one but you for me, ever."

Bella Books, Inc.

Women. Books. Even Better Together.

P.O. Box 10543
Tallahassee, FL 32302

Phone: 800-729-4992
www.bellabooks.com